Jean Mead moved to North Wales twelve years ago, changing lifestyle dramatically. A regular commuter between London and Liverpool, managing and script writing for a busy and lucrative video production company, she chose to live peacefully and economically in a converted chapel on a mountainside in Gwynedd.

On long walks, she discovered derelict and abandoned slate quarries, some slumbering giants scarring the mountainsides, whilst others long since flooded, shimmering lakes lying in the valleys. Dorothea Quarry of Talysarn, an astoundingly beautiful and haunting place inspired Jean to write *The Widow Makers*.

THE
WIDOW MAKERS

Jean Mead

THE WIDOW MAKERS

Pegasus

PEGASUS PAPERBACK

© Copyright 2005
Jean Mead

The right of Jean Mead to be identified as author of this work has been asserted by her in accordance with the Copyright, Designs and Patents Act 1988

All Rights Reserved

No reproduction, copy or transmission of this publication may be made without written permission.
No paragraph of this publication may be reproduced, copied or transmitted save with the written permission of the publisher, or in accordance with the provisions of the Copyright Act 1956 (as amended).

Any person who does any unauthorised act in relation to this publication may be liable to criminal prosecution and civil claims for damage.

A CIP catalogue record for this title is available from the British Library

ISBN 1 903490 18 9

Pegasus is an imprint of
Pegasus Elliot MacKenzie Publishers Ltd.
www.pegasuspublishers.com

First Published in 2005

Pegasus
Sheraton House Castle Park
Cambridge England

Printed & Bound in Great Britain

DEDICATION

To my beloved husband
Lt. Commander Anthony James Mead.

May the Gods be with you and all who sail with you.

Chapter One

Joe Standish a skinny pale boy, imaginative enough to be afraid of the dark, a weakness he would never have admitted to anyone, least of all his father, had become a miner on his eleventh birthday. Although the event had been cataclysmic for Joe, it had gone virtually unheeded by his numerous siblings; harassed mother or bullying father.

Joe had known better than to query his father's decision to send him to work at the infamous Galloway pit. A stinging clip around the ear would have been the reward for his boldness, along with a piece of advice he'd heard often, 'Thou'll work if thee wants to carry on eatin' an livin' in style thee's become accustomed. Work or knuckle pie for thee, lad, suit thesen.' Amused by his own wit his father would give a gap-toothed grin as he delivered a clout and the homily. Joe would have been surprised and thankful if all he'd received was a cuff and not a lashing that would leave him unable to sit comfortably for a week. Joe's blood might boil at the injustice of his father's domination, but he would have no more considered challenging him than fleeing to China.

So to the Galloway he went, along with his ten-year-old friend Frank, both boys still dreaming of fishing in the nearby canal, and chasing girls with pigtails to pull down the dirty alleys of their slum homes.

Twenty-two years on, Joe was a married man with an infant son, Tommy.

Joe's bullying father was long dead, killed in a public house brawl. With his premature death it had fallen to Joe, then a thirteen year old boy, to fend for his younger siblings and his mother, until the day she surprised her family by marrying the local baker, a proud veteran of Wellington's Waterloo.

In the two decades that Joe worked in the Galloway, the pit had changed little save that now the deepest levels had reached hundreds of feet, making labouring more arduous and dangerous.

He and Frank were still mates, often working the same shifts, and drinking together in the crowded Collier public alehouse on a Saturday night.

Today, Joe had been below ground since the start of the early morning shift. Ten mind numbing, muscle crippling hours ago. The hot airlessness had increased steadily and now it was stifling, draining the last of his energy. Wiping sweat off his brow, he closed his eyes against the moving shadows beyond the flicker of his lamp, playing tricks with his vision. In the deep darkness, shrouded in a circle of solitude it was too easy for imagination to take flight. A shadow to become the bent back of a miner long lost to a pit disaster. A scrape of an unseen tool, the rasping cough of a friend long perished. The cathedral high vaults and the three-foot burrows were sanctuaries of memories. Standing there, the black rock at his back, he put aside his whispering spirits turning his mind to the moment.

For all the shift's rough exertions and the constant clamour of picks torturing the coal face, he knew he'd been luckier than most working in this old gallery. Here he had the pleasure of stretching his sore muscles occasionally.

The newer galleries were a nightmare, claustrophobically narrow and so low a man was compelled to lie on his back to hack at a black ceiling no more than inches above his head. It was hot filthy work, and depending on their modesty, many laboured naked or nearly naked.

It embarrassed Joe that men shed their clothes and worked alongside children and women. Reason told him that the women, or at least most of them, bare breasted against the heat cared little. Only last week he'd got into a debate whilst having a drink in the Collier public house regarding the women and children working illegally in the Galloway. A husband of one of the collier women defended the Galloway manager's decision to let women work below ground if they wanted too. Joe's view matched that of parliament, the work was too dangerous and arduous for women and bairns. His argument had fallen on deaf ears, rather like Lord Ashley's new bill. John Searson, the pit manager, flouting the new law allowed children as young as four, and women in their last years into the pit. The cheaper the labour the higher the profits, and his bonuses depended on profits.

Going over the row in his head, face screwed with aggravation, Joe grabbed his pick and swung it with all the energy he could muster, the blow vibrating through his muscles sending new sweat in all directions, and coal flying from its solid foundation. Pausing before the next punishing blow his eye caught the foreman, Fanshaw, hurrying up the gallery, feet thumping, fat belly shivering above the waistband of his moleskin trews, hell bent on putting an end to shenanigans in the tunnel ahead.

It was always the same at the end of the Saturday shift, high spirits would get the better of the youngsters and some tomfoolery would follow. Thoughts of a free day and how to spend it making monkeys of most, and for all their high spirits it was doubtful that the lads would escape their parents' religious Sunday rituals. It'd be a rare treat indeed to spend a day as they'd dreamed and planned of doing.

Fanshaw disappeared into the gallery and the noise there stopped instantly. Joe heard a few yelps and whimpers as the foreman swung his knotted rope amongst the culprits' heads.

Taking the weight off his feet, reckoning that it would take the fat bully minutes to clout the lot of them. He was longing for a smoke; his nerves parched for a drag, but his baccy had run out yesterday, and he wouldn't have more until he'd collected his wages.

A disturbed mouse ran over his shins. Expecting Fanshaw to appear, he started to get to his feet, then inched down again recognising the dry bark of George Thomas. Coal dust had claimed the man, and now his lungs were hard.

He was buttoning his trousers after relieving himself. 'No bloody wonder it's as hot as buggery down here, the bloody trap door's shut. Looks like the blasted thing's been shut all day, it's clogged wi' muck.'

Joe's knees creaked, as he inched up. 'The bairn, Mary O'Hara supposed to be there. Didn't tha see her?'

'Course I didn't bloody see her. I just said the bloody trap door's shut, if the wench were there she'd be opening the bugger.'

Thoughts of an accident ran through Joe's mind. 'Didn't tha think to look to see if the youngster's alreeght?'

'It's not my bloody job to check on the bairns around here. More than likely the little runt just took off. A good hiding is what she needs, a clout to remember, an' I'll be the man to give it her.'

Joe's eyes narrowed. 'Thee'll have me to answer to if tha lays a hand on any of the little one's down here.'

Balling his fists the man pushed his face forward. 'And who will tha get to give thee a hand with this hiding?'

Joe caught a whiff of his breath, tainted with last night's beer and onions. His hand snaked out, grabbing the man's shirt. 'I'll need nowt but mesen to throw thee in the dirt, George Thomas.'

Released suddenly, the man staggered back, grunting as his shoulder smacked the black wall. Shoving himself off, he scowled. 'Nowt but an old woman, that's what thee is, Standish.'

Fighting his anger, Joe grabbed his lantern from a hollow in the rock, the flame flickered, and expecting it to smoke and die he kept his eyes to it, but it steadied. Turning away from George Thomas he strode towards the far end of the gallery.

A hundred yards on, several men were sitting with their backs to the wall, taking advantage of Fanshaw's disciplinary errand.

Shouting to them he tasted the dust on his lips. 'Has any of thee seen little Mary O'Hara? The bairn from the trap door.'

A young man unknown to Joe, his face ravaged by smallpox, looked up from the pie he was chewing. 'Trap door's been shut most of the day, mister. It's hot enough to roast conkers down here.'

Joe held up his lantern. 'So tha hasn't seen her then?'

A near naked man stuffed his pipe with a plug of tobacco; his eyes turned to the job. 'I saw her first thing, but not since.'

Shingle clinked as Joe shifted his boots. 'Hasn't anyone said where she might be? Fanshaw or anybody?'

A bull shouldered man got to his feet. 'It ain't our job to go hunting missing nippers. If tha wants her, thee go and find her.' Wiping sweat off his baldhead, he grinned. 'She a bit too young and scrawny for me own taste.'

The men joined in his laughter.

Lowering his lantern, Joe moved on. Behind him, someone called 'And too bloody dirty too. Kid's lousy.'

Curbing an uncharitable remark, Joe kept walking. Beyond the beam of their lamps the darkness was infinite. He was walking in the tiny circle of light of his Davy. The air was cheesy, and from far off down the seam he heard the drip of water, and the ominous creaking of old, worn props. The height of the ceiling had dropped considerably, and it was hotter, like standing near an open oven door. He thought of the bath that would be waiting for him when he got home, he'd finish it off with a dousing of cold water in the back yard, then he'd sup ale after his wetting.

Arriving at the opening of gallery six, he stooped to enter, and saw a sight that never failed to arouse an emotion as keen and invasive as pain. The cheapest labour were working here, children as young as five, not greatly different from his own son, Tommy, save that these poor bairns had a sick pallor, and hollow eyed fragility. The children were stuffing coal into sacks; one little girl missing her infant teeth gave him a gap-toothed grin. He smiled, and was rewarded with a shy, babyish giggle.

Joe was asking an older boy if he had seen Mary, when a truck came rumbling out of the darkness, the children collecting the coal moved aside to let it pass. For a moment he thought he recognised the small boy harnessed to the truck's shanks. As it drew nearer he winced seeing the red graze mark around the child's middle where the rough belt bit into his tender belly. Chains attaching him to the haft clinked like gaoler's keys, swinging against skinny childish flanks. His tiny hands and knees had been transformed into hooves with rough padding, protecting his precious skin from the sharp shale. Neither the boy that pulled the truck, or the small girl pushing it, gave Joe a second glance; they passed him like small, wheezing donkeys.

A clot of hot bile rose in his stomach, in his mind he saw the rich owners with their satin clad women, riding in fine carriages drawn by muscular, well-fed horses.

He was powerless to help the little colliers, and it shamed him.

As he turned away, he heard, then saw, two more trucks rumbling out of the darkness. It was impossible to see if the four children shifting them were boys or girls, the shadows were too deep, and as the little beasts of burden crawled out of the blackness, the minute hairs on his body rose.

At the far end of the tunnel a dangerous light was struck and in the white flash Joe saw a replicate scene of Dante's Inferno.

For a moment he thought his eyes would fill. Then turning away he went in search of little Mary O'Hara. Finding the trap door shut and gathering a line of black dust around it, he called 'Mary' into the darkness, his voice echoing down the long tunnel. There was no response so he made his way back to his tools. Reaching his work place as Fanshaw's bellow of 'Shift's over' reverberated down the long galleries.

With thoughts of home, he stooped to pick up his pickaxe and hammer, securing them to the chain on the wall.

Joining the men making their way to the shaft, he discovered that the foreman had sent Mary home. Her mother in labour with her seventh child, Mary was needed to mind the smaller bairns. He was glad the little one was safe, and made a mental note to inquire after the family when he reached the top.

Nearing the shaft the crowd was thick, the smell of so many hot dirty bodies potent enough to taste, a filthy odour that would cling like a leech to the back of his mouth until he'd washed it down with the first quart of ale of the evening.

Females at the head of the crowd were laughing, making enough noise to wake the dead, and then the laughter turned to angry voices as a spat broke out. How they found the energy to fight was a mystery to him. A couple of men joined the row, and the women banded together against them.

The crowd moved forward, and a frisson of apprehension checked Joe's thoughts. This was the time of day he loathed, fearing the perilous climb back to the surface on ladders that should have been condemned to the fire long ago. A hundred or more men had died in this shaft over the last decade, and it wasn't for the want of trying to get something done about the terrible death toll, colliers pleas had fallen on deaf ears, and their threats had gone to nothing. They were aware that the other mines in the district had installed man hoists, but the Galloway was to be the last of the Lancashire mines to do so. High casualties had not persuaded the owners to invest in newly invented machinery.

His jaw clenched as he anticipated the nightmarish ascent, the fear that a man above him would miss his footing and crash down, taking them to a shared death, playing havoc with his nerve. He took a deep breath of fouled air; it would be the best he'd get before he reached the top. Six hundred ladder rungs stole what little air a man had in his lungs; the climb never failed to leave his head spinning and legs trembling. Moving forward with the thought that to get out thee had to go up, he grasped a ladder rung and began his climb.

He'd gone no further than a hundred feet when his lungs started to labour on the coal dust spiralling upwards in the draught. A miner climbing above him faired no better, Joe could hear the man's breath rasping louder than his own. His neck ached from watching the fellow's unsteady feet. A racking cough crippled the man, he hunched over and for a terrifying instant Joe thought he would topple, his bowels cramped. Holding on tightly, his knuckles bone yellow, he was prepared to swing away, to clutch the side of the ladder should the sick man lose his precarious hold. Eyes glued to the worn soles of the man's boots, he prayed that he'd hang on. It seemed an age, the seconds elongating out of all proportion as the man fought for breath.

Twenty feet below them a collier called rudely. 'Get a bloody move on.'

Another joined in. 'Move it tha lazy buggers.'

More added to the bedlam. 'Got all bloody day up there.'

'Stopped for tha bloody tea have tha?'

Joe's temper flared, angry he shouted down. 'Think we've stopped for our own bloody enjoyment tha selfish bastards?' Ignoring the rude replies, he glanced up at the sick man, his racking cough had eased, but he was battling for air.

Joe spoke kindly. 'Take tha time, never mind those impatient buggers.'

Fighting the fire in his chest, the miner wheezed. 'I'll be all right in a minute.'

'Aye course tha will, nowt a bit of fresh air won't cure.'

Nodding, the collier shuffled upwards.

Joe kept his eyes on the frayed trouser hems, and worn boots, as the man progressed. He was remembering the last time a leading man had tumbled, the youth had flailed passed him, terror blazoned on his face as he screamed his way to death. The memory of the lad's fear filled eyes still had the power to sicken him. He glanced down as though following the path of the boy's unnatural flight. The despair in the lad's long and inhuman screams echoing once more in his mind.

Thank God that they had nearly reached the top of the fourth ladder. The risk of climbing was bad enough without following a chap on his last legs. It was with a silent prayer that Joe swung off the ladder, landing on a wide ledge. Now he wished more than ever that he had a poke of tobacco to steady his jangling nerves.

He'd really thought that he had breathed his last back there, he couldn't imagine how the poor devil was going to reach the top under his own steam. If Fanshaw got to hear of it, it'd be the last time the collier would be allowed down, safest thing for the other colliers, but not the best thing for the poor bugger's family. He gave the man a chance to be well out of the way before swinging back onto the ladder.

Fifteen minutes later he came above ground and took a long pull of air laden with fumes from the local foundry, after several hours below ground the air was sweet enough, the April sun had enough warmth to dry his sweat, a bonus.

Feeling more cheerful than he had all day, he hitched his satchel onto his shoulder and made his way to collect his wages. He'd pay for the hire of his tools, square up for the lamp oil, then he'd get his baccy and fill his pipe, and all would be well with the world.

The queue at the wages hut had dwindled to a half dozen when Joe got there, there was a slight altercation between him and Fanshaw, the foreman insisting that Joe had not paid for last week's oil, grinning cheerfully, Joe proved him wrong.

With his wages in his pocket, he set off to meet Frank at the Gower street entrance. There was no sign of him when he reached the wrought iron gates, but Joe expected he'd be along within a few minutes. Leaning up against the iron palings he took out his pipe and stuffed it with tobacco, lighting up he dragged the smooth Virginia smoke into his lungs.

A light breeze blew across his face; he turned to the sun, feeling the last rays of warmth penetrating the muck. His eyes wandered beyond the mine workings to the barren mountain of slag that former Galloway miners had built. The sun was setting, silhouetting the sharp summit, black as jet against the coral pink sky. The stark contrast was brutal to his pit dry eyes; he redirected his gaze east of the Galloway, to the recently built cotton mills belching yellow smoke into the spring air.

A group of men came out of the ramshackle wages hut, they were enjoying a shared joke, Frank was with them, a big barrel-chested man with a mop of unruly hair the colour of wet, rusting iron. Joe watched them crossing the pit yard, coming alongside him they wished him a collective 'goodneeght' without breaking their stride. Frank held back, then falling into step he and Joe followed the men out of the pit gates into Gower Street, boots sparking on the old cobbles.

Frank hitched the jacket he was carrying over his shoulder.

'I'm not a bit sorry that shift's over, it was as hot as the devil's front porch down there.'

Joe smiled; he was well used to Frank speaking of the devil as an old friend, there were times when he wondered if the pair hadn't formed some sort of an allegiance. 'Aye it was certainly warm. Fanshaw sent little Mary O'Hara home, her Mam was bearing another bairn by all accounts.'

'What another? How many is that now?' Frank was astonished.

'Seven I think.'

'Wouldn't thee think Irish O'Hara would know what caused the trouble and keep his breeches buttoned.' Frank grinned.

Joe chuckled. 'Wouldn't surprise me if Mrs. O'Hara hasn't snipped off his buttons, she's saucy enough and buxom with it.'

Frank sighed. 'Aye she's certainly a bonny lass. But forget the O'Hara's and their bairns. It's Sunday all day tomorrow, and not a blessed piece of coal to shovel, or misery face Fanshaw to suck up too.' He sighed contentedly. 'And several ales to sup in the Collier toneeght. What more could a man ask for?'

Matching his grin, Joe said, 'I'm looking forward to sinking a few.'

They fell silent until they rounded the corner of Tanner's Row, then Frank said: 'What did tha think of the rumble this afternoon?'

Joe wasn't prepared to admit that he was worried. Trying to explain the noise away as nothing more than the creaking of old props or the growl of the rock. It was Saturday afternoon, the week was over, and he didn't want to dwell on trouble before it jumped up to greet him. 'Maybe it were nowt to worry about, just the old girl whispering her discontent, telling us to go easier with her.'

Surprised, Frank gave him a sidelong glance. It wasn't like Joe to disregard the warnings that the pit gave out. 'I don't like it, I think it's a warning. I tell thee, Joe I'll be glad to see the back of that place. Maybe it's time to get meself off to the slate quarries, not wait until the summer.'

Joe closed his mind to the brewing disagreement; head down, he said, 'Aye, happen thee's reeght.'

For weeks now Frank had talked of the slate quarries. Joe thought the idea of uprooting and moving to North Wales was nothing more than a pipe dream. But if Frank should go he'd miss him like buggery.

Frank was grinning like a lad. 'Why don't tha think about it, Joe? A move to Wales could be just the thing for thee and Emily.'

Joe sighed. 'I don't know, Frank. It'd be risky giving up a sure job for one that I know bugger all about. I'd have to give it a lot of thought.'

Glad that he had Joe saying he'd think about it, Frank veered off towards his own front door. Shouting back, 'I'll see thee in the Collier later.'

Thoughtfully, Joe completed the journey to his own.

The old red brick alehouse, The Collier, had stood on the corner of Rotherman Street and Brickhouse Lane for as long as anyone could remember, gathering dirt as Anne MacBride, alehouse keeper for sixty years or more, grew too old to allow a bit of muck to worry her.

Affectionately known as Dirty Anne's by her more regular customers, the alehouse did a fair trade in cheap gin and homemade grog.

Crossing the threshold, Joe acknowledged Anne who was squatting on a stool at the hearth, piling wet wood on a smoking fire. Her mongrel dog lay asleep at her feet, impervious to the clatter of the crowded bar.

Anne threw the last of the wood on the spluttering fire; rheumatically she straightened her back, cursing the ache in her spine that never left her now. Thin as a pick-axe shank, nearing ninety, born and bred locally when the district had been nothing but green fields, Anne had seen more changes than most. Wellington's Waterloo, the French revolution, and the declaration of American Independence were events as clear as yesterday.

Raising a hand crippled by arthritis, she beckoned. 'Joe, come over 'ere, lad.'

Joe had a lot of time for Anne, a survivor with a tale to tell when the gin was in her. Hunched on a stool by the fire hearth, she would gather an audience, and take her customers back to the time of highwaymen, revolutions, rebels, and heroes.

Crossing to her, Joe lifted his cap. His brown hair was short and dense. A scrubbing in the tin bath had rid him of the colliery muck, and now in the lamplight his face appeared as pale as old ivory, revealing the hours he lived below ground. A scar on his forehead showed pink where a rafter had cut into it. Recently, little creases had appeared around his china blue eyes, not laughter lines but lines brought about from squinting against the slivers of coal that flew from beneath his pick.

Anne considered him a big handsome chap, although he wasn't tall at five foot ten, but the rough spun shirt he wore did not hide his broad shoulders and wide back.

Anne had already enjoyed a glass or two of gin, and as Joe drew alongside, she turned her ancient face to his and he saw the spark of flirtation in her eyes.

'And how's my big 'andsome lad toneeght?'

Joe pressed her thin shoulder. 'All the better for seeing thee, Anne. Let me get a tuppence of gin for thee.'

Anne struggled to her feet. 'I'll not hear of if. I'm going to treat thee to a quart of me best ale.'

'There's no need, Anne.'

'There's every need, lad, unless thee's given up drinking on a Saturday neeght. If thee's done that what are thee doing in this hovel of mine?' Laughter made her old eyes weep, whipping a dirty rag from her garter she mopped at the scant tears.

A collier warming his backside by the fire, hollered, 'Granny it's no good thee lifting tha skirt, we've only come for our grog.'

Anne frowned. 'Thee old devil, Kirkshore. Everyone knows tha privates have shriveled from lack of employment.'

Henry Kirkshore received a slap on the back from another customer. 'Is it yer wife or unhappy mistress that's been talking?'

Henry spluttered, spilling his ale.

After wiping her eyes again, Anne stuffed the rag into her frayed garter, letting the hem of her skirt fall.'Even if it had been in good order, Henry, tha's missed thy chance.'

With a promise that he would drink ale with her the next time he called, Joe left the small crowd gathered around the fireside and crossed the room to Frank.

Frank had been sharing a table with Jack Brodie; Brodie had risen and worked his way back to the bar as Joe approached.

Frank pushed a quart of ale across the table as Joe sat.

'Thanks, Frank, I've been looking forward to this all day.' He took a long satisfying pull.

Frank watched him drink, when he had put his glass down, he asked, 'How's your Emily?'

Joe wiped his mouth with the back of his hand. 'Lass is alreeght. She's been busy most of the week whitening the outhouse, always finds a job to do does our Emily.'

Emily had been working in the pie factory attached to the local slaughterhouse when she and Joe met. They had married the following spring, and Tommy, their only child was born ten months later. The family now lived in a cramped, rented house, in a dirty alley.

Joe's face lit as he spoke of his young son. 'Tommy's growing so fast it's hard to keep up with the little beggar.'

For the next few minutes they spoke of family life.

They were drinking a second quart when Frank's face became serious. 'That rumbling this afternoon has really worried me. It's happening too often lately, and this time I felt the trembling under me feet.'

All Joe wanted was to enjoy a few ales and forget about work. He'd put the Galloway out of his mind the moment the pit gate was to his back.

A bunch of men were playing dominoes, their sudden shouts drowned Frank's words.

'I told our Betty about it, and she agreed with me, that we up-sticks and go to the slate quarries as soon as possible.' Hitting the table with the palm of his hand, he spoke earnestly. 'I have to leave that bloody pit, the place is driving me crazy.'

Joe leaned forward, elbows on the table. 'It's nowt but madness, Frank, tha can't really mean to pack-up and go, just like that. With no job guaranteed.'

Frank was used to this argument. He let Joe run on. Listening to the reasons why he shouldn't take the risk.

Joe was aware that his words were falling on deaf ears. Frank had made up his mind. Sighing, he straightened. Lifting his glass, he took a long draft.

Months before, Frank had met a Welsh quarrier, the man had been visiting relatives in Oldham. The conversation they got into had stuck with Frank, firing him up to make the move. Nearly word perfect Frank repeated the exchange.

Without interruption Joe heard him out. Then with a frown creasing his brow, he said, 'So tha's saying there's plenty of work in these quarries? Guaranteed?'

Frank grinned. 'Aye, I'm saying exactly that. There's plenty of work, and it's above ground in the fresh air. Think of it Joe, working in clean mountain air.'

'Aye and perishing cold air in the winter months.' Adding sarcastically. 'To say nowt of the spring and summer rain.'

Frank's smile melted. 'I know it won't be all bloody roses, but it has to be better than working hundreds of feet below daylight.'

Joe repented. 'Aye, I'll grant that.'

Frank drained his glass. The day had been hot and tiring, the fears of a rock fall bedeviling every hour. There wasn't a morning that he trekked to the Galloway that he didn't have a sweat on. Fear grinding at his nerves. Would this be the day that the world caved in? Thinking of it now made his belly quiver. All he wanted was to get shut of the place, and take his mate with him out of harms way. Shouting wasn't going to help; it was no way to make a man see sense.

There was a plea in Frank's voice. 'Will tha think about it, Joe?'

Joe nodded. 'Aye I'll think about it.'

Failing to leave it there, as he knew he should, didn't he have the man saying he'd think about it, Frank pushed his case. 'By all accounts it's a reeght pretty place as well as being prosperous. Emily would take to it in no time, and Tommy's young enough to settle anywhere. The fresh air would be good for the lad.'

Joe's mind flashed to Tommy; he pictured the boy playing on grass not blackened by coal dust. Where trees grew and the ground yielded crops. A world of difference from the dirt and black grit the lad was bred too. His heart skipped a beat. Perhaps he and Emily could uproot, this might be a chance of getting out of the Galloway, leave all the rotten uncertainty behind him.

Frank lit his pipe, eye on the flame, he said:

'I could see how the land lies and send thee word about a job. ' Holding his breath he waited for opposition.

'Aye that would be the way to do it, Emily might go for that.'

Frank couldn't have been more amazed. Eager to get roots on the idea and make its survival more certain, he tried to sound positive, but not too enthusiastic. 'As soon as I get there I'll look for a likely place for lodgings, and a job in the quarry.'

'Do tha not think that we're a bit long in the tooth to be making such enormous changes?'

Frank snorted. 'Long in the tooth! Good God man, were not passed it yet. We're not so far off thirty that we need measuring for our shrouds.'

Laughing, Joe picked up his glass.

'Sometimes, Joe Standish, I worry about thee. We can make it work, and it wouldn't take us too long to get fixed up, we could be settled by summer.'

There was a smile on Joe's face, as he rose. 'I'll get another in. Same again?'

'Aye, go on then.'

He had to elbow his way to the counter and once there he had to wedge himself in between a young lad and a women spoon feeding gin to a teething baby. With a coin he rapped on the marble top.

Polly Skite served him his ale and he made his way back to Frank.

Emily was in bed when Joe arrived home. Coming in through the back door, he closed it quietly, and stepped into the kitchen. The scent of recent ironing lingered in the room. Emily had left the oil lamp burning low for his return, the thin blue flame glimmered in the glass chimney, the watery light dimmed the scarlet of the tablecloth, and cast pale shades across the dun walls. The fire in the grate still glowed, and after the chill walk home, an easterly wind fanning down the narrow alleys, the warmth was welcome.

Shrugging off his jacket he hung it on the hook behind the door, and sitting in the high-backed chair by the hearth, he eased off his heavy boots and propped them on the fender. Legs outstretched to the heat, eyes glinting in the firelight, he pondered on the things that Frank had told him, and although he was tired his mind was alive with possibilities, he knew that sleep would not come easily.

Picking up the old poker he stirred the fire until it flared. For a while his mind drifted, and in the dying flames he saw the mountains and valley of Wales.

The next morning Joe came awake slowly; primrose rays of the April sun filtering through the thin curtains warmed the remnant of the chill night air. Emily had risen; he could hear her downstairs. Usually on a Sunday morning he'd turn over and listen to his wife going about her domestic rituals until he dropped into a doze. This morning was different, something he couldn't put his finger on, a sliver of lingering pleasure left by a happy dream, lazily he searched his mind trying to recall the reason for his content, it was something green, he knew that, green and fresh. Frank's words came back to him "a chance to work in fresh air." Sleep was forgotten as his mind raced over all that Frank had said last night. Recalling his excitement, he smiled.

The bedroom door opened, and Emily walked in carrying a cup of tea; he put his thoughts away for the moment. Now wasn't the time to tell her about Wales, later, he promised himself, I will tell her later, who knows she might just go for the idea.

Throughout the day Joe planned how he would tell Emily about the quarry and the chance of a new life. Several times he tried to ignore the cold finger of uncertainty, he had doubts of his own but he feared that Emily's would be greater. He couldn't bear the thought that she would dismiss the idea and crush his chance to dream. By nightfall that's all it was, a dream, his doubts had surfaced too often for it to be anything else. He didn't tell Emily.

Four thirty the following morning he left for work with dozens of other colliers, their nailed boots ringing on the dark, wet cobbled street as they trekked towards the sound of the Galloway's pealing bell.

Joe's heart was heavier than at any other time, he wept silently, for himself and all the souls forced to work below ground in a dank God forsaken place, just to exist, not to live, living didn't come into it.

The rumble began as a distant growl. Heads lifted, each man his face etched with fear met the eyes of the nearest collier.

Joe felt his heart lurch sickeningly, he waited like a hundred others, pickaxe and bare arms frozen in the act of breaking black glistening coal.

The silence lengthened. Hearts dared beat again, breath held for long agonising seconds escaped in stifled whispers. Paralysed with terror they waited for a deeper silence to proclaim the all clear.

Terrible moments later the world shifted, a trembling shiver ran through the dark corridors of black gold.

Flinging aside their tools they ran towards the nearest ladders, sounds from hell marked the path of the screaming exodus. Men, women, and children stumbled, crushed they died in the wake of fleeing feet.

Like an avenging God the black pit shook itself, roaring angrily at the mortals that chipped at its core each day, a vertical crack opened, timber split and twisted, snapping like dried twigs under the unbearable weight of toppling rock.

Neither Joe nor Frank heard the pit bell tolling, summoning wives, lovers, mothers, children, and fathers, to the new graves of their loved ones.

Joe came out of his dead faint into a solid barrier of silence, his throat felt rough and dry, his nose clogged with dust, beside him Frank lay deathly still. He rose to a crouch, his head striking a splintered prop, tentatively he felt around it, reckoning it would hold he bent to Frank, he was unnaturally still. Placing his hand on his chest he felt for his breath, but there was no reassuring movement.

His own breath caught as fear and panic rose in his throat like bile, he fought it back, concentrating on doing what he could for his friend. Gently, brushing away the rubble he pressed an ear to his shirt, listening for the slightest sound of heartbeat, he couldn't be sure but he thought he heard a shallow pulse.

There was little he could do for Frank until help arrived. With a few whispered words he left him and went to search for a way out. Crawling across the ragged ground he came to a solid wall of fallen coal, backtracking he inched towards Frank and then beyond. With a hand outstretched he explored through the blackness until he came to a rampart of rock, icy tentacles gripped his bowels.

The sound of the tolling bell tore along the cobbled streets and dirty back alleys surrounding the stricken pit, freezing hearts and purging houses of women and children. Kettles boiled dry, and abandoned wet washing lay on the dirty yard tiles, an acrid smell of burning food hung over the narrow streets.

Wooden clogs clattered on the cobblestones as women ran towards the pithead, in their wake the streets were left stripped and silent.

Gathering Tommy in her arms Emily ran barefoot, an aching breathless mile of agony with dread in her heart.

Afraid, Tommy held on to the bodice of his mother's grey dress, he knew that something terrible had happened, women were shouting, calling to their children. Terrified, he buried his small head into his mother's breast and cried for his Dada.

Joe knew that Frank was dead, afraid of the truth he'd checked several times praying that he was wrong. His throat ached with the effort of swallowing tears, it was important not to cry here, he would mourn Frank in a clean place, not in this hellhole that had claimed him.

Men were already busy; those that had recovered from the initial shock were tunnelling through the rock and coal that blocked the corridors where colliers and animals lay. The gnawing fear of further falls buried deep within every man as they wrestled in the dangerous filth to free their comrades.

Joe felt the vibrations and a tendril of fear crawled through his belly, another rock fall would sound his own death knell. To fight his fear he thought of Emily and Tommy. They would be waiting at the top. Picturing the scene above ground, the community gathered, agonised and waiting to count their dead.

'Aye and they'll be many of those,' he muttered. His words marred the first sound of metal tools hacking through the fallen coal. A moment later he heard a chink and his heart surged with hope, and for all his sorrow for Frank a smile curved his lips.

It was many hours before Frank's body and Joe surfaced. Night had fallen and amber light from hundreds of candles lit the pithead. Then he was burying his face into Emily's hair, smelling the clean lavender fragrance.

A lump in his throat threatened to choke him, as he said, 'Don't worry Lass, I'm alreeght.' His arms supported her as she clung to him, and her tears streaked the filthy dust that cloaked him.

The following morning, before dawn, men rendered speechless by the horror of the previous day, trudged along the starlit streets, their boots ringing in quiet parlours where the dead lay.

Unaware of his own footfalls Joe trekked the lonely mile, Frank's voice was with him. "Betty and me are going to make our way to Wales as soon as we can. I'll be reeght glad to leave that bloody pit. Work in fresh air, think of it, fresh and clean air." Joe bit back the pain. His barren thoughts brought him to the place he had dreaded reaching, Frank's home. The parlour curtains were drawn, a barrier against the living world, he knew that Betty would be keeping vigil.

A terrible blinding pain of loss crushed him, a silent scream swelled his throat, and he fought to contain his emotions, suffocate his grief.

Long minutes later he walked through the Galloway gates and saw the manager's office window glowing with lamplight. Filled with an urge to thrash the man for his penny-pinching that had caused the tragedy Joe turned in that direction, then checked his stride.

'Bugger won't be there this morning; he'll still be in his bed, getting over the shock that there'll not be much brass made today.' Angry, he turned away

Joe was wrong, the manager was at the pit and a frock coated, silk hatted, delegation stood with him at the shaft entrance.

'Pit's Shut!' The cry started near the pithead, rising to a crescendo it reached the men tramping through the Gower Street gates.

Throughout the night many of them had tunnelled for their comrades, and now after taking a short rest they expected to begin again, refusing to believe that all that were still down there were dead. There was a faint chance, but a chance that they might bring more out.

'Shut? What, closed completely?' Joe roared over the noise.

The man nearest to him shrugged, resigned to the will of the bosses. 'They say it's not safe. Likely to be another fall before the day's out.'

Joe's anger erupted, shouting hard enough to crack his voice. 'Not bloody safe, it never were bloody safe. Bastards!' His raw emotion fuelled other colliers' bitterness.

A man inches taller than the rest, hollered 'He's bloody reeght. It were always a death trap. How many men, woman, and bairns have to die before you buggers' change your ways? Shylocks the lot of yer. Corrupt buggers living off the backs off us workers.'

Agreeing with him they shouted in anger, then shoulder to shoulder the mob pushed forward. A stone was flung, followed by another. Fists were raised. Someone began a chant of 'Shylocks. Shylocks.' A hundred voices joined in. Iron-tipped boots ringing as the men advanced.

Stoically the threatened coal masters held their position. There was fear in some eyes, but loathing of the labouring classes was plainly written in every face.

Taking control the manager shoved forward, commanding above

the roar of voices. 'Where's your respect for the dead?' Instinctively the men faltered at his authority.

Taking advantage of the flicker of uncertainty he pulled himself up to his impressive height, six-foot-two, built like an Irish navy, large hands balled fist by his side; he stared into the faces of the leaders of the rabble, shouting, 'The pit is flooded!'

He was still in control; he had the upper hand. A surge of power made him bold, he'd quell the bastards' single handed if necessary. His massive voice reached the far gates. 'The Galloway is closed! There will be no more rescues. Those down there must stay.'

The threatening black tide halted, and as they stood shoulder to shoulder impotent rage was written in every face. That friends and work mates were to be denied a Christian burial damned them all to bitterness, and the sound of their collective anger was silence.

Rage, futility and sorrow, pressed down on Joe, and through his tears he saw the rose tints of dawn flushing the sky.

His walk home took him passed Frank's home, a dray stood on the cobbles before the front door that only last week Frank had painted moss green, the horse in the shafts had its nose in a feed bag, ignoring the men piling the cart with furniture.

Joe crossed the street, walking towards the house he spoke to a man lifting a mattress onto the boards. 'Is missus in?'

The man thumped the mattress down. 'Betty's round at her Mam's, I'm taking this lot round there now.' He spat onto the road. 'Bugger of a landlord wants the place emptied so he can rent it out toneeght.'

He could hardly bear to say the name. 'And Frank.'

'I took him to his Mam's house.'

Joe was speechless. Smouldering with rage, he walked home.

Emily was tidying the kitchen when she heard the street door open, she jumped so violently that she nearly dropped the dishes she was carrying. 'Is that thee, Joe?'

The kitchen door opened. 'Aye, Lass it's me.'

Her heart recovered, but seeing his drained exhausted face, she was anxious. 'Are thee alreeght, Joe?'

'Don't fret, Em' I'm alreeght.' He slumped into the chair by the hearth.

Earlier she had tried to keep him home but he had insisted that he must help in the rescue. 'What happened?'

'The Galloway's shut.'

'What for good?'

Joe sighed. 'I don't know, Lass, the bosses told us the place isn't safe. As though we didn't bloody know it.'

'Is everybody out then?' Her voice was a whisper.

'No.' it was as much as he could bear to say.

'Oh the poor families.'

Taking a paper spill from the hearth he stuck it into the flames.

'I suppose one grave is as permanent as another, and just as bloody cold and dismal.' He lit his pipe.

Emily's thoughts went to the relatives who would not have the chance to say a last farewell to their loved ones. Glancing at Joe she counted her blessings, it could so very easily have happened to her.

Although she counted herself amongst the lucky ones, the closure of the Galloway brought its problems, the rent was due on Friday, and she owed the corner shop for candles. Only last Tuesday she'd been into Fred Hogarth's shop for some belly pork for tea and found her purse short, and put the bill on tick. Joe would understand and settle up with the tradesmen, but come next week there'd be no money to settle up with unless she dipped into the bit they'd put by.

A door slammed in the adjoining house, and she guessed that Charlie Gormley, a Galloway collier must have come home with the same bleak news.

'What will we do for money?' The question was out before she realised it.'

His eyes caught hers and he saw the effort she was making to remain calm. 'Don't fret, Emily, I'll think of summat.'

Turning to hide her tears she busied herself putting the kettle to the hob.

'Go back to bed, Joe, there's not much thee can do today. Tha looks worn out, love.'

'Aye I will when I've had a cuppa and finished me pipe.' He settled back into the chair, his eyes staring vacantly ahead.

Glancing at him she could have wept, his poor bruised hands and face, and the pain of grief for Frank etched in his eyes. Yesterday she had never expected to see him again, thought this beloved man lost to her forever. Swallowing her tears, she dipped her head to kiss his hair. He was still with her, together they'd get through whatever life offered. Lifting the singing kettle, she poured water into the pot.

The mantel clock was striking the hour as the latch on the kitchen door lifted. Emily turned from the fire, the teapot in her hand.

'It's only me.' Bertha Rushton's familiar voice preceded her into the kitchen.

'Emily do thee want me to take care of your Tommy for a while?' Noticing Joe, she started. 'I'm sorry, Joe, I didn't know thee was at home.'

'Aye I'm home and likely to be for some time to come.'

Bertha looked puzzled, she knew that Joe had come out of the stricken pit virtually unscathed, although he'd lost friends, Frank included. 'Thee's not hurt are thee, Joe?'

'Tha hasn't heard then?'

Bertha's big face clouded.

'Heard what? Not more heartache surely?'

'Aye thee might say that. The Galloway is closed. Likely to be the end of the colliery round here.'

Joe's words sunk slowly into Bertha's mind. If the news were true the unemployment would bring the already poor district to its knees. Bertha owned the local corner shop, supplying the community of Rotherman Street, Houndsditch, the cottages along the Cut and Salford Street with their staple diet of bread, potatoes, suet, cooked pies, ale and vegetables, when she could get them. Most of her customers lived on credit, paying for the goods on payday. Just about everyone owed her money. Naturally optimistic she tried to brush away the threat. 'It doesn't bear thinking about.'

Joe sighed. 'Aye thee's reeght there, Bertha, it doesn't bear thinking about.'

Emily stirred the teapot. 'It's a kind offer to have our Tommy. Joe's all in and could do with a rest. Are thee sure it wouldn't be too much trouble? Our Tommy's a reeght handful at times.'

'He won't be any trouble, our Freda can look after him.' Turning to leave she said as an afterthought, 'Don't bother to give him breakfast he can have something with my lot.'

Before leaving she touched Joe lightly on the shoulder 'Get some rest, lad.'

Emily went to rouse and dress young Tommy, and a few minutes later they left the house together.

Joe heard Tommy's complaints, then a sharper tone of Emily chastising him as they walked along the street. The house fell quiet he could hear the ticking of the mantel clock. Picking up the coal bucket he tipped nuggets onto the burning embers in the grate, the fire crackled as the new coal caught; staring into the flames he saw Frank's smiling face.

'I'm taking mesen off to Wales, Joe. Why doesn't tha come with me.'

His tears flowed, his throat burned with the effort to stifle them, and moments later his body heaved with the bitter cry of loss.

Emily found him like this. Fighting her own tears she went to him and held him tenderly. When he quieted, she coaxed him to their bed and covered him with a blanket. Unbuttoning her bodice she slipped it from her breast and let it fall to the floor, naked she came to him, pushing her fears of pregnancy aside, this wasn't the time to consider the awful possibility. Slipping into the bed she felt the warmth of his body along hers, and then she was in his arms.

Later, Joe slept, the look of exhaustion at last fleeing from his face.

It was much later, when Tommy was in bed and the lamp was lit that Joe told Emily of the slate quarries in Wales.

When he had finished she took his hand, kissing the grazed knuckles. 'We could make a life there, a better life for us and our Tommy.'

Joe smiled. 'We could do that, Lass, it might take a bit of planning, but I reckon we could.'

She looked so unsure and vulnerable; he ached with love for her. Drawing her close he kissed her hair, smelling the fragrant lavender trapped in the dark, silky tresses. 'We would have to find out about work, and get an idea of how easy or difficult it would be to find a home.'

The thought of moving away from the drab street where she'd spent most of her adulthood was terrifying, and thrilling. Would Wales resemble the wild Lancashire moors where she had spend her early years? It would be easy to fall under the spell of adventure. Curbing her growing excitement, she said, 'There's a lot to think about. There's bound to be some difficulties, but we are good at dealing with difficulties.'

She sounded so like her late mother it made him smile. 'I don't even know which road we'd need to take or how long it'd take us to get there.'

She smiled. 'Thee'll find a way for us, Joe, just like tha always does.'

Her faith touched him. 'It's a big step leaving all this.' His eyes wandered over the room.

Her eyebrows rose in surprise. 'The house is only rented, we could rent another somewhere else.' Her hand slid over the wooden back of a kitchen chair. 'We could sell the furniture. We wouldn't get much for it but what we did get would go to pay for basic replacements.'

Taking her mother's wooden tea caddy from the mantel she emptied the contents onto the table. 'We've a bit put by.' Eyeing the meagre pile her nerve faltered. With the Galloway closed it was all that stood between them and the pawnshop. Forcing a bright smile. 'It's enough to get us started.'

Joe heard the fear behind the bold words, and his mind went back to the night when his father had been killed in a pub brawl, his mother reassuring her hungry offspring that all would be well. Her look then, had been so like Emily's now, naked and defenceless.

Taking her hand, he squeezed gently. 'I'll go and see Betty first thing tomorrow, and find out how the poor girl is coping. If I can, I'll ask her how she and Frank planned on getting to Wales. If she's in too bad a way, I'll put it off a day or two.'

Gathering the coins Emily put them back into the caddy. She was a lot luckier than most, many of the colliers wives had a great deal less. Like Betty, who now had nothing at all.

Joe broke into her thoughts. 'I wonder if Betty will mind if we do go to Wales? After what's happened to Frank…'

She was placing the caddy back on the mantel. 'No, I don't think she'd mind. Betty's a practical lass, she'd know we have to do summat now the Galloway's closed.'

'I hope tha's reeght. I wouldn't want to hurt the lass, she'll be suffering terribly.'

'Aye I know, but she's not going to want us to stay here and starve, when we could be better off elsewhere.'

He gave a long sigh. 'I know tha's reeght.'

'Joe, stop worrying. Make a brew while I finish this tidying up.'

Joe found Betty in her mother's parlour, her eyelids swollen from weeping. She was wearing a dress that was new to him, grey and as dismal as an English November sky; it hung off her slim frame, looking as though it had been borrowed for the event of her sudden widowhood.

Joe found it impossible to believe that only a few days ago she had been a happy carefree girl in love with her husband, and looking forward to a new way of life.

A lump was in his throat. 'Are thee alreeght, Lass? How are thee coping?'

Her hands clutching the back of an old dining room chair looked chilled the bones of her knuckles pearl-white. 'I'm alreeght, Joe. It was good of thee to call.'

Fresh tears filled her grey-blue eyes.'I've made all the necessary arrangements for our Frank. Mam and me have done him proud.'

Joe's eyes blurred. 'I'm sure thee has, Lass.' Again the vision of Frank sitting in the Collier pub last Saturday night rose in his mind. From the street came the clatter of a horse and cart on the cobbles.

Betty moved stiffly from behind the chair and came to stand by the empty fireplace; her eyes fixed on the sprinkling of cold ash at the bottom of the swept grate.

Often he'd heard the phrase I though my heart would break now looking at Betty he understood the full meaning of the words, for her heart was surely beyond repair. He thought he'd shed all his tears and was mortified to feel a trickle of moisture running down his cheek, brushing it away with the back of his hand, he swallowed deeply.

Betty spoke in a flat, quiet voice, without lifting her head. 'The funeral's arranged for tomorrow at twelve.'

There were no words of comfort that he could offer; the girl was too steeped in grief to listen to platitudes. 'Is there anything that me and Emily can do?' As soon as the words were out he regretted them, the mention of Emily, a loving partner, seemed heartless, a reminder that other couples had survived, life together went on.

She made no answer, but stood staring into the empty grate.

He made a step towards her, his cap still clutched in his hand. 'I'll come round here at eleven see if anything needs doing.'

She didn't want to say that Frank's body lay at his own mother's house, explaining the landlord's harshness in repossessing her and Frank's home was too much of a sacrifice of her emotional reserves. Joe would demand details, and the man's blood. There was shame enough in not burying Frank from his own home.

Lifting her head her eyes met his. 'Thanks, Joe, I'll be glad of the support and so will Mam. She was fond of Frank, he could do no wrong according to her.'

The news of the closure had reached her, and she said, 'With the Galloway closed what will thee do for work? Last Sunday Frank said it was possible that you and Emily might go to Wales with us. Will thee still be going?'

Before he could answer, she said earnestly, 'It'd be the right thing to do. Then at least summat good would have come out of all this horror.'

Moving quickly, as though there wasn't a moment to lose, she opened a corner cupboard. 'Frank's stuff is in here.'

Rummaging through a pile of papers she drew out a small bundle. 'Here's a rough map the quarrier drew for him, and a couple of useful addresses for lodging.' Fingering through the papers. 'The chap's name and address is here somewhere, he has a team of men working for him, and said there was always a job available.'

She held the wad of paper out to him, and for a split second the thought that he was stealing Frank's place made him hesitate.

Lifting his cold hand she placed the notes onto his palm. 'Since childhood, Frank and thee were best friends, do you think he wouldn't have wanted thee and Emily to go. It was all he thought about lately, how he could convince thee that it was the best move.' She smiled. 'He told me about the squabbles, and how hard it was to get thee to talk about Wales.' Her eyes filmed. 'It's the right thing to do, Joe. Do it for Frank.'

Sniffing back tears, he nodded. 'Aye, I'll do it for Frank.'

Standing on tiptoe, she kissed his cheek. 'Thee get off to Emily. I'll see thee tomorrow at eleven.'

Several days after Frank's funeral, Emily and Joe's furniture graced the pawnbroker's shop window. There were a few things that Emily had flatly refused to be parted from; one was her mother's tea caddy and a sampler her grandmother had stitched when a small child.

Emily often ran her hand over the imperfect work imagining the small girl labouring over her stitches. Mary Ellen Hanover, born in the year of our Lord 1780 in Roebuck Cot, Ashton.

Joe had raised his eyes to the heavens as she packed the precious material and the caddy in the bottom of a bag. The mantel clock, Tommy's monkey on a stick, a pipe rack and three pipes, and a few home necessities were well placed between a variety of clothes.

The day to leave their house and everything familiar dawned. Emily watched the sun climb over the rooftops, and for a brief moment saw the windows along Rotherman Street flame crimson as the first amber rays lit the panes of glass. A sight familiar to her, but this morning it brought a pang of regret that never again would she witness God's spectacular glory reflected on the parade of windows of the terrace of red brick houses.

For days butterflies had fluttered playfully just beneath her breastbone, ruining her appetite and adding nausea to the string of symptoms her anxiety had created. There were so many things to organise, the selling and removal of the furniture, selecting what they could or couldn't take, then packing the bare necessities. Tommy constantly underfoot made the smallest chore a difficult task.

Whilst she was busy she had no time to worry and ponder on the uncertainties of their future in Wales, and for that she was grateful, as a few of her symptoms left her and she had less need to continually trot to the privy outdoors.

Now they had done all they could, everything was ready and Emily stood beside Joe in the empty room waiting for George Fanshaw, the drayman to arrive. Joe had stacked the bags and roll of blankets beside the open front door, and as protection from hungry stray cats Emily had the large basket packed with food at her feet.

Nervously Joe checked his pockets for the umpteenth time to

assure himself that the map of Caernarvonshire and their planned route were stowed safely.

During the early hours, unable to sleep, Emily had sewn a small pouch in her wool skirt and placed their few coins in it.

'Any robber would be a foolish man indeed,' Joe had laughed seeing her handiwork, 'if he tried to lift her apparel and steal her treasure.'

Sniffing, Emily had dropped the hem of her skirt.

Wisely, Joe knew when not to pursue a joke.

Young Tommy was standing on an old discarded wooden chest, nose pressed up against the window, his small hands spread on the cold glass.

Joe had a moment of sheer panic, looking at his young son, he knew they had to make the journey, but the uncertainty of their future was like a physical ache at the pit of his stomach.

The clatter of iron rimmed wheels on the cobblestones halted his thoughts.

Shrieking, Tommy leapt off the chest and ran to the front door.

Emily's butterflies rose. This is it then, she thought, there's no turning back.

Emily heard Bertha caution Tommy. 'Just thee mind thesen young man tha'll tumble running like that.'

Joe was oblivious to her words, his mind had wandered back across the years to his earliest memory, burying his nose in the worn cotton of his mother's apron and smelling the dough and yeast clinging there. Standing in the bare room he fancied that he could feel the heat of the old oven on baking days as though it was alight now. His glance fell on the cold empty grate. It was going to be as hard as he had feared to say goodbye to this old house that had sheltered him through boy and manhood. Things that had up until this moment been nothing more than familiar objects suddenly took on a new light of valued treasures, his mam's washing tub in the back yard, the stone sink where his father had washed pit muck of his hands and face. Childish carvings in the back door, done by young siblings that never survived beyond childhood, names etched roughly in the thick wood. Birthdays, Christmases, wakes, the old house had seen them all, laughter and tears.

Looking across to him Emily saw the way of his thoughts, the memories flowing unbidden.

Speaking softly, sorry to hurry his last moments here. 'Are thee ready, Joe?'

He smiled. 'I was just remembering our wedding day. Thee looked so pretty all done up in tha Sunday best, with that daft hat borrowed from our Nancy. All pink and white frothy stuff.'

Emily's eyes filled. 'That were a great day.'

'Aye it was that, Lass. A great day. Carried thee right over that very threshold. Weighed nowt more than a bundle of washing.'

George Fanshaw poked his head round the door. 'Are you folks ready for the off?'

'Sorry, didn't mean to delay tha, George.' Joe gave the room a last look then took his leave. Bags stuffed under his arms, he walked out of the house.

Emily's hand trembled as she reached for the basket at her feet. Then with a sad sigh she gave the parlour a final glance, whispering goodbye. For the very last time her hand held the familiar brass doorknob, battered by time and worn thin by many hands. Winged moths of apprehension came fluttering to life below her belt, willing them away she closed the door, then with forced calmness she turned and had a smile ready for Joe and Tommy.

It was between nine and ten in the morning and the day was warm, the sun glinting on the brasses adorning the black and grey Shire horse, clumping his great hooves on the cobbles. George Fanshaw had the animal's bridal held firmly, steadying his massive head.

Joe had stowed the bags and blankets on the cart, and was lifting Tommy aboard as Emily stepped out of the house.

He returned her smile. 'Come on, Lass, let's get tha aboard.'

Shrugging off their winter woollies, neighbours had gathered to see the Standish family off. Ancient relatives drawn out of hibernation by sons or daughters leaned against rickety doorframes.

Emily acknowledged everyone, and was beginning to chatter to Bertha, when Joe took the basket from her and pushed it under the plank seat.

Then with a grin that said 'women' he steered her towards the wagon, lifting her aboard with a flourish that spread her skirt and flashed a hand stitched edge of her white petticoat.

Emily reddened at the show of her husband's affection.

Bertha gripped Joe's shoulder. 'Take care of the Lass and the little un.' Then grinning. 'And thesen, Joe.'

Emily's chin was up; she was biting back tears, clutching Tommy's shoulder.

George called over the chatter. 'Are ye about ready to set off?'

Joe kissed Bertha's cheek. 'Take care.'

He turned to George. 'Aye we're ready. Let's go.' Jumping up, he sat beside Emily.

Loosing the bridle George patted the animal's head affectionately, then taking the reins he settled on the driving board. 'Up and at um Billy.' Swishing the reins above the horse's rump.

The wagon jolted.

Joe caught Emily's eye, and she put out her hand to touch his.

From a doorway, an old man called, 'God speed Joe an Emily.'

The cart moved forward.

Joe saw an image of Frank has he had been on that last Saturday night in the Collier.

"What does thee say Joe, will thee come with us to Wales?"

Aye Frank, he thought, I would have gone with thee.

A man called from an entry opening. 'Be happy, Joe.'

I'll be happy. I have a chance to be that. He squeezed Emily's hand.

Chapter Two

For Emily and Joe the journey through the back streets and the roads leading out of the parish had been a revelation. Everything was so much cleaner, better kept, the further away they got from the factories and slums. The size and grandeur of the houses improved to such a degree that an hour after leaving Ashton they were passing homes where small patches of grass grew behind iron railings.

When the streets narrowed to lanes and green fields were either side of the cart, Emily was in her element. A country girl at heart she took great breaths of clean, fresh air. Exuberant, she told Joe how remarkable everything was every few minutes. From the trees being nearly in full leaf. That pale primroses were peeping through new grass. And linnets were singing in flight.

Delighted by her sheer enjoyment, Joe listened to her, and added a few observations of his own.

The road narrowed further, cutting through an old forest where the overhanging branches formed a long, dim tunnel. Passing out into the sunlight once more, George pointed out the canal; it was down in a slight valley, running straight as a ribbon. They lost sight of it as trees obscured the view.

Tommy became restless.

Turning in his seat, George smiled at the child. 'Not long now, young fellow, just another minute or two. A quick trot down a bit of a hill and then we'll be there.'

Finding his coat, Joe slipped it on, checking again that Frank's notes were still safe in the pocket.

It was near midday when they came to the redbrick bridge spanning the canal; with gentle words George coaxed the horse up the incline.

Craning his neck, Joe looked over the parapet.

The canal here was cleaner than the canals and wharves that were familiar to him; those at the city's manufacturing heart were filthy cesspools. Industrial greed had turned the watery thoroughfares into stagnant open sewers, running with the waste of iron ore, coal, cotton, bone, lime and more obnoxious minerals to season the pestilence. The once verdant banks were now barren. Although the scene here was different, pastoral and picturesque, he knew there would be no flash of silver fish in the grey water, they had long gasped their last.

He got a better view as Billy crested the crown, and he saw several hundred yards upstream to a lay-pool where three black, work barges were moored, the small quay looked deserted but for several horses grazing near an old warehouse. The doors of the building were propped open with planks of wood, and a rope swung from an overhead gantry. Along the canal bank several brightly painted narrow boats were moored.

Billy clip clopped slowly down the cant, the wheels of the cart rumbling.

George halted the horse.

The animal snorted loudly, moving restlessly in the shafts. George explained, 'Billy doesn't like canals. A bargee owned him before me, the careless bugger let poor Billy fall into the water, hell off a job to get a horse out, 'specially in a tunnel with bricked banks, where Billy nearly met his Maker.'

Looking down at the almost motionless water, Emily imagined the terrible calamity, the terror of the poor horse struggling in the darkness.

Joe muttered his concern, but his mind was already on the next stage of the journey. Jumping down, he retrieved the baggage. 'Thee should get back, George, I don't want to delay thee more than we have already.'

'I'll give Billy a few minutes rest before we head back home.' He searched successfully for his pipe and shag in his tattered coat pocket, and then lighting up he sighed with satisfaction.

Catching a whiff of the sweet tobacco smoke, Emily was transported back to her grandfather's parlour, the old man in his chair by the fireside, his pipe clamped between what remained of his front teeth. She wondered at the power of fragrances to send a mind hurtling back years.

Beside her Tommy started to fidget and whine.

'Thee can stop that now, our Tommy. Sit still and wait.' Giving him a look, which said mark my words or else, she scooped up her skirt and climbed down.

Joe was looking up-stream to where the first of the boats was moored. She stood beside him, her hand on his forearm. 'What should Tommy and me do, Joe? Stay here and wait or come with thee?'

His hand covered hers. 'Stay here. I'll come back if I can get us a ride.'

He met the eyes of his young son. 'Behave thesen, young man.'

Without waiting for a reply he stepped over the low stone wall and clambered down the steep embankment. The grass was long, spiked with towering nettles, a tiny wilderness speckled with flowers; he took a long deep breath, and for the first time he really looked forward to the adventure. Jumping the last couple of feet he landed sure-footed on the towpath.

Stopping at the first boat he knocked on the cabin roof. There was no reply and he was just moving away, going to investigate the warehouse for signs of life, when a dirty, militant looking lad appeared.

'What do yer want mister?'

Ignoring the lad's question, Joe said, 'Is tha father or mother about?'

Before the youngster replied, a heavyset man appeared from the cabin, he was unshaven and by the look of him had been so for several days

With blatant suspicion in his eyes, he grunted, 'What can I do for you?' Stooping he claimed a thick rope off the deck and started to coil it around his massive forearm, wielding it like a weapon.

Joe had rehearsed the conversation in his mind several times, but when faced with asking a stranger a favour he felt awkward, thick tongued and embarrassed. 'I'm trying to get to Runcorn. I'm looking for a boat that's heading that way. I'm willing to pay summat for the ride.' He spoke hastily, judging that the man thought he was scrounging. 'If thee's going to Runcorn or if tha knows of a boat that is, I'd me glad of a lift.'

Slinging the rope down the bargee ordered the boy to stow it.

Joe thought he was going to be ignored. 'I'll work.'

'Know a lot about boats then?'

Joe's face flamed pink. 'No nowt at all. But I do know about work.'

The bargee took several slow breaths.

Joe was of a mind to leave it and find someone else to hitch a ride from, as he didn't think he and this rude bugger would be the best of friends by the time they reached Runcorn.

He was about to turn away when the man said, 'What's your reason for going to Runcorn?'

Joe kept his thoughts about Nosy Parker's to himself. 'I'm making me way to Wales, I'm trying to find work there. I have me wife and nipper with me.' He glanced back to the bridge. 'If we can get to Runcorn, it shouldn't be too difficult to get a boat from Liverpool to Caernarvon.'

The man pushed back his cap, wiping sweat from his hairline with a dirty rag. 'Well if that's the case I'll take yer.'

Joe's face relaxed. 'Thanks a lot. It's appreciated.'

'No thanks needed. Yer'll have to do a turn of work, help the lad here. I'm short handed today, Old Macgilligudy, me usual helper is laid up, broke his leg falling off the lock gates yonder.'

'I'm sorry to hear that.'

The man grinned for the first time. 'You'd have been a lot sorrier if he hadn't. I wouldn't be taking yer to Runcorn.' Pleased with his joke he laughed, wiping his eyes on the rag. 'You'll need to be on board in the next ten minutes.' The scowl was back, his face like a bloodhound's. 'I'll wait for nowt or no one.'

'We'll not keep thee waiting.'

Emily knew that Joe had good news when he turned to wave. She wondered why she had worried, if anyone could fix things Joe could. Smiling, she returned his wave.

Hurrying back along the towpath he climbed the embankment.

Tommy was standing on the parapet of the bridge, George's arm around his waist. The child was giggling with excitement, clapping his tiny hands, as his father scrambled up.

Joe was slightly out of breath. 'It's all fixed. The boat yonder is leaving in a few minutes, but we'll have to hurry, the chap doesn't look like a man blessed with patience. He said he'd not wait above ten minutes.'

Flustered, Emily grabbed a bag and reached for another.

Joe took control. 'Hold on, Emily. Calm down, sweetheart. Just take the blankets. I'll deal with the rest. More haste less speed remember.'

Taking Tommy from George, he lowered the child to the ground. 'I'll lift the stuff down when I've taken this little ruffian.'

George picked up the basket. 'Let me help with that lot.'

'There's no need thanks, George. Emily and me will manage. Thee's done enough for us today.'

Joe slung Tommy onto his shoulders.

Giggling, the child curled his tiny fingers into his father's hair.

Carefully, keeping the child steady, Joe climbed down; reaching the towpath he lifted the child down and stooped to draw level with the three-year-old. 'Don't move till I fetch tha Mam.'

Tommy nodded, acknowledging the seriousness of his father's voice.

His mother repeated the warning. 'Don't move, our Tommy.' Without taking her eyes off the youngster, she hoisted her skirt above the snaring weeds and scrambled down, there was no reassuring smile on her lips, and when the soles of her boots slipped on the grass she gave an unexpected cry.

Tommy shrieked.

'Take care, Emily!' Joe's tone mirrored Tommy's alarm.

Reaching the path she stooped to Tommy, holding him close. 'It's alreeght, love.'

Laden with baggage, Joe drew alongside them. 'Come on, our Tommy. We're going to have a great day.'

From the bridge George called to them. 'Don't forget us. Send a letter to the dray office, let us know how things are.'

Emily waved. 'We will, George. Promise. And thanks for everything.'

Turning, Joe called, 'Goodbye, George. Thanks for the ride. We will write soon.'

Hurrying, Emily moved as quickly as her long skirt would permit, but every few steps the hem caught in the brambles growing out of the hedgerow, cursing she pulled it free once again and hurried on. God knew how long they might have to wait for another boat if they missed this one. With visions of huddling beneath the hedge for the night in the freezing cold, she caught up with Joe and Tommy.

As they drew alongside the barge, the elderly man elbowed the boy forward. 'Help the lass with her bundle and show 'er where to stow it.'

Emily, reluctant to allow the filthy child to touch her newly washed blankets, clutched the roll. 'Thankee but I can manage it for mesen.' She tried to hide the snap in her voice with a smile.

The boy shrugged.

Joe bent to Tommy, swinging him off his feet. He caught the faint whisper of the child's breath on his face and an immense feeling of love checked him. What if I fail him? He thought, as he planted the child on the deck of the Alexandria.

The boy unlocked the cabin hatchway. Then with a leap he landed on the narrow deck, and jumped down to the towpath.

Admiring the lad's vitality and agility, Joe sighed for his own lost boyhood. Taking off his coat he slung it down carelessly and rolled up his shirtsleeves. Turning to the boatman he smiled. 'Makes a man envious, all that energy.'

'Wasted on 'im, he's a lazy bugger generally. He just showing off.'

It was impossible not to smile. His eyes flicked to the boy. 'Show me what I can do to help.'

'Catch the ropes as the lad chucks 'em on board. Wind 'em up and throw 'em down below. Then when we get to the other end yer can fish 'em out, tie 'em on, and sling the other end to the lad. Easy.'

It hardly constituted a day's work and he expected more would be asked of him before they reached Runcorn. Believing that forewarned is forearmed; he asked, 'Are thee taking on any cargo?'

A wry smile was on the fellow's lips. 'Oh aye. We'll take a bit of a load on later. You'll come in right handy then.'

Obviously the man wasn't going to be more forthcoming as to what the load would be. It didn't matter; he'd know soon enough. Picking their bags up off the deck, Joe stacked them in the cabin.

On deck, the bargee turned his craggy face to Emily. 'You and the nipper can sit at the stern. Little beggar might like to see the bridge as we pass under it.'

'Thanks very much, I'm sure he'll be interested in everything that's going on.' Wondering if she might have given the wrong impression, that the child was likely to be a nuisance, she held the boy firmly to her skirt. 'He'll be no bother.'

Her eyes flashed a warning to Tommy, and under her breath she warned him. 'Thee had better behave thesen, me lad.'

Tommy was more interested in the horse, now harnessed, than listening to his mother as she tried unsuccessfully to tow him towards the stern. Pulling in the opposite direction he whined.

Emily tightened her grip. 'I've told thee behave thesen or I'll give thee a reeght wallop.'

Astonished by his mother's tone he submitted and walked quietly towards the narrow perch near the tiller.

At the bow, Harry tugged the horse's head free from the last bite of grass he was stealing.

Emily took in the scene, at peace for the first time since the Galloway disaster. Joe was at the running block at the bow, as though all his life had been spent on boats. Harry was whispering into the ear of the Shire. His skinny arm lying affectionately along the animal's neck. The bargee at the helm was gauging the readiness of the boy and horse. Tommy leaned against her, smiling she hugged him close.

'Ben's ready.' The lad sounded eager to be away.

'Get a bloody move on then yer daft sossidge.'

The boy gave his father an affectionate grin, used by now to his old man's crabby disposition. He had learned early in life to accept the long silences and irrational, unearned chiding's.

With his fingers looped through the bridle he coaxed the horse forward. Three steps and the rope attached to the halter was taut, the muscles on the animal's back rippling as he took the strain. The barge moved slowly, once in motion it was easier, slipping gently through the water. Catching a long blade of grass as he walked, the boy put it between his teeth and chewed the end.

Emily would often recall the moment when the horse trod beneath the bridge and into the tunnel. The sound of his great hooves clomping on the paving beneath the dank and mossy arch. It was much dimmer beneath the vaulted roof than she expected, echoing and strange, and the circle of yellow light ahead looked far away. Beside her Tommy inched closer, the warmth of his little body warming her thigh. The child's face filled with awe as he looked up to the dripping, brick roof.

Long minutes passed before the *Alexandria* glided from the shadows and into the April sunshine.

Soon they were moored at a factory wharf. The horse left to roam the towpath found untrodden grass to eat. As Joe and the bargee loaded bales of Lancashire cotton destined for shops in Wales, Emily and Tommy took a walk.

On the move again, passing by the cotton mill wharves where workers lucky enough to have a break sunned themselves for a few precious minutes. On into pastoral England, unchanged but for the canal for hundreds of years. Cows grazed, farmers sowed crops, thatchers wove their intricate craft, children played, chanting rhymes as old as time, it was all to see as the barge meandered through the rural communities.

The sun set at seven o'clock, the air growing chill after the warm spring day, and as they cruised up the canal nearing their destination Emily and Tommy retreated to the warm cabin. Through the partially open door the men's desultory conversation came to her, and occasionally she glimpsed either one or the other of them, their faces lit by lamplight. The boy stayed with the horse, coaxing and guiding the creature, padding softly now on the bare soil of the towpath.

The men started to ready the boat for mooring. Emily hearing the thump of heavy ropes on deck, and the rattle of the lamp swinging as they changed course to meet the dockside, came up on deck with Tommy.

The night sky was immense, pricked with starlight, a crescent moon riding high in the ink black. The industrial harbour was silent but for the sound of water lapping at the dockside and along the hulls of the berthed boats.

Jack Duffield brought the *Alexandria* to her berth, easing the boat between a pair of butty barges moored there.

Joe, although no expert, jumped off and tied the mooring lines to iron rings set in the flat stones, then stepped back on board for the baggage.

The horse had his nose buried deep in a feed bag as Joe finally disembarked and joined Emily and Tommy on the dockside.

She was stooped buttoning Tommy's coat. Glancing up. 'Everything done, love?'

'Aye it's done.' Fondly he glanced back at the *Alexandria*, the darkness had robbed her of her bright paintwork, reduced her gypsy shades to dull oxblood and dark grey. Twin slivers of lamplight showed through chinks in the drawn curtains. He took a final glimpse of the day, it had been one to remember, a good day.

Emily was tying a red woollen muffler around Tommy. Wriggling he tried to break free as she tied the ends in a tight knot at his back.

'For goodness sake, Tommy hold still.'

'Mam?'

'Yes, love.'

'Where we sleepin' toneeght?'

She kissed his warm, baby soft cheek. 'Tha dad will find somewhere for us. So don't thee worry.'

Stooping to his tired child, Joe swung him onto his shoulders. 'We'll stop at the first likely place we come to and get lodgings.' Rubbing the palm of his hand along the child's cold leg. 'Then me little pet can fall into his bed an' sleep till morning.'

Crossing and tying her shawl, Emily glanced at the pair. 'Aye, stop at first place we see, Joe. Our Tommy is all done in, poor little beggar.' Covering his small bony knees with his coat, she planted a kiss on his leg. 'We'll soon have thee in bed, sweetheart.'

He gave her a wan smile and laying his cheek against his father's hair he closed his eyes.

Sharing the baggage between them, taking the most cumbersome herself, she checked Joe's protest. 'Hold on to our Tommy watch he don't fall, he's all but asleep.'

'Just say if that bag is too much for thee, Emmy.'

For all her tiredness, she grinned. 'I will an' all.' Hoisting a heavy bag and settling the roll of blankets beneath her arm, she fell into step with him.

Following Jack Duffield's directions they swung away from the canal, leaving the deep shadows of now silent warehouses, sheds and stockyards behind them.

Emily's elbow was never far from Joe's, the narrow street empty and desolate at this time of night brought thoughts of departed and restless spirits into her mind. Trying to convince herself that she was being, as Joe would say, too fanciful, she tried not to heed the sound of their lonely and overloud footfalls, which she was sure would alert every ne'er do well in the parish, and probably Old Harry himself of their passage through Runcorn. Catching Joe's eye she immediately dismissed the idea of asking him to step more quietly.

'Penny for tha thoughts, Emily.' He gave a crooked smile quite aware that she was having what he considered being one of her spirity moments.

She knew what he was hinting at and wouldn't give him the satisfaction of knowing the way her mind was running. With a sniff, she said, 'They're worth a sight more than a penny, Joe Standish.'

He stifled a giggle. 'If I offered thee a shilling would thee take it?'

Haughty now she raised her nose. 'Thou hasn't a shilling to spare, and me thoughts are still worth more'n that anyway.' Her eye caught a shadow moving between buildings and thoughts of besting Joe fled. Her voice dropped to a whisper. 'Did thee see that?'

'What?'

'Summat moved.'

'Probably a cat.'

'No, Joe, it were too big fer a cat, it was as big as a chap. Look, there, it moved again. I'm scared, Joe.'

Coming to a standstill he focused his eyes to the shadows, his breath stationary in his chest.

Emily clung to his forearm. 'Joe.'

'Shush, Emily.' Listening intently he heard slow footsteps. Keeping his voice light to reassure her but aware that someone lurked in the shadows, he said, 'Whoever it was has gone now.' He was more pleased than he would have liked to admit when they reached a row of redbrick cottages where light shone from small windows.

Emily downed her baggage.

Holding onto Tommy, Joe bent to retrieve it. 'Here let me take that heavy one now.'

'No I only stopped to change over.'

'Emily.'

Recognising the stubborn tone, she gave in. 'Well just for a minute or two.'

They walked to the end of the street searching for notices in windows advertising that the occupants took paying guests.

'Perhaps we'll have more luck yonder.' Emily's mind was on a cup of tea and a warm bed. She was tired, probably as tired as Tommy and he was asleep. Joe had the stamina of a dozen men, nothing and no one would break his back. How she loved him, his strength and dependability. Glancing up into his face she gave him a smile. 'I love you, Joe Standish.'

Bending his knees he planted a kiss on her cold brow. 'An' I love thee, Emmy. You're a great lass to be upping sticks and coming all this way wi' me.'

'I wouldn't be anywhere else in the world, Joe.'

A few steps on they glanced through an open door of a terraced house and saw several horses tethered there, they looked content enough in their unlikely home chawing on dry hay bundles. There were few of the trappings of the parlour save that of an ancient stool by the empty fireplace and a lit candle on the mantel top. A hostler, his garb the tattered remains of an infantry conscript, back bent by worn bones, was tending to their needs.

At a glance Joe counted seven horses then his attention was taken by the stick thin man. Old enough to have known Wellington himself and fought alongside him in his early campaigns, Joe spoke with a certain deference, touching his cap. 'Goodneeght to thee.'

Startled, the old man slopped water from the pail he was clutching.

'I'm sorry I didn't mean to alarm thee. But I'm looking for a night's lodging hereabout for me wife and bairn. Can thee tell me where we might find such a place as takes lodgers overnight?'

The man raised his face and in the light of the single candle flame he looked as wrinkled and dried out as last Christmas's apples.

Straightening slowly, his hand clasping his painful hip, he groaned. 'Plenty of folk round here take in boarders but I know nowt of 'em. Nor have I a wish to. You'd be better served by asking the chap that keeps the provision shop around the corner. He's nowt but a few steps further on.'

Joe started to thank him.

'No need to tell him who sent you. There's no reason to let locals know that I'm going soft in me old age. Now be off wi' yer I've me 'orses to mind.'

'Thanks anyway.' Joe smiled with amusement. 'And trust me I'll not let anyone know that thee's taken to being kind and gentlemanly.'

'Tosh. Away with yer.'

Joe was still smiling as he and Emily fell into step.

'Poor old fella.' Emily spoke sympathetically.

'Poor old fella my arse. He looked as happy as a pig in swill to me.'

'There's no need for coarseness, our Joe.'

'I'm not being coarse, I'm just saying he looked content with his 'orses. That house made a fine stable for 'em all. I suppose the old fella lives above them. A cosy and warm billet if thee asks me.'

'Well, Joe Standish I only hope tha's got better ideas for our Tommy and me. Cosy indeed.'

Rounding the end of the street the aroma of ripe cheese and fresh fish wafted to them through the open door of McGregor's provision shop.

Emily's stomach rumbled. 'I'm famished. It seems ages since we had a bite back on the boat.'

'Thee go in and get what we need for a bit of supper and a drop of milk for our Tommy. We'll wait out here. Don't forget to ask about some place to stay.'

Her eyes went to the heavens. 'Course I'll ask, Joe. I'm not completely daft just yet. Men.'

Grinning, he watched her climb the three steps into the shop. 'Women.'

Rummaging in her basket she brought out a small tin container and spoke to the women behind the counter. 'Would thee fill this with fresh milk if tha's got it? And I'll take a piece of that cheese.' She pointed to a large round. 'And if tha has got a good sized loaf I'll take that an' all.' It was a novelty shopping for a loaf and Emily's thoughts went back to her kitchen and the smell of warm bread baking, a weekly chore normally done on a Sunday morning. Inwardly she sighed.

Mrs. Mcgregor, as Emily supposed the woman must be, for surely no self-respecting shop owner would employ a woman with such a sourpuss, looked up from cutting the cheese. 'Will you be needing fresh butter to go with this?'

Emily felt a tinge of pink rise to her cheeks, obviously the woman understood that the pennies in her purse had to stretch a long way and found some mischievous delight in reminding her of the fact. 'A ha'p'orth of lard is all I need.'

Wiping her greasy hands on her pinafore the woman glanced at Joe and Tommy standing in the doorway. 'Just lard then.' Spooning a dollop of the white fat onto paper, she weighed it carefully.

Emily was glad to push her purchases into the basket and remove herself out of the shop, away from the scornful eyes of its mistress. Outdoors was less frosty than the atmosphere within.

Tommy was still fast asleep, his small head drooping over his father's shoulder.

With his hand on his son supporting him, Joe looked expectantly at Emily. 'Did she say where there might be some place to stay tonight?'

'I nearly forgot to ask. The woman was such a misery. She gave me such an eyeful our Joe, I hope the folks down here are not all so unfriendly.'

'It doesn't really matter, as we are not staying in the place above a night. That's if thee'll furnish me with the information the she gave thee.'

She smiled sheepishly. 'Am I going on a bit?'

'It's to be expected, I know that tha's tired out and worried.'

She began to walk on.

'I know that tha likes having a bit of a secret, our Emily. But tha might tell me where we are going.'

She grinned. 'I just might.'

'Tha's mighty playful for someone so tired.'

Half-turning she grinned back at him. 'We are nearly there. Sourpuss said the house with the green door and green gate takes in lodgers. She was sure that none were staying tonight, because the landlady had been in the shop ten minutes ago complaining about it.'

'Stop a minute, Emily and take our Tommy. Those bags are too heavy for you.'

'No need to stop, we're here.' She dumped the bags on the step at the front door.

Lifting Tommy from his shoulders he cradled his limp little body in his arms.

The child stirred and whimpered.

'Shush, love.' Emily coaxed, stroking his cold leg.

'Get down, Dada.' Shuffling out of Joe's arms he stood forlornly rubbing his eyes with his knuckles.

As there was no knocker on the door, Joe thumped it with his fist.

'Mind, Joe, they'll think we've come to knock the 'ouse down.'

He was just about to start a discourse on folk not attending to their business of admitting lodgers, when the door opened. An elderly woman in a rusty black dress, her iron-grey hair coiled like two fat snakes over her ears, and her thin mouth drawn tight like a purse string, gazed down at them.

Tommy backed into his father's legs, and Joe put his hand on the lad's shoulder to reassure him.

The woman had no business to stand there frightening bairns, if she chose to take in lodgers the least she could do was run a hospitable house. His mood bordering on short-tempered he met her withering glance.

'We are in need of lodging for the night and we were told that tha might be able to accommodate us.'

Now that they had stopped traipsing, Emily felt a stab of cold night air creep under her shawl raising goose-bump on her arms. She shivered.

Casting a glance over Emily, she said, 'You are in luck.'

Joe doubted it. Reminding himself that beggars can't be choosers, he forced a smile.

It must have melted her frost for she opened the door wide and gave what might have passed as a smile. 'I have an empty room at the front of the house, the bed is big enough for the three of yer wi' a bit of a squeeze.'

Joe had no qualms haggling the price of the room to what he considered fair, the house only just passed muster, by the woman's own admission they'd need to breathe in if they were all to fit on the bed. What's more they'd need to see in the dark, for he'd never seen such a lack of light in any house. There was not above two candles lit in the hall and the old woman was holding one of those fairly close to her chest.

Following Mrs. Collins, she had introduced herself the moment the bidding ended, they trailed behind her up the uncarpeted staircase.

Joe had Tommy in his arms; there wasn't an ounce of energy left in the little lad. It would be a wonder if he were still awake when the milk that Emily had bought and Mrs. Collins had promised to heat, arrived.

Guided by her candlelight they passed along the narrow corridor towards the front room, mindful of the uneven floor and miscellaneous steps. The temperature of the house was little different from the outside air, but as Mrs. Collins opened the door of the bedroom a colder blast escaped.

Reading Joe's mind she preempt his complaint. 'I'll send me son Gerry up wi' a bucket of hot coals from our own stove, you'll have a blazing fire in no time. Our Jenny will warm the milk for the little one. A couple of hot bricks for the bed and you'll be right as rain.'

She lit the candle in the old fashioned candlestick, Joe hadn't seen the like of it since his own grandfather was alive, then seeing his expression she lit its twin. Departing with her candle she took a good portion of the light with her.

Gently, Joe eased Tommy down onto the bed. He looked vulnerable and forlorn, his little legs mottled with cold. Joe would have given anything he had to give, to see Tommy asleep in his own bed, lying between clean, aired sheets.

Understanding what was in Joe's mind, for the same thought was not far from her own, Emily tried to sound cheerful. 'This is certainly a bit of an adventure, Joe. Me an' Tommy loved the boat ride today. Didn't we, Tommy?'

Smiling sleepily, Tommy nodded. 'I liked the boat, and Ben the 'orse, he was nice, Dada.'

Joe kissed the child's forehead. 'Maybe we'll go on another boat tomorrow. Will that make thee happy?'

The room was too cold to tug off her boots as Emily longed to, doing the next best thing she took the weight off her feet. Sitting beside Tommy, she pulled her shawl close. 'The three of us will have a great day tomorro' but now it's Tommy's bedtime. In two shakes of a lamb's tail we'll have my pet in a nice warm bed.'

All three looked up as a timid knock tapped the door.

Joe called, 'Come in.'

Jenny, Mrs. Collins daughter stood on the threshold, with a tin mug of steaming milk in one hand and a candle in the other, she had the look of a terrified gazelle. Her dark eyes darted to Tommy.

Eagerly he held out his baby hands for the mug.

Joe came up from his crouch. 'Thank you very much. Our Tommy will enjoy that, it'll warm the little bairn.' He spoke quietly aware that the young girl was painfully shy.

Her adolescent cheeks blushed crimson; free of her small burden she fled, running down the stairs.

'Girls,' he said, as though that explained everything.

The milk was steaming; he tested it with his lips before offering it to Tommy to drink. Clutching the mug the boy warmed his cold hands.

Emily was opening one of the bags when she heard hurried footsteps on the stairs.

The door practically blew in, a young man speckled with ginger freckles and an impressive auburn beard, came dashing in clanking a bucket of burning coals, hot fumes trailing in his wake.

Rather breathlessly he blurted his name. 'Gerry Collins.' Tipping the smoking contents into the small barred grate. He tapped the bucket with his boot. 'It's only a matter of time before the hot coals falls through the bottom of that, but Ma won't listen. Carrying hot coals around this house from morn to night, she is. Burn her bloody feet off one of these days.'

Sitting on his haunches, he took lumps of coal from a nearby scuttle and threw them onto the fire. 'Soon have a good blaze going.'

Emily came alongside him, frozen to the marrow. 'Thanks ever so much, we are really grateful.'

He blushed to the roots of his hair. 'It's no trouble.'

Jenny stood in the doorway; no one had heard her steps on the stairs. She was holding a tray. 'Mam asked me to bring a hot brick for the bed and a pot of tea.'

Gerry spoke sharply. 'Stop hovering, Jenny, and come in.'

The girl's face turned hot carmine. Without meeting his eyes she put the tray down and made her escape.

Embarrassed, he tried to explain. 'She's always been amazingly shy. Not like her twin, our Martha. A regular little vixen that one.'

Emily frowned. 'Twins? That must be a terrible burden when they are very young.' Pouring tea into the two mugs on the tray. She glanced over at Joe, who had the hot brick in the bed, and was taking a top layer of clothes off Tommy before putting him into bed.

Sighing, Gerry said, 'They are all a burden, Mrs. All twelve of the buggers.'

'Twelve!'

'Aye.' He sighed again. 'And our father dead this last five years.'

Emily pitied Mrs. Collins. Twelve and no man bringing in a wage. No wonder she looked a surly woman.

'Sam, that's me brother, helps me with the fishing now.'

Tommy settled, Joe crossed to the fire.

'So yer a fisherman, Gerry?' Conscious of his accent Joe made an effort to drop his tha's and thee's.

'Aye. Sam and me use our father's old boat. We just about manage to keep the family afloat between us.'

Sitting on the scruffy chair at the fireside, Joe ferreted in his pocket for his pipe.

Handing him a mug of tea Emily sat on the chair opposite him, her feet crossed to the fire.

Pleased to see a drop of milk clouding the strong brew he took a sip before speaking. 'If yer know the port you'll be able to give me some advice.'

Emily's face came up and she looked puzzled.

Joe grinned. Not much got passed Emmy. She'd quiz him later, and he'd get a roasting for trying to be what he was not.

Gerry smiled. 'Fire away. Anything I can do to help, I will.'

Leaning forward, Joe poked a paper spill into the fire. His eyes turned to Gerry as he lit his pipe. 'Would you know of a boat that sails to Caernarvon in Wales?'

'Aye, I do. The Hardwick Lady sails on the tide three times a week, weather permitting. Her route takes her beyond Bangor to Caernarvon.'

Joe grinned. 'Do you happen to know the captain? Or is that asking too much?'

'Me mother know him better than I do.' He sounded amused. 'The poor devil has taken quite a fancy to her.' He laughed. 'It won't do him any good though, she'd rather swim the Mersey than take another chap on.'

Joe laughed with him.

Keeping her thoughts to herself, Emily sipped her tea.

'Sam and me will be going out on the first tide; we can cross to Liverpool docks on the full tide to the *Hardwick Lady*. I'll introduce you to the man.'

His pipe empty Joe knocked the ash out in the grate. 'We can't put yer too that much trouble. It'd take up too much of tha's time.'

'Tosh. Sam and me only said yesterday that we need some advice off yonder rigger, so it will suit us both to go and see the chap on the dockside there.'

Joe looked serious. 'If tha brother isn't happy wi' the plan, I expect to be told. There'd be no offence taken.'

'Sam won't mind. We need to go over to Liverpool dock anyway. The tide will be full at nine in the morning; we'll be across the water and be in the docks in two to three hours and with a bit of luck, The *Hardwick Lady* should sail on the top of the tide. So we'll need to sail at half tide, three hours before her, at six o'clock.'

Joe had expected to lose a day or two looking for a ship. Now with everything more or less settled he could relax. Reaching for his pipe, ignoring his self imposed rationing; he filled and lit it. For the next few minutes he relaxed, listening to the chatter between Emily and Gerry.

Joe opened his eyes to see the watery light of a grey dawn showing through the chink in the curtain. Tommy's small body was folded into his. Emily, asleep the other side of the boy, slept deeply. He was loathed to wake them. Gently, disentangling himself from the child he climbed out of the bed and walked over to the window. The air was chill not a vestige of last night's blazing fire glimmered in the grate. Shivering, he parted the curtains and was disappointed to see neither the canal nor the river Mersey. Roof tops and drab streets were all there was in view. A few workmen were passing the house, on their daily pilgrimage to work.

Behind him Emily stirred, raising herself on one elbow she said sleepily, 'Joe tha'll catch cold standing there. Put summat warm on, those combinations won't keep out influenza.'

'Aye in a minute. I'm just trying to make out in which direction the river lies.' He wiped away the condensation his breath was forming on the cold glass. 'I reckon it's only a couple of streets away. There's a break between the set of houses just beyond...'

Sitting up, Emily ran her fingers through her long tangled hair, twirling it into some sort of a topknot. With a hairpin between her teeth, she said, 'It can't be far away.'

Turning, he saw her with both hands raised above her head, her loveliness still had the power to astonish him.

Taking the pin from her lips she slipped it deftly into her hair securing the knot. Then pushing the blankets from her she started to rise.

He watched as one bare leg as pale as ivory slid from beneath the grey blankets, a flash of thigh and its twin emerged. As she stood, her white shift spilled down, hiding her nakedness.

A wave of desire swept through him, and forgetting the imminent appointment with Gerry, the close proximity of Tommy, and the certain opposition from Emily, he turned to cross to the bed.

Emily brought him back to reality. 'Put summat warm on, Joe.'

Sighing, he pulled his woollen shirt from the pile of discarded garments on the chair.

With his back to her less she should see the evidence of his passion he dressed quickly.

Belting his trousers he looked over his shoulder. 'I'll go and find Gerry, and see if I can rustle up some tea from Mrs. Collins.'

'Aye tha do that. I'll get Tommy dressed and the bags packed.' She gave him a pleading look. 'Do tha best with that tea, Joe, I could murder a brew.'

Mrs. Collins was spreading dripping on a stack of toast as he walked into the kitchen. She looked less formidable with her hair unbraided and her face soft from sleep. Hardly raising her eyes from her chore, she pointed with the knife.

'You'll find warm water for a wash and a shave in any one of those three kettles on the hob.' Her eyes went back to the toast. 'You can use the scullery sink. I'll make a brew whilst you get on with it.

'Thanks. Is Gerry about yet?'

'He's looking around the yard.'

Joe took this to mean that he was using the privy, so made no comment.

He was stripped to the waist standing at the stone sink in the scullery when the back door opened and Gerry walked in.

'Morning, Joe. It's a bit nippy out there, but it looks like the rain'll hold off for a bit.'

'Let's hope so. Emily has a natural dislike of foul weather.' He grinned. 'It seems it has the impertinence of ruining either her bonnet or her hair.'

Gerry laughed. 'Women, who'd be with out 'em?'

Joe finished his shave. 'Not me. Our Emmy wouldn't hear of it.'

Sam came into the kitchen as Joe was drying his razor. Gerry outlined the plan to sail to Liverpool docks.

They were still talking about the times of the tide and state of the weather as Joe returned upstairs.

Seeing that he came with a mug of tea, and a plate of toast and dripping, Emily kissed his cheek. 'Thanks, sweetheart. Thee's a marvel.'

At a glance he saw that they were ready, dressed and packed, the blankets on the bed thrown back neatly.

Ten minutes later, they were standing in the hall, bags at their feet. Sam appeared, Gerry following was buttoning his coat.

Outdoors it was chillier than Emily expected, and tying her shawl, she stepped onto the pavement. Joe walked by her side, Tommy on his shoulders, the boy mumbling happily about boats and the seaside. Sam and Gerry walked ahead leading the way down to the wide tidal river.

As they neared the water the smell of wet mud, seaweed, and dead shells was on the air.

Considering that he hadn't a lot of sleep, Tommy was quite cheerful. 'Will we see a nice bridge like we saw yesterday.'

'Which nice bridge, sweetheart.' Emily was only half listening to the child; her attention was fixed on the water ahead, white plumes tipped the small waves on the slate-grey surface. She didn't dare to contemplate its depth.

'Mammy will we?'

Before she answered, they came to the river, and Tommy was shouting in delight.

Moored at the dockside were several boats, most of them sitting unbelievably low in the water.

Emily's heart missed a beat. She almost cried out, We can't get in one of those Joe, they don't look safe.

Stooping, Joe took Tommy off his shoulders. 'Now just mind thesen I don't want to have to pull you out of the drink.'

'What drink, Dada? I want a drink.'

Gerry took the child's hand. 'Never mind a drink, come and see the boat you're going to sail across to Liverpool in.'

'What's Liverpool?'

Bending to the boy Gerry pointed to the far side of the river. 'Over there, as far as you can see, is Liverpool.'

'It's in the fog.'

Butterflies fluttered in Emily's stomach. 'It's a lot further than I expected.'

Pointing to a boat with a black hull, Gerry said 'That's *Pretty Polly*, she's a Morecambe bay Shrimper, or Prawner as they're called here. She was built nearly twenty years ago, but the newer ones are much the same.'

'It's low in the water.' Emily was nervous.

'That's so the nets can be hauled in easily.' He grinned. 'Not the driest boat in the world.'

Emily glanced at the sky. Rain was imminent. If that didn't drench them, there were no below decks on *Pretty Polly* she was open to the elements; then they'd cop a wetting for sure from the waves already dancing along the hull. And they hadn't set sail yet or got into the middle of the great mass of water. Bracing herself for a wetting of a lifetime, she climbed aboard with Joe's help, and settled where Sam instructed her to with Tommy beside her.

Sam and Gerry made ready to sail.

Joe sitting on the upper edge of the side of the boat, he'd learn later to call it the gunwale, watched their actions intently, eager to learn and make himself useful. His eye had already caught the copper boiler and guessed it was for boiling the catch before it came ashore. Had he not been born in a landlocked town he wondered if he might have gone to sea, it would have been a life that would have satisfied him. Too late now, he'd never see thirty again and besides he was a married man and father. He hid a smile as he thought how Emily might take the news if he said he'd changed his mind about working in the slate quarries and decided to go to sea. Glancing at her he saw her face was pinched, and she looked a little green.

The black sails were hoisted, gently flapping in the breeze as they began to unfold.

Gerry took the tiller, nudging it to port.

Sam drew in the lines linking them to the shore. Unfettered, the boat moved gently from the dock, heading for deeper water. Catching the breeze the sails unfurled with a crack like an old tree splitting in two. An untied sheet slashed out; caught by Sam he held the rope tight in his massive hands binding it around a belaying pin. The black sails filled with God's own energy and *Pretty Polly* heeled to the stiffing breeze, her bow cutting through the water, scudding faster than the overhead clouds, on the river in full flood.

They seemed to be moving at an amazing rate, Joe turning to Gerry asked how fast were they going. He looked to the shore then to the water and said, 'Five knots. Maybe a little more.'

They were getting into deeper water, the bow lifting to meet the waves and falling back with a small bump that vibrated along the bottom of the hull.

The smell of fish, Stockholm tar, sea and the slight aroma of the lard Tommy had eaten with his morning toast sent Emily stomach quivering. Praying that she wouldn't embarrass herself she concentrated on the clouds racing behind the black sails.

Beside her Tommy wriggled more than any unfortunate shrimp that had found itself destined to the copper boiler. Joe took him from her. He was full of questions and Joe wondered if it wouldn't be his son that took to the water when he became a grown man.

Sam said he was going to make a brew, eyeing the copper that he proposed to brew upon. Emily longed for a hot drink but cringed at the thought that it might be tainted with the aroma of fish. Risking all, she said she would love a cup and could she help.

Sam laughed saying, 'The old boiler likes a lot of attention before it condescends to build up a head of heat and as I'm used to it and its nefarious ways I'll deal with the brute myself. But thanks for the offer. Not many women come on board and offer to help.' He laughed again. 'Most wenches were too busy holding on to the sides or feeding the fish.'

The picture made Emily's stomach tremble.

Other boats were passing them now, some crossing the river and others making their way to Liverpool or Wallasey. Emily gave them all her attention; it was better than thinking of the other unfortunates that had suffered a queasy stomach before her.

'If all the trees still stood that made masts for the ships moored in Liverpool docks it would have made a veritable forest,' Joe said as they drew nearer to the shore. 'And if one thought of the amount of timber that had been sawed for ships planks it might have covered the entire soil of England.' He was stooped, hands on the gunwale, to get a better view of the thicket of ships that blocked the sight of the warehouses, inns, shops houses, markets and buildings beyond.

'Lord how ever will we find the *Hardwick Lady* amongst them.' Emily said.

Pointing to a smaller copse of masts, set slightly apart from the main forest, Gerry said, 'She's berthed amongst that lot there.'

'I have never seen anything like it.' Joe gaze was on the dockside. 'And if I hadn't seen it wi' me own eyes, I reckon I wouldna believed that there were so many ships in a port all at the same time.'

'There's a fair amount in there that's for sure. But nothing like as many as in Nelson's day or so our old father was fond of telling us.' Sam grinned reliving the memory of the oft-repeated family anecdote.

Turning his head Joe looked over his shoulder. 'I suppose he was a young man in Nelson's day?'

'Young enough. He couldn't have been above ten when Nelson died, but he swore he'd seen the man himself standing on the dockside yonder.'

Joe's eyes went to the dock, in his mind he saw the great man casting a glance at the small Morcambe Bay Prawner making its approach to the shore.

Fixing a line at the bow, Gerry called to Sam. 'We'll be alongside in a few minutes, best make ready.'

Rising from his knees Sam made his way astern.

To keep out of the way Joe sat back down on the gunwale, clamping Tommy between his thighs. 'There, now thee can't escape me.'

Feigning an escape bid Tommy giggled, wriggling to be free.

'Hold still, Tommy, we don't want thee falling overboard. What would Mama say if we lost thee to the fishes.'

Emily's head shot up. 'Mind what tha father says, Tommy and hold still, there's a good lad.'

As they approached their destination, the dockside wall loomed above, overshadowing the brown water.

With her heart in her mouth, surely the boat would never stop in time, Emily watched Sam and Gerry who had long mastered the art of bringing in the thirty-five-foot boat, prepare to bring her alongside. Reducing the canvas at just the right moment, and handling the tiller with the expertise of long-time mariners, they had her lying along the dock wall with barely a bump.

Leaping ashore with a line Sam hauled on the rope, tying it to the nearest bollard, a shiver ran through the boat as the power changed from wind to man. Then held fast she lay still on the water, submissive and docile as an ancient pussycat. Few knew what a she devil *Pretty Polly* could be in a storm, and not all had lived to tell the tale. But for now, lying alongside, she bobbed contentedly, the tidal water running beneath her hull.

Remaining on the dock to give what assistance he could to the family as they disembarked, Sam drew his tobacco pouch out of the pocket of his fisherman's smock, and filled the bowl of his clay pipe. Half an eye to the moored boats expecting to see a familiar face, he waited for Emily to master her sea legs and make her way to the portside. There was quite a step up to the dockside, and he was ready to give her a tug up to land her safely.

The glance she gave Joe said it all, and putting down the bag he'd just picked up, he said, 'Nothing to worry about, Emmy, I'll give thee a shove up and Sam'll give tha a pull. This was no time to stand on her dignity and with a small acknowledging nod she put her boot on the gunwale and outstretched her arms to Sam.

Her long skirt flapping in the breeze covered Joe's head as he placed his hands on her behind. Stifling the bout of laughter that threatened to land him in trouble and Emily tumbling back in the boat, he gave her a push up. She was ashore before she'd glanced down into the dark water between the hull and the wall.

Sam glanced away from the amusement in Joe's eyes, one more grin from Joe and he'd end up in a fit of laughter himself, and looking at Emily's stern expression he knew that it would bode no good to anyone if either of them gave way.

Gerry lifted Tommy to Sam and caught the look of mischief in his younger brother's face. To hide his smile, he said, 'Check that stern line, our Sam.'

'Aye aye, skipper.'

Joe almost leapt ashore.

Still standing on her dignity, Emily snapped. 'Just mind tha self, Joe and don't show off.'

'Sorry.'

Ignoring him, she picked up her food basket and roll of blankets. Turning her attention on her young son. 'Mind theself Tommy and stay away from the edge. Tha'll fall in.'

Finishing tying the sails Gerry came alongside them. 'I'll take you to the *Hardwick Lady* while Sam finishes off here. It is not too far, shouldn't take us more than a few minutes.'

Joe called goodbye to Sam then turned to Gerry. 'I really appreciate everything tha's done for us.'

'I'm glad to help, Joe. It is not easy setting off new like you and Emily are doing. Sam and me are glad to assist. We only ask one thing in return.'

'Anything I can do I will.' Joe looked puzzled.

'I just want to hear from you both when you've settled.'

Keeping pace with them, Tommy's hand in hers, Emily said, 'We'd be glad to let thee know how we've faired. Won't we Joe?'

'Course.' It meant a lot to Joe to think that the two young men, comparative strangers cared.

The *Hardwick Lady*, an old topsail schooner, a sturdy workhorse of a ship, defaced and blackened by scores of cargoes, was a hive of activity. Her crew making ready to sail closely watched by the Captain at the taff-rail. His voice could be heard along the dock swearing at the men either to haul cargo aboard or those on the main deck to shift faster.

Emily felt sorry for them, if straining muscles and sweat were the measure of their effort they were working to their limits and his admonition was a waste of breath.

Grinning, Gerry muttered for Joe's ears only. 'What a tartar.'

The captain was a tall, very large boned man with an enormous breadth of shoulder. His features were harsh, bushy white eyebrows overhung piercing eyes, similar whiskers poked from beneath his cap.

Seizing the opportunity of greeting him during a very brief lull in his criticisms, Gerry lifted his hat. 'Morning, Captain. How are you today?'

As though there hadn't been a bad thought in his head that day, the man looked down at the small group. Joe could see now that he had a capacious mouth and when it curved in a smile the man looked almost human.

'Gerry Collins, we don't often see you walking the quay. How are you? And how's that lovely mother of yours?'

'The whole family couldn't be better and Mam sends her regards to you.' It was a lie but he judged it to be worthwhile. As he was about to ask a favour of the man it was well to have him better tempered. He was about to elaborate on his mother's conversation, but reckoning she'd wallop him if she got to hear of it, he explained his mission simply.

'I have some passengers for you if you've a mind to carry 'em.'

'Oh yes.' The captain's stern face returned.

For a moment Gerry thought he'd failed at the first hurdle. To put a better slant on things he told another lie. 'These good people are family friends, you'd be doing Ma a favour in taking them to Caernarvon if that's where the *Hardwick Lady* is bound for.'

A smile lit the captain's face. 'If they are friends of your mother's that's good enough for me. But mind, we don't put on airs and graces for passengers.' Addressing Joe. 'You'll be expected to stay out of the way of my men and keep below if we run into any bad weather.'

'And you are sailing to Caernarvon?'

'Of course we bloody are. Where else does this ship ever go?' Pausing to holler at one of the hands, before saying, 'Get on board sharpish we sail on this tide not the bloody next.'

Joe clasped Gerry's hand. 'Thank you for…'

Embarrassed, Gerry released him. 'You heard the man, get on board. All the thanks I want is the message from you that you have settled. So mind that you don't forget.'

'We won't, I promise.'

Reaching on tiptoe Emily kissed his cheek. 'It was really nice to meet you, and Sam. And thanks for everything that thee has done for us. We are really grateful.'

He'd whipped his hat off as Emily reached to plant her kiss.

'Say thank you to Gerry.' Emily pushed Tommy forward.

'Are we going to feed the fishes, Mister Gerry?'

He stooped to the child. 'I most certainly hope not.'

'Tha friends fed the fishes thee told Mama that's what they did.'

Laughing, Gerry tumbled the child's hair.

'Whatever will he think of next.' Emily looked with amusement at her young son. 'Feed the fishes indeed.'

Scooping the child up, Joe laughed. 'Come on, young man let's get thee on board with Mama.'

Emily bent to pick up some baggage.

From his place of power the captain yelled down to her. 'No need for that, Madam. I have a ship full of lazy beggars that can assist with that lot.' With an ear piercing bellow heard in every corner of the ship. 'Merriman at the double get that dunnage on board NOW!'

Watching the family board, Gerry felt regret that they were leaving, He had got to like Joe, he was the sort of bloke he would have liked to go fishing with, and enjoy a drink with in O'Flaherty's public house.

Emily glanced back at him as she stepped onto the deck, then bent to Tommy who's bootlace had come unfastened, when she straightened, Gerry had disappeared, lost in the throng of dock workers.

'Merriman.' The captain roared near Emily's ear startling her. 'Get that stuff down below now.'

The unfortunate mariner the captain was favouring with his orders was skeletally thin, squint eyed, his skin the colour of an old nutmeg, but for all his unhealthy appearance he jumped faster than a big cat to the pile of baggage he'd dumped.

Bending his back, he gave Emily a sidelong glance, grunting, 'Follow me.'

Catching a whiff of his foetid breath she held her own until he had turned his head away. Joe was several feet away, holding on to Tommy's hand, answering one of the little lad's interminable questions.

Attracting his attention. 'Joe we are to go with the chap who has the bags.'

Stopping mid-sentence Joe scooped Tommy up. 'Righto. We're coming.'

Merriman was at the companionway ladder, juggling the baggage for his descent. Under his breath he cursed all passengers, an anathema, their only useful purpose being that the more nervous of the bunch allowed for a bit of sport now and again.

Afraid that she'd lose sight of him and their few belongings, Emily lifted her skirt above the damp planks hurrying after him, trailing down the companionway steps.

Merriman stood with his back to a stove warming his backside.

Joe clattered into the large open cabin, Tommy in tow. Feeble light from two suspended lanterns barely lit the wooden panelled place but there was enough to discern a long table bolted to the floor, with a bench similarly fastened too each side. There was a stove, which was bright enough with hot coals to render it a useful companion to the lamplight.

Holding Tommy's hand, Joe made for the plank seat where their luggage lay. 'Thanks for fetching the bags down.'

It wasn't in Merriman's nature to accept a word of gratitude and as he wasn't troubled with compliments, one had never come his way, he reacted in his usual surly fashion by saying, 'Weren't my idea.'

After long years working underground with men a great deal more sullen if not downright vicious, Joe was unfazed by the sailor's demeanour he pressed for the information he required. 'How long will it take us to get to Caernarvon?'

Scratching himself, Merriman pondered the question. 'Ten or twelve hours in fair weather, but today it's likely we'll meet a bit of a blow, so it'll take us a mite longer as the wind'll come from the direction it's a mind to.' Glancing at Emily he saw he had her full attention and he wasn't sorry to see her unsettled. Enjoying his brief malicious moment, he said. 'Baring accidents, or the ill fortune of running into a widow maker, we might make it in twelve.'

Panicked butterflies swirled in Emily's stomach.

Aware that the man's remark had reached its target, as he had intended it to, Joe matched Merriman's malevolent smile. 'There'll have a hard task ahead of thee if tha's aiming to frighten me wife. She doesn't scare easily and neither does me bairn. If tha's a mind to upset somebody I suggest tha starts wi' me, tha's already set on reeght road to do it.'

Wilting under Joe's hard-eyed stare, Merriman sidled from the stove and made for the companionway ladder.

'Widow makers indeed. The man's bloody feeble minded.' Jerking his head back Joe gave a short laugh.

The strokes of the ship's bell reached below decks. Joe made a stab at guessing the time. 'Must be eight o'clock.' Eager to get on deck to watch the crew make ready for sea, he settled the child beside his mother. 'Stay here while I go and find out when we are to leave.'

'This is exciting isn't it, Tommy.' To hide her nervousness she spoke cheerfully. The last thing they needed was for Tommy to take fright and make a fuss for the next twelve hours. Praying that he might sleep for most of the journey, she promised him a story if he was a good boy and sat quietly.

Glancing at Joe she saw that the chances of him sitting quietly, or sitting at all, were bleak. He was too anxious to be on deck.

'Go up, Joe. Bring back some news.' She smiled seeing him so eager. Like a big kid really. 'Go on.' She gave him a nudge.

Overhead, the captain barked an order.

Before Emily could change her mind Joe made for the companionway. Climbing up quickly.

The *Hardwick Lady* was a flurry of activity. Every man was on deck or in the rigging. Aft, the captain was pacing the quarterdeck. His big nose sniffing the breeze, his eyes on the horizon watching for rain.

Leaning his big body over the rail the second mate bawled to the longshoremen. 'Get ready to cast off.'

Joe turned his face to follow the captain's line of sight, and felt the freshening breeze on his cheek.

The helmsman looked up to the masthead to where the topsail would soon fly.

Joe felt a rush of excitement, a profound eagerness to be under sail. The last grains of sand of his previous life were running out, the unknown waited. His gaze moved slowly across the land in the distance, grey in the early morning mist. Focusing on a single distant point he wondered if it lay in the direction of the Galloway.

'Ready to cast off.'

The captain was at the helmsman's elbow. The second mate still leaning across the rail looked down to hawsers, thick as a man's wrist, holding the ship to the dock. Above him, men and boys clung like monkeys in the rigging ready to loose the canvas. Their shaggy hair whipping in the breeze. Trouser legs flapping against bare ankles.

'Let her go.'

The main topsail suddenly flapped like thunder and *Hardwick Lady,* the water running under her hull, began to turn to deeper water.

'Lay her on a port tack, Mr. Jones.'

'Aye aye.'

The wind caught the topsails and she began to lie over, gathering speed as she met the fast running tidal water, hitting the wake of a larger ship with her port bow she plunged into it, sending a spray of water flying across the weather rail. Joe, his face into the wind caught the stingingly cold spindrift, he laughed aloud at the gloriousness of it.

With her stern now to Liverpool, her sails braced sharp on the port tack, she was making her way to the open sea on the long beat to the bar. The captain with a telescope to his eye swept the water ahead and to port and starboard, with a precautionary glance to his stern where a big lugger and schooner were leaving the dock.

Squinting, Joe could just make out a buoy dipping and rising between the waves, here the water looked turbulent, white-tipped spray flying from it.

A handful of raucous gulls that had been following the ship turned landward, their cries lost on the wind.

They were nearing the bar, green water washing fast along the portside. The wind piping in the rigging as *Hardwick Lady* dipped her once majestic bows into the heavy seas, clawing her way to the treacherous bank.

The buoy appeared to rush by as they passed it, plunging and sinking into the dark water, close enough for Joe to make out the great chain holding it fast, green with algae and clinging weed.

This was an adventure that he would not have missed for the world; he was still far enough away from the unknown to make it possible to put thoughts of it aside for a few short hours. Out here in this glorious open space the Galloway didn't exist. God, he felt alive. Damp but happy, he thought, smiling.

They crossed the powerful water race and lifting her bows the ship headed for the open sea.

He waited until the endless sea was before them, the land fast receding, before he made his way to the companionway. As he appeared, Emily noticed that some of the lines, achieved at the time of the disaster, had disappeared. Wind and spray had given his completion a healthier colour.

'It's started to rain. Not heavy but enough to drench.' He pushed his wet hair off his forehead. 'It's great up there. The water is a bit choppy and the wind is picking up.'

A smile was on her lips. 'Joe Standish I swear thee will become a sailor yet.'

He laughed. 'I wouldn't mind that at all.'

'Joe tha wouldn't.'

'Don't be daft, Emmy, not full time, just now and again for sport.'

'Sport indeed. When did folks like us think of sailing for sport?'

'From now on I hope. This is a new life, Emily, and I mean us to enjoy it to the full.'

Riding a great wave the ship's bows rose, then came thumping down, jarring through her timbers.

Losing her footing Emily staggered, recovering, she clutched the edge of the table and held on. 'Well tha won't be finding me sailin' for fun.'

Just in time Joe caught the rail on the companionway. To humour her, he laughed. 'Perhaps I had better rethink this sport lark.'

Grabbing at anything stationary, Emily made it back to the seat by the stove. Behind the bench Tommy slept in hammock, protected from the pitch and roll of the ship.

'Takes a lot to wake that little tyke. Not a bit like you, Emily in that respect.'

She looked across at the still child. 'I hope he's alreeght. Poor little mite.'

Joe smiled fondly. 'Course he's alreeght. He's tough our Tommy, tougher than tha knows. And what better way to ride out a bit of a blow. He can't hurt himself snug up there.'

The day wore on, the weather improving as the ship changed course heading for the Cambrian coast. Tommy slept, exhausted with excitement and the effect of a late night.

Emily and Joe, her hand in his, talked of their future. During the late afternoon her head slipped to his shoulder and she dozed for a while.

Premature night had fallen when the *Hardwick Lady* rounded Anglesey.

After a late supper he left Emily and the boy sleeping, and went up on deck.

The breeze had strengthened, and he shivered at the chill of it. Finding a sheltered spot he lit his pipe. Absorbing the soft sound of the sea, he tilted his head to the sky and smoked contentedly. There was no moonlight, and against the clouds the sails were indigo shadows. Ahead, ink-black waves rolled towards the lights shimmering on the land. The solitary moments were perfect, calming his mind. Tomorrow, with all its uncertainties lay far enough away to be a shadow. Dismissing it from his mind he went over the events of the day. Knowing that, even if he could, there wasn't a portion of it that he would have altered in any way.

The Watch called an order, summoning the sailors. The bark of it was so much part of the ship that it disturbed him not at all.

A moment later from hatchways and dark, private recesses, men emerged, their feet clattering across the planks. The rigging creaked as many of the hands climbed aloft. A moment later the topsail was furled. *Hardwick Lady's* pace slackened and her bow dipped to meet the short waves. Ahead of her the dock was alight with lamps.

Joe's stomach fluttered with excitement.

When at last the ship's movement ceased Emily thanked God for their safe delivery. Calling Tommy to her, she dressed him in his outdoor coat and mittens. She was stuffing his scattered belongings into a bag when Joe came down the companionway steps.

His face glowed with excitement. 'We've arrived and no widow makers, storms, gales or catastrophes.'

She grinned. 'What's it like?'

'What?'

'Outside. What's it like?'

'Too dark to see anything.'

'Oh, Joe there must be something to see.'

Grinning. 'Well there's quite a big quay and an enormous castle. At least I think it's enormous. Like I said it's hard to see anything clearly.'

Her eyes shone. 'I can't wait to explore.' Hugging Tommy. 'At last. We have arrived, Tommy. Isn't it exciting?'

Sleepily, he rubbed his eyes.

Hurrying, Joe began collecting the bags together. 'I'll get this lot up on top and then come back.'

On deck Joe hunted for Captain Jenkins.

Emily, incapable of remaining still for a moment longer, collected the remaining possessions, and helping Tommy up the steep steps, followed Joe. Coming on deck she saw him chatting with the captain. Joe offered the man money only to have it refused. Pushing the coins back into his pocket Joe shook the captain's hand. A few more words passed between them, and then Joe, skirting around a bunch of sailors winding ropes, crossed to Emily.

'Wouldn't he take anything from thee Joe?'

'No. He said that his reward would be in a dinner we might offer him when we're settled.'

Catching the captain's eye she waved, calling. 'We expect to see thee soon. We'll keep an eye out for the *Hardwick Lady* coming into port.'

Giving her a cheerful wave, he chuckled. 'Expect nothing less young lady. Now you be on your way, and put that little lad in a warm bed.'

A last farewell, then laden with bags they walked gingerly across the rickety gangplank. Emily thought her legs were going to give way as she took her first step on terra firma. Gaining her sea legs had been difficult enough, now she wondered how she was going to rid herself of them. She had no notions of climbing aboard a ship again; it was all the same to her if the next boat she rode in was Saint Michael's. Gathering her shawl about her, she relayed this thought to Joe.

With laughter on his lips, he drew her to his side. 'There's an inn at the end of the dock. Let's make for it.'

'Lordy, does tha know everything, Joe?'

He laughed again. 'The captain gave me the information.'

Tommy listened to scraps of their conversation. The cold crawling under his coat collar. The promise of warm milk and a biscuit kept his chilled legs moving. He remembered little of that night except that he spent it snug between his parents warm bodies in a curtained bed.

Chapter Three

Overnight the weather improved and it was to a cool but bright morning that Joe led Emily and Tommy out of the seventeenth century inn and into the narrow street.

Standing under the timber porch, Joe stooped to knot Tommy's muffler and draw his mittens over his hands.

Emily, surveying the houses was amazed that there wasn't two the same shape, size or height the entire length of the street, so different from the long slum terraces and mucky alleys of Lancashire. There was poverty here like everywhere else, the run down houses were proof of it, but alongside the poorer dwelling were homes that evidently enjoyed better circumstances.

The front door of the house opposite opened, and a couple of middle-aged women wearing plain black dresses and mantles emerged. One was carrying a basket covered with a blue cloth, as she passed by her eyes took in the baggage at Emily's feet and she gave her a keen, reproachful look. The other, retying her bonnet riband didn't give her a second glance, but a word from the other woman and she looked over her shoulder and gave Emily a haughty look.

Unperturbed, Emily glanced at the young woman walking behind them, a baby in her arms. She was thin, thin enough for the olive dress she wore to hang limply. A black shawl wrapped around her shoulders was ragged at the fringe. The child stirred and whispering a word to it she dipped her head and kissed the tiny forehead. Emily's eyes followed her until she was out of sight.

Satisfied that Tommy would be warm Joe stood, his eyes meeting Emily's. 'Shall we take a look round? Or should we get ourselves off straightaway?'

Earlier, when he had first risen and poked his head out of the bedroom window he had heard the sound of the sea washing the shore. Last night it had been pitch-black when they arrived and now he was curious to retrace their steps from the dock and get a look at the castle, which had been a great looming shadow, eerily foreboding, easy to imagine its ancient ghosts were keeping watch.

'An hour shouldn't hurt, Joe. I would like to look at the tiny church.' Picking up the basket, she smiled down at her son. 'Come on, our Tommy take my hand.'

'Are we going to see the big ship, Dada?'

'Aye. There'll be lots of big ships I shouldn't wonder.' Joe smiled. He'd be glad to get a look at the *Hardwick Lady*. The old ship had not only gained his affection but had stirred a liking for the sea. He felt so full of energy it was hard to stay still, or keep to the slow pace of the three-year-old. He took a deep breath of the chill; salty air then expelled it with a loud sigh.

'Happy, Joe?'

'I feel better than I have for an age.'

She'd noticed that he had more of a spring in his step.

He grinned at her. 'Down here and turn right.'

'But, Joe the church is in the opposite direction.'

He looked back to the short way they had come. 'Don't fret, Em. We can walk back that way.'

A group of schoolboys, clean from an early scrubbing, rounded the corner. They were all carrying a book. The tallest was poking a tubby lad, teasing him until he was near to tears, the rest laughing maliciously.

Joe frowned at them, they fell silent, and the bully sticking his hand in his pocket stared ahead. Then as a pack they ran on shouting and laughing disturbing a dog sniffing a post, the animal barked and gave chase, the boys ran faster squealing with fright.

Joe gave Emily a grin. 'Boys who'd have 'em.' They both glanced down at the top of Tommy blonde head and laughed. Emily squeezing the child's hand gently.

As they reached the end of the street and turned the corner the sound of waves breaking on the shore was clear.

'Joe just look at that! I wonder how old it is?' Emily was looking to the farthest end of the narrow cobbled street to the gatehouse in the castle walls. The ancient archway was wide enough to support a building above, and deep enough for a man to take more than a dozen paces to walk from end to end.

'Centuries and centuries old I reckon.' Joe's eyes were on the water visible through the arch, the blue-grey expanse of the Menai Strait stretching towards the sea.

Emily admired the workmanship of the stone ceiling arching above her head, as they walked through.

Tommy delighted to hear the echo of his voice hollered several times. Then escaping his mother's grip he ran to the seawall.

Dropping a bag, Joe caught him by the coattail scooping him up. 'Tommy Standish tha is a reeght rascal.'

Giggling, he struggled to be free. Holding him tightly around the waist Joe put him down on top of the wide, flat wall. 'Look, Dada look. The big ships. Where are they going?'

'America perhaps or Liverpool. Everywhere.'

Excitedly he pointed. 'Mammy see the ships, they are going everywhere. Dada said so.'

Joe's gaze passed over the water and settled on the distant meadows of Anglesey. The land he could see was verdant, and looked thinly populated. In the valleys there were a handful of scattered farms or cottages. A straggling forest peaked the higher ground, the trees hazy green with the beginning of spring. Promising himself a day off soon to explore the island, there were several small open boats moored on a tiny sandy shore probably used for fishing or ferrying to the mainland.

If he could convince Emily to climb aboard a ferry, she'd been quite adamant last night that she would never set foot on a boat again, they could explore together. Glancing at her expression as she watched a lugger leave the safety of the quay he doubted that he'd ever convince her that as a mode of travel it wasn't dangerous.

But my God the scenery was beautiful. The air clear as crystals, the water shimmering in the early morning sunshine. The majestic castle seemed to rise out of the water.

'Emmy, did tha ever see anything as beautiful?'

'No, Joe. It's all so lovely. I can't believe that we are going to make our home here. Or at least near here.'

The tide had begun to fall, the water no longer breaking along the long stone wall, now the waves were curling, white tipped crests breaking onto the sandy mud. Exposing eel trails, long dead shells, broken weed, and an empty bottle stuck up to its waist in the brown seabed.

It was time to move on.'Let's take a quick look at the castle before we set off for Garddryn?'

Without replying Emily picked up her basket and a bag and with her mind on the dirty alleys of her former home, she walked on.

On the top of the wide wall, his hand in his father's, Tommy kept up a running commentary of everything he saw. Agreeing with everything the lad said, Joe kept his eyes on the castle, dreaming of its history.

The reality of its beauty took his breath away. Making mental notes to discover everything he could about its past, he walked across the worn stones of the great square tower, built to defend the entrance. It was so high, immense, looking up the majestic stone walls to the angular towers made his head spin, clouds racing across the sky toying with his sight. 'My God, anyone standing up there would see for miles around. We'll have to come back and have a proper look. It is amazing. And the mountains look at 'em, Emily they're beautiful.'

'I reckon that tha's pleased to be here, our Joe.' She smiled.

'Aye, Emily I am an' all. My God it's quite something.'
'Well let's hope that Garddryn has the same effect on thee.'
'Aye let's.' He grinned. 'Is that a hint that we should be on our way.'
'Aye, summat like that.'
The streets were beginning to fill with people. There were ten laden carts in a line making their way to the quay, a mule drawn wagon climbing the steep incline to the main street.

Stopping for a moment Joe drew the map out of his pocket. 'The road we want is up the hill. With a bit of luck we might cadge a ride.'

Following the quay road out of town they saw evidence of the slate industry everywhere. In complete contrast to the beauty they had witnessed. Here the ground was laid barren by waste, spoiled stock, and surplus industrial production. There wasn't a place in the land, he thought, that work didn't stain. Wales was not unlike England in that respect. And hadn't it been said more than once where there's muck, there's brass.

Turning, he gave the castle a final glance. Nowt would spoil that beauty for centuries. Man would come and go and his mucky work with him, but a thing that splendid should last forever.

Cheerfully, he settled the bags into a comfortable load. 'Come on, Emily, let's try to get a ride to Nantlle. It's not above ten miles at a rough guess. Once there we'll soon find a home to call our own. So look lively woman, grab a bag and the child.'

'A daft beggar tha is at times, Joe.'

He grinned. 'Aye so yer fond of telling me.' He gave another shot to dropping his northern dialect. Although he'd failed at his first attempt, he thought the locals here might be muddled by his thee's and tha's. He was explaining this to Emily as they walked out of the town on the road that would take them to Garddryn.

Until now Tommy had not asked too many questions, it was as though he had decided long ago to keep his own counsel and not puzzle himself with his mother's and father's interpretations of his small world. Since his arrival he'd fired questions non-stop.

'Why is that house so little?'
'What sort of bird is that big one there?'
'What's that there?'
'Why hasn't that little girl got any shoes on?'
'Why does everyone talk funny?'

Emily had a thousand questions of her own but doubting that Joe would have the answer she kept them to herself. Now and again her eyes met his and there was a smile on her lips, for no sooner had he replied to one question when Tommy, his small face peering up, sprung another.

The simple chatter gave her opportunity to survey the countryside. Impressed by the provident nature of most of the cottagers with their stacked faggot piles, cut logs, dried furze and heather stored under sturdy lean-tos. In her mind's eye she saw herself gathering her own stock, and taking water from a barrel at the back door to water gilly flowers growing in neat beds around a patch of grass. Perhaps Joe would find a place where they could keep a pig in a pen or hens in the back yard.

Her eyes did not dwell on the tumbledown cottages where poverty and neglect were barely hidden behind blossoming blackthorn hedgerows. Near naked children at open doors or dirty faces at broken windows were likely to prompt reminders of her family's present homelessness.

They had walked for over an hour during which time several farm carts, wagons and a smart carriage had passed. Joe was about to suggest that they stopped to rest when a wagon drew alongside them. A lanky youth with a mop of dirty blond hair was perched on the driving seat.

Seeing them walking ahead the lad seized the opportunity to earn a penny reckoning that folks with a small child and baggage were likely to be glad of the chance of a ride.

Drawing alongside, he shouted 'Where you heading for?'

Lifting his hat Joe wiped sweat from the band. 'Garddryn village.'

'Count it your lucky day I'm headed there meself and I'll only charge a penny to carry yer all. Be easier on your feet and the little chap will be a sight more comfortable aboard me cart.'

Relieved that the lad spoke a language he could understand and he only wanted a penny for his trouble, Joe smiled. 'We'd be mighty pleased to accept the offer.'

'Climb up then. Mrs. and the small un can ride comfortable in the back.'

They were aboard and the old brown mare coaxed into action with a 'Come on Dolly ol' thing.' In an unexpected little burst of energy that lasted more than five minutes the old mare trotted towards home.

Glad to be off her feet, for a moment Emily didn't pay heed to the disturbed skylarks scooted from the hedgerow by the racket of the cart. It took her long minutes to appreciate the grass fields dotted with newly leafed trees and the flock of sheep grazing by a fast running brook.

Two miles on and Tommy dozed leaning against her thigh. Her own eyelids drooped and it was as though from far away that she heard Joe's voice.

'Thee not from around here?'

'I am, born and bred. Me mother comes from Cumbria and father was a Welshman.'

Joe heard the anger and sadness at the mention of his father and wondered what the story was. There was a silence that lasted several minutes, and understanding, Joe left the boy with his ghosts.

Passing two children climbing over a farmer's fence and threatening to run off the grass verge and onto the roadway, he came out of his reverie to shout a warning. His mood changed with astonishing speed and a moment later he was chatting as though he and Joe were lifelong friends. Joe thought little of it, the lad was young, whatever had touched him to make him brood hadn't rooted itself so deeply that bitterness held the upper hand.

They passed a cottage, the door was open and an old dog slept fitfully on the step. A cat as black as night slunk along the boundary wall his yellow eyes watchful, wary of the dreaming dog. Joe gave the cottage more than a passing glance; it was low and narrow. A tethered goat was grazing, and several hens scraped in the soil raking for morsels in the soft earth. Beyond, there was a quarter acre of ground tilled and showing a green tipped crop.

David, as the youth had introduced himself, clicked his tongue, jiggled the reins to rouse the mare who had slackened her pace, her nose twitching at the scent of new cut grass. 'Dolly, I swear yer get lazier and hungrier by the day.'

Joe smiled, the lad's words spinning him back to childhood, riding on the back of his grandfather's cart, the old man chastising a lazy mare reluctant to trot further than a mile from her stable. All the giddy-ups and ensuing curses powerless to get the animal moving above walking pace.

He wondered to his penchant of moving back and forth in time today. Was it because everything was so new that he needed to remember the times when his life had been stable, virtually unchangeable? Or was it the countryside, green grass, trees and running brooks that put him in mind of his grandfather, a farmer in a small way.

David broke into his thoughts. 'So what are you and your family doing in these parts? Visiting relatives?'

'No. I've come to find work at the quarry.'

'Shouldn't be difficult. If yeh looking for somewhere to stay the woman at the grocery shop in the village has houses she rents out. Folk are always moving in and out of Garddryn for one reason or another.'

Joe pressed him as to why the families moved on, David wouldn't say anything further on the subject. For the next mile or so Joe pecked at the bones of his worries and not until they reached the first village was he distracted enough to cease fretting.

The village was a long untidy straggle of houses butting onto one another. A bake-house and grocer, tea dealer, draper, boot maker, chemist, a skin and feather importer, bonesetter and three inns made up the trade. The doors of the bake house and grocer's stood open, women with small children clinging to their skirts were gathered near the steps to chatter and enjoy the unexpected sunshine. At the south end of the village stood a square stone house set apart from its neighbours by a deep rhododendron hedge. A small Wellingtonia fir grew in a tiny circular bed cut into the velvet lawn. Weather washed pebbles surfaced the short driveway from the house to the stone pillared entrance.

Glancing at the polished brass plaque on the nearest pillar Emily gave a thought to the zealous polisher rather than the flamboyant script etched into the pale brass informing that the house and grounds belonged to surgeon, Neil Griffith.

The black iron spiked gates were open, and as the farm cart passed, a brougham with a dapple grey horse in harness trotted down the driveway, a middle aged, bald headed man in black breeches and a frock coat holding the reins.

David's hands balled into fists his youthful face puckered in malice. 'That's the bastard Griffith.'

The animosity was so unexpected Joe was jolted out of tiredness. Craning his neck he gave the doctor a second glance.

Staring at the man hatefully David raised his voice so that his words were sure not to be missed. 'Friend of the gentry. Quarrymen's worst enemy.'

Unbearably embarrassed by the boy's outburst Joe averted his eyes. Keeping his questions until later.

As they passed Emily looked at the brougham with feminine interest, watching as it fell a pace or two behind them. The doctor's eyes were on the wagon and his expression was far from friendly. Emily prayed that their paths would not cross, for rarely had she seen such hostility.

Twitching the whip across the horse's back, David tried to put distance between the brougham and the wagon. Raising his voice over the increased noise. 'The bastard fills out death certificates in favour of the quarry owners. Me own father was killed in a slate fall at the Garddryn, Griffith were the bloody surgeon that made bloody sure me mother got bugger all in compensation.'

Joe was about to ask how it had happened when David said, 'Enough of him, it really gets me dander up when I think what he did.'

Politely, but with many thoughts running through his head, Joe changed the topic.

They climbed steadily, creeping towards the dark towering horizon.

It was a different world for Emily. Spring had brought a flush of tiny green heads sprouting from the bare brown earth. Beneath the blackthorn hedgerows butter yellow flowers opened their petals to the sunshine, and she had spotted a first show of bluebells.

It's a long way, she thought, from the sooty cobbles and dirty bricks that had been home. It was quiet, pure and lovely, and she was so glad that they had come. That Joe had found the courage after the pit disaster to start a new life. She sent a silent prayer to Frank, for it was he that had brought them here.

Joe was picking up what nuggets of information he could of the village and what to expect when they arrived, when he noticed that the air had cooled and looking skywards he saw dark clouds passing over the sun. The mountains, near now, darkened as shifting shadows raced across the peaks.

Emily drew Tommy close.

Rounding a foothill Joe got his first glimpse of the Garddryn quarry. Towering black and immense above the gigantic pit was the mountain. Generations of men had blasted it to the spine, gouging deep terraces, cleaving and penetrating the underbelly of God's creative glory. Where once light had fallen was now stark shadow. Every square inch of available earth was covered with a litter of slate waste, rising hundreds of feet into the air, monumental memorials to former quarrymen's endeavours.

Joe's breath escaped in a rush. 'God in heaven!'

Behind him, Tommy in her arms, Emily was silent.

'So this is the Garddryn.' The words stuck in Joe's throat, he was looking into the rest of his working life.

David pointed. 'Hundreds and hundreds of men labour from dawn to dusk to fetch slate out of that hole. Surprising ain't it, that it would take hundreds of years to make a hole that monstrous.'

Blood had drained from Joe's face. 'It doesn't surprise me at all that it would take so many to create...' He was about to say Hades and only just stopped in time when he thought of Emily.

She was leaning so close he could feel the warmth of her body. Touching his shoulder she pressed gently. Her understanding, gentle reassurance, was almost his undoing. Tears came to his eyes and a lump ached in his throat that he thought he might never swallow.

'Joe.'

He heard the love spoken in that one word and he took heart. Touching her hand, he said, 'It's alreeght, love. It were a bit of a shock that's all.'

It wasn't the first time he'd lied to her to save her heartache and he knew it wouldn't be the last if they were to survive this place.

Emily's thoughts went to the home they had left, dirty back alleys, the Galloway pit and the poverty. Turning her eyes from the Garddryn she looked out over the sloping green hills and the tiny toy like village nestling there.

As if reading her brighter thoughts, David piped up 'It'll only take us half an hour to reach the village.'

A pale golden afternoon enhanced the long line of cottages, the sinking sun gilding the stark granite stone, as the cart rumbled into Garddryn village.

David was happy to be near home. 'I'll stop at Maisy Lloyd's shop. If Maisy hasn't got somewhere that you can stay she's certain to know who has.' He elbowed Joe in the ribs. 'Cheer-up, yer look right miserable to be arriving in yer new home.' He turned his attention to the mare; she was reluctant to dawdle with the smell of home in her nostrils. 'Now whoa there, Dolly just be still.'

Joe grinned. 'I guess I'm a bit like that horse, restless to be in me own place.'

Catching his smile, Emily relaxed. Perhaps they had been too ready to judge the place. The village looked nice enough, and David was certainly friendly and very helpful. If everyone around here was half as nice they'd manage well.'

Tommy woke and stirred fretfully.

Climbing down, Joe said, 'If there are so many men and boys working yonder where do they all live? Not all in this village surely?'

'No they don't all live here, most of them travel a fair distance. Some come from Anglesey. They get the ferry across on a Sunday evening then go back to the island every Saturday.'

'Not much of a home life.'

'Probably don't want too much.' David grinned.

Tommy struggled to be free of his mother. 'I want to go with Dada.'

'Tha can stay and look after Mammy or get a clip round tha ear.'

Tommy's face crumpled. 'But I wanna…'

'Shush, Tommy and do as father says and wait here with me.'

'But, Mammy…'

Joe followed David through the shop door before the dispute was settled.

Maisy, a plump middle-aged woman, her wiry grey hair partially covered by a white bonnet was dusting goods on a low shelf. Straightening, her knees creaked and she gave a small huff. David being one of her favourite customers and the son of her close friend she gave him the benefit of a warm smile. 'David there you are! Your poor mother has been fretting all the day.'

David chuckled. 'Frettin' should have been her middle name.'

'David yeh a bad lad.'

'No doubt about it, Maisy. But forget all that I want yeh to meet Joe Standish. He's from the North Country and he's looking for somewhere to stay.'

Seeing the spark of interest in Maisy's brown eyes he hurried to explain before she made calf eyes at the man. 'His wife and little son are waiting outside. If you can offer something until they find their feet, it would be very helpful.'

'There's an end cottage at the far side of the village came empty recently. If your wife would like to look it over then come back to me and let me know if she'd like to have it...'

It was hard to believe his luck. Before he spoke he knew that they would take the cottage, it would be foolish not to grasp the opportunity of a roof over their heads. Emily would be delighted.

His relief was so evident Maisy saw that he had every intention of taking the property before he'd seen it. Before someone offered him a more reasonable and less damp home, she hunted in her cash box for a key. 'David here will show you where it is won't you, lad? It's the very last house in the village. You can't miss it.'

Joe took the offered key. In the back of his mind playing like a mischievous imp was the thought that it had all been too easy. He should expect a disappointment.

Maisy was busy extolling the virtues of her houses, Joe nodding when it was required of him. Politeness kept him stationary looking into her muddy brown eyes, when the urge to run out to tell Emily of their good fortune, to clasp her to his chest and hug her was making his feet itch to be moving.

David said that although it was smashing to be in the shop and smell the aroma of a bit of home baking, they really must be going, as he had the famished horse to feed.

Joe hid his sigh of relief.

Walking to the door with them Maisy threatened to keep both longer while she lauded the good points of the three-roomed house.

Glancing through the tiny window at the side of the door, Joe watched Tommy and Emily playing patter-cake. The thought ran through his head that, whatever the problem the house might have in store it couldn't be beyond the wit of a healthy man to correct to provide a home for his family.

Closing the door on the pair Maisy sighed and went back to her dusting.

In three strides Joe was standing by the side of the wagon. 'Emily tha won't believe our luck. We may have a house.' He held the key up. 'It's at the end of the village and David has agreed to take us to it. If we don't like it I'll bring the key back to the shop.'

'Joe I don't think we have a choice as to liking or not liking, if its a roof over our heads we must take it. For now at least.'

'Aye, yeh reeght.'

'Is it expensive?'

He jumped up sitting beside David but half turned to his wife. 'We can afford it. If I get work tomorrow we'll be okay.'

'Oh, Joe. What if?'

'Now don't start what iffing. Let's go and see it, we can iron out the problems later.'

David took pleasure in Joe's excitement. He'd taken a liking to him and although there was more than a decade between their ages he felt that they would become friends. Anxious now to discover what state the house was in, he lifted the reins. 'Come on, Dolly wake-up yer lazy bugger. You'll soon be home me ol' darling with your head in the fodder.'

Moving slowly the horse ambled down the street.

'What is the house like? And who lived in it before?' As Joe asked the question a picture came into his mind of Betty made homeless by a monstrous landlord and Frank moved to his mother's home to await burial.

'It's more of a cottage than a house. Last I knew there was a family there, the Hanson's if I remember correctly.'

Emily leaned forward. 'What were they like?'

'He was lazy. Mrs. Hanson's a nice enough woman but she was forever getting into debt. I suppose she owed Maisy and there's been summat of a row. Maisy wouldn't stand for any nonsense. She might look like butter wouldn't melt but she can be a real Tartar. She could curse for Wales if she had a mind too. As her poor husband could attest.'

Looking surprised, Joe said. 'I hadn't thought that she was married. She wasn't wearing a ring.'

'He left long ago. Went back to England, Somerset as I remember.'

'So the poor woman is on her own now.' Emily was sympathetic.

Looking over his shoulder, David answered, 'Nothing poor about her. She owns a load of properties around her. Left to her by her father, a vicar.'

They were coming to the end of the village; the houses thinned out and beyond the last one, open land stretched to the edge of a thick wood.

At first glance the house, or cottage as it turned out to be, looked substantial enough, built of cut granite, the slate roof although slightly rickety in the centre appeared sound. The paintwork was peeling and the bare wood of the window frame and door was exposed to the elements. The tiny front path was choked with weed and to negotiate it Emily had to lift her skirt from the thorny bracken. Thick, green ivy climbed up the gable wall reaching to the apex of the roof, disappearing beneath the overhanging slates.

Joe was pleasantly surprised, he had expected much worse. There appeared to be nothing that a bit of love and attention and a pot of paint wouldn't put right. He was forced to rethink this when he opened the front door and the smell of musty damp wafted out to greet them.

Anxious, Emily glanced at him.

While she was looking at the living room, inspecting the fireplace and the dirt on the shelves either side of it, Joe went into the kitchen, he called from there. 'I've found the source of the smell and I think we can sort it out.'

Lifting her skirt off the dirty floor she joined him.

Hunkered down he was inspecting beneath the cloth floor covering. 'Mind it's wet in here.' He lifted the edge to show her the sodden slate tiles beneath. 'This is why it smells awful. If we get rid of this and clean up the tiles I reckon it will get rid of the stink.'

'Joe I hope so. It's wet through in here.'

'Don't fret, Lass I'll find where the water is coming in and fix it.'

David came through from the living room, Tommy in tow.

Joe had the back door open inspecting the doorstep. 'I reckon rainwater is seeping in through here. Now't that can't be put reeght.'

'I told you that Hanson was a lazy bugger.' David wrinkled his nose. 'Pity his poor wife living with this stink. Maisy, by rights, should fix this.'

'I'll mention it to her when I go back to the shop.' Joe turned to Emily who was wiping Tommy's nose. 'What does tha think, lass? Shall we take it?'

'If the rents not to high I'd say aye.

Escaping his mother, Tommy ran upstairs his boots echoing on the bare boards. Peering through the low window he hollered down. 'I can see a big mountain and lots of trees and things. Come up, Mama and see.'

David smiled. 'I must be off or that poor mare of mine will die of starvation.'

Joe took his hand and held it for a moment. 'Thank you, David.'

'It were nothing much, just a ride.'

'But a Godsend to us.'

Emily added her thanks.

To cover his embarrassment David pushed his hair back off his forehead. 'Joe I can give you a lift half way to the shop but I can't take you all the way as I turn off at Plas Morfa.'

Grinning, Joe looked to Emily. 'I wonder how long it will take us to get used to the strange names of places. Plas Morfa sounds really...'

David shrugged. 'Take yer no time at all.' As an afterthought he added. 'Welcome to Bryn Tirion, I hope you'll all be very happy here.'

His words touched Emily. 'Oh is that the name of the cottage? It's lovely. Do you know what it means, David?

'Bryn Tirion, it means gentle hill.'

Emily beamed. 'But that's beautiful.'

Closing the back door, Joe slid the bolt. 'Let's get moving, David, before that horse of yours comes in to fetch us.'

'I reckon she would if she thought she could get the cart in and all.'

Laughing, Joe kissed Emily's cheek. 'You get sorted as best as tha can. I'll be back soon. Don't fret if it takes me a little while. I'll fetch the bags in and then tha can start to unpack.'

Suddenly she was excited. 'I'll feed Tommy and put a bit aside for later. There's still be a bit of meat pie left.'

'Don't fret about food I'll bring summat back from the shop.'

They were gone and Emily had the living room to herself. She took a moment to assess the scanty possession. A very battered oak table and two chairs and in the corner a forlorn looking high backed chair, very like the one she had sold to the pawn dealer a few days earlier, the only difference being this one was in dire need of a coat of polish. A pot blackened by age and use was pushed to the back of the dirty grate, a kettle in similar condition beside it. A lone candlestick that hadn't seen a duster this side of Christmastide stood on the grey ashes that had fallen in the hearthstone. Beside it a long bent poker and a stained kettle trivet. Mismatched crockery as dusty as everything else in the room was untidily stacked on the shelf alongside the grate. Standing in a cup an assortment of cutlery spoiled by misuse. There was no curtain to the small window and in the falling dusk the trees on the far bank of the stream swayed in the increasing breeze.

Tommy was unusually quiet, she called to him and as there was no reply she persuaded herself he couldn't be getting up to much trouble and went to the kitchen to inspect the cupboard and drawers. Finding them empty she slipped the bolt on the back door and went in search of the privy.

It was near twilight, and she wished she had started her search here instead of indoors, the trees moved menacingly the new leaves beating against the branches. The stream although not deep was fast flowing, and very near to the house, in the gathering darkness the whiteness of it rushing passed the half-submerged boulders gleamed, eerily. There was a footbridge fording the stream with a wooden structure on it, stepping onto the bridge she tried the door. Inside the sound and vibration of the water rushing beneath was astounding, frightening. It was so obviously the privy, a plank of wood with a hole cut into it and a corresponding hole over the maelstrom, left nothing to her imagination. A picture came into her mind of all the cottages and houses they had passed coming through the village and she wondered how many people lived there. Although she was reluctant to make use of the facility, she lifted her skirt, muttering, 'Needs must when the devil drives.'

Coming back into the kitchen, several logs in her arms, she had found them in a small stack beneath a lean-to on the back wall, she heard Tommy calling from upstairs.

Smiling, she dumped her trophy in the hearth and climbed the stairs.

Soon she had a fire burning and the battered kettle simmering on the grubby hob. The one candle spread a meagre light over a small portion of the room but she was reluctant to light another.

The bed, old enough to have been fashionable in her grandmother's time, now had clean linen and the blankets she had carried from her previous home, for all the inconvenience she was now heartily glad that she had done so.

Her treasures were unpacked, as few as they were, her mother's tea caddy being the most precious was now in pride of place on the dusty mantelpiece. Joe's pipe rack and pipes lay on the table waiting for him to decide where he wanted them.

Before settling Tommy she had given him the leftovers of the meat and potato pie. Now left with an idle moment she realised that Joe had been gone an age. She was beginning to fret when she heard his step on the path.

Running to open the door. 'Joe I was beginning to worry that summat had gone wrong.'

Stepping over the threshold he kissed her cheek 'Thee worry's too much, our Em. Where's Tommy?'

'Fast asleep in our bed. It's the only one, so I put the little beggar in the middle, we'll manage till we get him summat of his own.'

He looked tired, running her fingers through his hair, she said, 'What happened at the shop? What's Maisy really like? Is she really a harridan like David reckons? How much is the rent? And can we stay? And where have thee been all this time?'

Laughing he caught her hand kissing her fingertips. 'One question at a time.'

'Come on, Joe tell me everything.'

'I will if ye'd get me a cuppa tea. I brought back some sausages so I hope you have a way of cooking them.'

'Course I have Joe. I'm not that simple as to come wi' out essentials.'

'Thee's a great lass.'

'Now tell me everything while I cook the sausages.'

It was much later, when Emily lay in bed waiting for sleep to come, listening to the ill-fitting window panes rattling so furiously she imagined herself back on the *Hardwick Lady,* that she made plans for their new home. In her mind's eye she saw a rag rug before the hearth; curtains to the window, blue ones. Two comfortable chairs to replace the old high backed one, done in pale grey upholstery. A bed for Tommy, the little beggar wriggled unmercifully in his sleep. Maybe a cat for him too. It would keep the mice down.

Beside her Joe's mind circled, he had a wish to turn, beat his hard bolster but the thought of waking Tommy kept him still. What he had heard in the inn after leaving Maisy's, had disturbed him. His visit had been on the advice of David; men from the quarry went to the inn of an evening and that was where he was most likely to meet the steward or the little steward. He'd met neither but he had garnered a lot of information, little of it good. A strike had been mentioned, the men were not paid as regularly as they should be, dirty barracks, unsafe work practices and blinding wet days. He'd told none of this to Emily. Sleep eventually claimed him, not a restful refreshing slumber but one of ghosts and suffocation.

Chapter Four

Joe rose from his bed early, before the sun had risen above the horizon. Donning the clothes he had last worn in the Galloway he crept quietly out of the bedroom and down the stairs. Lifting the latch on the staircase door he stepped into the living room. The aroma of warm oatmeal greeted him. A pan of it had been left beside the hob overnight and now all it needed was a stir to make a quick breakfast. The table had been set the previous night; cups and dishes had been laid out, a board and a knife for cutting the loaf, and a crock basin of dripping. The last chore before retiring had been to measure tea leaves into the pot, a wetting and the first brew of the day would be ready.

Yawning, he sat in the fireside chair and pulled on his boots. The leather impregnated with coal dust had hardened, and he gave a little stamp to settle his feet then tied the laces tight.

Standing he lifted the large chunk of wood from the hearth where it had been left to dry and settled it on the still glowing embers, blowing on the hot ashes until tiny flames took hold.

He'd wash and shave in cold water whilst it caught properly, and heated the kettle for the brew.

His breakfast took only a moment to eat; porridge washed down by a cup of strong tea. Putting the used dishes into the deep sink in the kitchen, he glanced out of the tiny window. The day was dry, but the sky visible through the branches of the trees was too scanty to see if it might hold.

Deciding not to wake Emily he made his way out of the house quietly. A bottle of tea under his arm and a bit of bread in his pocket, he was as prepared as he could be to do a day's work.

There was hardly a light burning as he trekked through the village; the only glimmer he saw for the first mile was that of the grocery store and the doctor's front window.

The village ended with the doctor's house and the small infirmary attached to it. Passing this he turned onto the narrow track leading to the quarry. It was still early; there were no workmen about. He could enjoy the solitude, just the sound of his boots on the shingles, birds in the trees and in the far distance a cockerel's crow.

Looking across the valley to the river winding between green banks he imagined how the scene would change with the seasons. With the fullness of summer when everything was at its peak it would be glorious, bountiful. Then the slow change to the splendour of autumn, the gorse, bracken, and woodland, bronze with spent leaves. Winter would be harsh, the mountains snow peaked and bitten with frost, the landscape carved out of glass and diamonds. Impossible for man or beast to survive in the bleak terrain but it would be a sight to behold.

Ahead of him the path widened, several tracks branching from it. Ignoring these he took the widest and most used. The way opened up, firs; oaks and mountain ash had been felled close to the ground, any grass that grew was sparse, littered with slivers of blue-grey slate. Scuffing his boots he set fragments clinking.

The path ended suddenly and he was staring at the great abyss that was the Garddryn. Immense terraces layered one upon another like a Babylonian temple magnified a thousand times. Yesterday from the road it had looked monstrous, but the sight of it then did nothing to prepare him for the reality of it today. Hades he had thought then and he did so again. David had said it took hundreds and hundreds of men centuries to dig it.

Well, he wasn't surprised. It made the Galloway look puny by comparison. What would Frank have thought of it? Narrowing his eyes, he counted the wide galleries or terraces, he made out ten and one in the process of being fashioned. The distance between them he reckoned to be at least fifty or sixty feet. The platforms looked to be fifty feet or so at the widest. Offshoots, narrow ledges were only a few feet wide.

He made out several small buildings nestled in crannies, the nearest built of layers of slate was well camouflaged. Although it had a doorway there were no windows. He was speculating on its use when a breeze brushed his face, the last vestiges of winter in it. Buttoning his coat he turned away and followed the wide track to a house beyond. He had a thousand questions, he didn't doubt that he'd have the answers to most of them before the day was out.

Hands buried deep in his pockets, he thought of the day ahead. His reason for arriving so early was to find the manager or a steward before the man got caught up in his daily routine.

The sound of voices came to him from much further down the track, from the route he had come, camaraderie of working men. His thoughts went to the Lancashire streets, walking with Frank to the Galloway. How they could talk the two of them, there were few topics that weren't discussed as they trekked to and from work. With pictures of Frank in his mind he walked to a building that looked most likely to house the office. It was locked and shuttered. Resting his back against the door he lit his pipe.

Several men rounded the curve in the track and made their way passed him. One held back, greeting him with a nod that shook his shaggy, iron-grey hair. 'Bore da.'

For a moment he was tempted to answer Bore da but thinking better of it he responded with a cheerful 'Morning.'

The man took a step towards him. 'English is it?' Although his English was rusty he was pleased to show off his skill to the other men.

'Aye.'

A rare smile crossed the man's face. 'If you are waiting for Griffith the steward, you'll have a long wait, he's never about the office until after eight o'clock.'

Pipe smoke escaped Joe lips. 'Oh, I expected that someone would be about early. I'm looking for work and hoped I might get taken on today.'

Glancing over his shoulder the man checked which quarrymen were listening. Nosy all of them; they didn't miss a thing, and ready as the next man to take advantage of a novice. Closing the gap, he dropped his voice. 'What work you looking for?'

'Any work I can get. Until recently I was a Lancashire collier but a pit collapse has put paid to that.'

'You a miner long?'

A smile flitted across Joe's mouth. 'Aye, man and boy.'

The stranger glanced over his shoulder to where Tom Hughes and Fergie Ferguson were standing. Running their own teams they were equally eager to get their hands on strong men and they'd pay more than he would. He tried and failed to wipe the sly expression off his face. 'I might be able to help you there. I'm in need of a rubble man.'

An old hand at dealing with men, and hard men at that, Joe noted the glance. Taking his time he relit his pipe and through the first drag of smoke, he spoke casually 'Do I have to apply through the quarry office.'

The chap wondered if he hadn't been too hasty with his offer, the man was obviously suspicious and he wasn't as grateful as he should be. But with his team a rubble-man short he was desperate to lay someone on and quickly. Time was money and nowhere in the world was it truer than in the Garddryn. If he took him on he would have to watch the bugger; he'd be looking for a better share before the week was out.

Surly now he answered brusquely. 'No need to worry with the office. You're looking for work and I'm offering you a job. Take it or leave it, it's no skin off my nose.' He began to saunter off.

Joe took a hurried step forward. 'Hang-on I didn't say I wasn't interested. What work are yer offering?'

'Simple enough. You just collect the rubble and dump it. The easiest job in the Garddryn.' It wasn't a helpful job description or even accurate. 'Job's yours if you want it.'

Joe forgot to smile. 'I'll take it. Just show me what to do and I'll do it.'

'Follow me and I'll get someone to show you the ropes.' He held out a work-scarred hand. 'I'm Jack Dickens but you can call me Boss.'

Clasping it Joe barely felt the scarred and hardened skin his own hands were beyond being sensitive. Falling into step with the man they walked towards the quarry workings. There was a lot about his new boss that was much like his old one, and he hadn't liked him either. Both were surly, full of themselves and bullies.

Jack Dickens was not convinced that he'd done the right thing in offering Joe a job. Had it not been for the strength and breadth of his shoulder and hands that were so obviously used to hard work, he wouldn't have bothered. Retreating into a sullen silence he quickened his pace.

Reaching the team, Jack Dickens bellowed to a young lad working on a ledge sixty feet below the path where they were standing. 'Thomas.'

Scrambling up a ladder the lad came alongside. A hurried conversation none of which Joe was able to follow, then the lad stood grinning at Joe.

'Mr. Dickens says I have to show you what to do. I'm to give you a quick shufti round the quarry so you can get your bearings. Then you're to take the sled and load it. I'll show you where to dump the burden.'

They walked away from the men beginning their shift.

Looking back Joe watched with amazement, as one of the men secured a hemp rope around a boulder then looping the other end around his thigh launched himself over the precipice. Several of the other men followed him and their shouted banter bounced off the rock-face as they descended.

Joe wasn't afraid of heights but he didn't relish the thought that before the week was out a similar climb might be expected of him.

Thomas's eyes followed Joe's line of sight. He gave a short laugh. 'Don't worry about that lot they've been at it for years, safe as houses that job.'

Doubting it, Joe glanced back to where a last man was disappearing from sight. 'Do you do that?'

'No. Worst luck. They get a better share of the bargain for doing it. But it's a job that takes years to master. A man's got to know a lot about the rock before he can start blasting it or shifting it off the face.' Nudging Joe's elbow he grinned again. 'Don't worry you'll not be following that lot for many years, if ever.'

'I'm grateful for that.' Joe was familiar with the bargain as David had explained it to him on the ride to Garddryn village. He was considering the ways it would surely be open to exploitation when Thomas broke into his thoughts with a warning.

'The most important, thing to remember is to keep your head down when you hear the whistle. If you don't, you're likely to get it blown clean off.'

Shielding his eyes the boy looked to the far rock-face. 'Before a blast there's a red flag hoisted and after a few minutes you'll hear a whistle blown, that gives you time to get to cover. The all clear is three whistle blasts and a white flag flying.'

Joe's eyes hunted the deep clefts for signs of the flag. 'Where exactly...'

With a disregard for danger peculiar to youth, he said nonchalantly 'Don't worry, someone will be near you all day and they'll holler before the blasting.'

Sensing that the lad was bored, Joe saved his questions for someone older and less fearless he might meet later. The quarry was very different but equally as dangerous as the Galloway and good council would help him stay safe.

An hour passed before Joe witnessed his first blasting. Although he took cover and felt relatively safe the experience was unexpectedly ear shattering. The roar of the explosion was noisier than he had anticipated, and then came the unbelievable reverberation as the entire quarry face trembled as the slate was torn free of its roots. Every eye turned to the eruption praying that only the selected rock would fall. The second blast of the day had gone awry, a flaw creating a near catastrophe. Men had run for their lives as a section of a gallery began to collapse. Thousands of tons of slate tumbling down the cliff, a terrifying avalanche of rock, slate, and mud hurtling down into the man-made crater. The pandemonium had been unbelievable and that only two men had been injured by falling debris was a miracle. Blasting had been suspended for the rest of the day whilst the damage was examined and an inspection made for other dangerous fissures.

Despite the bedlam he had shifted many hundredweight of rubble, his strength and energy adding to the ancient tips. At the end of the shift he was stinking, his clothes stiff with dust and new blisters had erupted on his palms.

Parking his tools he took a breather, resting his back against a rock he swigged the last of the cold tea in the bottle.

The sun was creeping behind the mountain, chilling the air,

cooling the sweat on his skin. Glancing at the sky he saw that the weather was changing, there was a good chance that it would rain tonight or tomorrow. But what did it matter, sweat or rain, both drenched.

The promise of another day of work tomorrow lightened his step towards home and Emily. Pausing at Maisy's shop he bought tobacco for himself, a sugar mouse for Tommy and a few apples for Emily.

The doors of the Half-Way inn were open, the noise of men slaking a quarry thirst too tempting to ignore. Stepping inside he pushed between equally sweaty bodies as his and made his way to the bar. A pewter tankard in his hand he smiled with satisfaction. He'd earned it.

Emily placed a log on the fire, and for the umpteenth time removed the simmering kettle to one side of the hob. She'd been on tenterhooks all day. First wondering if Joe had found a place, then wondering how hard the work would be on him. Then worrying about what time she might expect him.

A few men had passed her open door making their way to the next village, and then there had been a lull in pedestrians. Eventually she guessed that Joe had stopped off at the Half-Way and she stopped worrying. Joe would neither come home worse for drink, or too late for his dinner.

At last she heard the catch lift on the door. He came in bringing the chill of the evening air and the smell of pipe smoke from the crowded bar.

Pleased to see him, she tried not to sound a nag. 'Joe I was beginning to worry.'

He was matter-of-fact. 'No need. Is Tommy in bed?'

'Oh aye. I put him down some time back. But don't mind him. Tell me everything. How did it go? Who did tha meet? Is the work hard?' A frown followed the question. 'Tha did get a place?'

'Aye, course I did. I don't usually get this mucky standing drinking ale.'

'Don't be daft, Joe. It's just that I worry.'

'Aye, I know tha does. Come here and give me a kiss. I'll tell yeh everything as soon as I have had a bit of a wash and me tea.'

She had to be content with that. Listening to him swilling himself in the kitchen, she stirred the pot of beans and knuckle of pork.

He shouted over the splashing water. 'It were a reeght eye-opener. The place is amazing.' He walked into the parlour drying the back of his neck with a cloth. 'The folk are a bit different from the Lancashire crowd. They talk a lot about chapel and the brass band. To fit in I reckon I'll have to learn to play a musical instrument. I could begin with the trumpet?' Blowing down an imaginary trumpet he mimed a player.

Carrying the pot of food to the table Emily nudged him out of the way with her elbow. 'Don't be daft, tha couldn't play a tambourine if someone else were holding it.' The pot was settled on the table beside a loaf recently out of the oven.

'Thee's a hard women, Em.' He lifted the lid. 'That smells good. I hope our Tommy ate some of it before tha put him down for the neeght.'

'Aye. But under protest.'

'Scamp.'

She tapped the back of his hand with the serving spoon as he filched a bean out of the hot gravy

'Hurry up, woman. Serve it up, I'm famished.' He began to cut the bread as Emily ladled stew onto the plates.

Joe's eyes were on the gravy flowing like a spring tide to the rim of his plate. 'Yer know the way to a man's heart, our Em.' Pulling a chair out he sat, drew the plate towards him. Throwing salt on his potatoes, he said, 'Did tha know there are five chapels in the village? Nearly one for every day of the week'

'There's also a church in the next village. We can attend there. We could take a look at it on Sunday.'

It hadn't been Joe's intention to attend church on Sunday. There were other more pressing matters to deal with.

In the caban, the hut where the men gathered to eat the midday meal and drink tea, there had been little else talked about but a threatened strike. Late payment of wages seeming the principle aggravation. If what the men had said were true, and the management likely to be tardy about settling wages a week on Saturday, he'd need to find a day's work come the weekend. Emily would dip into the bit of money they'd put by for emergencies and say nowt about it, but that wouldn't stop her worrying, and if he could save the lass from fretting, he would.

Looking at her, flushed from the heat of the fire, her hair dark wisps around her face, and a smile on her pretty mouth. He'd be buggered if he was going to upset the apple cart by explaining that a strike looked imminent and doubtful that he'd be paid for his work on time. Revelations like that didn't create a restful evening.

'Summat wrong, Joe?'

'No. Why should there be?'

She looked quizzical. 'It's just that thee looked so cross there for a moment.'

His knife and fork clattered on the earthenware plate as he finished his meal. He gave a satisfied sigh.

'Another spoonful, Joe? There's some left.'

'I couldn't eat another thing.'

Rising, she put the kettle to the hob.

Glancing at her, he wondered how long it might be before she found out about the dissention for herself. Emily was far from stupid. One word picked up from the local shop and she'd be down on him like a ton of bricks for keeping things from her.

Turning to the table, she gathered the plates together, carrying them into the tiny kitchen.

Returning, she lifted a basin from a hot pan. 'There's a plum duff for pudding.'

'I'll give it a minute, Emily. I'm stuffed.'

'While tha's waiting for that lot to settle then tha can tell me about the day. Who did thee meet? What's the quarry's like? Tell me everything, Joe. I've been like a cat with its tail smouldering, all day. '

'It's no good me trying to explain how big the quarry really is, I haven't the imagination to begin to describe it. I'll take thee and Tommy to see it. As for the folk, thee had probably best meet them too.' He laughed. 'They're nearly as hard to describe as the quarry itself.'

'Joe yer hopeless. I've waited all day to hear about it.'

Seeing that she wasn't to be put off, he began to tell her. 'The quarry is made up of about ten terraces or galleries as they're called. These are about sixty feet deep and about the same wide. Each one has a name of it's own. There's Nazareth, Jericho, and Bethlehem. I've forgotten all of them. I'm working with a team on Jerusalem.'

Omitting to mention the catastrophe of the gallery ruined by the rock fall, he went on. 'Imagine a big piece of rock say six yards square that's called a bargain. The steward, he's like an overseer, offers this bargain to a team leader. The team leader has to agree a price for working on the piece of rock. It is up to him to get the best possible price and the best rock to work with. I'm working for Jack Dickens. There are six of us in his team. The better the bargain he strikes with the steward, the higher the profits, and so more wages for his team.'

There was no fooling Emily. She must have seen a fleeting expression cross his face because her next words came quickly.

'How often does this team leader, Jack Dickens pay his crew?'

'Every four weeks.' He smiled. 'It's called sadwrn setlo, it means settling-up Saturday. That's probably the first bit of Welsh that stuck with me.'

'Hang on a minute, Joe.' She was frowning. 'When is the next

Saturday pay out?'

'Week Saturday.' He rushed his words. 'Emily I know it's not what we expected but that's the way they do it here. There's nowt I can do to change it, Lass.'

'I'm not getting at thee, Joe, I'm just trying to figure out when we'll have money coming in.'

'Look on the bright side, there'll be some months when I'll earn more, if the bargains gooduns.'

'Aye there is that. But on the other side of the coin, Joe, if Jack Dickens isn't popular with the bosses or goes out of favour what happens? It is relying on management paying him and him paying the team. And doing so on time. '

She was cleverer than he'd reckoned. She'd spotted the flaw in the bargain system and uncovered the reason why the men were threatening to strike. Pay out was not guaranteed, and the bargain system was open to bribery and corruption. He'd seen the defect the moment David had explained the system. Good rock, easier access, made profitable bargains and they would go to those prepared to grease, or buy their way into favour with the management. Second and third-rate bargains would leave hard-working men out in the financial cold.

'It might stick in me craw, Emmy, but there isn't a thing I can do about it. I'm nowt but a new man, with no say and no chance of ever having one.'

Chapter Five

Winter arrived early, the frost killing the few flowers that grew in the beds around the tiny patch of grass in Emily's garden.

Icy draughts blown straight off the turbulent sea penetrated the loose window frames rattling the panes, whistling beneath and around the ill fitting doors, until the old house moaned a lament to the coming season.

The afternoons grew dark early, and before Emily had put a pan to the hob for Joe's tea, the candles were lit and the first half of the wick burned down. She was bemoaning the extravagance as Joe came through the kitchen door.

Dumping his bag on the table he glanced at the candle in question. 'You'll have us going back to old fashioned tallow sticks next.'

'Don't be daft, Joe.'

'Daft is it, woman. There's not a night I come through that door that you're not of a twitter about the price of a pound of candles.'

Picking up the corner of her apron she wiped her damp hands. 'Sorry, Joe. But it's true, candles have never cost so much.'

'Never mind the bloody candles. What sort of a day have you had and as Tommy behaved himself?'

Scooping the bag up from the table she removed the tea bottle and tin box. 'Tommy's been a right little perisher. I'm sure that since his fourth birthday his behaviour has got worse.'

'I'll have another word with him.'

'Words, Joe. I wonder if a clip round the ear wouldn't make more of a difference.

'A terrible day I've had with him.' Then against her better judgement she blurted out, 'Jack Dickens kids came calling with their mother, two black eyes she had, Joe.'

It was no surprise to Joe that Mrs. Dickens might suffer at her husband's hands, he was a bully at work so it stood to reason that he'd be much the same at home, behind closed doors.

Six months he had worked for the man and every one of them purgatory. Not that he'd let on to Emily, she had enough to worry about with their Tommy, he was turning out to be a real handful. Another bairn might help; she'd soon stop spoiling the lad if she had another to fret over. But feeding another was a different kettle of fish altogether.

They were just beginning to put a bit of his wages aside, if another child should come along it would put paid to the notion of buying a tiny small holding. A dream they both shared.

Neither of them could get out of this old house quick enough. Cold, damp, cramped and for all the cleaning and airing the smell in the kitchen hadn't gone entirely.

Tommy had a mortal fear of the privy perched over the stream, and who could blame the lad. The water hurdling beneath a sitter's behind was enough to fright anyone. At least there was no fear of boys lighting a rag and floating it down the gully-way to singe a backside for a bit of fun. Smiling he recalled when he and Frank, seven-year old heathens, had done that in the big six-hole privy back of Rotherman Street. Seven o'clock on a Sunday morning and the toasted occupants' language not fit for the Sabbath. What a wallop he got from his mother. Frank could hardly sit for a week after coming into conflict with his father's belt.

The memory brought a smile. Sighing, he pulled his baccy pouch out of his pocket. Thinking of Frank, he filled his pipe. 'Have I got time for a smoke before supper?'

Emily took a pan off the hook. 'Aye. I'm cooking a few herrings they won't be ready for another twenty minutes or so.'

Standing over the fire, turning the fish with a fork, she felt queasy. It was the second time today, first thing this morning she'd felt quite dreadful. Surely she couldn't be... she was too afraid to complete the question, even to herself.

Upstairs Tommy yelled.

Easing himself out of the chair, Joe said, 'No rest for the wicked.'

She turned the fish onto a warmed plate. 'Thanks, Joe. If he can't sleep bring him down, he can have a bit of supper with us.'

Later, when the dishes were done and Tommy was back in his makeshift bed, Emily her skirt raised above her ankles was toasting her toes in front of the hearth. Most of the day she had debated with herself as to the wisdom of telling Joe about the missing pennies. Coming to a decision she looked up from the flames she was watching. 'Joe you know I said that Mrs. Dickens had called with her bairns, Mary and Ifan.'

Lowering his newspaper slowly he looked over it. 'Aye.' The tone of her voice warned him that she'd keep him awhile from the news.

'And she had a black eye.'

'Aye.' It was going to take longer than he first thought.

'Well there were some pennies, not many, on the table. I knew exactly where I had left them, but when the family left the pennies were no longer there.'

She had all his attention. 'How many?'

'Five.'

'And who does tha think took them?' He fell back into his northern dialect.

'Well I don't know, but it had to be one of them.'

'Are tha sure that the pennies were there?'

'Course they were, Joe. When did thee know me to be daft with money.'

'I know yer careful, Em. But it's best to be sure before we start to accuse anyone.'

'Well I am sure. The pennies were on the table.'

Joe took a minute to think through the implications. Telling his boss, an unreasonable man, that he suspected that either his wife or one of his bairns was a thief was out of the question. The loss of the money was bad enough but knowing that there was little he could do about it would rankle every time he looked at the belligerent bugger.

'What should we do, Joe? I feel really bad about it.'

Slowly he folded the paper. 'Besides taking care not to leave anything lying about there is nowt we can do, Lass. I hate the loss as much as you do but if I say owt there'd be hell to pay. For certain I'd lose me place at the quarry. No one there is taking on workers. The strike is still a threat and there's no knowing from one day to another what will happen. I'd say all we can do is take care and hope it doesn't happen again.'

'I can't close me door to her, and if the kids come a calling I can't keep them chatting on the doorstep.'

'Likely as not the thief will call again and soon, see if the pickings are as easy a second time.'

Throwing the hem of her skirt over her ankles she started to rise. 'Oh, Joe you don't think that they would, surely?'

'Aye, I'm certain of it, Lass. So hide tha purse or keep it about tha person.'

Thoughtfully she nibbled a snag on a fingernail. 'Aye, a will.'

Unfolding his paper he shook it straight. 'No need to panic, they're not likely to come at this hour and certainly not with me here.'

'I suppose you're reeght.' But for all his calming words she gave the door another glance. Settling again, she gave the fire a brisk poke sending sparks flying up the chimney, then looking into the dancing flames she tried to think of a better solution, one that would satisfy her simmering anger.

The herrings would need to suffice for supper for two days if the loss of the pennies was to be made up, so Emily, having no reason to go down to the village shop the following day, took Tommy for a walk, hoping to tire him.

It was impossible to walk the length of the village without passing the Dickens house and as they neared the run - down property, afraid to encounter any member of the family Emily quickened her step, pulling Tommy along with her. Almost at once he started to whine and before they had negotiated their way passed the dry stone wall protecting the straggly patch of land, his whining had become full-blown noisy complaints. Although sorely tempted to give him something to moan about Emily kept her hand in the folds of her shawl. If she were still in a mind to smack him when she got him home, he'd go to bed with a sore backside. Trying desperately hard not to raise her voice on the street, she told Tommy what might be in store.

He looked so aggrieved; his little mouth hard with anger then tears spilled from beneath long, dark lashes. Relenting at once she was tempted to kiss his pretty cheek and cuddle him to her. As she had on so many other occasions, stooping to him she tried to pull him close.

'Horrid Mammy. Bugger off.'

Nothing could have amazed Emily more. Later, when describing the incident to Joe she could not have said if it was because the child swore, or the anger that was so evident in his young voice.

As Joe was not with her, she had to deal with the matter herself. Swiping Tommy across his bottom, she hauled him towards home.

It would be the first of many occasions that Tommy would spend the afternoon alone in the cold bedroom, seething, sore bottomed, and planning his revenge.

Emily spent the afternoon cleaning furiously, dabbing at her wet eyes one moment and tight lipped with anger the next. What was going to become of her little boy? Why had he become so difficult?

Eventually, she closed the curtains on the raw afternoon and lit a candle.

There was no sound from upstairs and again she dithered on the bottom step listening. If she had heard a cry she might have gone to comfort her child, but the thought that he might swear again and she would lose her temper, kept her rooted to the ground floor.

For the next half-hour she prayed for Joe's speedy return, then wished him held up on route home. Wavering between dreading telling him, and needing his comfort and calming hand.

Throughout the dreadful afternoon bouts of nausea filled her mouth with saliva.

As Joe walked through the door, she was passing her hand over her stomach, instinctively aware that another heart had begun to beat there.

Closing the door he crossed to her, a look of concern on his dirty face. 'Is everything alreeght, Lass? Tha looks hot and bothered.'

Lifting her chin gently with his fingertips. 'And tha's been crying.'

Tears brimmed onto her lashes. 'Joe. Tommy has been so awful.'

'Come on sit down, and tell me everything. Where is the little perisher?'

Her eyes went to the stairway door. 'He's upstairs I sent him to bed. I just don't know what to do with him any more, Joe.'

'Calm down and tell me what's happened. I'll do what needs doing.'

When the tale was told, Joe went to Tommy, his footfall ominously loud on the bare wooden stairs.

Emily listened to the muffled voices.

Content that Joe would deal well with the situation, not lose his temper as she had done, she began the supper, it was almost cooked when Joe came down with his shamefaced child in tow.

His small face was pink from recent tears and he brushed his tiny fist to clear them. 'Sorry, Mammy.'

Stooping, Emily opened her arms. She was near to tears herself.

Reluctantly, assisted with a small nudge from his father Tommy went to her accepting a cuddle.

The following day Tommy remained on Joe's mind. He was trying to fathom when the trouble had begun, certainly not before the move to Wales. For quite a while after that the child had appeared happy, then all of a sudden something seemed to disquiet him and since he'd been a regular little devil.

Hauling a load of waste slate to the dump, his back near breaking with the strain, perspiration and rainwater running off his bare arms, slate dust muddy rivulets dripping from his elbows, the answer came to him. At first it was too astounding to take in, the child was so young, but the more he went through it in his head the answer kept coming back to the same thing, Henrietta Bellamy's tenth birthday. That's when the trouble with Tommy had begun, the visit to the big house nearly three months ago. All the quarry workers kids had been invited to the birthday party at the owner's mansion. Tommy had been really excited about it for weeks. Afterwards he'd been reticent to discuss what had happened and since that day he'd withdrawn and had been a reeght pain for his mother. Little devil.

Throwing another shovel load onto the dump he humphed with the effort. Then relaxing for a moment he leaned on his shovel looking down onto the village. His own home was out of sight, but Plas Mawr was visible. Even from this distance he could make out the green lawns, the long tree lined drive. His eyes went to the mansion itself, he could see a corner of the edifice, the second and third floor long windows dark smudges in the cut granite.

Trudging back to collect another load he went over the afternoon of the party in his mind.

He and Tommy had walked from home to Plas Mawr. At the front door a liveried servant had welcomed the lad and whisked him inside. Joe had caught a last glimpse of the child before the imposing door had closed. Tommy had stopped moving and was standing in the middle of the marble-floored hallway looking up. Following his line of sight Joe saw that he was looking at the great crystal chandelier hanging in the massive stairwell between the first and second floor banisters. The youngster was staring mesmerised, and although the flunkey had tried to push him forward young Tommy had stood his ground. Not until another little boy had called to him from behind an enormous potted plant did Tommy move, but his eyes had stayed on the crystal shimmering with candlelight.

It was still something of a mystery but at least remembering the incident he was nearer to solving it, and when he got home by heck he would do just that, he'd sit the lad down and he and Emily would find out exactly what happened at that birthday party. With a bit of luck before the evening was through they would have their smashing little boy back to normal.

The afternoon progressed quickly. Completing another punishing delivery, he raised his head and saw that the sun was sinking quickly behind the mountain. Birds were turning to their roosts. The early twilight was colder, his hot breath visible on the cooling air.

The siren went, and collecting his tools he made his way towards the quarry track. He'd not stop of at the Half-Way for his usual quart of ale; he was for home and his boy.

Tommy was sitting in front of the fire, an old newspaper beneath him to protect Emily's most recent addition to the room, a brightly coloured rug. Joe came in bringing the cold damp air with him.

Looking up Tommy grinned. 'Dada, Dada come and see what I've made. Isn't it nice, Dada?' He was holding up a green paper lantern, messy with glue. His chubby baby fingers searched in the small pile beside his knee, and plucking out a red lantern he held it out to Joe. 'This one is the nicest.'

Stooping, Joe kissed his forehead. Carefully he took the miniature Chinese lantern from the child's sticky fingers and made a show of admiring it.

Delighted, Tommy grinned. 'We made loads of them. It took us all afternoon and we made a long, long paper chain. Mammy said we could hang it up on Christmas Eve. Do you think it will look nice, Dada?'

'I think it will look very lovely. Just what this old room needs, pretty lanterns and paper chains.' He stood, pretending to inspect the thick beam over the door. 'I reckon if we put a nail in this it would take the weight alreeght and then if the chain was long enough we could fasten it to the beam over there.' With a serious expression he glanced at the beam on the far side of the room.

Tommy clapped his hands gleefully.

Looking at his son's beaming face he admonished himself for worrying. The child looked like a perfectly happy little boy should. Briefly he wondered if having that chat with him about the Plas Mawr birthday party really was necessary. Perhaps the boy was just a bit wilful. Might even be because he's very bright and likely to bore easily. Who knew the reason, he stifled a sigh.

Jumping up Tommy clapped his hands 'I can make it that long. Look I've got loads more paper and Mammy will help.'

'Mammy will help doing what?' Emily came in carrying rumpled clothes in her arms. She smiled at Joe. 'I didn't hear you come in.' She kissed his mouth lightly. 'How was the day?'

'Wet.'

Throwing the clothes on a chair she looked at his trousers, from the knee down they were wet, thick with mud. 'Get changed, then I'll dish up supper.'

Noticing that she looked tired he slipped his hand around her waist. 'Tell me what I can do to help.'

'Nothing, Joe. I've had a bit of lamb simmering in the pot all afternoon.'

Closing his eyes in feigned ecstasy, he sniffed the aroma. 'I thought I could smell something nice cooking. I'm starving.' His hand tightened around her.

'Off with you, Joe. Get out of those filthy clothes, thee'll make a reeght muck of me and the clean floor.'

Undressing in the back scullery, he dumped his caked clothes in a bucket at the back door. Pushing them under the soapy water, the thought passed through his mind that Emily was thickening around the waist, yet he hardly saw her eat more than a morsel at any one meal. A clean vest and trousers were hanging from a peg on the back door and lifting them off he shrugged into them. Fastening his belt, he went back to Tommy to help him with his paper chain.

Sitting crossed legged on the rug, listening to Tommy's advice of how to paste a perfect chain, he watched his wife as she checked the dinner pot.

Looking over her shoulder, she smiled. 'What are you thinking about then.'

For all the tea in China he wouldn't tell her what was running through his mind. It'd take a braver man than him to tell a woman that her waist was not a narrow as it had been. Even after Tommy she'd got back to...The thought stopped him dead in his tracks. A bairn, surely not. She wouldn't keep such a thing from him. Would she? He had gone on a bit about affording another place. But surely she...

Standing with the firelight behind her, the candle on the mantelpiece shedding light on her dark clean hair, he thought he had rarely seen her look so pretty, fragile but with a bloom about her that made her radiant. So like when she was first carrying...

'Penny for them, Joe Standish.'

Sure his face had paled he dipped his head to the paper he was gluing. 'They're worth a sight more than a penny, Mrs. Standish.'

Lifting the lid off the simmering pot the aromatic steam wafted into her face. Her stomach turned, and dropping the lid back into place she flew out of the room, her hand covering her mouth.

The doubt left Joe's mind. A sliver of happiness, maybe a girl child would be theirs, slipped into his heart. But the smallholding he had so longed for would be lost, there would be no chance of saving a penny towards it. Beside him Tommy muttered, his sticky hand touching Joe's. He glanced down at the chubby fingers and an emotion stronger than love rent his heart. What sort of man was he to weigh a child against a tiny farm, a couple of pigs and maybe a cow were all it might amount too, nothing in comparison to a child.

Tommy was pretending to count the links in the chain.

Joe's eyes dropped to the tousled hair on his small head. But the expenses, another mouth to feed, clothes for her back, shoes for school. He stopped himself. Joe Standish tha's not even certain a bairn is on the way and tha mind is running on like a spinster's. Putting aside the paper chain he rose.

'Dada it isn't finished yet.'

'I'll be back in a moment, lad. I'm just going to find tha mother.'

Emily had her back against wall, arms wrapped in the skirt of her apron staring up into the bare branches of the trees. In the faint light escaping through the kitchen window she looked pale and drawn.

Stepping through the kitchen door Joe glanced towards the privy then saw her standing motionless, gazing into the darkness. 'Emily it's too cold out here, come in, Lass.'

Pulling herself erect she gave him a wan smile. 'I came over a bit faint.'

'Aye and sick as well by the colour of tha face.'

There was love and concern in his voice and she thought that she didn't deserve it. She was holding a secret from him and she had no right to do so. Tears brimmed onto her lashes.

'Come here, sweetheart.' His arms opened.

'I'm sorry, Joe.' She sniffed against his vest. The words she must say stuck to her tongue like soft toffee.

Kissing her cheek he tasted her tears. 'Tell me what it is that's fretting thee so.'

The face of a newborn baby came into mind and she was finally forced to meet what had haunted her for weeks, Joe's hidden resentment and despair. She made the delivery fast as though the very speed of her confession would counteract his anger. 'I'm carrying a bairn.' She waited for the heavens to fall.

A slow smile crossed his face. 'I know that you silly wench. Come here and give me a hug.'

'How did...'

'How did I guess? Easy.' Pulling her closer he kissed her brow. 'We'd better get inside before the little bugger we already have sets fire to the place.'

She pulled him back. 'Joe, tha doesn't mind too much?'

'Mind. Don't be such a silly beggar, course I don't mind.' Putting as much spirit as he could muster into his words, he said 'And as for the small-holding we'll manage that somehow.'

Emily wasn't so sure. A baby cost money and that was a fact. Following him inside she bolted the door.

In a rush Emily went back to the cooking pot and stirred the meat. 'Lordy I forgot all about this.'

Dropping the glue and the paper, Tommy stood. 'What's for supper, Mammy?'

'Lamb and potato.'

His mouth turned down. 'I don't like that.'

Dreading a tantrum, Emily kept her voice calm, hoping to divert him. 'Aye, Tommy you love lamb and spuds.

'I don't like it. Didn't you hear me.'

Emily dropped the spoon back into the pot. 'Tommy do not be a naughty boy.'

This was the first time that Joe had experienced one of Tommy's outbursts and his first reaction was to land him a smack. Holding onto his own temper, he spoke slowly. 'Tommy Standish say sorry to Mammy now.'

The youngster his face red with anger stamped his foot. 'No!'

Joe had never lifted a hand to the lad. Victim of his own father's temper it was not Joe's intention that his own son should suffer in the same way. He was firm. 'I said say sorry. Or sorry you will be, my lad.'

Tommy held his ground. 'I'll not eat pig swill.'

Where on earth have you ever heard such a thing?' Emily was in tears.

His face dark, Joe lunged at the boy, catching him by the scruff of his collar. 'Then tha'll not worry that there's no supper tonight and there will be none until Tommy lad apologises to his Mammy.'

Screaming abuse Tommy kicked his father on the shins.

Pain seared through Joe's legs and he gave a thought to the bruises that would show there tomorrow. Grabbing the child around the waist he carried him struggling towards the stairway door.

Slumped in a chair Emily heard the child screaming his way up the stairs. Above the racket she heard Joe's stern voice. With a sigh that was more of a sob she rose from the chair and removed the supper from the hob. No one, she reckoned, would be in the mood to eat for quite sometime.

Eventually Tommy's screams ceased, he had screamed himself hoarse and now Emily heard the occasional sob coming from upstairs. Her heart went out to him but how she was to manage such a defiant and rebellious child. Dreading the day that Joe took matters into his own hands. It would be bad for her and Joe, and bad for little Tommy, for he would have no respect for either of them then.

She was poking the fire into a blaze as Joe came back into the kitchen. His face looked pale beneath his quarry tan.

'He's asleep. Thank God.' Sighing he slumped into the chair opposite Emily's. 'I owe you an apology.'

Reaching out she touched his hand. 'No, Joe...'

'Let me finish, lass.' He sounded weary to the bone. 'I known that you said he was getting to be a handful but I never thought that he was that bad.' Leaning back he gazed into the fire. 'I tried to find out what's worrying him but he says nothing is. He's as stubborn and bad tempered as me own father was.' He gave Emily a worried glance. 'You don't think that he's taken after that evil tempered bugger do you?'

'Joe he has you as a father, a kinder more gentle man no one could be. You're a good father to him, it's our Tommy that's the little heathen.'

He gave her a wan smile. 'I'm glad of your trust. You don't know how close I came to walloping him and I don't think it would have been a tap either. It's frightening to think a little bairn can make a man forget himself.'

'But you didn't, Joe.'

'No I suppose you're reeght.' Rising he put the kettle to the hob. 'I need a cuppa.'

After supper, which was a quiet affair, Emily worrying that Tommy would wake hungry during the night and Joe would remember his words to the lad, "an apology comes before another meal."

When they had finished and Emily had stacked the dishes in the sink and returned to the living room, Joe threw another log on the fire and in the light of the blaze he explained to her where he thought the source of Tommy's temper had stemmed. Leaning forward in his chair elbows on his knees, he spoke quietly. 'Do you remember when I took him to the big house to the birthday party? I think something happened there at Plas Mawr that disturbed him, but I'll be buggered if the little mite will tell me.'

He turned hopefully to Emily. 'Perhaps you can get it out of him. If we can't get to the bottom of it I don't know how we will fare especially with the new bairn on the way.'

The thought of a new baby in the house and Tommy throwing fits of temper didn't bear thinking about. Her soft brown eyes were full of anxiety. 'I'll try Joe, but you saw how he was it's impossible to reason with him.'

'Perhaps we are going about it the wrong way. If we try talking to him when he's relaxed and happy perhaps we might get to the bottom of the problem. A walk or a trip to the shops, something that he likes to do might be the right time to talk to him.' He lowered his voice glancing at the stair door. 'It's not long before we need to do some Christmas shopping, we could make a treat of it and take him to Caernarvon or Bangor!'

Emily wasn't sure if it was a good idea to give the lad treats for being naughty, perhaps a sound clout was the answer. But she'd try Joe's way first and if that failed she'd box the little beggars ears herself.

Sighing, she looked into the fire. 'Aye it's worth a try. But you take him it wouldn't be wise for me to go rattling along in a wagon for hours at this early stage.' Her hand went to her stomach, silently she prayed for a well-behaved and sweet baby girl.

They were no further forwards in solving their dilemma when Tommy's fifth birthday dawned on the eighteenth of December. For a few days prior to the big day Tommy had curbed the excesses of his temper and given his mother and father a small respite. But they were both surprised and disappointed when he refused to entertain the children of the village to his birthday party, he would have no one but

Henrietta Bellamy.

Joe put his foot down refusing to visit Plas Mawr to invite the ten-year-old girl.

Tommy sulked.

Emily cancelled the plans for the party.

Tommy fifth birthday passed quietly with nothing to celebrate it but a special tea and a gift of wooden farm animals that Joe had made and painted lovingly. Enthralled by the little farmyard Tommy played quietly.

For Emily it was a relief when the day was over. She went to bed disappointed that she hadn't tried harder to change Tommy's mind about inviting some of his young friends from the village.

Snow fell on Christmas Eve and for the first time in years it looked as though Christmas would be white. Through the window Emily could see the boughs of the trees transformed to silvery white. The snowflakes falling silently against the glass, cast a thick mantle on the window ledge.

She looked across the room to the table, where a candle guttered in the draft from the chimney. Beside the candlestick a tiny feast was laid out for Father Christmas and his reindeer. Lovingly positioned a hundred times by Tommy, to be sure that the old man would find them.

The child was kicking his heels in the chair beside the fire, his eyes turning to the plate of pies and the glass of ale and then to the chimney itself, head bent to one side he would stare up into the sooty blackness.

Watching him brought back wonderful memories for Emily of her own early childhood Christmases in Chorley. Her father keeping the farm for his ancient parents and in the early years even her great-grandfather had been present. She could see the old man now, smoking his pipe beside the fire, a massive old dog at his feet. What days! When folk lived off the land and the fat of it most times. Never short of a goose or a pair of ducks for the table. The Christmas puddings had been something, great round wonders wrapped in the remnant of an old sheet. The pot would be boiling for days above the fire, in the wisps of steam a fragrant aroma of expensive spices and fruit. Remembering that it wasn't only appetising aromas from the pot; there was also the less appealing smell of boiled linen and if the pot should ever run dry...

Joe was coming down the tiny path to the front door, stamping the snow off his boots before coming in. His face and bare hands red with cold. Entering he brought the chill air into the room. 'It's a bit parky.'

Tommy jumped off the chair. 'Dada do you like the feast Mama and me have put out for Father Christmas?' Crossing to the table he lifted a small pie off the plate. 'This one is for the reindeer.'

Joe rumpled the boy's hair. 'Oh he'll love that. He'll be pretty hungry by the time he gets here I shouldn't wonder.'

Grabbing his father's hand he tugged. 'Tell me again about where he comes from and how he gets down the chimney. Tell me, Dada. Tell me.'

Joe laughed. 'I'll tell you on the way to the church and all the way back again.'

Tommy's eyes were glowing. 'Promise.'

'I most certainly do promise.'

Joe turned to Emily. 'Will you be alreeght for walking in this weather, lass?'

Tommy, swinging on his father's arm turned his face up to him. 'Why won't Mammy be all right? Mammy walks everywhere. She's always walking about.'

Smiling, Emily touched his cheek. Participating in Tommy's excitement was as good as being a child again, resurrecting the magic of Christmas.

Checking the time, Joe said, 'If we are to make the church service at seven we had better start thinking about setting off. It's over a mile and in this weather...'

'I'll get Tommy's coat and muffler.'

He caught her arm. 'Are you up to walking to Llandfydd?'

'I've looked forward to it, Joe. I wouldn't want to miss the Christmas Eve service. The church is so pretty...'

'Let's get a move on then.'

Joe dressed Tommy in a dark blue outdoor coat; a hand-me-down that would see another year on the child's age before it fitted him properly. Pulling up the collar Joe wrapped a muffler around his neck, tucking the fringed end into the belt at his waist. Buttoning his boots, he hitched up his long socks almost covering his knees. 'Thee'll do, little fella.'

It wasn't often that Joe fell into his natural dialect it took a loss of temper or some other emotional moment for his Northern origins to surface. His thee's and tha's had been hard to drop and had taken a concerted effort but he knew that the men he worked with understood him better, so that was reward enough. For Tommy, already picking up snippets of Welsh, his father's previous speech was quite foreign. Emily had the most trouble with the Welsh language and as her roots were firmly buried in rural Lancashire soil, her dialect surfaced more often than not.

Tying her cloak, newly acquired from a second hand shop that had recently opened in Caernarvon, Emily glanced at her reflection in the spotted looking glass. The dark green material suited her brown hair and brought out the green lights in her brown eyes. Pleased with the way she looked; blossoming now the first few months of her pregnancy were behind her, she smiled at Joe. 'Ready?'

He checked his pocket for a couple of pennies for the church collection plate. 'Let's go.' Extinguishing the candles, she had banked the fire for their return; Emily opened the front door.

'Dada will Father Christmas come while we are at church?'

'No, Tommy he'll not make an appearance until you are fast asleep in bed.'

'Are you sure?'

'Positive.'

Holding the boy by the hand, Joe stood on the tiny garden path, Emily pulled the door closed and locking it put the old key into her pocket.

There were no sounds except the crush of snow beneath their boots, the wind had dropped and the garden and beyond was solemn and quiet. Twilight had passed and the sky was dark with night, the clouds purple and sloe black, occasionally edged with silver from the rising moon. Snow had piled up against the stone walls, thick and crisp twinkling in the light of Joe's lantern.

Tommy ran ahead kicking at the drifts, scattering snow with his boot caps.

Emily linked Joe's arm. 'It's a really magical night. I love it when it snows for Christmas.'

He pulled her closer. 'Aye I know what you mean.'

'Are thee happy, Joe?'

He smiled down at her. 'Course I am.'

The sound of church bells rose from the valley.

They were five minutes late for the service, and as Joe quietly lifted the latch on the old door the choir and congregation were singing the first verse of a carol. Quietly they made their way into the nearest pew.

The snow fell heavily throughout the service obliterating the congregations' footprints on the pathway between the gate and the church porch. The nearby holly tree heavy with berries was cloaked in snow, and the ancient yew tree in the graveyard was bending its great boughs with the weight.

Tommy was delighted.

It took longer to walk home. The night was colder; the wind rising, clouds coming in off the sea were banking up on the mountaintops. There were no breaks between them to allow a sliver of moonlight to silver them.

The flame of the lantern helped them to keep a sure footing, and the promise of a hot drink and a warm pie by the fire speeded them on.

In the lane, near home, Tommy squealed when he saw animal tracks. 'Look reindeer footprints. Dada he's been and I was not at home.'

Stooping to get a better look at the disturbed snow, Joe held Tommy's hand. Keeping his voice very serious he looked into the child's eyes. 'It doesn't mean that he's been but it might mean that he's around and waiting for you to be in bed before he calls.'

Tommy's face brightened. Running ahead he yelled over his shoulder. 'Hurry. Hurry. Hurry. Mammy, please hurry.' He was standing on the front step of the house looking anxiously towards the white roof as Joe and Emily made it to the gate.

'Look up there, Dada can you see if his sleigh has been on our roof.

Joe made a show of looking. 'No he has certainly not been here yet but I think we had better hurry to bed just in case he comes very soon.'

'Let me in then, Dada, be quick.' His little legs were jiggling with excitement and when the door was finally opened he ran to the stair door, stretching his small body to lift the latch, he ran headlong up the stairs. 'I'll have a wee in the po. I can't wait to go out to the privy.' He shouted down.

Emily and Joe's eyes locked and they had difficulty stifling a giggle.

Joe took Tommy's warm drink up to him in bed and sat with him until his excited eyes finally closed in sleep.

Grinning, Joe closed the stair door quietly and came into the living room. 'I didn't think that it would be that easy to get him off to bed tonight.'

Emily was sitting by the fire warming her bare toes.' Small mercies are very welcome and especially on Christmas Eve.'

Taking off his jacket, Joe eyed the fire. 'He went off as good as gold. Thank heaven for fox tracks.'

Emily smiled. 'Is that what it was?'

He laughed. 'Well did you think they were reindeers?'

'No. Don't be daft, Joe. I thought that they might have been old mother Harris's mongrel making his way home.'

Rubbing his hands together he looked expectantly. 'Well where's Father Christmas's treat then. Pie and ale was mentioned.'

'It's on the table, behind you, Joe.'

'Smashing.' He took a bite of the meat pie and with his mouth full, he said. 'Merry Christmas, darling.'

She smiled. 'Merry Christmas, Joe.'

Chapter Six

The morning was bitter, since Christmas the weather had worsened. With the arrival of the New Year the villagers gripped in the fiercest winter in living memory hoped that the new month would bring a respite to the freezing temperatures. It wasn't to be, and now in the second week of January there looked like little hope of milder conditions until the winter months had rolled by.

Emily, heavily pregnant, was virtually confined to the house the roadway being too treacherous for her to negotiate.

If she'd had the price of candles to worry her last year now she had the price of fuel and against all her wishes and protestations the Standish family, like many of the other householders in the district, was burning dried cattle dung for heat. It wasn't ideal and Emily swore that it left a tainted smell to the house that made her sick. Joe thought the real culprit was her pregnancy, women in that condition were renowned for fickle stomachs.

This morning Joe gave no thought to either the cattle or their combustible production. Head bent he trudged down the track towards the quarry several layers of flannel failing to protect him from the biting wind. With only the sound of his boots for company, the cold had silenced the birds in the black branched trees weeks before. Shoulders hunched, breath a smoking cloud, and chill tears pulled from his eyes, he passed a stand of bushes rimed white with frost offering a few seconds respite from the icy gusts.

Harsh as the conditions were he'd count himself lucky if he did a day's work. There was every chance that the threatened strike would take hold and every man, for or against the intended action would find himself unable to work.

Late on Saturday night in the Half-Way there had been talk of little else. The dissenters opening their mouths and pouring ale down their throats for hours before they found the courage to speak in public.

Aware that a group of quarrymen was coming up behind him Joe quickened his pace not wishing to get into a debate. He might agree that bargains set of late had been grossly unfair but he was too much of a newcomer and in bad need of his job to openly rubbish the steward's ethics. The last straw had come at the beginning of the month when the steward had awarded his brothers and brothers-in-law, not for the first time, the best bargains. The rock that was either hard to yield, or less profitable, going to the men whom had not sucked up enough, greased palms or openly complained.

In the short time that he'd been here he'd made friends and they would expect him to stand with them if it came to a vote behind closed doors. But his common sense told him that he'd not get back into the Garddryn if he opposed the steward and walked out. There were too many other men willing to work, Amlwch copper men with their ore running out, Irish fleeing a famine, blacklisted rioters from the South, immigrants from Liverpool and the North Country, not to mention the local Welshman seeking better wages than the land could offer.

The ugly picture of men making a mad rush for his job set his mouth in a hard line. A fine old temper he was working himself into and not a minute of the working day accomplished. He kicked a stone out of his path sending it yards ahead of him. If it was as easy to transplant problems as it was stones...

Iwan Williams breaking away from the group caught up and came alongside Joe. He was a big brawny man with a gut nurtured by ale, he was nearer fifty than forty and his face was coarse, marked with infantile smallpox, on the occasions that he was clean his mop of thick hair was salt and pepper grey. He would have looked brutish but for his pale baby blue eyes which gave him an appearance of mildness. He had a long moustache and thick beard, twin furrows from nose to mouth buried in the wiry hair. The jacket he was wearing was worn and filthy, barely buttoning over his paunch. A dark blue muffler kept the worst of the weather off his neck, and around his stout middle a thick belt of flannel kept the draught from his kidneys.

English didn't come easily to him and faltering over the seldom used words he scowled. 'We can depend on you Standish when it's put to the vote.' His hand had found its way to Joe's arm.

Fighting the impulse to shake the man off, Joe forced a smile. The last thing he needed was an open confrontation. Choosing his words carefully he looked candidly into the man's degenerate face. 'Depend on me. I should hope that any man could.'

'Good. So if it comes to a vote tonight in the Half-Way we know where your loyalties lie.'

Falling into step, Joe's eyes turned to the man walking beside him. 'And what vote would this be?'

Scowling, Iwan Williams drew up, caught Joe by the arm again but now his grip was brutal. 'Don't play silly buggers with me and don't forget, English,' he used the word as an insult, 'while you are working in this quarry you're taking the job of a Welshman.'

Joe glanced down at the broad hand gripping his arm. Speaking in a tone that was respectful but at the same time declared he wasn't to be bullied, he didn't want to start a war. 'I wouldn't have thought I'd qualify to vote on quarry issues. I'm only a rubble man and an apprentice at that when all said and done.'

Releasing Joe's arm Williams balled his hands. 'Apprentice.' He spat the word. 'Bit long in the tooth for that.'

Joe had no answer, so it was with mixed blessing that he saw a woman, a neighbour running towards the group of men that stood nearby. Hearing his name his heart missed a beat.

One of the men cupping his hand to his mouth shouted. 'Standish go home at once, your wife has taken a fall.'

Beneath his weather tan Joe's complexion paled. Scarcely heeding the woman's breathless words, he turned, and with the sounds of the Garddryn stirring to a new day he raced down the track towards home, shale flying beneath his boots.

Miss Roscommon and Miss Hogarth, two elderly women who shared a cottage in the village, were standing over Emily as Joe, his lungs burning from effort and the freezing air rushed into the cottage.

Emily was propped in the old ladder-back chair, her face as pale as her whitened apron. Struggling up her hand covering her swollen belly. 'Joe there was no need for you to come home.' She sank back slowly, pain written in her face.

Crouching down beside her, Joe took her hand. 'I'll go for the doctor. Don't move until I get back.'

Her eyes filled with tears. 'I'm sorry, Joe. I only stepped out for a moment.'

Miss Roscommon retying her bonnet explained the mishap. 'She fell on the ice. It was lucky we were passing. Took a real tumble she did. Good thing that someone was on hand.' The intricate bow complete and now partially hidden beneath her several chins Miss Roscommon began fastening her cloak. 'It would be better if you stayed with her and we fetched the doctor.'

Martha Hogarth ever acquiescent to her dominant companion, nodded agreement. Although she hardly knew Joe, she placed her rheumatic hand lightly on his shoulder and sighed compassionately. 'A cup of sweet tea would be the thing for your wife, Mr. Standish.'

'Good idea, Miss Hogarth, I'll make a brew.' He was glad of the mundane, anything to occupy his time until the medical man's arrival. He had the kettle on the hob before the two women departed.

Nervous after witnessing Emily's fall, their progress was slow as they trod carefully on the snow and ice. Watching at the window Joe wished that he had gone to fetch the doctor himself, he would have been there and back in no time, he was about to suggest that he go after the two women and send them back when Emily caught her breath.

Turning to her quickly he was shocked to see her grimace of pain. 'Shall I carry you up to bed? It'd be more comfortable than the old chair.'

'Aye, Joe. It might be better for the babe.'

Although heavily pregnant she was still light in his arms, and as he made his way up the narrow stairs fear that he might lose her terrified him.

The wait for the doctor was interminable and Joe spent it walking to the window watching for his carriage, or sitting beside Emily listening for it. It could have been an hour or even longer, he lost track of real time, before he saw Miss Roscommon and Miss Hogarth returning along the lane, bedraggled, their clothes wet with newly falling snow.

Stumbling over his feet Joe rushed down the stairs to open the front door.

The two elderly women were gingerly skirting around a snowdrift. Joe met them at the gate.

'Mr. Standish the doctor's wife assured us that he would be along presently.' Miss Roscommon was uncharacteristically agitated.' I'm afraid we have nothing more definite to tell you. The doctor has an urgent call at the quarry.' She sighed. 'It is a bad day for accidents I'm afraid.'

His mind raced over the options open to him, another doctor, the nearest was too far away. It would take hours to reach him and then return…Remembering his manners he opened the gate. 'Please come in and warm yourselves.'

'No. No.' Miss Roscommon waved her gloved hand. 'We had better be getting back to our own home.' Her old rheumy eyes searched the laden sky. 'This snow looks like it is setting in again and we are afraid that it might become more difficult to get about.'

Martha Hogarth nodded her agreement. 'Best to be getting back. Unless of course we can be of some use to your wife.'

'No, ladies, you have done more than enough for us and I thank you for that. Get off home. I will call round later if I have any news.'

Holding her bonnet as a gust of bitter wind threatened to send it flying, Miss Roscommon looked belligerently at the lowering clouds. 'We'll be anxious to know how she fares. We will not be venturing out again this day or tomorrow by the look of it, so call at anytime, Mr. Standish.'

Watching them as they negotiated the now obliterated roadway Joe felt kindly towards the two women who had done him such a service. The conditions were terrible and neither of them would see seventy again. Trekking to the doctor's and back must have been quite an ordeal. In his mind he made a vow to see what he could do for them to repay their kindness when his own family crisis was over. There were always plenty of jobs that needed doing around an old property that might not get fixed by two old girls. They had rounded the bend and were now out of sight. Shivering with cold he made his way back into the house. Rushing up the stairs two at a time he entered the bedroom. 'The doctor will be along presently.'

'Oh, Joe, did those two lovely old dears walk all the way back?'

'Aye.' Leaning over her, he wiped beads of perspiration off her brow.

She did not voice her fears that the babe might be harmed. Her guilt was immense, drawing her into a pit of despair that she dare not share with Joe. Would he ever forgive her if something were to happen, how could she expect him to when she would never forgive herself. Tears filled her eyes and she brushed them away before Joe should notice. There was still her other child. 'Is Tommy alreeght?'

'Aye. Nelly next door is minding him.' He didn't mention that he had found Tommy sitting in the corner of his bed, hands covering his eyes terrified by the calamity. Or that in a temper tantrum he'd screamed that he didn't want to stay with Nelly and then proceeded to bite the youngest child of the family. He would deal with that problem later, when he was certain that all was well with Emily and their unborn baby.

A spasm of pain gripped Emily. 'Joe I think thee had better send for Ma Jones and not wait for the doctor. I reckon this baby will not be long in coming.' She grimaced as another contraction took hold.

'I think I can hear a carriage.' With his cheek pressed against the windowpane he looked up the lane. 'It's the doctor, Emily.'

Clattering down the stairs he opened the door and dashed once more to the gate. Doctor Lidell, Surgeon Griffith's partner was hastily ushered into the cottage.

The clock ticked the minutes away and Joe with nothing to do but wait, paced back and forth in the room downstairs. After a preliminary examination the doctor had called Joe to the top of the stairs and explained that the birth might be difficult. After such a heavy fall it was unlikely that a premature child would survive and there was no guarantee for the mother.

The hours slouched by on iron shoes. With nothing but Emily's imminent danger to focus his mind on, the waiting was an agonising torture. The curtains had not been drawn across the cold, dark windows. The fire had burned low, a few embers glowing in the grey ashes. The kettle grew cold from the last brew at two o'clock. Occasionally his belly rumbled for lack of food. Unaware of anything but the room upstairs he sat hunched before the cold grate. The clock struck six startling him. Still no other sound bar the shuffling step of the doctor as he crossed the bedroom.

The horse and carriage had been collected long ago and would not return until asked for. There was nothing he could do. Visiting Tommy was out of the question; he wouldn't dare leave the house for a moment in case... The clock struck a single note and out of habit he looked at the dark face and cursed it for its constancy. Then he watched as the hand crept to seven.

Emily cried out, an agonising wail of pain. Startled out of his chair he covered his face with his hands and a great sob wrenched from deep in his belly.

A faint infant cry followed the mother's.

He had crossed the room, his foot on the first step of the stairs, afraid to climb up and too frightened to resume his terrible waiting ordeal.

The bedroom door opened and the doctor poked his head out.

'Mr. Standish you have a daughter, and although small she looks healthy enough.'

'And Emily? His voice was a whisper.

'Oh she'll do. They must breed 'em tough in Lancashire.'

The door closed and Joe crumpled onto the step. He felt like crying and it was long moments before he grasped that his face was wet with tears.

His daughter Chloe was thirty minutes old before Joe looked into her startlingly blue eyes. But by then he had the fire blazing, the curtains drawn blocking out the cold inhospitable night, the kettle singing on the hob, a loaf sliced and buttered, and an egg ready for boiling, should Emily feel like eating it. He had also taken a moment to shave in preparation for the first kiss he would plant on the soft cheek of his already beloved daughter. Many times in his life he had known true joy, the day he had married his Emily had been joyous, as had the birth of their son, and now today he felt truly blessed.

Emily was sleeping peacefully, her dark hair splayed across the pillow. Her face as white as alabaster save for a livid purple bruise across her cheekbone. In the candlelight her long dark lashes shadowed the faint blue hollows beneath her eyes, mark of her childbirth pain, her small hand resting above the bedcovers was grazed and red from the fall. He had a great urge to stoop to her and lightly kiss the bruise as though his love would wipe away the hurt. Beside her, the baby stirred, her bright eyes slowly opening she looked into her father's face. His whole being was suffused with love, how apt the biblical words *my cup runneth over*. Gently he placed his hands beneath her tiny body and drew her up, holding her to his chest for the first time he kissed her small brow. 'Chloe. My darling Chloe.' Her searching miniature fingers found his lips and very gently he kissed the tiny perfect nails.

Afraid that the baby would disturb Emily, he carried her downstairs. Pulling the comfortable chair close to the fire he sat with her in his arms admiring her, dreaming off her golden future, marvelling how bright she was, watched her eyes focus on the flickering flames.

The back door opened and Tommy and Nelly came into the room. Joe hadn't planned that Tommy should meet his little sister like this, Emily and he had talked about it and decided that the introduction would be made when the new baby was in its own little bed. But of course events had ridden over all their plans and now faced with the dilemma without Emily's good counsel and commonsense he made the best of a bad job.

Tommy rushed across the room and stood beside the chair. 'Where did that come from?'

Protectively Joe held the little girl closer. Putting his other arm around his son. 'Jesus sent her.'

With a sticky finger Tommy touched the baby's cheek, the soft flesh dimpled. 'When is he coming to get her.'

Joe pulled him close, kissing his brow. 'He's not coming to get her, he's given her to us as a special and precious gift. She is your new sister. Say hello to Chloe.'

'Shan't.'

'Oh, Mr. Standish she is lovely. Isn't she tiny.' Nelly, awe struck, lifted the tiny hand from the soft blanket. 'She is so perfect.'

'I want me supper.' Tommy poked his finger into his nostril.

Nelly turned to the child. 'Tommy you had your tea hours ago and you had a piece of bread and jam since then.'

'Haven't.'

'Oh, Tommy don't be naughty again. You'll wake your mammy.'

'I want me Mammy now.'

Joe placed the baby in Nelly's arms and stooped to his boy. 'You can see your mammy when she wakes up.'

Stamping his foot. 'I want to see Mammy now.'

Joe was firm. 'Tommy if you wake her up, my lad, tha'll have me to answer too.' None of this was going to plan, any minute he and Tommy would be in confrontation, the baby would start crying, Emily would wake and everything would go haywire. Why did this son of his always create mayhem where moments before there had been harmony. Drawing on his euphoria and happiness of only moment before he contained his temper.

'As soon as Mammy wakes we will go to see her together. Now that's a promise. So be a good boy and help me get a little supper for her.'

He looked into Tommy's defiant eyes. 'Is that alreeght?'

The child remained silent, and with a sigh Joe put the kettle to the hob.

Emily's recovery was slow, and a week had passed before Joe announced that as friends would help out during the daytime, he planned on returning to work.

Tommy had been a pain during Emily's lying in, there had been days when Joe had wondered if he could manage the boy without resorting to smacking him. How on earth did Emily cope...?

A visitor arrived as Joe was putting his working clothes to air ready for the following morning. Opening the door Joe was pleased to see Tudor Williams, a man who was becoming a close friend. Cold from his trek from the quarry barracks, he warmed himself by the fire. 'How's Emily?'

There was still the beatific look of a new father about Joe, he beamed, glad of the opportunity to speak of his little miracle. 'Little Chloe is thriving. She's so tiny yer wouldn't believe it, she's sleeping now or else I'd show her off.'

'I'm glad to hear it, at times like this that we need of a bit of good news.'

A look of concern crossed Joe's face. During the past week he had virtually been cut off from village and quarry life.

The thought that the strike had begun flashed through his mind. 'As summat happened then?'

'Aye. Gerallt Jones the chap that had the fall off Jerusalem...'

Joe interrupted. 'Now I remember. That's why Surgeon Griffith couldn't come at Chloe's birth, because he'd been summoned to the quarry. It had completely gone out of my head. So what happened to Gerallt ? How bad an accident was it? Is he alreeght.'

Solemnly, Tudor explained. 'I'm afraid he died this morning.'

'Dead. Gerallt. But he's only thirty summat.' He felt faint with shock. The young man and he had worked on the same team. A day never went by when he didn't teach Joe a Welsh word. There was always a bit of raillery when Gerallt was on form.

Sad, Tudor shook his head. 'It's no age. Terrible waste of a life.'

There was a slight tremor in Joe's hand as he took a spill from the holder on the mantelpiece. 'Aye. Terrible.' He lit the remnants of tobacco in his pipe, taking a slow drag to get it burning.

Tudor watched the flame. 'That's the reason I called. The lads are getting a bit of a collection together to help his widow and the three boys.'

'That's a good idea.' Joe went to the tea caddy taking a few coins from it. 'Me and Emily will be glad to do whatever we can.' He handed the money to Tudor. 'I wish it were more. I really liked the lad.'

Tudor gave him a weak smile. 'It all helps. Money will be short for them from now on.'

'Aye. But his wife will get some compensation for the loss.'

Tudor smirked. 'She'll be lucky to get the time of day after Surgeon Griffith has had his say.'

Recalling a recent conversation, Joe said, 'I've heard he's a hard bugger. The men at the quarry say he favours the owners more than the quarriers.'

'You never said a truer word, Joe. Griffith, I will not dignify him with the title of Doctor or Surgeon, Bastard runs off me tongue better. He's saying that Gerallt must have had a fainting fit, which caused him to fall. Says that he was already ill when he went to work that day, as the man died of pneumonia. He's said nothing about his broken legs and smashed hip, besides a nasty wound to his head, pneumonia indeed.' His voice rose. 'For God sake, the man fell sixty feet when a pillar of rock broke free. It was lying across his legs with a chunk of ice as tall as a man still clinging to the rear side of it.' Taking several breaths he tried to calm himself. Explaining more slowly. 'That morning the conditions were bad. It stood to reason that ice packed in the fissures would be a problem. But no, the steward wouldn't have it, said if they wanted to keep their places they'd work while there was light enough to do it. Plenty more men would be glad of the jobs and he'd be delighted to offer 'em. His exact words. He's another bastard.'

Joe was imagining the scene. That morning, the morning Chloe was born my God it had been cold, packed ice underfoot, total whiteness as far as you could see. It had started snowing again. He remembered the two old ladies trudging through snow to get to the doctor's place and at the self same time poor Gerallt was lying with the weight of the rock across his broken body.

Tudor broke into his morbid vision. 'Some of the men have got together and decided to try and oust Surgeon Griffith as quarry doctor.'

'What!'

'Don't look so surprised, Joe. You know what a bastard he is.'

'That might be so, Tudor but how do you propose to get rid of him. Shoot the bugger?'

Tudor gave a faint smile. 'Don't be daft. We weren't thinking of going that far.' His smile deepened. 'But it sounds a right good idea. But seriously, we would prefer it if he went under his own steam. For now we'd be happy if we could get another doctor to say that Gerallt died of his injuries. Pneumonia as we know from past experience, generally follows such cases.'

Joe knocked the ashes out of his pipe. 'I don't know that there'd be much of a chance of another doctor going against Griffith's word.'

'This is where your help is needed.'

Joe raised his eyebrows; he couldn't for the devil think what he had to do with the scheme.

Upstairs the baby began to whimper. Emily spoke softly. In the following silence both men were aware that the child had been put to the breast.

Tudor lowered his voice. 'The doctor that attends at the Alice Quarry is a reasonable chap; he has regard for the workers. We need someone to approach him, get his advice and find out if we can have another opinion on Gerallt. If we can prove that he was healthy, as his wife swears he was, she and the kids would be taken care of.'

'I still say that the man will not go against another of the same profession.'

Tudor looked despondently. 'I know you're right. But the lads want to try anyway. The least we can do for Gerallt's widow is to try for another opinion. Let's forget trying to oust the bugger for now. Let's just knock his lying diagnosis on the head.'

'I reckon that's all yer can do in reality.' He waited for Tudor to come to the reason for his visit. Riddling the fire with the poker he threw on a rotting log, a treasure found beneath the hedgerow.

Tudor coughed. 'We need you to approach the Alice Quarry doctor.'

'Me!'

'Don't look so shocked. This doctor chap is English, he even comes from Lancashire, your home county. So we thought that you would be the best man for the job. He'll understand you better. You know, English to English, Welsh to Welsh.'

Taking a minute to think things through, Joe took his tobacco pouch off the mantelpiece and refilled his pipe.

Tudor was silent.

Putting a lighted spill to the bowl, Joe puffed out smoke as he spoke. 'Be hell of a bloody risk. What happens if the steward or the little steward finds out, not to mention the bloody manager, or the

Marquis himself.'

Tudor's voice rose. 'He's nothing to do with us at the Garddryn.'

Forgetting to keep his voice low Joe alerted Emily to the discussion. She caught the tail end of Joe's sentence. 'Aye, I know he isn't, but his arm stretches a long way in these parts. The owners stick together. What I'm saying is, if this should come to anyone's ears I won't find meself another job in any quarry in Wales.'

Mediating for the stricken family Tudor went on, 'I know there is a risk. But think, if this should happen to your Emily and the two children you'd want your mates to do the best they could for them.'

Joe frowned. 'There's always that argument to fall back on.'

'Yes, but it's true isn't it, Joe.'

'Aye it is.' He spoke softly looking into the fire.

Tudor leaned forward in his chair. 'Look, the funeral was supposed to be tomorrow but we've persuaded the widow to put it off a day or two. That'll give you time to ask the Alice doctor for his help.'

Joe's eyes widened. 'And when am I supposed to do this?'

'Tomorrow.'

'But I'm working tomorrow.'

'As you've had all week off, what's another day?' Tudor became earnest. 'We can't leave it any longer, the poor bugger's got to be buried. Before that happens we need the doctor's report.'

Joe looked at his clothes airing beside the fire. 'I'll not be needing these for work tomorrow then?' He sighed.

'No, but you'll be wanting them to walk to Feichnan won't you?'

'Aye, I suppose you're reeght.'

Emily wasn't thrilled at the scheme, but could not find it in her heart to talk Joe out of going. If, as he had said, it were her and their bairns going hungry and homeless he would expect his mates to put up something of a fight for her.

The following morning under the cover of darkness he left the cottage, the fewer eyes to see him leave the village the better. In his coat pocket he had a chunk of bread spread with lard and a bottle filled with sweet, strong tea. His coat collar was pulled up against the penetrating wind; he walked briskly to keep his circulation moving. With a bit of luck, and if the weather didn't hinder him, he'd cover the eight miles to Feichnan before sunrise.

Cold, tired and now dispirited, it had taken longer than Joe had expected to tramp the miles, ice lay beneath the snow making the going difficult, at times the way was so treacherous that he was slowed to almost a snails pace.

To cap it all, the loss of a day's work, the biting cold, and the return journey to overcome, had all been in vain. Doctor Luke Mason, sitting in his comfortable sitting room beside a roaring fire, was absolutely adamant that his help could not be procured. He had got quite heated that Joe should think that Surgeon Griffith's professional conduct should be put in question.

It was with his words ringing in his ears that Joe found himself once more outdoors facing another onslaught of wind and snow. Wrapping his muffler around his neck and pulling it up around his cheeks he began the long, slow trek home. During the next two hours he saw no one but a shepherd, high in the hills checking his stock, muffled against the weather and carrying a lantern against the murk of the falling snow. No carriages or carts passed, the drifts had closed the narrow roadway, the snow covering the top of the hedgerows in places.

Cutting down a sapling tree he fashioned a thick stick, tall as a herdsman's crook, using this to steady himself, and for testing the depth of the drifts, he followed what fences and hedgerows were still visible and trudged towards home. The wind was behind him, and the sack he placed over his coat although heavy with melted snow still kept the worst of the wind off.

Nearing his destination, although snowflakes obliterated the lights in the windows, he knew how close to the village he was as he passed the barn at Shanks farm and heard the lowing of the cattle sheltering there.

Through the murk he made out the old workhouse, he wondered how many people it now housed, and felt ashamed that he knew so little of the people living in dire straits there.

This thought brought Gerallt's face to mind, and the consequences to his widow and sons because of his failure to secure Doctor Mason help.

Hangman's cross, now unused, was thick with snow softening its grim outline. Why it wasn't pulled down was beyond him, was it left as a monument to the poor devils that had suffered there, or did the local gentry hold out hopes for its revival, a useful tool to obliterate the quarries of dissenters. What a thought to carry home.

He was passing by the Morgan cottage, Mrs. Morgan and her simple son, Billy's home. Billy must be nearly twenty-five and not a day's work in the poor bugger. What a burden to cope with, feeding and minding a big strapping man like that.

Today hiking to and from Feichnan he'd probably given more thought to Garddryn and the people that lived there than at any other time.

He reached the bridge fording the stream, the going was

treacherous here, thick ice clinging to the rails, the rocks were freezing over, and only the water at its deepest was still flowing freely. If that froze the village privies would be another problem. The ground was too hard... There was a moving lantern ahead, and then out of the darkness he heard a familiar voice.

'Joe. I've been worried about you man. I called at your place and Emily said that you hadn't returned, so I thought I'd come searching. Expected to find you buried in a drift. Merciful heaven, you're safe. But you must be frozen to death. Look at you; frost on your eyelashes and a frozen dewdrop on the end of your red nose. Still, you are a sight for sore eyes.'

Joe's lips were too numb to make a comprehensible reply.

Concerned, Tudor didn't think he'd ever seen anyone looking so cold, and the poor man still had the length of the village to tramp before he reached home. Peering through the falling snowflakes he looked across the street. 'Let's go over to the barracks, there's always plenty of tea on the brew, when you've warmed through you can tell me what happened.'

'No, no. I'm for me own fire.' It was difficult to form the words his lips were so numb.

Tudor was concerned. 'Well at least let me walk with you.'

Joe leaned heavily on his makeshift staff as they trudged on, the blanket of snow absorbing every sound but for the scrunch of their boots.

Emily was at the window, seeing them approach the gate she rushed out in her nightgown and shawl. The sight of him terrified her. His face blue with cold and the sack on his back crusty with ice. 'Joe, God in heaven look at the state of thee.'

Tudor steered him through the front door.

Beside the fire Emily began to remove the sodden sack and coat. He was shivering with cold.' Take tha shoes of, Joe I'll wrap tha feet in a blanket. Tudor get the blankets off our bed.'

Noisily, Tudor made for the stairs.

'Try not to waken the little ones.' She turned to Joe. 'Joe tha looks a reeght mess.'

'Aye. I feel it an all.' Shivering, he sneezed. 'It wouldna be so bad, 'Em if I hadn't failed.'

'Joe, I won't listen to that sort of talk. Tha's done the absolute best tha could. Even risked tha life to do it. What more could be expected of a man.' She looked up from rubbing his shins as Tudor stepped back in the room.'

'Take the rest of tha clothes off Joe and wrap these blankets around thaself.'

She turned to look at Tudor standing near the fire. 'Spoon some of the broth from the pan on the hob into that dish on the table. Warm food and hot tea is the only way to heat his frozen body.'

Speaking quietly, she didn't want Tudor to hear, she said, 'Joe, why did tha go in this weather. When I woke and found that tha gone I was so worried.' Her eyes filled.

'Oh, Emily please don't fret yerself. I'm back now. And safe.'

'Aye. But it's likely to be thee with pneumonia. I couldna bear to lose thee, Joe.'

'And tha's not likely too. Come here.' His arms sheltered her. 'Now, me bonny lass, get back to bed. Tudor and me will manage. We have things to talk over. I'll be up shortly. Now stop worrying or that bairn of ours will be without her milk for breakfast. It would be murder around here if she were as grumpy as our Tommy tomorrow morning.'

Sniffing, Emily gave him a weak smile. 'Promise that thee'll be up to bed soon.'

'Aye. I promise. Soon as I've thawed through and had summat to eat. Now go to bed.' He shrugged off a blanket. 'Here take this, I'll not need two sitting beside this roaring fire.'

Taking it from him, she held it close feeling the warmth of the fire on it. Then quietly, so as not to waken either child, she climbed the stairs to the cold bedroom.

Tudor handed Joe a brimming dish and a spoon. 'Don't say a word until you've got that down you.'

'I wouldn't know where to start.' Joe sighed deeply.

Tudor frowned. 'I should never have asked you to go. I should have realised that the weather was too bad to venture to Feichnan. I was so anxious to get some help for Gerallt's family that I put another life at risk. I'm sorry Joe. More sorry than I can ever say.'

Joe slurped broth. 'Don't be daft, man. I wouldn't have gone if I didn't think I'd get back safe. What do yer take me for, a simpleton?

'No of course not.'

'Well then let's forget about the bloody weather. More important to talk about the Alice Quarry doctor.'

Tudor moved forward in his chair. 'Was he helpful?'

'Was he buggery. Sent me off with a reeght flea in me ear. I suspected summat were wrong when I saw the size of the bloody house. The driveway looked to be half a mile long. Great fir trees either side of a high falutin gate.' He took another spoonful and swallowed before going on. 'Fine furniture, and a young maid to answer the door.'

Nonplussed, Tudor mouth gaped. 'But it wasn't like that last time

I saw the man, he was living over the tailor's in the high street. He had rooms there.'

The spoon clattered in the dish. 'Well he's moved. Got himself wed.'

'Married.' Tudor couldn't have been more surprised.

'Aye, he's married alreeght, to the Alice Quarry owner's daughter.'
'Never.'

Joe scraped the dish and licked the spoon. 'It is as true as I'm sitting here.' His feet and hands were beginning to tingle unpleasantly as the warmth penetrated.

Tudor sat thoughtfully, arms folded. The news was bleak. 'This change of allegiance will be hard on the Alice workers. Up till now the doctor had been fair to them. If they were sick or injured they could rely on him doing something about it. Everyone liked him even though he was a bit of a Nancy boy. That's why I was surprised when you said he had wed. He didn't look the sort, if you know what I mean.'

'Aye, whatever. It takes all sorts to make up this rum world of ours.'

Standing, Tudor reached for the dish. 'Shall I fill this again?'

'Go on then. It's a nice drop of soup.' Watching as the broth was poured, Joe said sadly, 'I suppose you can tell Gerallt's widow that she can bury him now.'

Tudor sighed. 'I can't think what else can be done. There isn't another doctor to help us. Old Griffith will have his way after all and Gerallt will be buried with pneumonia written on his death certificate. There'll be a bit of help from the parish for his family.' Handing the dish of soup to Joe, he slumped back in the chair, sighing. 'I'll go up first thing and have a word with the preacher from Salem chapel. Gerallt worshipped there. He was going to join the choir again. Like a lot of other young men he'd given it up when he got wed. Nice to think he felt settled enough to go back to it.'

Thoughtful, Joe tapped the edge of the dish with the spoon. 'One thing that has surprised me about quarrymen, they're different in many ways from the miners of Lancashire, here they actively belong to choirs or societies of one sort or another. I know they have their games and sport back home but here they're more community minded. Do things more in groups.'

Tudor nodded. 'It's been like that since I can remember. It's the influence of the chapel. The luckier chaps, those with an ear for music get to play in a band. I was in the choir, same as me father and his brothers. Three nights a week for practice, a night for home-life, and the rest of the time taking up with church meetings.' He grinned. 'On a good day we might even get to Caernarvon. Best were the fair days, those days were fun, and after we'd ride back on farmer Pendryn's cart. Starlit nights with a pretty girl sitting close, to keep the cold at bay...' Glancing at the clock, he jumped up. 'Look at me, keeping you from your bed. Talking of choirs and the like when I should be making me way back to the barracks and letting you get your well-earned rest.'

Clutching the folds of the blanket, Joe struggled up.

Tudor started to put on his coat. 'No. You stay put I'll see myself out.' The buttons fastened, he raised the collar to cover his ears.

'It's no trouble, Tudor. I have to lock up anyway.'

Opening the door on a white, silent world Joe looked to the heavens. 'Look at that. It's stopped snowing at last.'

Tudor sniffed the air. 'Now the wind's dropped, I reckon it's warmed up a bit.' Pulling on his gloves, he waved Joe inside. 'Don't stand on the doorstep you'll only get cold again.' With a final wave, he stepped onto the pathway

The bare twigs in the meagre hedge had made a re-appearance, and the icicles that had clung to the eaves for the best part of a fortnight dribbled drops of water.

It was a long way from being perfect weather for a stroll but it was still a great improvement. Tudor felt confident that the worst was over. Although his right foot might get damp, the wad of paper inside his boot covering the small hole in the sole wasn't up to dealing with this amount of wetness. Closing the gate behind him, he started out to the quarry barracks.

Joe turned to close the door, then stopped, he thought he had heard footfalls other than those of Tudor on the road. Imagination, he decided, as he turned towards the warm interior of the cottage.

The next morning, with the baby sleeping in the crook of her arm, Emily sat at the table. Joe was brewing tea.

'I didn't hear thee come to bed last night, Joe. Were tha very late?'

'Aye. I suppose I was. After Tudor left, I sat thinking for a little while.'

The baby whimpered. Emily rocked her gently. 'So what happened about the doctor? Is he going to help Gerallt's widow?'

Joe frowned. 'No, the bugger isn't.'

Sleepy, Tommy came down the stairs and into the room, rubbing his eyes with the back of his hands. He went to Emily's side, scrutinised the sleeping baby. Crossly, he whined. 'You woke me up, Mammy.'

Lovingly, Emily held him close, kissing the top of his tousled hair. 'I'm sorry, Tommy.'

Reaching out, Joe touched the boy's shoulder, giving it a light squeeze. Then pouring milk into a mug, he tapped the seat of a chair. 'Come and sit here, by me.'

Tripping over the hem of his nightgown Tommy went to his father.

Steadying him, Joe lifted him onto the chair, and carefully placing the mug in his hand, he watched the child drink.

Looking across at the pair, Emily smiled. 'So the doctor's not going to help at all? Why not?'

Wearily, Joe sighed. 'The young doctor has had a change of allegiance. He's gone over to the gentry's way of thinking.'

With her eyes on Chloe, who was slowly beginning to stir, Emily lowered her cup of tea. 'How can that be? Tudor thought that he would be sympathetic.'

Joe smirked. 'Not now he's the husband of the quarry owner's eldest daughter he won't.'

Emily's eyes widened in surprise. 'Never. When did that happen?'

'Very recently.'

'So that means that the Alice workers have lost a friend.'

'Aye. They've lost a friend alreeght. But he's gained money and influence.'

So his great effort had been in vain. It made her feel like crying, he'd been so cold, so tired. She saw him as he was on the path last night. Frozen snow clinging to the sack on his back. His eyebrows white with ice. 'Oh, Joe. So that means that all the effort of yesterday, trekking through that awful weather, went for nowt.'

He was wearied to the bone. 'Aye you could say that.'

Tommy, sounding older than his years, piped up. 'Will the doctor be very rich now he's married the rich lady, and have lots and lots of money to spend, and a big house to live in?'

Joe was flabbergasted at Tommy's grasp of the situation. His eyes locked with Emily's. 'Out of the mouths of babes.'

Frowning, Emily snapped at Tommy. 'Just drink tha milk. I'll not hear another word. Children are supposed to be seen and not heard. Just remember that, my lad.'

Tommy stuck his tongue out at his mother, but as she had turned to look down on the sleeping child in her arms, she missed this rude gesture.

Joe hadn't missed the rosy tip of it as it drew back, and he frowned. 'I'll have a word with you young man when I get back from work. Now try to be a good boy for Mammy today.'

Tommy scowled.

Giving him a long dark look, Emily tutted. 'A closed mouth

catches no flies. Just remember that, our Tommy. Sometimes I wonder what's to become of thee.'

Pushing his chair back from the table, Joe stood. Fastening the top button on his flannel shirt, his eye turned to his son. 'Listen to Mammy and try to help her today.'

Bending to Emily he kissed her lips, then kissed his tiny daughter. 'And you be good an' all.'

Passing Tommy he ruffled the child's hair. 'If you are a good lad we'll have a battle with the toy soldiers when I get home. Would you like that?'

Tommy was sulking. 'S'pose.'

Glancing at his wife. 'I'll be back same time as usual, Emmy.'

She raised her hand. 'Bye, Joe, take care.'

He was gone. The breeze blown into the room by the opening and closing of the door wafted smoke down the chimney. Looking across the littered table, the ashy hearth, and the dust gathering on the rungs of the ladder-back chairs, and then to her son, she sighed. The baby woke, and screamed her discontent at the world she had so recently entered.

Outdoors the thaw had continued, so it was to a wet and dripping morning, the clouds lying heavily on the mountains tops, that Joe began his walk to the quarry. Before he got to the heart of the village he was amongst a hundred or so men, all going in the same direction. Their boots sloshing through the water running down the lane.

The thaw had cheered everyone, and for a short time Gerallt and the impending funeral was forgotten. An early spring was talked of and the first signs looked for.

With the bottle of hot tea in his pocket, warming his hip, Joe could even believe a little in the season's early arrival.

'Before we know it it'll be Easter.' Someone said near him. The optimism made him smile. Listening to them, who would believe that they were going to work for as many hours as there was daylight? In temperatures cold enough to torment the marrow in a man's bones. Suspended on ropes over precipices hundreds of feet deep. Loading, shifting, and carting tons of rock. The luckier ones, those that had an aptitude and expertise would split and dress the rough slate with their backside on a hard bench, and the elements tearing at their clothes seeping beneath the thickest flannel. And all around, fierce explosions cleaving the workplace every hour or so. Men!

These thoughts brought him to the quarry, and bidding those he had walked with a good day, he climbed down to his team on Jerusalem. Obeying Jack Dickens orders, and if these were not politely given at least they bore a succinct quality, Joe dug at the rubble, hauling it to the mountainous slate dump. Within the hour he was sodden, the dripping ice and snow merging with his own body fluid to soak his clothes. The flannel next to his skin was damp and cold. If he'd skinned his knuckles once this morning...

A whistle blew, glancing up to the highest point of the quarry he saw the red flag flying. Dropping his shovel he climbed upwards. He had a few minutes to reach a shelter before blasting tore at the quarry wall. He wondered if he would ever become accustomed to the moments between the whistle and the blast. Those few minutes always flew by. The shelter would seem far away and the more he hurried the more his feet would slip and slide on the shale.

Cursing as he slipped now, scuffing the palms of his hands as he saved his fall, he heard the familiar two blasts of a whistle in rapid succession, announcing that the fuse was already alight. Wiping the grazes free of grit, he ran towards the stone building. Glancing around he saw that no one else was making a similar dash for it, and rushing through the door he slammed it behind him. The place was filled with men, standing shoulder to shoulder.

A familiar voice shouted from the back of the crowd. 'Made it then, Joe. We thought you were staying outside to watch the fireworks.'

Before he could call back a reply the whumff of the explosion shook the building. Scattered birds screamed overhead. Then their raucous cries could be heard in the distance, as they flew away from the Garddryn, heading for the safety of the shore or fields. The roar of splitting and falling rock ricochet around the galleries, filling the great cavern with thunder. Then silence.

A young man brushed passed Joe, and before anyone could stop him or shout a warning, he pulled the door open, just as a second explosion roared.

'Ffwl.' A loud shout from the rear of the shelter.

Joe had picked up enough Welsh to understand that at least one man thought the intrepid quarrier, a fool.

Three whistle blasts announced the all clear. It was back to work, two more hours before the lunch break. Walking back to his shovel, Joe took a swig of his cold tea. After shifting another hundredweight of rubbish rock, his muscles were sore, his throat parched for a hot drink. Breakfast seemed an age ago and his stomach rumbled for the cold pie in his bag.

The awaited, and looked for lunchtime eventually arrived, and relieved that half the day was over, Joe made his way with dozen of other men to the cabanod. He was tired.

Yesterday, trekking so many miles through the blizzard had

sapped his energy, only the thought of hot strong tea and a bite to eat kept him moving now.

The cabanod, was a rough building constructed from layers of thick slate. The slate floor scarred and ruined by countless hobnailed boots. A good stove in the middle of the room radiated a welcome heat on bitter or wet days. For the men working on the inhospitable galleries it was a welcome retreat, somewhere to rest, drink tea, eat and socialise.

Joe was one of the last men to arrive, and as he came through the door the smell of wet and dirty clothes steaming by the blazing stove reached him.

Ignoring the odour, his clothes would smell no better to a fastidious nose, he made his way to the fountain, or as others knew it, the tea urn. It had been brewing on the stove for over an hour, it was steaming, and the fragrance coming off the strong, stewed, tea was like sniffing nectar. He helped himself, filling a mug to the brim. Before moving away, he took a mouthful, sighing with gratification as it swilled his parched throat. Careful not to spill a drop, he made his way to the bench where Jack Dickens team sat. As he inched his legs under the table, an argument broke out near to the stove.

An older man, cuffing a lad's ears gave him some advice. 'Boys don't take the heat of the stove from their betters. Lad's brawn is for stopping the draught. So get back where you belong, beside the door. Don't let me find you warming your backside again.'

It had been the first thing that Joe had learned about the cabanod; men sat in strict order around the stove. Boys were relegated to the draughty benches near to the door. It had amazed him, being used to the roughness of the colliers, to find how fierce the hierarchy, and how important the intellectual side of the cabanod was. There would be times when a man would start off a recitation and before long several men would have joined him. Rich Welsh voices reciting poetry of the day, or from the old books they carried to work with them. Competitions, debates, there was always something going on. These men had a relationship with each other, different from the rough and ready camaraderie of the colliery workers. Not that it was always friendly; there were spats from time to time. But in the pit it wasn't spats that they had it was more like bloody murder. The women were worse. He nearly laughed aloud when he thought of George Thomas, he wondered what the fat bastard would have thought of the cabanod, and the intellectual entertainment. Or come to that, the President. A man highly regarded, elected by the majority, and renowned for his wisdom and integrity.

Reaching into his bag for his pie he took off the protective paper and stuffed it into his bag to use again tomorrow. A faint aroma of pastry and cold gravy reached his nostrils, saliva filled his mouth. Closing his eyes, better to taste the glorious flavour, he bit into the succulent pastry.

A man sitting alongside watched enviously. 'Your misses looks after you, Joe.'

Joe's mouth was stuffed. 'Mmmm you could certainly say that alreeght. But this pie I made mesen.'

There was awe in his companion's voice. 'An' is it a good un?'

Joe swallowed. 'Aye. It is an' all.' He took a swig of tea. Sighed with pleasure.

The man's voice dropped a note. 'Lucky beggar. Me wife wrapped a bit a bread and lard for me. As if that fills a quarrier's stomach.'

Joe finished his pie in silence. His thoughts had turned to Frank and how he would have fitted into the cabanod. The choir, he would have liked that, joined up the minute he got here. The chapel would have rung with his big baritone voice. Reminiscing, he finished his tea.

The gravedigger had watched the weather closely. It was a good thing that Gerallt Jones's funeral had been put off for a few day's, the ground had been hard as iron. Now it was wet through, and every time he struck it with his spade it seeped muddy water. He had an hour to complete the job before they carried the coffin from the chapel. Thrusting his spade in again, he moaned with weariness.

The job finished he stood under the old yew tree and watched the procession of mourners approach. There were hundreds of them; they'd fill the spaces between the old gravestones and spill over into the lane. The minister would have to shout if he wanted to be heard.

It was always the same, when a man died in the quarry; every one of the workers took a day off work. Respect day they called it, he wasn't so sure, a lot of them would never have met the man.

Gerallt Jones widow was crying, dabbing at her eyes with a piece of cloth. A rare moment of pity swept over him. It was sad, leaving a young wife and three healthy sons behind. They'd have a devil of a job making ends meet. The village was in an uproar, but there was nothing unusual about that. The quarriers always started to bleat about Surgeon Griffith the moment somebody was killed. It was said that he looked after the quarry owners' interest and ignored the plight of the quarrymen. They always had something to bleat about, the men from Garddryn. If it wasn't a strike, it was the doctor that had got it wrong again. Mind you, the chap had fallen a bloody long way, broke his legs and hip. But the surgeon said he died of pneumonia, so he must have.

Striking a light for his pipe, he sucked in the aromatic smoke.

The crowd had reached the hole now, he hoped to God it wasn't full of water. No, all must be well, he could see that they were lowering the coffin into it. He sighed thankfully. Ten minutes and the job would be done, the poor bugger planted, it was up to him then to fill in the hole. With luck he'd be home for his tea before five. No point visiting the Half-Way for a few ales tonight, the place would be steaming with quarrymen. They'd all be having their say, and not a sensible word between them.

Watching, he saw the first leave the graveside and begin to make their way into the lane. Taking the spade he'd left leaning up against the tree, he sauntered over to the new grave. It didn't take him long, then turning his back on the freshly turned earth; he made his way back to the chapel shed to store his tools.

Martha would be pleased to see him early; there might even be something decent to eat for his tea.

Chapter Seven

It was the morning of Chloe's third birthday. Joe had been looking forward to the day for weeks, his dark winter evenings being spent in making her birthday present, a wooden cradle for her dolly.

The three intervening years had seen several changes. Gerallt Jones widow was a married woman again, her boys no longer fatherless. If the match were a good one only time would tell. Her new husband wasn't the friendliest of men, and he had a temper, which flared up at the smallest upset.

Tommy was attending the small school in the village. Joe and Emily really couldn't afford it, but as it made life easier for Emily, he was still the most wilful child, hard to control. Smacking didn't work; reasoning with him proved to be a failure, so it was decided that school might be the answer. Keeping the boy occupied was their prime concern.

They hadn't been able to move house as they had wished. The expense of Tommy's schooling and the arrival of Chloe had put paid to that idea. Instead, they had rented the acre field at the side of the cottage. Working on Sundays and after work when the evenings were light enough, Joe had managed to remove the largest stones off the land, he'd used them to build a wall around a lean-to sty in the corner of the field. Digging and turning the soil working as much muck as he could into it, the ground that had lain fallow for as many years as anyone could remember now held the promise of fertility. His first crop was to be potatoes and root vegetables.

Last April, a piglet, the runt of the litter had been bought for pennies, and now, after careful nurturing, she was a good size sow, and enjoying the run of the walled patch and sty. There were six brown hens sharing the pig's quarters, they weren't laying yet but in a few weeks time there should be eggs from them.

Shortly after Gerallt's funeral, Jack Dickens suspecting that Joe had a hand in interfering between the Alice Quarry doctor and Surgeon Griffith's treatment of the sick man had fired Joe.

Fortunately, Tudor Hughes was working on his own bargain on Bethlehem gallery, it wasn't the most advantageous of bargains, but it was good enough for him to afford to pay Joe a cut of the profits.

Tudor was a better boss, solicitous of his team of men and a great deal less abrasive than Jack Dickens. Working for him took some of the stress out of the job but didn't make the grinding toil any easier.

The strike that had threatened three years back never came too much, due mainly to the workers at the heart of the dissent being dismissed. The rest of the men might simmer with the injustice of it but they were too fearful of their own jobs to raise much of a fight. Time would tell. Joe believed that ultimately the strike would take hold, and because of the delays and procrastination it would be a great deal more militant.

It was early, and as Joe put the kettle to the hob he was thinking back to Chloe's birth. That morning, Emily had fallen at the gate, and he had rushed home to find two old ladies, Miss Roscommon and Mary Hogarth in the cottage watching over her. What an agonising day it had been, waiting, praying. Then he had heard the baby's cry and Emily was pronounced in good health. Watching the kettle coming to the boil, he relived the relief he had felt at that moment.

Chloe was a beautiful child, eyes as soft as dark blue pansies. Good-natured, a happy smiling child.

The cradle he had made was standing near to the fireplace. Admiring his handy-work, he wiped imaginary dust off it. The wood was smooth and glossy, the little rockers moved silently. He was pleased. Little Chloe would be delighted with her birthday present. It was worth the effort, the nights rubbing down the wood and trying to do it quietly lest he wake her or Tommy.

Pouring water into the teapot, he heard her climbing cautiously down the stairs, one step at a time, then pushing the door open, her dolly tucked under her arm, she made the final step into the room.

'Chloe darling come and see what the birthday fairy has left for you.'

Seeing the cradle her eyes lit. She ran headlong into his arms.

Scooping her up, her chubby small hands clinging to his neck, he kissed her cheek.

'Happy birthday, darling girl.'

Wriggling to be free. He lowered her to the floor gently, smiling at her excitement.

She couldn't get the little covers that Emily had sewn off quickly enough and lay her dolly down. 'Dada it's lovely. Daisy May loves it. She's going to go to sleep all day.' She kissed the doll. 'Daisy May you be good and go to sleep.'

Emily came in from the privy. 'Poor Daisy May will miss Chloe's birthday if she has to sleep all day.' She smiled.

Snatching the doll up, she said 'She can go to sleep tonight.'

Thumping down the stairs, Tommy came into the room, grumpy.

Dashing to him, Chloe held up her doll. 'Look, Tommy, Daisy May has a new bed. Isn't it nice?'

His small face furrowed in a frown, he pushed the doll away. 'Stupid doll.'

Emily tried not to look cross. 'Don't be naughty, Tommy. Wish Chloe a happy birthday.'

Shaking his head and sighing, Joe put his bottle of tea into his workbag. 'Let's make this day a happy one for Chloe.'

Tommy scowled. 'Stupid doll.'

Thankful that today was a school day for her son, Emily poured buttermilk into his cup and began spooning steaming porridge into his dish.

Sitting beside him Chloe chattered happily about her dolly.

Tommy ate in silence.

Walking to work, Joe gave Tommy the benefit of his charitable thoughts. It was to be expected that Tommy would be jealous that it was his sister's birthday, and Tommy being Tommy would find it impossible to hide it as other children might try to do. Little Chloe was so pleased when it was Tommy's birthday and shared his pleasure. The boy just didn't have the generosity that was second nature to Chloe. He sighed. Perhaps the lad would grow into a hard man. He hoped not. Men like his father, hard-nosed bullies, missed so much of life. He hoped that the harder side of his son would mellow with the years, but in his heart he knew that it was not going to happen. He sighed again, but this time with sadness.

A few minutes late for work, he made a last minute dash. He could have saved himself the trouble, because when he reached Bethlehem gallery the men were not working they were in deep conversation, a sombre mood about them.

'What's up?' He asked Tudor quietly.

'Allan Fiedland's not working today, a message has come from his home to say one of his children has cholera.'

The news was like ice in Joe's stomach. Everyone knew that infectious and poisonous vapours caused the disease. Few miles separated Feichnan and Garddryn. .

Guessing what was running through Joe's head Tudor put out his hand touching him sympathetically. There was a lot to be said for being a single man and having no offspring to scare yourself witless about. He spoke compassionately. 'This is probably an isolated incident. The Fiedland's live miles away. There's no report of it in Garddryn village and there's been no cases in Feichnan or Llandfydd, and no mention of it on Anglesey.'

Although shaken Joe found slight comfort in Tudor's words. Perhaps it was true, this was an isolated case and there was nothing to fear. Chloe's face came to him, her pansy eyes shining with happiness. Please God be kind, he prayed silently.

Putting his arm around Joe's shoulder, Tudor said, 'Let's get some work done. If there is any report of new cases we'll hear about it at lunchtime.'

'Aye, your reeght. Best take our minds off it until something definite is known.'

The morning crept by. Working at the quarry face, hanging over the precipice on a hemp rope, Joe cleared the precarious sections of rock left by the last blasting. His mind was not on the job, it was on his home where Tommy and Chloe were playing, healthy, happy and alive. Then a moment later, in his mind's eye he saw his two beloved children lying deathly still upon the bed. The morbid scene had the power to cramp his bowels and raise a sweat on his flesh, though the easterly breeze dancing around him was raw.

The morning progressed slowly, the blasting and the climb to the shelter failed to take his mind off the dreadful possibilities of the disease affecting Garddryn village and more specifically his home.

Men would gather at midmorning in the cabanod, their gossip although not always accurate was as informative as a Snowden Gazette. Trekking from Cym a Glo and on ferries from Anglesey they brought the news. Joe made a dash for the cabin minutes before the whistle for knocking off time blew. He kicked his heels for several minutes before the other men sauntered into the warmth.

He shouted over their chatter. 'Does anyone know if there's cholera in any of the villages beside Feichnan?'

There was a moment of stunned silence; it was news to everyone that there was cholera in that village.

Someone shouted. 'Are you certain they've got it?'

Joe answered 'Aye they've got it alreeght. Allan Fiedland's child has gone down with it.'

'Jesus.' The speaker lowered himself onto a bench. 'My little girl was playing with the Allan children two days ago. She stayed overnight at Feichnan.

Anxious to know where the man lived, Joe almost shouted 'Where's your home?'

The man had paled. 'Half-a-mile from Garddryn village.'

Joe felt that he'd been clouted with a stout pole. 'Good God. There's no chance that we'll escape it. Oh Jesus.'

The President, Steffan Roberts stepped forward. 'Let's be calm.'

The quarrier was leaning forward his head in his hands, around him men were all speaking at once.

Steffan Roberts thumped the long table with his fist, calling for order. When he had their attention, he said, 'There's no saying that the child will go down with it.' Calmly he spoke to the unfortunate father. 'Thomas Davies is your little girl healthy?'

'Yes, she's robust.'

Endeavouring to sound encouraging. The last thing he required was panic flaring. 'Well then, everything could work out fine. If she's a strong child nothing untoward should happen. Go home man and see how she is. There's little point in you working whilst you're worried out of your mind.'

Slowly the man rose and crossed to the door. Opening it, he turned and looked back, then was gone, the door closing quietly.

All eyes had followed him out. There wasn't a man there that didn't pray to God that his turn wouldn't be next to be sent from work.

A naturally ebullient man, Steffan Roberts tried to brighten the gloomy atmosphere. 'Not like you lot to forgo your brew. So come on lads fill your mugs and lets talk of things other than disease.' He pulled a rolled newspaper out of his coat pocket. 'There's a report here in the newspaper that'll amuse you all. I'll read it out.' His rich voice filled the muggy room.

Few paid much attention, the cholera taking precedent over the small piece of local news, however amusing.

When the meal was eaten the men fell into talking quietly of other things, as though by not discussing the arrival of the disease in their community it would relegate the problem to where it belonged, at the back of their minds. Time enough to face it tonight when they were at home with their families.

Emily knew nothing of the calamity in Feichnan until Joe arrived home. He was in an unnaturally quiet and thoughtful mood.

Watching him as he emptied his bag and washed out the bottle he used for his cold tea, she asked him what was wrong.

Reluctant to discuss the problem he lit a lantern and went out in the early evening gloom to check on the sow and gather the chickens into the coop. It was fully dark when he returned.

The children were playing with Tommy's wooden farm animals on the table.

Tommy looked up from placing the sheep in a tiny pen. 'Do you want to help us with our farm, Dada?'

Joe hardly glanced at the child. 'Not now, Tommy. I want to sit down and rest for a moment.'

Sighing, Tommy whined. 'You're always tired.'

Emily snapped. 'Leave your father alone. If he wants to rest let him. He works hard all day long.'

Rudely, Tommy waggled his tongue at her.

Emily had her attention elsewhere; her eyes were on Joe. 'Are you feeling poorly?' She had almost forgotten her thee's and tha's, but under extreme duress, generally created by Tommy, they surfaced and she was back to speaking with her old dialect.

'It's nothing.' Patting her hand, he spoke quietly. 'I'll tell you later.'

'Secrets, secrets, secrets,' Tommy chanted in a sing song voice.'

Chloe giggled. Picking up her doll she swung her about. 'Secrets, Daisy May, secrets.' She giggled.

Joe smiled for the first time that day. 'No good being tired in this house.' Standing, he crossed to the table. 'Move over Tommy and let me be the farmer for a while.'

Grinning, Tommy inched to the edge of the chair and let his father share the seat.

Content that Tommy would be quiet while the game was in progress, Emily put a pound of salted herrings into the pan.

After supper, the children went to bed. Emily was washing the dishes in the old sink in the scullery, her mind on the weather and washing the clothes tomorrow, or more importantly, drying them.

Joe, sitting at the table was mending a broken toy.

Drying her hands on a cloth, Emily came through from the cold scullery. The tip of her nose pink from the freezing temperature in there. 'What happened today to upset you, Joe?'

He put the toy down carefully, laying the two parts side by side. 'Come and sit down.' He patted the chair next to his.

'Oh, Joe don't tell me you've been laid off.'

'No nothing like that.'

A long sigh escaped her. 'Thank the Lord for that.'

He looked serious. 'You might not say that when I tell you...'

Filled with apprehension her voice was intense. 'Just tell me, Joe. Whatever it is, I'm sure we can weather it.'

As he told her he watched her face pale.

'Cholera. Oh God no. The poor Fiedland family.'

'I'm afraid it gets worse than that, Emily.'

Anticipating his next words she felt a sickness in her stomach. 'Not in Garddryn village is it?'

His hand covered hers and he felt the chill in her flesh. 'It's not quite that bad, but one of the Davies children was playing over at the Fiedland's only the other day she might have picked it up.'

'Oh, Joe. What are we do to?'

His hand pressed hers tightly. 'Short of leaving the area until it passes I don't know that we can do anything.'

She clung to his hand. 'I'm not going anywhere without you, Joe.'

'If we could afford it, I'd say it was the best idea. But as we can't...' He sighed. 'I was thinking about my sister in Manchester, but I haven't heard from her in an age. I don't know if she's still living there.' He grinned. 'You couldn't say that we were a close family. As for our Sam, if he's alive he'll still be on a prison ship or in Australia by now.' He gave another long sigh. 'As for the other three I wouldn't house a dog with them.'

He tried to smile. 'I think it's best if we have as little contact with others as possible, and keep indoors as much as practical. I'll not mix with the men in the cabanod until all this is over. I'll eat my lunch outdoors.' He met her eyes. 'It should lessen the risk.'

Emily saw the flaw in this. 'But you can't stay away from the men when you're in the blast shelter.'

'So I'll not go in there. I can put my head down, duck behind something.'

'No, Joe. It's far too dangerous.'

He held her hand tightly. 'So is cholera, Emily.'

The next few days brought the infection to Garddryn, claiming both of the Davies children and their elderly grandmother. The Feichnan doctor had more than his fair share of the sick as the disease there rose to almost epidemic proportions. Llandfydd was not spared, and several there succumbed. It was the same story from village to village.

In the few days since the beginning of the outbreak Joe and Emily had become nervous wrecks, watching their children for the first sign of the sickness.

The school closed when the mother of the schoolmistress became another Garddryn victim.

The depression hanging over the village was immense as day by day the graveyard filled.

Few men were at work, every morning the long walk there brought news of further losses overnight.

For a few days Joe stayed away from the quarry, then as the news came that men who had been absent since the beginning of the outbreak were succumbing to the disease, and he saw no signs that his own family was affected, he returned.

Taking precautions, he stayed away from the cabanod, eating and resting outdoors whatever the weather. Blasting was at a minimum, there were not enough men working to make it a regular ritual, so he remained outdoors keeping his head down, suffering the explosions and flying shale to stay out of the shelter.

The evenings he would rush home, dreading that the children had developed a symptom during his absence. Discovering none made the remainder of the day almost a celebration. Then during the darkest hours of the night, the terror would return. The stress caused he and Emily to lose weight.

Chloe was sick for less than twenty hours. The grief that tore at Joe at the loss of his beautiful daughter was a bottomless, dark pit.

The burial, standing beside the tiny coffin, sharing the priest's words with other parents with similar coffins to bury was a terrifying nightmare, one that he knew he would never awake from. His pansy-eyed child was lost to him and he could find no solace. The days were dark, the nights darker still.

Weeks passed and the reports of new cases dwindled. The unaffected could begin to believe that they had been spared. When the turf was flattened on the last burial site, and the cost counted, the ultimate roll call was long. Twenty-five dead in Garddryn, thirty-nine in Llandfydd, forty-four from the Alice quarry, making the total for Feichnan the highest at seventy-nine. Outlying villages had victims; most homes had lost a loved one or more.

A week with no cases and the villagers of Garddryn dared to lift their hearts; filling the chapels and churches they raised their voice to the Almighty and sang his praise.

Spring came, the ground fulfilled its promise and new crops emerged.

Tommy returned to school.

Evenings, Joe came home to the empty place in his heart. Whilst there was daylight he worked in the acre field. It seemed an eternity since he and Emily had talked. He watched her go about her chores, her shoulders drawn in as though to protect herself from another devastating blow.

Summer passed slowly. He was aware that the flowers emerged, and the beeches beyond the woods swayed in the evening breeze, the ripening cornfields were bejewelled in a blaze of red poppies, but these miracles were no longer a joy, just a sore reminder of the walks he'd taken with his darling girl.

When the autumn harvest was in, Joe began to take evening walks to the graveyard, there he would sit for awhile beside Chloe's little headstone, smoking his pipe, telling his little girl of the day that had passed. When it was almost dark, and the midges had ceased to mist beneath the trees, he walked back to his home. Empty and desolate in his grief. A few words with Emily and he would make his way to his bed, and in the small hours cry silently.

The months passed slowly for Emily, the pain of watching Joe in his deep grief was like a knife twisting in her belly. She was lonely for a word from him, but knew that she couldn't reach into the place he had retreated to and for him to climb out of the abyss was impossible.

At night, in her lonely space in their bed, she would relive the birth pains she'd suffered bearing little Chloe into this world. The pain of her death was so much greater, stabs of it grinding into her body and heart throughout the day. There was only one solace and that was that one day Joe's soul would come back to her. She would wait, and in that time learn to remember her daughter, her happiness, smiling face, baby smell, and laughter, without pain.

Chapter Eight

There was joy in Emily's heart when two years on there was something to celebrate, she was sure that she was pregnant. It was almost a miracle; Joe's deep mourning had kept him from her but for one or two occasions.

It worried her that he rarely spoke of Chloe, if he was not bitter, his mind was still turned inwards with grief. A week didn't go by that he didn't lay fresh flowers, or in wintertime, leaves and berries on her little grave.

If the baby turned out to be a girl, would she be a constant reminder of his darling, which might spoil the relationship between father and new daughter. Perhaps it would be better if the new one was a boy.

There was no knowing how Tommy would take the news of an addition to the family; he hadn't been pleased when Chloe arrived. Not that he would need to be told until it happened, boys were not known for their close observations of their mother's figures.

He was still a wilful child, sometime surly, at best he brooded, but they had put this down to the loss of his sister. It was odd that he had buried Daisy May, Chloe's doll, in the acre field. In those first few days they had been too caught up in grief to pay the strange act much attention, and as the months rolled by it seemed silly to bring it all up again and have it fresh in everyone's mind.

His schooling had gone well, a prodigious worker, Tommy was always top of the class. Passing his exams to get him into a college would be child's play his teacher, Mr. Raglan had said. Tommy gloated on the elderly man's attention.

These thoughts were running through Emily's mind as she kneaded dough, a Saturday morning chore that she enjoyed. The warm kitchen, the smell of yeast in the rising dough, and then that lovely warm bread straight from the oven with a lump of cheese or a dollop of home-made blackberry jam.

Tommy loved the berry jams she made, spreading it on a thick slice of bread; he'd wrap it carefully, slip it in his pocket and then take himself off to the quarry to meet his father coming off shift. Then together they'd trek around the old place until Joe's legs were worn out. Tommy was always full of questions, and every one of them about the quarry. There was never a mention of a bird, or a flower, or even a tree.

At seven-years-old he could recite the names and sizes of the slates. Grinning because he was sure he wouldn't make a slip, he'd call them off one by one in his sure little voice. 'The queen at thirty inches, countess...'and when he'd finished he would recount the prices they fetched compared with the previous year, and similarly the tonnage extracted. He was a regular little marvel.

She gave the dough a final clout. Pity he could be so naughty when he was in the house.

But then he could be dreadfully precocious when he was out of it too. Only last week Joe had told her that they'd met the manager on the road, and the man had asked Tommy what he wanted to be when he grew up.

Tommy had answered without hesitation. 'I'm going to own Garddryn quarry and be extremely rich.'

The manager had laughed. 'He's the makings of a regular little Marquis of Anglesey has Tommy Standish.'

It might have amused the man, but not Joe, for he had seen the glint in the boy's eyes as he had said it and knew that it wasn't just a childish dream, but a true goal. It made the hairs on the back of Emily's neck stand up when she thought of it.

Putting the dough back into the big earthenware bowl she covered it with a cloth. Wiping the flour and dough off her hands she lifted the kettle, pouring boiling water into the teapot.

With a mug of piping hot tea in her hand, she sat in the old chair dreaming of her new baby pondering a few Christian names that would ring well with Standish, while the dough rose.

The bread was out of the oven, cooling on the table when Tommy ran in, breathless. 'Mammy, I'm going to meet father.'

'Hold on, young man, take a piece of bread and cheese for him. If you're going to have him walking over the quarry all afternoon he'll need something to eat.' She started to cut into a loaf. 'Pass that jar of jam, there's a love. What the pair of you find to look at there, every Saturday afternoon, I'll never know. Now get me the cheese from the shelf in the scullery.'

He was gone, racing down the lane, his pockets crammed with two parcels of food.

Thankful for the peace and quiet Emily looked to her pile of mending.

Joe was watching the birds gathering material for their nests as Tommy appeared, red faced from running, and a little breathless from the climb up the hill. Putting out his arm he surrounded the boy's narrow shoulders. 'Thought you'd forgotten to come.' He grinned. The chance of Tommy forgetting this Saturday ritual was a slight one indeed. It was the highlight of the lad's week. But what fascinated him so about the Garddryn was a mystery, but as it made the boy happy what did it matter.

Skirting the perimeter, looking down into the great hole, Tommy was silent. Then taking his father's hand he said, 'I wonder where all that slate is now.'

Joe imagined every gravestone, roof slate, fireplace, floor tile, candle stick, sundial, clocks, fencing post and the hundred and one items man had fashioned out of slate, pouring back into the hole. 'God knows.' He sighed. Turning his gaze to the sky he saw rain clouds gathering over the ocean. 'Think we'd better get back home. It looks like it'll rain very soon.'

Tommy moaned. 'I wanted to go and look at the old horse whim.'

'Why? We could look at the new pump house instead.'

Tommy's brow puckered. 'We could look at the pump house later. I want to see how the whim is constructed.'

Would this strange boy of his ever cease to amaze?

Emily had the supper laid out on the table when Tommy and Joe arrived home.

Joe noticed that she looked unusually pleased with herself. Smiling, he kissed her cheek. 'What you looking so happy about?'

Emily feigned innocence. 'Do I, it must be because I've finished all me mending and have an empty basket at last.'

Looking quizzical. 'I don't think it's much to do with mending, Emily Standish. I think you've been up to something. But no mind, you're extremely bad at keeping a secret, so all I have to do is wait until you come out wi' it.'

'Well that's where you're wrong. I can keep a secret, you wait and see.'

'Ah! So you admit to having one then?'

A faint blush pinked her cheeks. 'I didn't say that I had.'

'Oh, yes you did, Emily.'

Laughing, she turned to Tommy. 'Did you have a nice time?'

He replied pompously. 'I don't go to the Garddryn to enjoy myself but to learn, Mother.'

It was the first time he'd called her Mother and Emily didn't like it. Somehow the way he said it made it sound disparaging. Saying nothing she turned away, she wasn't going to let the little imp ruin her new found happiness, neither was she going to spoil the look on his father's face, it was the first smile for many a long day.

Brooding, Tommy sat through the early evening with a look of dissatisfaction on his face. Several times, asked by each parent what the matter was, he would shrug his shoulders and reply, 'Nothing.'

A game was suggested, or a book to read, but nothing would bring him out of his melancholy mood. Eventually unable to stand the long sighs, Joe told him to go to bed, obviously the boy was tired. Groaning, and with a backward glance of disgust, Tommy climbed the stairs.

When all was silent above their heads and they were sure that the boy had dropped off to sleep, Joe touched Emily's knee. Keeping his voice low, he said, 'So are you going to tell me, or do I have to guess?'

Looking up from her knitting, Emily smiled. 'I think that you have already guessed.'

His brow furrowed. He was at a complete loss. 'I'm afraid you'll have to tell me. I'm not clever enough to know what goes on in a woman's mind.'

Lowering the knitting onto her knee, she gave him a long thoughtful look. 'Really, Joe. Haven't you guessed?'

'Honest, Em. I haven't a clue what you're on about.'

Happiness swept over her. 'Oh darling, Joe. It's simple really. We're having a baby.'

He was stunned. He'd hardly touched her since... Chloe's little face came into his mind. 'Oh God, Emily I couldn't go through all that again.' Tears filled his eyes, brimming onto his cheeks.

His words were like a knife in her gut. Frantic, she rose out of the chair and knelt before him, her hands on his thighs. 'Joe, my darling, I thought that you'd be happy.'

Distraught, his face twisted in pain. 'I couldn't bear to lose another. I loved Chloe so much.' He gave a heartbreak sob. 'I could no more stand in that awful churchyard looking into the tiny hole waiting to receive my baby again.' He sobbed. 'Chloe was full of life. When she went she took a great part of me with her. I can't love another, only to lose them to some disgusting disease.'

Cradling him, she made soothing noises. 'Joe, please listen to me. It doesn't have to be the same again. This time everything will be different.'

His voice broke. 'We can't know that, Em.'

There was a slight trace of impatience in her tone. 'Joe, nothing is guaranteed. Chloe was a blessing from God. We should remember that.'

He smirked. 'If all this pain is a blessing from God, I'd prefer it if he turned his eyes from me, and mine.'

Staggered by his words, she spoke hotly. 'You can't mean that, Joe.'

'Mean it! A day doesn't go by that I don't curse God. If he gave us another child there is a chance that it could be snatched away.'

She was fighting for her unformed child, desperately trying to reach the Joe of old, whilst her heart was breaking for her lost daughter. Her voice almost failed her.

Tears brimmed. 'No. We can never be sure that it wouldn't happen, but we have to hope. We can't stop hoping, Joe.'

He had no hope left in him, why couldn't she understand that. He didn't want another to climb on his lap, to feel the wetness of baby kisses on his lips. The lump in his throat was so hard that it hurt to speak. 'I can't give up on Chloe, replacing her would be an awful thing to do.'

Emily forced herself to sound calm. 'Chloe can never be replaced, she was and always will be our very special daughter. Nothing or no one can take that away from her.'

He was crying silently.

She rested her head on his thigh, tears trickling into her hair.

They were both lost in their separate misery, listening to ticking of the clock and the fire falling in on itself as it burnt low.

Her thighs ached from kneeling, but she hadn't the heart to move, or the strength to continue the unhappy scene.

Joe touched her hair lightly. Since Chloe's death he'd kept his grief a solitary agony, knowing, but not wanting to accept that Emily was suffering as much as himself. Anger, like a deadly serpent had wound itself around his grief, not to crush it, but to inflict greater pain. That anger he had used against everyone, and to his shame that meant Emily, and Tommy to some extent. But now in a few short hours it was as though a healing balm had cloaked the monster. Maybe Emily's hope had reached down into his abyss and hauled him free. Now, all he wanted was to cry, not the tears of anguish, the heartbreaking sobs that had torn at his guts for two years, but cleansing tears that would begin to heal his soul.

He spoke softly. 'I am so sorry for all the hurt I've caused you, Emily.'

She didn't dare to stir, to stop his words before all his pent up emotion had broken free.

His voice choked. 'Losing Chloe broke my heart. When I should have clung to you for support I cast your love aside, I was too angry to love anyone. I blamed myself, you, God, even Frank for suggesting we came, here. If we had still been living in Manchester this might never have happened. If I had made more money I could have afforded to send the three of you away, where you would have been safe from the disease.' He sighed deeply. 'And I blamed darling Chloe for not trying harder to get better, and that made me angrier with myself because it was ridiculous. Chloe loved life. She was a free and happy spirit. There wasn't a bad thought or unkind deed in her. I wasn't as big, or as unselfish as little Chloe, I was just stupid. Will you ever forgive me?'

Stirring, she met his eyes. 'Forgive you, my darling, there is nothing to forgive. We lost a child what greater reason to be unhappy.'

He drew her up, held her close to his chest. 'Our girl inherited your compassion and kindness.' Kissing her hair, he gave a watery smile. 'And now we have another on the way.'

She smiled. 'We do, and whoever this one is, he or she will not replace our lovely daughter, they will be special in their own right.'

'I know. But another little girl might be hard...'

'Shush, Joe. This baby might be a boy.'

He hugged her close, his smile widened. 'Oh God forbid, Emily, not another like our Tommy.'

She laughed. 'Probably.'

The next morning, Sunday, Joe rose early and without stopping for breakfast made his way through the village to the churchyard. Sitting beside the little grave he told Chloe what was in his heart. For the first time he could walk away without a great depression claiming him. Today he had a slight spring in his step, as of old, and walking beneath the old sycamore tree he noticed that the leaves were bursting open.

The baby arrived on time, following a fairly easy pregnancy. It happened on a Sunday morning so Joe was home, the moment he heard the child's cry he rushed to the bedroom and witnessed Doctor Lidell severing the umbilical cord.

Emily had thought it an unnecessary expense to have the doctor attend the delivery, but Joe remembering how she had suffered at the birth of Chloe, and how near he came to losing her, had insisted. To pay the doctor's fees he had taken on several small building jobs in the village.

Now seeing Emily safe, her pale faced wreathed in smiles, was worth every hour of hard graft.

Glancing up, the doctor made some remark about impatient fathers, but Joe wasn't listening, his attention taken by Emily, who was holding out her arms for her whimpering child.

Carefully, wrapping the child in a soft cloth, the doctor placed the small bundle in Emily's arms. He glanced at Joe. 'A fine son, Mr. Standish.'

Joe's eyes misted. A boy was wonderful. It took away the anxiety of replacing Chloe, but if he dared to be honest with himself wouldn't he have loved a replica. Might it not have been like having Chloe back?

Emily looked elated, and exhausted. Hair damp with perspiration, her eyes full of unshed tears. Joe wondered if she were having the same anxious thoughts, was this a step away from Chloe for her too.

She held a hand out to him. His eyes were watering, making the image of mother and child swim before him. Taking the one step to the bed he grasped her hand and sat beside her.

'Joe look, isn't he lovely. He's so tiny. See his little fingers, the nails are like pearls.'

The child was sleeping lightly.

Gently, Joe lifted the small hand from the flannel wrap. It was a little miniature, a marvel that it was so perfect. His tiny fingers curled around Joe's, the small pressure was delightful. Whispering softly, he said, 'Hello, son.'

With the baby's hand still clutching his, he looked to Emily. 'If you don't mind, I would like to call him Frank.'

Emily had prayed for a boy, afraid of the consequences for Joe had she been delivered of a girl. In her happiness she was willing to concede to any wish. 'I think that would be wonderful. We could ask Betty to be godmother.'

Joe's eyes lit. 'Betty would love it.'

He kissed her cheek, then bending low he kissed the small, moist brow. 'Welcome, Frank.'

The doctor coughed gently.

Joe had completely forgotten that the man was in the room. 'Sorry, Doctor Lidell.'

The doctor smiled. 'If a mother and father can't be a bit fond the first few minutes after the safe arrival of their son, when can they be?' Although he had delivered scores of babies, the moment of birth never failed to stir a keen emotion in him. The lad might turn out to be the devil incarnate, but those early days were magic.

Collecting his instruments, he pushed them into his bag. He was away to get a glass or two of good port. Then he'd put his feet up for an hour or so and read the Chronicle. With a few last minute instructions to Joe, he left the house. Walking down the lane he expected to meet his carriage.

When the birth was imminent, Tommy had been dispatched to the doctor's home with instructions to ask that the carriage be sent on. After delivering the message at the front door, Tommy dashed to the stables at the back of the house, and as the carriage passed him he leapt on the rear. A grin split his face as he stole a lift through Garddryn village. Several of his mates saw him and gave him the thumbs-up. He felt bold, and devilish. Grinning till the apples of his cheeks hurt.

Peeking, he saw Dr. Lidell walking towards him. With a

schoolboy curse on his lips he made a jump for it, rolling onto the grass verge. Landing, he tore his trousers, grazed a knee and clouted the funny bone in his elbow. Stifling the howl that would have alerted the doctor and the groom to his misdeed he lay in the long grass swearing under his breath. His knee stung and his elbow throbbed with pain. His temper flared.

Scowling, he wiped the mud off his clothes, crossed the lane to the cottage, opened and closed the gate with a loud slam, thudded down the short pathway, opened the front door slamming it so hard that it shivered on the hinges. Passing the stairway door, he shouted up the stairs. 'I'm back, Mam.'

The baby howled.

Assuming they had visitors, Tommy went to find the fresh loaf of bread, or pie that would have been baked in anticipation of their arrival. He was in the scullery looking in the bread crock, as Joe clattered down the stairs.

Joe's heart was thumping hard. Breaking the news of the arrival of the baby to Tommy wasn't going to be easy. He and Emily had decided not to tell him until after the birth, as he was sure to take it badly and sulk, making the last few weeks of Emily's pregnancy more difficult for her to bear.

Tommy called from the scullery. 'Where's the pie? I'm hungry.'

Joe was just about to tell him off for eating when it wasn't a mealtime, or taking food without permission, when he caught himself. What he had to announce was a great deal more important than pinching food. 'Tommy, come here I want to talk to you.'

'But I'm hungry.' The boy was rummaging through a cupboard.

Joe walked into the scullery.

Tommy was standing on a small wooden box, inspecting the dry ingredients in Emily's store cupboard. He gave a quick glance to his father. 'Who's come? I heard a baby yelling.'

Looking at his nine-year old boy, his filthy face and state of his clothes, he wondered what sort of lad little Frank would grow into. Bracing himself for the inevitable tantrum, he said 'Tommy I have something to tell you. Will you please get off that box and come with me.'

It was unlike his father to be so precise; guessing that whoever was cadging a sleep upstairs must have upset the old man. He climbed down without argument.

Sitting in the old ladder-back chair, Joe didn't know where to start. He wished that he and Emily had done this together a few days before. Memories transported him back to the birth of Chloe. Tommy had been a little heathen that day. Nelly, a neighbour, had taken care of him, and when the birth was over she had brought him home, Tommy had stood over the new baby, asking when Jesus was going to come and fetch it. The memory was so vivid that for a moment he felt that Chloe was back in his arms.

The boy was standing quite still, watching him, his eyes wary.

Blinking, he brought himself back to reality. Taking the boy's hand in his, he met his eyes. 'Tommy, Jesus has sent us a new baby, a brother for you, his name is Frank.'

Pulling his hand free Tommy looked defiant. 'Why would he send one, if he listens to my prayers he'd know that I don't want a brother or a sister. I didn't like the last baby we had, so I'm not likely to want another one. Am I?'

The words cut into Joe. Hurt and angry, he wanted to slap the boy. His eyes flamed, and although he endeavoured to keep his voice low there was no mistaking his fury. 'Where do you get your wicked tongue from?'

Tommy saw that he had overstepped the mark. Backtracking, before his father landed him a wallop, he lowered his eyes. 'It's just that I love you and Mam so much I find it hard to share you both.'

Joe wasn't sure about this remark; it sounded like a hasty defense, but the boy did look slightly contrite.

Giving him the benefit of the doubt, Joe pulled him close. 'Babies are very precious. I'm sorry that you didn't want Chloe, and it hurts me to hear you say such a thing.'

'I didn't mean it, Father.' Tommy's eyes filled with tears.

Joe was sure that he did, the tears looked too well staged. But if he did or didn't wasn't the issue at the moment, introducing him to Frank was. Harmony in the house was important for all of them, but especially for Emily if she were to be successful in feeding Frank.

His arm around the boy, he coaxed. 'I think we should go and have a look at this baby together. His grip tightened around the lad's hips. 'Tommy I want you to remember that it is important to me that you are especially nice to Mammy.'

Tommy's lips were drawn in a tight line. 'I will be nice, Dada.'

'Good. Now let's go upstairs.'

Joe watched Tommy closely, as the child looked down on the baby. What he saw in the boy's face worried him. It wasn't just jealousy he had seen written there; it was darker emotion than that.

Alerting Emily to the problem just wasn't an option. When Emily was up and about, that was the time to talk to her. For now little Frank was safe, he had his mother's constant presence.

Over the next few weeks the baby was watched carefully, and at the slightest indication of a cold, flu, bronchitis or any ailment in the vicinity, Frank was kept indoors and carefully monitored. Emily became an over anxious mother, a broody hen fussing over her chick.

Tommy was not impressed, and as the months moved on, and Frank thrived, his consuming jealousy grew.

Winter took hold, the days shortened to brief interludes between the long hours of darkness.

Frank grew into a bonny, happy baby. Joe was delighted with his new son, pleased that the child had a different temperament to Tommy. He was docile, easy to feed, and slept for long hours during the night.

Joe and Tommy still kept to their Saturday afternoon ritual of trekking around the quarry, Tommy firing questions and absorbing all the information his father could supply.

One sunny winter afternoon Tommy was running to meet his father when he saw a crowd of men, thirty or more, his father included, walking through the Garddyrn entrance.

Seeing his son, Joe broke his step and shouted 'Go back home, Tommy. We can't go around the quarry today. There's other business to attend too.'

Disappointed and disgruntled, Tommy kicked the heels of his boots in the dry dirt. Watching as the men, a tight packed crowd tramped towards the track that led to the fields and the old disused quarry. When they were far enough ahead, he began to trail them, using the shrubs and trees as cover. Too far away to hear the conversations, he narrowed the gap, and from behind a hawthorn bush listened to Jack Dickens, his father's old boss, rousing the men.

He was shouting, gesticulating wildly. 'I say that when we catch him we deal with the matter ourselves, and not wait for the law to take its course.'

Tommy ever observant saw that there was something inhuman in Jack Dickens face now that he was angry. The slackness had gone and he looked horrid, like one of the gargoyles beneath the church eaves. The mass of his matted grey hair, wild as an old wolf's pelt. He was too far off to see that the man's eyes were glinting at the prospect of giving someone a good whipping, but he watched as he raised his fist and beckoned the men on.

Hollering, Joe shouted over the men agreeing with Dickens. 'We don't even know if Billy Morgan has anything to do wi' it.'

Dickens snarled. 'Of course he has, you bloody mad Englishman. Billy Morgan is the only lunatic we have in the village. Nobody has seen him for hours, and the girl has been missing since this morning, according to her mother.'

Someone from the back of the crowd, shouted. 'Billy isn't the only madman around here, Dickens.' Laughter followed this anonymous remark.

Dickens eyes flared. Spittle flew from his lips. 'Well are we going to find Beryl Richards, or what?'

In a pack, obeying blindly, the men rushed forward, trampling the weeds growing on the verges of the track. Destroying sapling trees. Kicking stones into the ditches. Passing an old building, derelict and falling into ruin, two men held back, shoved their heads through the gaping apertures, peering for signs of the girl or Billy Morgan. Seeing nothing, they ran forward, caught up with the mob.

Further on there was a stack of wood from a cut tree, eyeing a stout branch Dickens stooped and grabbed it. Bringing it down on his palm, he felt the solid weight of it, and gave a mirthless chuckle.

Crouching low, Tommy inched from behind the bush.

'Hist.' The whispery sound came from the cover of the long grass.

Startled, Tommy turned, watching wide-eyed as the grass and bracken parted. 'Beryl!' He spluttered.

Her round, simple face was flushed, the top buttons of her blouse undone. Crouched in the greenery she had the look of a hunted rabbit. 'Shush, I don't want me Da to know that I'm here.'

Lowering his voice, he inched towards her. 'They're looking for you. Somebody said that you've been missing for hours.'

'Bother,' she sighed. 'There'll be trouble then when I get back.'

Tommy looked to the men far down the track, then back to Beryl. 'I expect so.' Used to trouble of his own he sympathised. 'Where were you? '

Whispering, she met his eyes. 'If I tell you, do you promise not to say anything?'

He wondered if making a solemn promise to a girl counted. He gave a perfunctory nod, and kept his mouth shut.

Accepting that he'd vowed, she murmured 'I went with a boy from the barracks to the woods.' Watching his face, she became defensive. 'It was only a bit of fun. That's all.'

Tommy shrugged. He couldn't care less where she'd been; she was only a stupid girl. He kicked a stone, the aim wasn't good and it bounced a couple of feet. Kicking another a similar distance to show that was what he had really intended, he said moodily, 'You had better get home.'

Eyeing him suspiciously, she squinted. 'Why? What you going to do?'

Hands in his pockets, he half-turned in the direction the men had gone. 'I'll follow them and tell them that you're on your way home. I'll say that you fell asleep in the field.'

She grinned. 'Tommy Standish, *Cariad,* you are clever.' Her eyes were bright with relief. 'I'll dash home and tell me Ma that I was tired, and sat down for a minute and next thing I woke…'

He didn't want to listen to her explanation. Rudely he cut her off. 'Stop dithering, girl and just go.'

Her face fell. He wasn't as nice a boy as she had first thought. 'No need to be haughty.'

He wasn't listening he was running. Rounding two bends in the track, he had the men in sight. Using the bushes as cover, he crept closer.

They had formed a tight bunch, his father was somewhere in the middle of it, shouting, flailing his arms. Tommy was still too far away to catch his words but his anger was evident.

Then a gap opened up and he saw Jack Dickens screaming abuse at Billy kneeling in the dirt. Dickens swiped him with the piece of wood and blood sprang from a wound on Billy's ear. His mooncalf face crumpled in pain and bewilderment, he began to blubber.

A tingle of excitement, like when his father used to swing him high above his head, shivered deep in Tommy's belly. His hands were sticky, his face flushed. A small smile fixed on his wet lips.

Billy screamed as several more blows reigned down on him. .

'Enough!' Joe was close enough to catch a couple of vicious swipes off Dickens. 'I said enough!' He was shouting, coming between them and the crouching man. Blood seeping from a gash on his cheek. His eyes were flaming with anger, his face ugly with rage.

Most of the men backed off.

Jack Dickens still poised to fight, his breath short grunts, held the chunk of wood above his shoulder, threatening to flatten Billy if he moved.

Roaring, Joe took a step towards Dickens. 'I said put it down.'

Lowering the weapon, Dickens spat on the ground. 'I'll take the pervert back to the village.'

Joe's shoulder came close enough for him to nudge his adversary. His words were calm, precise and unmistakably angry. 'You'll do no such thing. He's coming with me. When we know what's happened to Beryl will be the time to decide what is to be done. Now back off, before I give you a clout you'll remember many a long day.'

Gripping Billy's arm, Joe hauled the blubbering man to his feet.

His ice blue eyes flashed a warning to Dickens. 'Come on, Billy, there no need to fear this stupid bugger.'

Billy was sobbing, brushing at his bloody nose with the back of his hand.

Fighting to contain his anger, Joe spoke calmly, 'Come on, lad, let me take you back to your Mam.'

'Mammy. I want me Mammy,' Billy wailed.

Joe's anger erupted. His roar loud enough to reach the quarry was magnified ten-fold by the defaced mountain 'Bloody bastards. You pick on a defenceless lad with the brain of a child, to beat. And not one of you, not one, knows if any harm has come to Beryl. This was just an excuse to batter a simple sod. It might have been anyone.' His chest heaved as he boomed. 'Where's your bloody Welsh pride now?'

Shamed, the men shifted their feet, and looked anywhere but at Joe.

Elbowing his way through them, he pulled Billy close.

Tommy scarpered.

It was another two hours before Joe got home, his anger festering with the injustice of it all.

After delivering poor Billy to his mother, he'd stormed to the Richards house and found Beryl indoors, calmly washing a pan of potatoes.

Mrs. Richards accepting Beryl's explanation for the missing hours was perplexed to find Joe in her kitchen, steaming with indignation.

Ignoring the mother's lame comments, he'd laid into the girl with a sharp tongue. 'How long have you been home, Lady?'

Glancing wild-eyed to her mother for support and receiving none, she muttered, 'Most the afternoon. Why?'

Joe almost snarled. 'Why! You little vixen. Because an innocent man was nearly killed because of you today.'

Unaware of the calamity her daughter had caused, but knowing the wilful girl capable of anything, Mrs. Richards rushed to Joe's side and grabbed his arm. 'What's happened?'

Her eyes darted to her daughter. 'Our Beryl came in some time ago but she'd been missing for a good while. It really worried me, so I asked Jack Dickens to look out for her.'

Joe gave the girl a look of disgust. 'It's a wonder that the man isn't to be hung for bloody murder.'

Mrs. Richards hands flew to her mouth. 'Oh! Beryl what have you done this time?'

Wide-eyed and innocent, she stared at her mother. 'Nothing, Mam. Honest.'

Joe saw his own problems with his Tommy mirrored. The child's lies making a mockery of a parent's affections.

Giving no warning of her intentions, Mrs. Richards cuffed the girl's ear severely. Beryl wailed.

Face red with anger, Mrs. Richards screeched. 'I'll give you something to squeal about my girl.' Her hand shot out again and caught Beryl across the cheek.

Beryl sobbed. 'It's not my fault.'

Mrs. Richards dander was up, and not likely to settle for some time. 'Never is. Is it!' She repeated the clout.

Beryl covered her ears with her hands. 'Mam, Tommy Standish said he'd tell the men I was running home.'

Joe grabbed her elbow. 'When?'

Beryl sniffed, wiping the end of her nose on the back of her hand. 'Couple or more hours ago. He was up by the old quarry. He said he was going to run to Jack Dickens and the crowd of men and tell them that I was at home.' She began to wail. 'He promised, Mam. It's not my fault.'

Making no reply to this, Joe slammed out of the Richards house. His strides were long and purposeful as he marched up the lane to his home. This time Tommy would not get away with his crafty lies. The boy would feel his belt across his backside. Temper at boiling point he slammed into the cottage.

Emily was preparing the evening meal; baby Frank sleeping on their bed, when the front door slammed closed.

Legs splayed, his chest rising and falling with his fast breath, Joe stood with his back to the door. His face distorted with anger, the gashes across his cheeks seeping blood. 'Where's our Tommy?'

'Joe, what's happened?'

'First things first. I want to know where that little bugger is, because when I catch him I'm going to murder the swine.'

Her hands covered her mouth, never before had she been frightened by the presence of her husband. Her voice was small, nervous. 'I thought that he was with you.'

His eyes flashed. 'I saw him briefly. But it's no thanks to him that a man isn't lying dead, and another preparing to meet his maker.'

Her face paled. 'My God, Joe.' She sank into the nearest chair. 'Tell me what he's done.'

From the cover of bushes, Tommy watched his father lead Billy Morgan up the track; the man was still blubbering and leaning heavily on Joe's arm. The other men followed at a distance, forcing Tommy to stay low until they were out of earshot. Anxious to move, to get to the safety of the Garddryn, he willed the men to move faster. As the last man disappeared, heading for the village, Tommy spurted forward, running towards the Garddryn. Then, if anyone asked where he was during the debacle, he could say that he was at the quarry hoping that his father would return. Thoughts of Beryl, and what she might add to the drama were brushed aside. As he ran, pictures of Billy getting a thrashing flashed in his mind, the splash of blood as the wood had crashed into his head still stirring the feeling of thrill in his belly. The bright red flash made him want to run faster, jump higher, take more dangerous leaps into the air.

Mr. Bellamy was sauntering through the Garddryn entrance as Tommy nearly sprinted into him.

Sprightly for his age, but somewhat overweight, Mr. Bellamy spoke a little breathlessly. 'Hold on, young man. What's the rush? You nearly bowled an old man over.'

Tommy was breathing fast. 'Sorry, sir.'

The portly figure bent slightly to see more clearly into the boy's face. 'Get your breath back and tell me who you are.'

Tommy recognised the man; he was Henrietta Bellamy's father, and owner of the quarry. Although he knew that he had no right to be on Bellamy property, he wouldn't be cowed by the important man's presence. Squaring his shoulder, he met the man's eyes. 'I'm Tommy Standish, sir.'

He didn't recognise the name, and couldn't recall seeing the boy before, suspecting that he was up to no good, probably pinching something or other, his small eyes narrowed. 'And what are you doing here?'

There was something instinctive in Tommy's reply. His young voice was firm, he couldn't be faulted on his knowledge, and knew it. 'I like to learn as much as I can about the quarry, sir. So when I'm not at school, I come here, ask questions.' There was pride in his voice. 'I know every name of the slates, and the prices they fetch now, and what they were worth last year.' He glanced up at the mountainous waste tips. 'The history is interesting, if you know about the past you can change the future.' He smiled. 'Mr. Fellows, my teacher, says that history teaches us to rectify mistakes. He's right isn't he?'

Mr. Bellamy nodded his head sagely. This boy was interesting. Not often you met a lad with a brain, and knew how to use it.

Tommy was in full flow; it was wonderful to have someone take the time to listen to him. His father listened but that wasn't the same as talking to someone like Mr. Bellamy. 'When the railway gets to the Garddryn it will grow to be bigger than Penryhn or Dinorwig.' His eyes shone as the vision expanded. 'Imagine it, everything moving so much faster and easier. Places like this are going to be really exciting. Faster inclines, more efficient Blondins, the problem of them fouling will be a thing of the past, no more need for a man to risk his life disentangling the things.'

The boy was fascinating, if only his own son, George, took such an interest. This lad was virtually obsessed by the place, he'd make a fine manager one day, he shouldn't wonder. It might be a good idea to nurture a lad like this, the last thing anyone wanted was a bright spark like this working for the competition.

Placing a hand gently on Tommy's shoulder he led him forward. 'Tommy why don't you walk with me and tell me all that you know of this quarry of mine. I'd really like to hear about the prices, this year and last.'

Tommy's eyes shone. 'I'd really like that. I can tell you lots.'

Bertram Bellamy, leaning lightly upon his silver handled walking stick, moved forward with a brisker step than was normal. Earlier, he'd tried to think of a reason why he shouldn't come to the Garddryn, a boring meeting and reconnaissance of the workings with the manager wasn't his idea of a Saturday afternoon entertainment. If he'd known what a gem was waiting to be discovered he'd have come like a shot.

The manager dashed out of the office as the owner and boy came into view.

Mr. Bellamy swinging his stick called to him. 'No need for your help after all today. Young Standish has offered to walk with me.' Gripping Tommy's shoulder more firmly he smiled down benevolently. 'Master Standish and I are going to do the inspection of the property together.'

Tommy couldn't have been more pleased had someone just announced that Christmas had come early. Grinning, he looked up at his benefactor.

There was little that escaped their attention during the long walk, and throughout, Mr. Bellamy quizzed Tommy on his knowledge. Impressed with the lad, a plan formed in his mind. Tommy would be good for his own son, George. It might teach the lazy rascal a thing or two. The boy needed a competitor. Rivalry encouraged a boy to try harder.

George wasn't so stupid that he would let a village boy, a quarrier's son, get the better of him. There would be a marked change in his son in no time if the two boys were together regularly.

They arrived back at the entrance. Tommy was sorry to see the end to his wonderful afternoon. Wishing he were brave enough to ask Mr. Bellamy if they might spend another Saturday together, walking around the Garddryn, but he wasn't. The man would only brush him aside as just another boy asking a favour.

Bertram Bellamy's next words raised his ambition skywards. 'How would you like to come to my house on Thursdays and Fridays and take school lessons with my son, George?'

Tommy's eyes glistened. 'Do you really mean it?'

Mr. Bellamy chuckled; the boy's excitement was infectious. 'As you get to know me, you'll learn that I don't say what I don't mean.'

Getting to know the Bellamys, incredible. Stunned, his vocabulary suffered. 'Golly.'

Chuckling, Bellamy explained. 'I want you to arrive early, be at the house before eight so you can breakfast with George in the old nursery. Then Mr. Faversham will teach you the intricacies of mathematics.'

'Coor.'

Bellamy chuckled again. The boy would be good for George. Surely he wouldn't be so stupid as to let a village lad get the better of him in his lessons. George would learn his place in the social scale.

Triumphant, Tommy ran home. Dashing through the door he came face to face with his parents, and was instantly aware that something was very wrong. Beryl's face flashed into his mind. The news he couldn't wait to announce died on his lips. 'What's up?'

Rising out of his chair, Joe hauled Tommy further into the room. 'You have the nerve to ask, what's up, I have a mind to wallop you now and not wait for your explanation.'

Tommy's eyes widened, and standing with a mystified expression on his face, said 'I don't know what you are talking about. Honest.'

Joe growled. 'Honest, you don't know the meaning of the word. I sometimes wonder if you ever had an honest thought in your head. You little vagabond.'

Tears welled in Tommy's eyes. His bottom lip trembled.

Emily began to rise from her chair, Joe put a hand on her arm, and she sank back down with a sigh.

Joe's face was unyielding. His anger bubbling below the surface promised to boil over for the umpteenth time today. 'I'm not as soft as your Mam, and I'll not be moved by your tears. So you can pack it up now. I'll have answers from you and I'll have them fast, truthful, and without any embellishment to save your own skin.' His voice rose. 'Do you understand me?'

Tommy sniffed. 'I don't know what I'm supposed to have done. I just went to the Garddryn.' If only he was standing here telling them about Mr. Bellamy, his father would be astounded, proud, humbled that such a great man wanted his son. Instead he was being shouted at and blamed for things he had nothing to do with. Squaring his shoulder, he met Joe's hard eyes. He blinked twice as though amazed that his actions were being questioned.

'I waited for you, Father, and when you didn't come I walked around on my own. I have come straight from the quarry. I haven't done anything wrong.' His eyes were wide circles. He had faith in the fib. His father was sure to believe him.

Joe gave a rumbling growl, his hand shot out and he grabbed Tommy by the collar.

Emily shrieked. 'No, Joe!'

Lifted off his feet, Tommy screeched.

Joe snarled. 'I'll give you such a clout you little, bugger.' Like a terrier with a rat, Joe shook him. Shouting 'You'll tell me the truth now, or you'll feel me belt across your backside, you lying swine.'

Distraught, Emily grabbed Joe's arm. 'Put him down, Joe. Let the lad speak.'

Grunting, Joe dropped him back on his feet. 'Start right now.'

Tommy straightened his coat.

Joe stared at his son, his face red with anger. 'I'm waiting.'

On the surface Tommy looked calm, but beneath the façade his tummy wobbled and he felt vaguely sick. 'It's like I said, I went to the Garddryn, and now I've come back again.'

Emily put a restraining hand on Joe's arm. 'Wait.'

He shook himself free. 'For what? Until he tells me more lies?'

Tommy opened his eyes wide. 'But I'm not telling...'

Joe's hand shot out, cuffing the boy around the ear. 'No you little, bugger you're not telling me any more lies. I'll have the truth out of you if I have to beat you to get it. Where did you see Beryl Richards?'

His ear stung, but he wouldn't lift his hand to it. 'Beryl?'

Emily was terrified that Joe would lose his temper completely. Something he would regret terribly later. She tried to be calm. 'Tell your father the truth, Tommy.'

Tommy faltered.

Growling, Joe unbuckled his belt slowly.

Words came flooding from Tommy's mouth. 'I saw her up near the old, disused quarry. She was hiding in the long grass.' Throwing Beryl's reputation to the wind, better that everyone was shocked by her misdeeds than threatening violence to him. 'She said that she'd been in the woods with a boy, the front of her blouse was undone and I could see her...' widening his eyes to express his horror. 'I was so shocked, father, that I ran away.'

Joe gave a hard laugh. 'Good try, Tommy lad. But you seem to have missed the part where she said she'd go home, and you promised to run to Jack Dickens with the news that she was safe.'

Tommy burst into tears. 'She never said that she was going home and I never said that I'd go and tell the men anything. Dada you've got to believe me.'

Sounding resigned and exhausted, Joe sighed. 'Sadly, I don't believe a word of it. I suggest you get out of my sight and stay out of my way until tomorrow.'

'What about me supper?'

Joe gave a hollow laugh. 'Supper. If I were you I'd go and ask Billy Morgan how he's going to eat his supper with hardly any teeth left in his mouth.' His eyes flashed dangerously. 'Now get out of my sight.'

'But, Father.'

'Upstairs, NOW!'

The stair door slammed behind the boy, and baby Frank wailed.

Joe started to move.

Emily held his arm. 'I'll go. You sit down. I'll make us a brew in a moment.'

'Don't bother for me, Lass. I'll take myself off to the Half Way, I could do with something to clear the stink out of me nose.'

The next morning Tommy was the first to rise, and creeping downstairs he laid the table for breakfast. Leaving the cottage he went to the acre field and released the hens from the coop, and collected three warm eggs from the nest. To get on the good side of his parents he was prepared for a day of small inconveniences.

It was midday and his father was beginning to look less stern, nervously, Tommy broached the subject of Mr. Bellamy's offer.

Lowering the journal he was reading, Joe listened to his eldest son, his mind racing ahead. Why would Bellamy want Tommy to take lessons with his own boy? What was in it for Bellamy or his son, George? Even if it was nothing more than a generous offer, should he allow Tommy to take advantage of it, when he had behaved so atrociously yesterday? Until he knew more about it, the answer had to be no. Looking directly into the boy's face he saw the determined set of his mouth, the ambition and naked longing there.

It took Tommy enormous willpower to stand still, and not beg his father to let him go to Plas Mawr, the beautiful house he had loved for as long as he could remember. If the old man said no, he didn't know what he'd do, fight, scream. Panic. Watching him mulling it over was agony, why couldn't he just say 'Well done, Tommy.' Couldn't he see how much he needed to go, had to go? What was there to think about?

Joe sighed. It was hardly worth asking the question, when the answer was plain to see, but he asked it anyway. 'Do you want to go, Tommy?'

Believing that he was consenting, Tommy dropped the façade, his eyes shone. 'Oh yes, very much.'

Joe's eyes went back to the newspaper. He wasn't prepared to give the boy an answer until he'd spoken to Bellamy. Neither was he acceding to the lad's wishes after yesterday's debacle. Noncommittal, he answered quietly, 'I'll give it some thought.' Aware that the lad was staring at him, he lowered the Chronicle. 'Was there something else?'

Tears of frustration stung the boy's eyes. 'I thought that you would be pleased. And proud enough of me to be sorry about yesterday.'

Throwing the paper down, Joe rose from the chair. 'You're right, I am sorry about yesterday.'

Blind to his anger, and misinterpreting his father's words a flicker of happiness flashed across Tommy's face.

Joe walked to the window and looked out onto the drenched fields. 'I'm sorry because what I should have done was whip you until you couldn't sit for a week. Then there'd be no use going for lessons. Not unless you were prepared to stand up for the buggers.'

Tommy's disappointment was too immense to be contained in the small room; his sight blurred by tears he made a dash for the door, slamming it viciously after him.

Emily called from the kitchen. 'Is that Tommy?'

A deep frown cut across Joe's face, crossing to his chair by the fire, he grabbed his paper off the floor. 'Who else.'

Frank was on his father's knee, playing with a twist of paper and gurgling happily, when Tommy returned a few hours later. Expecting another outburst from his older son, Joe tensed.

Closing the door quietly, the boy crossed to the fireside, and leaning up against his father's lap he took the baby's hand and playfully tickled his palm. Frank chuckled, holding out his other sticky hand for the same treatment. Tommy obliged.

Joe couldn't have been more surprised, at the very least he had expected another outburst from the boy, and demands that he should have his own way about the lessons at Plas Mawr. Grateful for the smallest of respites, he watched his children playing contently, if only it was always so. He sighed deeply.

Looking up, Tommy gazed into his father's eyes. There was no sign of revolt in the child's look, yet something untameable, and it unsettled Joe, for there was something there that he didn't understand, but knew that it was in marked contrast to his own open character.

Watching them, Emily glimpsed something immeasurably sad in Joe's eyes. Misunderstanding, she believed his thoughts were of Chloe, and she was seized by a great sense of bereavement that was actual pain. To find calm she gazed at Frank, and in his baby features she found a sort of peace. Her glance swept the room, the fire in the grate burned brightly, the curtains were drawn against the dark evening, the table with the candle flickering in the centre was set for supper, and on the hob a pot of stew simmered.

Time had taught her that distraction was the best cure for these terrible moments of loss and panic that still swept over her, and now, although she still felt shaky, she bent to the fire and lifted the pot of stew from the hob, transferring it to the table. Her tummy was still fluttering, the last thing she needed was food, but busying herself with the family and Tommy's usual complaints of the meal, what the boy wanted to eat she'd never know, would serve as a distraction. She began to dish the stew onto the warmed plates.

Although rabbit stew was the least of Tommy's favourites, he sniffed the aroma with appreciation.

Bemused, Emily dished him up an extra spoonful.

Earlier, when Tommy had left the cottage, he had raced down the stony road, running so fast and hard he felt every thump of his boots jar his spine. The force of his anger a wild animal in his chest, bursting to be free. He hated the meanness of the cottage, the small downstairs room, the shared upper and the smelly privy across the stream. It was hateful.

His father was a jealous and unreasonable man, afraid that his son would make something of his life. He was hateful.

Large drops of rain dashed his hot face. Tears welled in his eyes and he saw the village through a watery veil. The rain increased, falling hard and fast, the dark threatening clouds promising at any moment to send a deluge.

As he sprinted passed Salem chapel, the door opened and the minister looked out. He was about to pop back in when he saw Tommy. Waving to the boy, he beckoned. With a swift change of direction Tommy ran towards him.

The tall, lean man was standing in the open doorway, wiping raindrops off his sparse grey hair, as Tommy ran under the porch.

'Come in lad, whilst the storm passes.'

These were the first kind words that Tommy had heard in twenty-four hours.'

Smiling weakly, he had let the man lead him indoors. The high vaulted chapel was chilly, and dismal, but dry. Tommy slumped onto a wooden chair.

Eyeing the boy, the minister couldn't place him, he wasn't one of the regular worshippers offspring. But in desperate need of a replacement choirboy, he hoped during the interlude of the storm to convince the lad that his place was at Salem chapel, singing his exaltation to the Lord.

The boy was distraught; a helping hand in his moment of unhappiness, and a kindly word might work miracles. Turning his azure-blue, benevolent eyes on Tommy, he spoke gently. 'You look like you've been running for some time.'

Tommy shook his head. 'I have. I ran from…' he was about to say the name of his family home when he pulled himself up, he was too ashamed to acknowledge that he lived in that cottage., 'the far end of the village.'

Smiling kindly, the man nodded sympathetically. 'It's a fair step. Quite a way to run even for young healthy legs.' Sighing, remembering his own days when his limbs drummed with the magical blood of youth. Resigned to his own arthritic joints, he sighed again. 'Are you from around here? I can't say that I recognise you.'

A faint blush reddened Tommy's cheeks, how he hated owning to living in the last cottage of the village. Almost inaudibly, he confessed to his home.

The elderly man pondered, stroking his chin. 'I can't say that I know that house.'

Tommy was happy to leave him perplexed to the exact whereabouts.

There looked to be no let up in the rain and after checking the sky twice, the minister sat alongside Tommy and told him of the choir and what pleasant young men belonged.

Politely, Tommy listened, but when it became obvious that the minister was asking him to come along to a rehearsal, Tommy explained the impossibility of doing so. He was busy at the quarry on Saturdays. This disclosure led onto Mr. Bellamy's offer and the uncertainty that his father would allow him to go to Plas Mawr for lessons twice a week.

The minister, with a smile, explained to Tommy how he should get around the problem. Like conspirators they sat in the darkening chapel, listening to the rain falling on the slate roof, and the occasional rumble of thunder, forging plans.

The minister had taken a liking to the boy; it was plain to see that the lad was intelligent, and it was grossly unfair of his father, who no doubt was a dullard, to hold the boy back in his ambitions.

Tommy could hardly wait to put the plan into action, and before the rain ceased he ran out of the chapel, smiling as he waved goodbye to the man standing thoughtfully beneath the dripping porch.

His first port of call was to Billy Morgan's house. There, he spent half - an - hour talking to Mrs. Morgan.

Billy was fetched down from his bed and his injuries displayed. The grazes and gashes had no effect on Tommy, as they had yesterday, it was only the moment of impact that had been exciting.

Billy made him nervous, his actions were unpredictable, and his speech, although hampered by the lack of his front teeth since the beating, had never been very comprehensible.

Arriving home, showing a brave face and calm demeanour, just as the Salem chapel minister had suggested, Tommy spoke quietly to his father, taking care not to show the slightest abhorrence for the baby, although his sticky fingers were horrid to touch.

Pitching his voice low and confidential, he said, 'Father, I sheltered from the storm in Salem chapel today and spoke to the minister there. Then I went to see Billy Morgan to find out how he was. Mrs. Morgan made tea for me. I had a slice of pie; it was nice but not as nice as Mam's.'

Joe couldn't have been more surprised had the angel Gabriel appeared in the living room and announced that he was to make Tommy Standish a saint.

Unaware that his father's attention had strayed for a moment, Tommy looked up from beneath his long dark lashes. 'I'm sorry that I have been unkind to Frank. I mean to turn over a new leaf. From now on I will be kind to him, after all he is my brother.' His boots shifted. The minister's precise words came back to him and he used them with real emotion, a tremble in his voice. 'I promised God that I would not answer Mam back again, and I will help with the dishes, and clean out the hens and the pig every Saturday morning before I go to the Garddryn with you. I thank you for not beating me yesterday. I did deserve a punishment, but I have to thank Jesus that my father was kind and forgiving.'

The spoon in her hand forgotten, and the stew sending a spiral of fragrant steam to the rafters ignored, Emily stood open-mouthed, listening to her son's words, wondering if the boy was sickening for something serious.

Deciding that he'd done enough grovelling for one day, Tommy came to the end of his rehearsed recital. Turning to his mother, he smiled. 'Supper smells wonderful. Thank you for cooking it for us, Mam.'

The spoon dropped from Emily's hand.

Rising out of the chair with the baby in his arms, Joe didn't know if to cuff the boy for his impertinence, for surely the whole speech was a charade, or bless the Salem minister that had saved the soul of his boy and put him on the right road.

It was to an uneasy silence that the family sat for supper.

Chapter Nine

Tommy had behaved incredibly well since his visit to the Salem chapel several weeks ago, his eleventh birthday had been a small success, although he had declined to invite his school friends to the cottage the family had enjoyed a special birthday treat tea together.

The dramatic change of attitude towards his brother Frank, and kindness he had shown his mother recently, convinced Joe that the boy meant to keep to his new regime. By his small thoughtful actions it became evident that he had really turned over a new leaf.

Pleased that the boy had knuckled down at last, and not wishing to stand in the way of his progress, Joe prepared to pay a visit to Plas Mawr to determine if the offer of lessons still stood. On the Sunday before Christmas, donning his weekend clothes, he was ready, albeit very reluctantly, to go cap-in-hand to the big house.

He was opening the front door, looking out on the awful day; it had been raining hard since first light, when a barouche pulled up at the gate.

The manager of the quarry stuck his head from beneath the half hood. 'Message for you, Standish, it needs no reply.' Delving into his coat pocket he pulled out a folded sheet of paper, and held it out.

Trotting to the front gate, the rain drenching his face in seconds, Joe took it from him, and with a hurried doff of his hat ran back to the cover of the open door.

The manager gave Joe a contemptuous glance, and it was obvious the moment that Joe read the note that the man had read it too.

The carriage turned, then swaying to the motion of the horse, the small chariot headed back to the village.

Joe read the missive for a second time, then repeated it to Emily as she came alongside him. 'Mr. Bellamy wishes Tommy to commence his lessons with George, eight o'clock sharp, on the first Thursday after the holiday.

'Well that saves me a lot of bother and embarrassment. Breathing a sigh of relief he slipped off his coat, and slumped onto his chair by the fire.

Emily made a brew, and they sat for a while, Joe blowing on his tea, as Emily, somewhat harassed, listed the articles the boy would need if he were to go to Plas Mawr.

'It's going to cost money, Joe.'

Looking up from re-reading the note, he lifted an eyebrow. 'What doesn't?'

She saw an amused gleam in his eyes. 'What are you smiling about?'

'This letter.'

Emily frowned. 'I don't see what's funny about it.'

His smile widened. 'It's the bit about the holiday. It says lessons to commence the first Thursday after the Christmas holiday. I'd like to know what holiday. The quarry's shut for Christmas day that's all.' He snorted. 'Unluckily for the Bellamys this Christmas falls on a Thursday. Three years hence there'll be no extra day off; it'll be just like any other Sunday. Day off, all day.' Sighing, he rose. 'I'll be out the back.'

As he opened the back door, Emily shouted to him. 'Take your coat, Joe, it's perishing out there.'

'I won't be out long enough to get cold.'

When Tommy came in from visiting a friend and was told the news he was ecstatic, and for the next few days he put the festive season to the back of his mind and worked at fever pitch polishing up his geometry, long division, and algebra.

Joe was impressed.

The following Saturday afternoon, the visit to the quarry was abandoned; the weather was atrocious, wet and cold. Instead, Tommy stayed huddled beneath a blanket in the freezing bedroom going over a theory that had him baffled.

Joe, climbing the stairs suggested he left the mathematics for now, to go with him and Emily shopping in Caernarvon.

Tommy looked up. 'Can't, I'm too busy.' His head dropped back down, a frown furrowing his brow as he worked at the conundrum.

Amazed that the lad had refused the treat, it only occurred every six months or so, he went back down to Emily.

'Tommy's too busy.'

'What!'

He raised his voice so that the boy would hear. 'Aye. We have a regular scholar in the house now.'

'Tommy's never been too busy to go to town. He loves going. Go and fetch him, Joe.'

Joe was grinning. 'Can't do it, Lass. The boy's too caught up in his puzzles.'

Emily picked Frank up off the floor where he was playing, and wrapped a warm blanket round him. 'What time did David say he'd pick us up from Maisy's shop?'

Joe looked to the clock. 'In about half-an-hour.'

'We could start out now. I want a word with Maisy before we set off.'

They shouted a 'goodbye' up the stairs and Tommy mumbled a reply. Then the door closed and the old cottage fell silent. For a few moments he listened to their voices and Frank's laughter as they walked slowly down the lane. When he could hear them no more he exhaled a long held breath. It was good to be alone in the house; he had begun to feel the strain of forever being pliant and co-operative. Not that he wanted to get into mischief, he didn't, he was happy practicing his lessons.

What he did want to do was wallow in daydreams, for in twelve days time he'd be at Plas Mawr, and servants would be obeying him. It would almost be as good as being the son of old Bellamy.

With his hands behind his head, he lay back looking at the sloping grey ceiling, but what he saw was the wonderful ornate plasterwork of the other house, the hundred candle chandelier glittering brightly. With shining eyes, he pursued the illusion, seeking brighter and more costly items in other rooms.

Eventually his eyes grew heavy and as he fell into a deep slumber, the mirage developed and he could smell, touch, taste the magnificent opulence.

The banging of the front door and the clattering of boots on the stairs broke the spell.

'Hello, Tommy lad.' His father's cheeks were red with cold. 'Dropped off to sleep did you?'

The dream fragmented as Tommy struggled to wakefulness. The taste of the strawberry iced cream still lingering in his mouth turning bitter on his tongue. He could have wept to find himself lying on the bed beneath the dull, cracked ceiling, when only a moment ago above his head had been rich, red tapestry.

'Come down, lad.' His father patted his bare knee and Tommy felt the hard, dried skin of his hand.

Joe's face was split in a grin. 'As a special treat, and as a celebration of your good news, Mam has bought a real shop cake.' Laughter lit his face. 'What do you think about that then? Wonders will never cease. What say you, our Tommy?'

Clattering back down the stairs, Joe called to Emily unpacking the shopping into the cupboard in the scullery. 'Our Tommy will be right down, he can't wait to see the cake. Could hardly believe that you had bought one. It's a real treat for him.'

Muttering, Tommy scowled. 'Shop cake. In twelve days time I'll eat all the cake the cook at the big house can bake.' Reluctantly he threw his legs over the side of the bed, and rummaging for his boots he slipped his cold feet into them.

Christmas Eve, Joe returned home unexpectedly early, the clock on the mantelpiece had barely struck twelve when he walked through the door.

Emily looked up from making a fruit pie. 'You're back early.'

Shrugging out of his coat, Joe glanced at the clock. 'Aye. Tom Hughes was anxious to catch an early ferry he wanted to get back to Anglesey before this wind turns to a gale.'

Rubbing his dusty hands together. 'It's really parky out there. I was glad to get off the gallery so you'll not find me complaining about an afternoon off.'

'Poor Joe. Sit down, and I'll make a brew.'

'I'll get cleaned up first. Then we can get this holiday off to a nice early start.' Looking around, he asked 'Where are the youngsters?'

Emily raised her eyes to the ceiling. 'Our Tommy is upstairs making a present, and our Frank, the little beggar, is fast asleep in the bed.'

'Have they been good?'

Emily grinned. 'What child isn't good on Christmas Eve?'

'Suppose you're right.' Combing his hand through his hair, his eyes went back to the clock. 'I'll get cleaned up before you make that tea. I'll put me better clothes on, then I'll be ready for our visit to the church, later.'

Mid-afternoon Emily walked down the village street; Frank tied like an apache child in her shawl, and Tommy walking briskly beside her, quite the grown up young man. They were going to Maisy's shop; a delivery of special sweetmeats was expected from Bangor.

Left alone, Joe fell into a semi-doze, sitting in the chair by the fireside. His mind had wondered back to this time last year. Then there had been a terrible tragedy. During the Christmas Eve church service the parson had announced that five people had lost their lives in a boat leaving from Conway. There hadn't been a moment during that Christmas that he hadn't thought of those poor souls and the grieving families. The boat had remained unnamed, he assumed that the people aboard had been going home, or to visit loved ones over the holiday. This year, the first anniversary would be hard for them.

Since hearing of that disaster, he'd often thought back to sailing on the *Hardwick Lady* from Liverpool to Caernarvon. On board there had been a shocking seaman predicting a calamity. Perhaps he hadn't been all together wrong.

For since that time and it was only a few short years, there had been countless tragedies on the coastline here. Tommy, who seemed to know more than most about it, kept a ghoulish record of the shipwrecks that occurred in the vicinity. There had been a staggering thirty-two recorded losses, sixteen of those occurring during 1843, the year after they arrived here.

The weather must have been particularly bad at that time, but he couldn't truthfully remember, every winter day seemed appalling up at the Garddryn, but he did recall it being gruesome four years later, when seven more vessels were lost.

Tommy never ceased to amaze him. There wasn't a seaman visiting the village that he didn't questioned as to his knowledge of the wrecks. The loss of life faithfully recorded in his little book. The boy collected disasters like other lad's collected toy soldiers.

Getting more comfortable, he shuffled in the chair, putting his feet on the hearth to catch the heat of the fire. The *Rothsay Castle* now there was a terrible disaster and one that luckily Tommy had not yet discovered, although it had been well documented since the catastrophe had happened. Engravings of the ship floundering were still on sale.

Recalling the event, he lit his pipe. The paddle steamer had been on a day trip from Liverpool sailing to Beaumaris, on an August day in '31. There had been a hundred and fifty passengers aboard her, unaware that the timbers were rotten, and the one and only ship's boat had a hole in it. Under powered and worn out, she'd met a violent storm. The passengers had asked the captain to put about, but the man was drunk and abusive, and when he did appear on the deck it was too late, the ship was coming apart at the seams. In his mind Joe saw the terrible tragedy unfurling, it made him cold to the bones to imagine what those poor people must have gone through. The cabins awash, the ship deprived of steam, the pumps broken, and the only bucket to bail with lost overboard. It must have seemed like God had deserted them. It didn't take long before the ship was caught on the unseen Dutchman's bank. The drunken captain was the first victim; the iron funnel collapsed taking the main mast with it sweeping him to his doom. But the tragedy was far from played out. Grounded on the sandbank with no help able to reach them, the passengers watched the rising tide, then one by one it picked them off. Despairing parents held their children above the waves only to be forced to lower them as their own strength ebbed. Mr. and Mrs. Tarry had their five little ones with them, how did they manage? Thinking about it made him want to cry. The people on the shore watched, helpless, the wind was too fierce for them to put the boats out. Only nine survivors made it to the shore at Penmaenmawr, on drifting debris and using a lady's skirt for a sail.

Wiping away a tear, he sniffed. It was Christmas; he ought to try to put it out of his mind. Oh, but the poor lost children.

Emily returned with the Frank and Tommy, their faces pink from the cold air, excited with the small parcel of treats from Maisy's shop, it was to be Tommy's job to hang them on the decorated hoop along with the gingerbread stars. The festive mood they brought in dispelled the ghosts of the *Rothsay Castle*.

Cutting some lengths of cotton Joe looped it around the paper wrapping and handed them to Tommy to string up. Nimble fingered, Tommy had the job finished and was standing back admiring his handiwork when carolers from the protestant church began to sing at the front door.

When the last verse of the old Christmas song was sung, Emily handed mince-pies to children. With Tommy standing beside her, she watched them retrace their steps to the village.

Back inside, she picked Frank up off the rug and hugging him to her chest she sang a song that had been one of her old grandfather's favourites.

"Observe how the chimneys do smoke all about; The cooks are providing for dinner no doubt. Good cheer, mince-pies and plum porridge, ale and strong beer; With pig, goose, and capon, the best that may be. The boar's head in hand bear I, bedecked with bays and rosemary; And I pray you, my masters, be merry. Tra lala, tra lala."

Joe's arm circled her shoulders, and dipping his head he kissed Frank's brow.

A pang of jealousy seared through Tommy, feeling neglected and set apart, he wanted to slap or pinch Frank's fat arms. He was just about to say something rude and nasty when his father turned to him.

Smiling warmly. 'Shall we go out and cut some holly and ivy and decorate this old room?'

Tommy could have wept with relief, he had come so close to blurting out something unpleasant, which would have lost him his chance at Plas Mawr, just for a momentary and idiotic need to be horrid and make everyone feel bad. He didn't have to fake sounding cheerful when he yelled, 'I'll fetch a knife and some string to tie it with.'

Kissing Emily and patting the baby, Joe said, 'We won't be gone long. I saw some good holly with lots of berries on it just down the track. On the way back I'll put the hens in, and lock up the pig. I'd hate to lose them to somebody's table.'

Putting Frank down, she gave him Tommy's old monkey on a stick to play with, and as Joe untwined a length of string, she knelt beside the baby singing to his upturned face. *"The poor shall not want, but have for relief, plum pudding, goose, capon, minced-pies, and roast beef."*

Joe was reminded of her country upbringing, and until the death of her grandfather, a farmer, her life had been one of, if not luxury, certainly plenty.

Tommy came from the scullery carrying a formidable looking knife.

Taking it from him Joe winced. 'I'll take that before you cut yourself.'

'Oh,' Tommy grumbled. 'I can manage it, I am eleven remember.'

Joe smiled. 'Come on, before it gets really dark, or someone else pinches all the best stuff.'

Listening to their voices growing faint as they walked away from the house, Emily turned her attention back to her baby son. Wrinkling her nose, she picked up the wet bundle, and carried him out to the scullery to change him.

Joe and Tommy walked side by side, their boots crunching on the hard frosty ruts underfoot. The air was freezing, chilling their cheeks and turning their noses red, but it was good to be outside, doing something festive together.

Changing direction, walking beneath the now bare, black branches of the stately oaks, Plas Mawr seen in the distance, smoke rising from the many chimneys, and at the edge of the park behind the metal fence, red deer grazing on frosted blades of grass.

It was beautiful, and so far away from the Galloway and the mean terrace of houses on Rotherman street.

A ray of sun shone from a gap in the clouds, and shadows like tiger stripes crossed the ground. The clear, diamond light glistened the dark evergreen foliage beyond the trees.

For a moment his friend Frank walked beside him, silent, companionable, sharing the moment of nature's magic.

The beauty of the late afternoon was lost on Tommy; he had other things to occupy his mind. He was thinking of his mother, and turning to Joe he surprised him with his question.

'Where did Mam learn to sing such pretty songs?'

'Oh, so you think them pretty do you?'

'Well, I like the Christmas ones, they are always so jolly. I remember when she used to sing them to me, when I was little.'

There was a strong bond of companionship between them, much like the times when they walked the paths of the Garddryn together. Joe was glad of it, he made a point of nurturing these precious times with his elder son, he didn't always understand the boy but that didn't stop him loving him. He might be a right tinker at times but he was still his boy.

Slipping a hand on the lad's shoulder, he said, 'Your mam grew up on her grandfather's farm, high up on the Lancashire dales. Where geese roamed with the cattle and poultry, and never a scant plate on the table.'

It was an enormous surprise to Tommy, until that moment he had not considered his parents early lives. They existed only after his arrival. He had thought of his mother living in the old cottage, always scrimping and saving to put meat onto the table, and clothes to their backs. It was a never-ending subject of conversation, where this or that was coming from. Deep in thought he walked on silently, then head bent to a gust of wind, he asked, 'If the old grandfather hadn't died would it have meant that we would have been rich?'

'If the old man hadn't died your Mam wouldn't have come to the town with her mother, and we wouldn't have met and married and had you and Frank.'

He walked on thoughtfully and Joe wondered what was going on inside his head.

A moment later Tommy said, 'Father.'

'Yes.' He spoke the word slowly; a premonition of what was coming already in his mind.

'Where did I come from?'

He squeezed the lad's shoulder. 'Now that is a big question and one I will answer another day. Today, we are going to cut holly and see if we can find a bit of mistletoe in the old abandoned orchard up yonder.'

'Oh goodie. I love going up there.'

It hadn't been Joe's intention to roam as far as the old house with the overrun kitchen garden, and he wondered how long it might take them to do it. It was sure to be dark when they reached home. But what the hell, walking was better than answering Tommy's big question. He needed time to think what he was going to say to the lad next time he brought the subject up.

The holly was bountiful, with juicy scarlet berries nestling in the dark glossy leaves. He cut a reasonable branch, instructing Tommy 'We won't cut more than we need, as the berries feed the birds during the winter months. Their need is greater than ours is.'

With the bunch tied, they made their way to the old house. The wind was getting up, and Tommy's next question brought a smile to his lips.

'Do you think it might snow tonight?'

What child didn't wish for a white Christmas? In a poorer home, snow was compensation for the meagre fare on the table. The delights of sliding down hillsides, building snowmen, snowballing and all the other outdoor activities, albeit freezing enough to raise chilblains for weeks to come. Glancing skywards. 'It might.'

Tommy, taking swipes at the undergrowth with a long stick, said, 'Will you be going to the literary festival tomorrow?'

'Hadn't thought about it. Why?'

Poking a snail with the end of the stick, Tommy took a moment to answer, and then, as though it hardly mattered one way or the other if the family attended, said, 'Mrs. Frobisher has asked me to read a piece about the Garddryn quarry.'

Joe's eyebrows rose in surprise. 'Really? That's good isn't it? I didn't know that the Sunday school teacher was interested in the quarry.' Smiling. 'Who wrote this great masterpiece?'

The stick swished through the dead bracken. Tommy didn't look up, but kept his eyes on the brown particles flying through the air. 'I did.'

Joe stopped walking. Disappointed that this was the first he'd heard of the project, he found it difficult to smile, but accomplished a bright and cheerful reply. 'Well done. I'm proud of you. Read it to me later? Or would you prefer that I hear it for the first time tomorrow?'

Resting the tip of the stick on the ground, Tommy, his face expressionless, answered plainly 'It would be better if you and Mam stayed away, you being there will distract me, and you know how difficult Frank can be, he'll start crying or gurgling and ruin everything.'

Joe could have cheerfully taken the stick and swiped him. Hiding his hurt, he lifted the holly. 'You're probably right. Best if you go alone. You can tell us all about it when you come home.'

Delighted, Tommy thrashed the hedgerow viciously. Mr. Bellamy was to award the prizes tomorrow, and expecting to receive one, Tommy did not want his parents presence reminding everyone of his niggardly origins.

Merry bloody Christmas, Joe thought miserably, stepping up his pace.

Chapter Ten

The morning was grey; a heavy bank of clouds promising rain was sweeping across the ocean and creeping towards the land.

With his eye to the sky, Tommy stepped up his pace, afraid that he'd get drenched if he dawdled. He still had a fair way to go before he reached Plas Mawr. The name had become like a sacred mantra, he muttered it between his teeth continuously, and it was the first and last thing on his mind when he rose or lay down to sleep. Starting to trot, he began again. 'Plas Mawr, Plas Mawr, Plas Mawr.' His excitement was so large it was too big to contain, and as he ran beneath the black branches of the oaks, with each footfall he repeated the chant. 'Plas Mawr, Plas Mawr.' A feeling of being swept along on a tide of happiness, in love with everyone and everything, the breeze blowing through his hair, and his feet as light and fleet as the sea's spindrift.

Two miles lay between his home and the mansion, and he had almost covered those, but it was the last half mile he was looking forward to most of all, the long avenue. On the superb, tree lined approach he would have a chance to admire the house, see it in all its magnificence. Built on the back of the sugar plantation slaves, so its detractors said, he didn't care on what backs, black, white, or yellow it had risen from, that it existed was enough.

Breathless, he arrived at the impressive double gates, wide enough to allow two carriages to pass, rising to a height of twelve feet, and above, a great decorative arch, the family crest blazoned upon the centre. The gates dwarfed him. His touch as light as a lover's, he caressed the metal.

There was a narrow pedestrian gate in the wall, the metal work replicating that of the main, lifting the latch Tommy stepped through and stood looking down the avenue. The wind at his back, hair blowing over his forehead, he took a long moment to savour that at last he had arrived, and to thank God that he had seen fit to place Tommy Standish where he belonged.

With a spring in his step he began to walk towards the house, admiring the fine architecture. The morning was too grey for the mellow stone to be seen at its best, it took the rosy light of evening or morning sun to bring out the honey shades. But the house still appeared beautiful. Built at the turn of the last century, it compared well to mansions built hereabout at that time. Its main rival was the Pennant's new Penrhyn Castle, completed a few years ago, built on the site of the old, in a fine park with a scenic view of mountains and sea. In many ways Plas Mawr was superior, more elegant and splendid. The mansion too had a fine park, the staged terraces to the side of the house and the Italianate gardens overlooked a good expanse of ocean. Where on a fine day a magnificent display of the setting sun sinking into the water could be admired. At the rear of the mansion were the glorious mountains of Snowdonia, an impressive sight whatever the weather.

A ray of sun shone through a hole in the clouds and the stone work warmed to honey. The great arched windows at ground level becoming golden fans of light. Spellbound he stopped and took in all the grandeur.

Today he would enter as an outsider, but there would come a time, not so far in the distant future that he would walk beneath the door lintel of Plas Mawr as the rightful owner, of that he was certain. Smiling, he began to walk towards his destination.

A liveried servant opened the door to Tommy. Stiff and aloof, the man was about to chastise the lad for the audacity of coming to the main door and not the tradesman's entrance, but Tommy's firm expression checked him. Prudently he waited for the boy to speak, so was saved from the ignominy of being upbraided by a mere village boy by the library door opening and the Master calling out.

'Tommy Standish you have arrived, and you are early, good boy. Come in here.'

Glancing at the servant, he spoke sharply, 'Draycot, fetch Master George to me.'

Wiping his feet with a thoroughness that would have astounded his mother, Tommy stepped over the threshold. He was in a kind of ecstasy, heart thumping with excitement. Glancing up into the enormous well of the stairs, as he had when a very small boy, to the magnificent chandelier, unlit now, but not less beautiful for that.

Stepping out of the doorway, Mr. Bellamy wearing an elderly, green velvet jacket, black trousers, and showing a little ruffle of white shirt at the neck, his pre-lunchtime attire, circled Tommy's shoulder and drew him into the warmth of the oak-panelled library.

The twin windows were tight shut, the heavy burgundy drapes not fully drawn across them. On a desk in the centre of the large room a lamp with a white globe was burning fiercely, casting a bright light on the papers that were strewn untidily across it. A matching lamp, with less of a flame, was on a small table between the two windows.

Tommy's eyes were drawn to the outdoors, to the trees lining the avenue; it had begun to rain heavily. He had only just made it in time.

Mr. Bellamy began to collect some of the papers, shuffling them into a tidy bundle. 'Take a seat, Standish.'

Sitting on the edge of the chair indicated, the fire at his back, Tommy could feel the heat of it through the sleeve of his coat. The double, glass-fronted bookcase caught his eye, one of the doors was open, and a book had been pulled out, opened, then discarded with its leaves lying face down. His love of books kept his eyes there, considering the damage to the spine.

Bellamy went to it and picking the edition up, muttered beneath his breath, 'If I've told that young rascal George once, I've told him a thousand times, not to leave the books in this way.' Passing his hand over the binding, he sighed, then slid the slim volume carefully between the others.

Rising, Tommy crossed the room, coming alongside the elderly man he smelt cigar smoke trapped in the fabric of his clothes; it wasn't unpleasant, but distinct after his walk in the fresh air. Scanning the spines of the books, his head tilted to a high shelf, he said, 'Is there anything here about the Garddryn?'

Re-opening the glass door Mr. Bellamy pulled out a book bound in red cloth. Turning it over in his hand, he ran his eyes over the gilt lettering. Pleased that Tommy had asked the question, it reaffirmed his belief in the boy's abilities and intelligence. That they shared the same interest, the Garddryn, was a bonus, an important one. Opening the cover he examined the first page. 'It has a mention in this one, featuring in the chapter pertaining to quarries that the Roman's were believed to have worked.'

'Phew! Roman times, that was a long time ago.' Enthusiastic, Tommy sounded his age.

Bellamy smiled, a man without benefit of a formal education, he was pleased to show off the knowledge he'd gathered with his own quick brain. 'Of course they didn't take the quantity that we do today.'

'That would have been difficult without...' interrupted by a light knock on the door Tommy turned.

A boy near his own age entered the room; his resentful eyes darted to Tommy, and in the glance he took in Tommy's cheap clothes and boots. Without acknowledging him, he turned his attention to his father.

His upper class speech clipped. 'You wanted me? sir.'

Waving the boy in impatiently, Mr Bellamy said, 'George, come here lad. Don't skulk in the doorway. I want you to meet Tommy Standish. As I have already explained, he is to take lessons twice a week with you. Nothing like a bit of competition to spice a boy up. Aha.'

George's eyes went to the ceiling, he answered sulkily, 'Yes sir. If you say so.'

Paying no attention to George's mood, his father went on brightly. 'I do say so, my boy, and in the end you'll thank me for it. Now, greet your new companion and take him into breakfast.'

George's mouth fell open in surprise and faint disgust. 'He's to eat with us?'

Bellamy's voice rose, and with an exaggerated gesture he flung his arms in the air. 'Of course he is. I don't expect he eats out of a trough at home.' He caught hold of Tommy's shoulder, his eyes glinting. 'Do you, Standish?'

Anger simmering, Tommy stood motionless. 'No, sir,'

Bellamy's eyes went back to his son. Where did he get his devilish notions, putting himself above and beyond everyone? As exasperated as he was, he portrayed a façade of calm. 'What is a matter with you, George? I told you that Standish is to be your companion, and I expect you to treat him with some respect.'

Although his indignation was sorely affronted, George realised that the old man's ire was seriously up and answered with a contrite, 'Sorry, Father.'

Sighing heavily, and looking his age, Bellamy gave his son a resentful stare. 'You will be, my lad if I have any nonsense from you. I expect your mathematics master to report to me at the end of the day.'

Glancing at Tommy. 'You can tell him that yourself, Standish.'

Tommy nodded. 'Yes, sir.' Already hating the stuck up young prig, heir to the Garddryn fortune, and this house. He was as slender and as pale as a girl, if the milksop thought that he could upset him, he was wrong. Used to the rough ways of the village boys, he could flatten him with one blow.

Bellamy made a gesture of impatience. 'Go along, George, take Standish to breakfast. The boy will be hungry after walking from the far end of the village.

With a hateful glance in the direction of his adversary, George turned on his heel, crossing to the tall double doors, then looked back to motion for the boy to follow, but Tommy was already on his heels.

Before passing through the door, Tommy stopped and turned to Mr. Bellamy. 'Thank you, sir. I will not disappoint you, I propose to learn all that I can.'

Raising his voice so that this son might hear in the hallway, 'Did you hear that, George, pity you can't be more like Tommy.'

George stopped, and glaring at Tommy as he came through the door he made a rude noise.

Tommy grinned. 'Manners, Bellamy.'

The breakfast table was laid for the family, but neither the daughter of the house or her mother appeared. A servant in uniform stood by the deeply carved sideboard waiting to serve. Another took a position near to the table, and as the boys appeared he pulled out their chairs.

Afraid to make an ass of himself, Tommy refrained from staring at the rich draperies, plaid rug, or the gorgeously carved, heavy furniture. Turning his attention instead to the copious silver cutlery, napery, and fine china laid on the whitest of cloths. Cautiously he waited for George to make the first move. It wasn't just the lessons he planned to learn from, social graces were important too. Watch and learn, he told himself for the hundredth time.

It was to be a meal he would always remember, and with the best of reasons. Kidneys and steak, ham, poached eggs, muffins and buttered toast were brought before him beneath silver-domed serving dishes, the lids lifted the delicious aroma gave him a powerful appetite.

Sitting in silence, until Mr. Bellamy and the mathematics master joined them long minutes later, then Tommy found himself questioned on his knowledge of algebra and the theorem of Pythagoras by his new tutor.

Confident, Tommy began to explain another version of the theorem. 'By dropping one perpendicular from the right angle on to the hypotenuse, two triangles thus...' catching George's frosty glance, 'created, are similar to one another and to the original...'

Mr Bellamy's laughter cut him short. 'Enough, young man, your breakfast grows cold.' Glancing towards his son, his face lit with humour. 'George, I think you will have your work cut out keeping up with Standish.'

The mathematics master gave a small, meaningful cough, but refrained from adding anything to this fatherly observation.

Pleased with himself, Tommy speared a lamb's kidney with his fork and began to eat again. Boyishly he was unable to resist glancing at George, and he grinned at his sullen face.

Missing the malicious glances darting across the table, Bertram Bellamy launched into the topic of the Garddyrn, taking pleasure in revealing the extent of Tommy's knowledge of the business of quarrying.

George, arms folded across his chest, a sneering smirk turning his bottom lip, listened to Tommy's aggravating replies. In his imagination, he had taken him prisoner, dragged him to the dank cellars beneath the kitchen and scullery, and was inflicting great pain on him with terrible tools of torture.

Mr. Thorbes interrupted the removal of one of Tommy's fingers.

'Come along young gentlemen, we have much work to cover today.' He smiled at George. 'Pythagoras calls for your attention.'

George's spirits sank.

Alert and ready to get started, Tommy liked nothing better than solving a mathematical puzzle, he pushed back his chair and stood behind it.

Bertram Bellamy smiled at his protégé. 'Work hard, Standish.' Glancing at his son. 'Behave yourself, George.'

The morning passed on fleet feet for Tommy, but George found the hours trudged by. Luncheon was served in the old nursery, boiled beef and vegetables and apple charlotte. The pudding, wonderfully exotic for Tommy, a regular for George, he eyed it with scorn.

Mr. Thorbes, a good mathematician, forced into teaching through unfortunate family circumstances, was delighted with the morning's progress. Tommy was a spectacular student. Accustomed to teaching dullard's and dolt's it was revelation. The boy was responsive, enthusiastic, he had a brilliant brain, soaked up information like a sponge. Watching him, head down, putting his entire energy into solving a mathematical riddle, he wondered how people like his parents, just simple working class, had produced such an astounding child. Genius was the only word for it. He was remarkable. George was just fodder beside him; that boy was nothing more than a means to extract a wage off his poor misguided father.

At the end of the day, Tommy walked down the avenue, his thoughts on the house, recalling the smallest detail of the decoration, furniture, curtains, and the servants. He had learned that in all, counting the gardening staff, it took seventeen to run Plas Mawr smoothly. Pondering this he estimated the cost of keeping so many people then subtracted that from the profits he was sure the Garddryn was making after all expenses were paid.

George running down the back stairs had slipped into the empty pastry room, grabbed a Viennese tart off the plate on the cold marble, and made a dash for outdoors. Shoving the tart whole into his mouth, he chewed as he ran, making for the gates. Trampling fast over the thick ivy that lay between the park fence and the trees, his shoes wet with the droplet of rains, spotting the dark leaves. A startled blackbird sprang up in front of his feet, giving him such a shock he almost called out his surprise. The bird, squawking, flew into a branch, and he ran on, heart thumping. The scent of dank earth and fungi rose as he pounded the wet soil. Running with his eyes on the ground, his lips opening and closing as he cursed Standish, the interloper, the carrion, village shit.

Arriving breathless and hot, he hid in the deep shrubbery growing thickly beside the high boundary wall, waiting until he caught his breath before venturing to look out. A wicked grin curled his lips as he saw Tommy sauntering towards him. As he drew near enough to see the laces in his cheap boots, George drew a long breath and tore through the bushes, rushing with blind fury.

Knocked off his feet Tommy flew backwards, and as his elbows hit the ground a blaze of pain shot through his nerves.

Screaming obscenities, George leapt astride him and with heavy right-handed blows delivered several vicious punches to his face.

The pain was astounding, blood from a gash on his forehead ran into his eye and for a horrible moment Tommy thought he'd been blinded.

Seeing the damage, and satisfied that Standish would not return to Plas Mawr, George made a dash for the house, keeping to the trees he was hidden by the falling gloom of late afternoon.

Biting back tears, Tommy tried to staunch the blood flowing from his forehead with his handkerchief, the blood on his nose he wiped onto the cuff of his jacket. Sore, angry and ashamed that he hadn't pulverised George before he had an opportunity to land the first blow, or at least to catch him before he'd bolted and given him a really good hiding. Vowing to get the bastard at the first opportunity, he began to gather his strewn books.

Painfully, he made his way to a nearby stream, dipping his hands in the cold, mountain water; he started to clean his face and jacket. Swilling the blood from the handkerchief, watching the watery red stain flow away, he wrung it out and put it to his eye, freezing cold it relieved the worst of the pain.

For a while he sat on his haunches, staring into the fast flowing water, but instead of the stream he saw George sitting in the schoolroom, without an answer to some mathematical problem, and the tutor looking on derisory. The reason for his act of revolt became clear. George Bellamy's nose had been put out of joint because he couldn't bear to see a village boy get the better of him. Well he had, and he would carry on doing so, he wasn't going to lose the opportunity of lessons with Mr. Thorbes, or stop going to Plas Mawr because it upset bloody George Bellamy.

Taking the cold pad from his forehead he checked it for blood, the wound had stopped bleeding, but he could hardly see out of his swollen eye. Struggling up, his muscles sending messages of protest to his brain, he picked up his belongings. With a last glance back to the house, the windows now glowing with lamplight, he wondered if a hundred candles were burning in the chandelier, imagining it glistening in the well of the flying staircase, he headed for home.

The last few steps of his journey he took slowly, composing a lie to tell his parents to account for his injuries. Putting the last finishing touches to the story he opened the front door of the cottage.

Emily, sitting by the fireside looked up from dressing Frank ready for bed. Seeing blood on Tommy's face, she cried out, 'What on earth has happened to you?'

Dumping Frank on the floor, she rushed to him. 'Tommy look at you, are you alreeght, lad?'

Her anxiety weakened his resolve to be brave, and for a moment he felt like telling her everything, but that would mean the end of his visits to Plas Mawr. There was nothing he wouldn't bear to keep his place there. Focusing on that, he gave her a fierce little smile. 'It's all right, Mam. It probably looks worse than it really is.'

Holding his head, she kissed his brow. 'Oh, Tommy it looks terrible. Wait till Father gets home and sees this, he'll want to strangle whoever did it.'

She hadn't kissed him like that, like a little boy, for a long time. Gently he pulled away from her and crossed to the fire, it was easier to lie to her looking into the flames. 'I didn't recognise him, probably just a boy from the village out to get whoever came along the lane at that time. Just bad luck for me that's all.' Looking up he gave a watery smile.

She began to fuss around him. 'Get your wet jacket off, and sit by the fire. I'll make a brew. Father will be in any minute. He can decide what to do.'

Spent, he slumped into the chair, and began to pull off his boots. Bending hurt his ribs and it took all his willpower not to wince.

It was with a sense of relief that Emily heard the ring of Joe's hobnailed boots on the path as he approached the cottage.

Glad to be home, he called out as he opened the door, sounding jovial and proud. 'Has the scholar returned?'

Tommy's bottom lip trembled.

Stepping over the threshold he saw Emily stooping to pick up Frank, and Tommy like an injured bird hunched on the chair. Alarmed, his voice rose. 'What the hell has happened to you?' He crossed the room quickly, and kneeling held Tommy closely.

Tommy's reserves dissolved, and burying his face in his father's gritty work jacket, he began to sob.

Making soothing noises, stroking the boy's back gently, Joe glanced at Emily, mouthing, 'What happened?'

She shook her head. 'I don't really know. He came in like this just a minute ago. He says it was a boy from the village lying in wait for him.'

Joe gently pushed Tommy back into the chair, and taking a clean cloth airing by the fireside, he wiped his tears. 'Now, you tell me exactly what happened and where.'

Snuffling, Tommy repeated the lie.

Somehow the tale didn't seem quite right, but Joe saw little use in questioning the lad further, he was good at keeping secrets, prying would be to no avail. If Tommy wanted to keep something to himself, he would.

Sighing, Joe rose, his knees creaking. 'I'll get cleaned up, then I'll bathe your wounds.' Running his hand over the boy's hair. 'You stay sitting by the fire until supper time and then its an early night. You can tell me all about Plas Mawr when I'm washed.'

Sniffing, Tommy wiped his hand over his eyes.

Emily followed Joe into the scullery. 'What do you think really happened, Joe?'

'Lord knows. Tommy is not likely to say if he doesn't want too.'

She helped him off with his shirt, then hung it on a peg on the door to dry; it would air by the fire overnight. 'Could it be something to do with Plas Mawr?'

Climbing into a clean pair of worn-out trousers, he looked up from buckling the belt. 'Lass, your guess is as good as mine. If he doesn't want to say, he won't. Tight-lipped our Tommy, the little bugger.' He smiled with fatherly affection.

'Aye you're reeght there.'

He wasn't going to enlighten her of his own day it would only upset her. The weather had been atrocious, most of the day it had poured with rain, hadn't stopped until it was time to start the long trek home. But that had been a minor problem, the attitude of some of his work mates with their jibes and catcalls had been hard to tolerate. Men that knew him least had made spurious comments about the Standish family coming up in the world, mixing with the gentry, and turning their backs on fellow quarriers'.

In the cabanod at lunchtime, the man he used to work for had shouted across the muggy, overcrowded room, 'We'll have to watch our backs now that Standish has the ear of the boss. He'll be getting the best bargains, it'll be dross rock for the rest of us.'

Joe, tempted to cuff the man, had been pulled back by his mate, Tom Hughes. The comment had upset him, he, like most workers, abhorred the men that were willing to pay, bribe, flatter or plainly blackmail the letting steward for the best Bargains, the good rocks that were easier to mine and more profitable for the team.

If he'd laid hands on Dickens, he might have done some serious damage to his supercilious face. There was still at lot of animosity and unfinished business between them, the incident of the stolen pennies wasn't forgotten and neither was being forced to remain silent about it to keep his job.

'Is summat a matter, Joe?' Emily had come alongside him.

'No. I was just thinking about our poor Tommy,' he fibbed.

Tommy was settled early, and for a while he listened to the quiet chatter, and the snuffling baby noises coming from the wooden crib that Frank still occupied.

His head ached and his almost closed eye throbbed painfully. Battered and bruised, sleep wouldn't come easily. George Bellamy's face loomed large in his mind and it wasn't until he had reached a decision regarding his future and Plas Mawr that he slipped into a trouble sleep, and once again walked up the avenue to the house.

The following morning, George was not at breakfast, Bellamy and Thorbes coming into the dining room found Tommy sitting alone. The dark bruises on his face were livid and one of his swollen eyes completely shut.

Mr. Bellamy was first to speak. 'I'm surprised at you, Standish, fighting like a common lout.'

Tear brimmed in Tommy eyes. 'Sir.'

Thorbes, observant, noted that had he been fighting like a common lout, as Mr. Bellamy had put it, he might not now be looking quite so dejected. Familiar with the way of boy's, loutish, and well bred, he saw that there was more to it than a common fight. There was no bravado attached to this skirmish.

Sitting, Bellamy looked across the table to Tommy. His demeanour was considerably changed from the previous day, he was uncertain, hunched, as though he had taken a serious beating. Why wasn't George at table? The penny dropped and his face darkened. He bellowed, 'Draycot. Fetch me Master George at once. I'll not hear his mamby pamby excuses, I want him here NOW!'

Draycot, glad he wasn't in the firing line of the Master's anger, bowed from the hip. 'Yes, sir.'

A moment later, George not quite fully dressed entered the room. Seeing Tommy, his face darkened.

Rising slowly from his chair Bellamy appeared ready to launch himself at his son. 'What have you got to say for yourself? Don't look at Tommy, he's said nothing, but I'm not a fool, I can see your low dealing in this.' Standing fully, he roared 'Answer me boy, before I take me belt to you in front of the servants.'

George stood firm.

Moving from the table, Bellamy approached him. His voice hard and clear 'Answer me, or I swear I will swing for you.'

Throughout the scene Draycot had been standing impassively by the open door, he moved aside for Mrs. Bellamy to enter.

She was dressed ready for travel, and had taken considerable pains with her toilette, she had anticipated approval from her husband, but she had walked into what appeared to be a family war. Crossing the room she came alongside her son, her bulky frame in an extravagant lavender frock shielding him from his angry father. 'What is all the noise about?'

Waving her aside, Bertram said crossly, 'Don't interrupt me. I'm dealing with this young hound.' Governing his women folk as he did his servants, with a benevolent dictatorship, Bellamy did not expect to be brooked.

Aggrieved at being discounted, Mrs. Bellamy looked for a person lower in the social scale to mistreat, her eyes settled on Tommy's injured face. She gave him an unfriendly stare, then addressing her husband, she said scornfully, 'I told you that no good would come of this new arrangement.'

Bellamy hardly moved his lips. 'Mind me, lady, I am as angry as I have ever been, I will not be sneered at by him or by you.'

Sniffing, fully aware that the servants knew that she counted little in this household, Mrs. Bellamy lifted her hem and flounced to the table, and with much arranging of her skirt she sat in a chair as far away from the village brat as she was able to.

Draycot shifted his feet, making a mental note to stay out of her way; Madam could be a right tartar when her hackles were up. Mean enough to pinch the young maids painfully and keep them long after they were supposed to have finished work at ten thirty at night. Nodding for an underling to wait at table, he kept watch by the door.

Seeing no help from is mother, she was already fussing over the cup of tea being poured for her, George's eyes filled with tears.

'Standish.' Bellamy roared loud enough for Tommy to flinch. 'I want you to answer me truthfully. If I find that you have lied to me, you will not enter my house again. Do you understand?'

Tommy trembled. 'Yes, sir.'

'Did my son do this despicable injury to you.'

Tommy trained by his school and village comrades not to grass fought with his conscience.

Articulating each word slowly, Mr. Bellamy loomed over him. 'I said did my son...'

Tommy saw his future sliding away. His bottom lip trembled. 'Yes, sir.'

George's shoulders sunk into his body.

Turning, Bellamy faced his son. 'Was this act of folly of your own making? Or did Standish attack you first?'

Seeing his way clear to ridding himself of the interloper, George looked straight into his father's eyes. 'He started it. He attacked me as he was leaving last night.'

His father sighed. 'And how did he do that?'

'He punched me on the chin.'

Bellamy lifted Tommy's hand, giving the knuckles a quick inspection.

Coming from behind the table he crossed to George, and with the back of his hand swiped him fiercely.

Covering his reddened ear, George wailed.

'And you can quit that.'

Cowering, George sobbed.

His anger was almost out of control. Bellowing near to the boy's ear. 'That a son of mine should be such a dishonourable disgrace.' Grabbing his arm, nearly lifting him off his feet, he hauled him out of the dining room.

Thorbes had remained silent throughout the debacle; lifting his cup he finished the dregs of the now cold coffee.

In the hallway the library door slam closed.

Mrs. Bellamy called to Draycot. 'Would you go and hurry Henrietta. We must leave soon if we are to reach the Mannering's in time for luncheon.

She spoke over the wails coming from behind the closed door of the library.

Kindly, Thorbes glanced at Tommy. 'If you have finished your breakfast we will go to the schoolroom.'

Relieved, Tommy sidled out of the chair.

Ignoring Tommy, Mrs. Bellamy spoke to the mathematics master. 'Perhaps Draycot could send someone with a pot of coffee and a little breakfast. I see that you have eaten nothing.'

Thorbes smiled, bowing slightly. 'That would be most welcome, Madam.'

Tommy did not add his thanks, knowing that any kindness that this woman might show was not meant for him. George wasn't the only enemy he had at Plas Mawr.

Sometime later, George, tear stained, came into the schoolroom. Sitting gingerly he took his place, avoiding looking at Tommy.

Walking down the avenue at the end of the day, Tommy was cautious, not that he expected to meet George, his defiance had been successfully beaten out of him that morning. He'd be nursing a sore backside for many days. He was no longer a threat to Tommy's long term plans.

With this thought, and content with the way things had panned out, it was worth the black eye to have George cowed, he walked down the half mile avenue listening to the rooks cawing in the distant trees preparing to roost for the night. Outside the gate, and away from eyes that might be watching, he ran towards home, the pain in his eye throbbing with every footfall.

Despising George became a habit. The boy was a dullard, unable to think clearly, inclined to cheat, and had an extraordinary amount of money spent on him, and servants at his beck and call.

Mr. Bellamy, although a great percentage of the blame fell to him for the ruination of his son, as Tommy saw it, remained high in his esteem. Although if a fault were to be found it would be that the man did not extract enough out of the Garddryn men or the quarry itself. Production could be improved greatly, corners could be cut, and more slate mined.

During the last twelve months there had been four deaths due to two rock falls and one caused as a man fell from Jerusalem gallery. Blame had not been attributed to the Garddryn, the men involved had been found to be negligent. So why Old Bellamy was slowing production whilst he tested new safety methods was beyond Tommy's ken.

Mrs. Bellamy didn't warrant his attention, being just an appendage, and a useless one at that, to the Estate.

Henrietta Bellamy, the fifteen-year-old daughter, was a plain girl. Vaguely interesting because she treated her younger brother George, less than fairly. If it were not for George she would eventually be heiress to the Garddryn fortune. This fact was never far from Tommy's meditations.

As the summer months progressed and the small windows in the schoolroom remained open throughout the day, the drone of bees and birdsong, the perfume of sweet scented roses filled the room.

Listening to a blackbird in full song, George was glad of the small diversion from the mathematics lesson and the punctilious voice of Thorbes. Idly he daydreamed, waiting for the opportunity to run out into the warm garden. Lesson's were a drag, he hardly understood a word his teacher tried to ram into his head. He felt his father's disappointment, and only wished he could be the son the old man wanted him to be.

Tommy would have been perfect for the job. The thought often raised a smile, for however hard the village boy worked, and how many people he impressed, the Garddryn fortune would never fall his way. There was no chance of him rising above being a steward at the quarry. He might have brains but what he lacked was Clout.

Chapter Eleven

Joe, his eyes on the looking glass studied the grey strands streaking his once brown hair. Luckier than most it hadn't yet begun to recede. His father's hair had been thick, streaked very much like his now, but then the man had died before his forty-second birthday. Looking for traces of his father's face in his, Joe looked to the lines raked from nostrils down to his mouth, and the furrows embedded in the skin of his brow, those had become more prominent recently. Crows feet radiating from the corners of his eyes seemed to have been there for a lifetime, but they too were deeper, more pronounced. Not wishing to glimpse his father's face in his, he looked to Emily, sitting in the old chair sewing.

'I'm getting old,' he sighed.

Her eyes stayed on her work. 'Don't be daft, Joe, you're forty, that's not very old.'

As if by magnetic force the glass dragged his eyes back to it, and he noted the stubble on his chin was pocked with grey, he touched the rough bristles. 'Well I feel ancient.'

Putting her work aside, she leaned back in the chair. 'What about me? Don't they say that women grow old faster than men do?'

Brushing aside her comment, he said, 'You're beautiful, so age doesn't count.'

The compliment meant or otherwise, made her smile. Going to him she put her arms around his waist. 'What's worrying you, Joe? Don't tell me that being forty is bothering you. I know you better than that.'

Their eyes met in the glass and he compared her soft, unlined complexion against his own rough skin.

The corner of his lips raised in a smile. 'I don't really feel old.' Then he gave a little laugh. 'Least I don't unless I'm struggling out of bed in the morning. Or listening to our Tommy going on about the Garddryn.'

Her arms tightened around him. 'Aye, he is a bit of a tinker.'

Turning, he placed his hands on her shoulder. 'Tinker, the lad's obsessed with the place. If it's not that, it's Plas Mawr this, or Plas Mawr that.'

A frown creased her forehead. 'Joe, you can't begrudge the lad the education he's got out of it.'

He dropped his hands. 'I don't, Lass. But I worry about what's going to happen to him in the future.' He was not accustomed to self-doubts, but the decision to send Tommy to Plas Mawr had often plagued him, it had set the lad apart from his contemporaries, now he neither belonged in the village nor the big house.

Drawing away from him, she picked up the half-finished garment, scrutinising the last few stitches she'd put into it. 'I worry too. He won't be happy working in the Garddryn, he's too well schooled now for him to want to settle for that.'

Joe turned from the mirror, and taking his pipe from the mantelpiece, poked the residue of ash out of the bowl. He saw her take up the needle, then nimbly begin to sew. Although her face was from him he knew that he had her attention.

'I want a lot better for him, than a job in the quarry. I'm loath to let him go there and run risks with his life. Too many young men, thinking themselves indestructible, take chances and get killed. They are such arrogant buggers, youngsters. Think they know it all.'

Shaking his head, he shredded a wodge of tobacco and stuffed it into the bowl, and bending to the fire lit a spill. Whilst he got the tobacco to burn properly, he thought of Tommy at Plas Mawr. What was done was done, there was no use going back over it. No point worrying about what might happen in the future, chances were it never would anyway. Things that were expected to happen had a peculiar way of never happening at all.

Looking through the wisps of smoke from his pipe he watched Emily sewing, hearing the rustle of the cotton as she turned, then inspected the shirt she was making. There was something very soothing watching a woman restoring or fashioning a garment, head bent to her work, and the quick dart of silver as the needle ran through the cloth.

Relaxing he put his feet on the fender, and settled his shoulders to the back of the chair. 'Summat will happen soon. Old Bellamy will want to sent his boy away to finish his education at some posh college.'

Without looking up, Emily said, 'I don't suppose that'll happen, the lad's not bright enough. His father will have him working in the quarry office, or not working at all.'

Exhaling smoke slowly, he sighed. 'Aye maybe.'

The front door opened noisily and Tommy bowled into the room. 'Mam, I'm going for a walk with a couple of friends. Bye.'

Emily started to rise. 'Come back here, Tommy, you'll not go out in your Sunday school clothes.'

Eyes to the ceiling, arms akimbo, he looked the picture of tried patience. 'Oh, Mam.'

'Don't oh Mam me, young man. Change, or stay at home.'

Muttering, Tommy stomped up the narrow stairs.

Eyes to the ceiling, she smiled. 'What was it you said about feeling old when Tommy starts.'

Joe shook his head. 'Ancient as the hills more like.'

Furious, Tommy flung his boots to the wall. 'Grown-ups, why do they always wreck everything. Why would I want to go out in old clothes? What's the point of having half-decent clothes if you're not allowed to wear them when you go out? Bah.' Pulling on a clean shirt, he buttoned it hurriedly. Then slipped into the least worn of his trousers, they were too short, but better than the ones he'd torn last week. Boots back on; he rattled down the stairs. Flinging the door at the bottom of the stairs fully open, he came into the living room. 'Where's Frank?'

Joe turned to inspect what he was wearing. 'Playing next door.'

Thankful for small mercies, Tommy smiled. Now he wouldn't be expected to amuse the brat all afternoon.

Coming out of Sunday school he had plucked up the courage to ask Millie Barker to walk to the old water mill with him. The afternoon was hot and dry, the water mill a good two miles away, Millie was sure to divest herself of a couple of layers of clothes before she reached there. With luck he'd get to see her plump breasts. A couple of the boys had verified that Millie liked to lark about. Tommy, suffering the sexual frustrations of a thirteen-year old boy, going on fourteen, was eager to experiment.

Checking him over, Emily said sternly, 'I want you back here in time for supper, or else.'

Tommy with no intention of returning home until he had seen Millie naked, however long that might take to accomplish, dashed out of the house, leaving the front door vibrating on the hinges. With visions of Millie Barker lying in the long grass, naked as the day she was born, he raced to the bridge at the far end of the village.

Before he reached there he could see that the bridge was empty, and his heart sank. For the next ten minutes he kicked his heels, elated that she would be there at any moment, and raging that she saw fit to make him wait. With these twin emotions riling in his head he spotted her, sauntering towards him, still wearing the blue dress with the button through bodice she'd worn earlier.

As she drew near, he spoke more sharply than he had intended. 'I thought you had decided not to come.'

She gave him a cocky smile. 'The Mrs. wouldn't let me off straight away, she made me sweep the kitchen floor, said it wasn't done proper earlier.'

Millie, employed as a kitchen maid in the family home of a feather and fur dealer was entitled to a free Sunday afternoon, twice a month. At fourteen, Millie might have expected to move up the domestic hierarchy, but to stay in close proximity to her family living in Garddryn village, she accepted the long hours of work and the six pounds a year wage that Mr. Shipton, the dealer paid. Millie, a basically lazy and simple girl, generally could keep out of earshot of Mrs. Shipton, a domestic tyrant, whilst fulfilling a modicum of duties.

Tommy's ears were ringing, red blood pumping fast through his veins. Forgetting his old garments, and the rotten temper wearing them had engendered, his mind was now totally preoccupied on his small clothes and what lay beneath them. Perspiration had collected in every nook and cranny of his flesh, and his limbs felt weak and trembling.

It was hard to drag his eyes from the thin, blue material covering Millie's rounded breasts, the little hand-sewn ruches stretching across the flattened orbs.

The afternoon simmered with heat, he could smell the scent of his own sweat and hers. Was it in his imagination or could he detect the perfume of carnal urgency bridging the gap between them? The tangy smell that came after the erection of his intimate flesh, when he'd witnessed the prize stallion copulating on Preece's farm, or imagined the cleft between a woman's legs.

Millie's tight shoes were pinching; she was hot, sticky and uncomfortable, the seams of her dress digging into her armpits. Discomforts she would endure because she was so happy to be walking beside handsome, Tommy Standish.

Many times her Mam had said that he would be a great catch for some girl one day, because he was clever, in the pocket of the quarry owner, and he came from a respectable family. Millie couldn't see any reason why she shouldn't be just that girl.

Reaching the end of the dirt track, Tommy offered his hand to assist her over a stile. Giggling, and feeling quite the young lady, she held onto him for a moment longer than necessary, and when he followed her with an agile leap across the wooden barrier he took her hand again, and they walked in silence to the fast, tumbling millrace.

The wheel no longer turned, and the building abandoned years before was now a haven for sheep, and inquisitive jackdaws. The hedge that had once surrounded a tidy garden was overgrown, offering shelter from prying eyes. An elm tree, taking root many decades ago shaded the mill, the highest branches reaching well beyond the broken roof.

Leading Millie to the shade beneath the tree, Tommy slumped down on the springy, close-cropped grass, patting the place beside him. 'Come on, Millie, take the weight off your legs.'

Dropping to her knees, her skirt a blue circle around her, she looked into his handsome face. 'I hope you haven't brought me here for any other reason than for the walk.'

He pulled her down beside him, and collapsing with a giggle, she allowed his lips to brush hers.

'Don't be daft, Millie, I only want to spend a bit of time with you. There's nothing wrong with that is there?' Feeling the resistance in her tense body, he was persuasive, 'I like you a lot, Millie.' His lips teased hers. 'You are very pretty.'

Some of the tension slipped from her and she nestled into him. 'I like you a lot too, Tommy.'

His mouth lingered on hers, and the familiar feeling of excitement sent his blood pulsing. Her hips moved against his. Surreptitiously, so as not to alarm her, he began to unbutton his trousers. His kiss deepened, his tongue parting her lips found a warm haven in her mouth.

Cautiously, he'd be furious if her failed after getting this far; he began to unbutton the bodice of her dress. The third button made a soft popping sound, alerting Millie and she gave a token resistance.

Not to be beaten, he deepened the penetration in her mouth, and pressed his body into hers. Sighing, she nestled against him.

Swiftly now, feeling himself on the home run, he completed the operation, and parting the material bared her breasts. Ecstatic, he marvelled at the soft roundness, the warmth beneath his palms, the nipples ripening and hardening with his delicate touch. It was the most natural thing in the world to take a nipple into his mouth and gently suck. Beneath him, Millie gave a soft, gentle moan.

Later, when she was dressing, pulling up her stockings, she noticed the smear of blood on the skirt of her precious dress. She felt like crying, it had been so fast, he had pushed into her and a stab of intense pain had pierced her to the core, then she had felt the stickiness between her legs.

Tommy, buttoning his trousers gave her a grin. 'Smile, Millie, anyone would think you'd lost a penny.'

The last thing she wanted to do was smile, but she forced a bright one. 'Do you still like me, Tommy?'

'Yea, course I do.'

'Are you sure? You don't think that I'm cheap because I let you do that to me?'

He was pulling on his boots, watching the tiny insects in the grass, a ladybird flitting from one blade of grass to another. He pulled his attention back to the girl. 'Don't be soft.' It was hard to hide his grin; at last he was a man. Something to shout from the mountaintops, tell the world, run home and confide to his father that now they belonged to the same club. Women versus men. He glanced at her, humped shoulders.

She had every reason to look miserable, she had given her only true value away, now she had no bargaining power, she was defunct. Silly mare. It was hard not to laugh.

Tears were standing in her eyes, blinking them away she looked to the ocean and the far horizon.

The track of his thoughts changed. Tomorrow he might need her again, it paid to be friendly, he could make a regular thing of it, Sundays they could come up here and he could tup her to his heart's content.

Pulling her towards him he kissed her mouth, it no longer tasted as good, but he kept his lips to hers. Drawing away, with a new edge to his voice, he said, 'Stop worrying, Millie, you're my girl now, so at least look a bit pleased.'

Millie's heart sang. Tommy's girl, who would believe that she, plain Millie Barker could catch him so easily.

Retracing their steps to the village, they held hands, Millie leaning into his body possessively. In sight of the cottages, Tommy stooped to pluck a blade of grass, breaking the contact, then chewing the stalk he kept up a running commentary of how wonderful everything was going to be now that they had an understanding.

Millie went back to work, happy.

For the next few weeks it became a regular thing, every Sunday afternoons they walked to the mill hand in hand. As the season changed to an unpredictable autumn they fell into a pattern of meeting there, taking shelter within the derelict building when necessary.

Millie was hurt that he no longer walked there with her, but loved him too much to tell him so, afraid that he might leave her in the lurch she accepted the change in the relationship. Fearful of being discovered skiving off work every other Sunday, Millie began to comfort eat, gaining weight steadily.

Tommy took a good ribbing from the boys of the village, their lies that Millie liked to lark about had given him a false sense of bravado, deflowering the girl had been easy because he hadn't expected to fail. When the lie was exposed, it was a good joke, one often repeated amongst them.

As autumn turned to winter and Millie's hips spread, the joke turned to the possibility of pregnancy. Tommy began to sweat, and the next Sunday he didn't go to the mill.

Arriving at the usual time, Millie waited until well after dark, huddled in the corner of the old building, her dreams of marriage disintegrating as the pale sun sank into the sea, and the crescent moon began to ride high in the heavens.

The following Sunday she escaped the house of her employer, the family had taken the carriage and were not expected back from Caernarvon until the next day, Millie went back to the mill. During the week she had almost convinced herself that there was probably a perfectly good explanation why Tommy had not shown up the previous week. But every time she thought that the relationship might be at an end, and he was probably in the arms of a new girl, her heart lurched with unhappiness. Several nights she wept herself to sleep.

Convincing herself that it would be better to know than not know, she walked apprehensively, her eyes turning back to the way she had come, and then searching the lane up ahead for sight of him. There was no sign of him; perhaps he was at the mill waiting. With this thought she stepped up her pace. Arriving, she was almost too afraid to enter in case she should find the old building empty, and her life with it. Then with her heart in her mouth she gathered her courage and walked through the wrecked doorway. The main area was gloomy, only a few slivers of light filtering through the broken tiles of the old sorting room lit the place. Ahead, she sensed a movement and her heart leapt with joy. 'Tommy.' She nearly screeched his name.

The shadows shifted and she saw not one boy but two, neither were Tommy Standish.

Although she had seen them in his company many times, their faces were familiar but not their names, inhabitants of another village.

Slowly, grinning slyly, they advanced on her.

With her back to the wall, she instinctively measured the distance between her and the relative safety of the garden.

Which boy pounced first, she didn't know and it hardly mattered. They were on top of her, pushing her skirt up over her belly, one holding her down, and the other ramming into her with such violence that she thought she must surely tear and die.

Screaming, Tommy's name, she wept for her past bliss, believing that never again would rapture and happiness be hers.

The second boy was less brutal, physically. Thrusting into her, he laughed in her face, shouting 'This is from Standish, he couldn't be present himself, due to another appointment.' The malicious words tore into her, ripping out her heart.

Eventually, satiated by rape and violence the two youths, whispering and giggling, buttoned their trousers and brushed dirt off their clothes. Without a backward glance to the mute girl, they slipped away. The old door, hanging on one hinge, clattered as they passed. Their banter mingling with obscene laughter as they trod the path back to the narrow lane.

Dazed, she watched the darkness fall, then gathering her torn clothes, and covering her nudity and shame as best she could, she stumbled away from the mill. Place of love and burning hatred.

Stumbling in the direction of Garddryn village, unseeing, the pain between her legs intense, blood and sticky ooze trickling down her thighs.

Clutching the ruined blue dress, formerly her pride and joy, the ruches so painstakingly sewn, now ripped and tattered, the skirt stained with blood and semen and marked with muck from the mill floor.

Choking on a sob, she crossed the bridge and saw a light burning in the window of her home. Staggering towards it, she fell against the door and gave a long, moaning cry.

Beside the fire her mother shivered, hearing the pain of a wounded animal.

Millie's feeble knock was hardly heard inside the stone cottage. Her father, Mathew Barker, coming in from the privy, thinking he heard a sound, crossed to the door and opened it warily. The heap of clothes at his feet gave a weak groan. Millie lifting her head turned her face to him. He saw the blood seeping from a cut on her forehead, her nose was bloody, her chin bruised and sore. Breasts exposed through the tears in her bodice.

'God in heaven, come quick, Mother, it's our Millie. Jesus Christ.' Stooping to her he lifted the girl into his arms.

Mrs. Barker's head came around the door, and she shrieked as she saw the blood on her daughter. 'Oh, Millie darlin' what has happened to you? Who did this to you?' She began to cry.

Mr. Barker snapped. 'There'll be time for tears later. We have to get a doctor and a policeman.'

Wary of the law, Mrs. Barker took a step back. 'The police, in our home?'

His eyes were fiery. 'Whoever did this to our girl, will pay the price. If the law doesn't get him then I will, and he'll look a bloody sight worse than this girl does when I've finished with the bastard.'

Carrying her into the back room, a bedroom she had shared with her sisters when the girls had still been at home, he placed her gently on the bed. The vacant look in her eyes broke his heart.

Catching back a sob, he turned to his wife. 'Take care of her while I go and fetch the surgeon.'

He was gone in a moment, hardly taking time to dress against the chill night. Outside the tears flowed, running unchecked down his face. Half running, stumbling, he made it to the surgeon's home; the windows were ablaze with light, smoke from several chimneys spewing into the cold air. At any other time he might have cast a thought to the expense of such luxury, but he had more important things on his mind.

Rage had taken over from the initial shock, and it was with his anger bubbling that he banged on the front door.

A moment later, on the second battering of the wood, the surgeon drew it open. 'What is it, man?' Grumpy to be disturbed on a Sunday night, he scowled at Barker.

Breathless, angry, and suffering shock, he stuttered, 'Yer have to come quick, it's me daughter.' His voice caught. 'Me daughter's been raped and beaten. She's in a bad way.' Tears filled his eyes.

It took a second for it to sink in. In all the years he had been a doctor here in Garddryn such a thing had not happened. A father of daughters himself, he suffered a sudden pang of panic, where were his girls at this moment. Pulling himself together, he beckoned the man in. 'Now calm down, man, or it'll be you that needs a doctor.'

Barker tried to steady himself, what the doctor said was true, his heart was racing, he could hear it pounding in his ears, and his chest was tight. He took a deep breath.

The surgeon had his arm on Barker's shoulder, the man looked likely to collapse. He spoke calmly, reassuringly. 'I'll come at once, we can go together.'

He bellowed for a manservant and when the man appeared, he gave his orders. 'Go at once to the Special Constable send him to...' he glanced at the visitor.

Mr. Barker stuttered out his name and address.

Repeating it, he told the servant to take the gig and bring the constable at once.

A moment later the surgeon and Mr. Barker were hurrying down the main street on foot. Inside the cottage, the surgeon took charge, banishing Mr. and Mrs. Barker from the bedroom. He tended to the girl compassionately. There was no doubt that the girl had been raped, and viciously. The tears should mend, given time, but there was always the question of disease and pregnancy to contend with. He sighed. Such disasters would have to be dealt with as they arrived. The state of her mind was in doubt, the wench lay mute, seemingly paralysed by the event. As he stitched and dressed her wounds, she hadn't so much as flinched. Finishing, he tried to talk calmly to her but he wasn't sure that his words registered. Sighing again, he picked up his instruments, pushed them back into his bag and went out, leaving the door wide in case the girl cried out.

The special policeman, Twm Williams, was an imposing figure in his hastily pulled on uniform. Standing six-foot-two, the top of his head almost touched the low ceiling of the Barker's living room, and his muscular bulk filled the doorway. Lead tenor in the Methodist chapel choir, his voice boomed in his barrel chest.

'How is she?' he asked as the surgeon came to the fire.

'The girl's in a poor way. We need the wild animal that did this caught and caught fast.' Thinking of his own girls, he spoke angrily. 'A man that stoops to rape should be hanged.'

Twm thought differently. Girls egged a man on with their wily ways and flirting. Who could blame a man for taking what he thought he'd been promised? Prudently, seeing that the doctor's ire was up, and the father heartbroken, he kept his thoughts to himself. Now that the surgeon was involved, he as the law enforcer would have to see that the culprit was brought to book. It shouldn't be such a difficult task, the girl was sure to know the man that had sowed his wild oats. The poor bugger would pay for his moment of pleasure, and probably pay dearly.

Standing in the bedroom doorway, Twm, his great voice booming in the small room, and without a trace of compassion, wasn't she just another girl that teased and didn't get away with it, shouted 'So what's the man's name that did this to you?'

Millie was afraid of the big man, afraid of the police and the military in general. She wanted to be left alone, to forget, but his eyes boring into hers were spiteful, and she knew that he wouldn't leave until she had spoken of her shame. Then everyone in the village would know and her life wouldn't be worth living.

Hating Tommy Standish as she did, and sure that he had a hand in this, she almost blurted out his name. Serve him right if he went to prison, or slaved for a lifetime in the colonies. She was picking at the sheet, her hands restless, her mind whirling with the events, the violent scene going round and round in her head until she thought her brain might explode.

Hearing the buffoon questioning her wounded girl, Mrs. Barker went directly into the room and stood beside the bed. Touching Millie's hand gently, she coaxed. 'Millie, when you have told us what happened, I'll give you a dose of laudanum then you will sleep and forget for a while.'

Tears brimmed in the girl's eyes. 'Promise.'

Her mother smiled, patting her grazed hand. 'I promise. You'll have a long sleep. It will look better in the morning.'

Patiently, Twm waited.

Millie's tear filled eyes caught his, and she said in a small, quiet voice, 'It were two of them, in the old mill.'

The tale was told and repeated several times, when he was sure that he would get no more information, Twm Williams left the cottage. His first port of call was on the Standish household. Tommy Standish had some questions to answer. He had a hand in this of that he was certain. The English family was rising above themselves in Garddryn village, mixing with gentry; they had their noses where they ought not to be. Changing his opinions on rape and girl's getting what they deserve; he made his way to Bryn Tirion. The night was cold, a bitter wind had sprung up, but his mission of law kept him warm as he hurried to the far end of the village.

The day had been an uncertain one for Tommy, jumping at every sound, expecting that Millie Barker or a member of her family might knock on the door and ask him what he thought he was playing at. He feared the mother the most, a real harridan; she'd make mincemeat out of him if she found out that he'd been tupping her daughter. He wouldn't fair any better if his own mother discovered the dirty secret. God forbid that it should come to his father's ears, for then he'd get such a beating, it would be doubtful that he'd ever be fit enough to fornicate again.

Ten days ago he'd talked to the boys, his mates, and it had been decided that Millie should be left alone, it did look horribly like she might be in the family way. This thought brought a gloss of sweat to his skin. If this were so, he might be held accountable. But the lads had volunteered to say that she'd been with all of them at some time or other, so that should cover his back. He could only pray that they would stand by him.

A fist beat the door tearing Tommy out of his reverie; he almost jumped out of his skin.

Joe looked up from the book he was reading. 'Who on earth can that be at this time of night?' Laying the book aside, he sighed. He was rising out of his chair, when Tommy dashed from the room, making for the outside privy.

'Tommy,' Emily called, but the boy was already outside, the door banging behind him.

At the front door, Joe invited Twm Williams into the house.

Emily rose as the big man, imposing in his uniform, walked into the room. He was polite enough in his greeting, but she saw his eyes raking the furnishings.

Joe expecting that he had called regarding a neighbour's misdemeanour was civil. 'What can we do for you, Constable?'

The man's eyes went to Emily; her alarm was obvious. Directing his question to her, he said, 'Is your son, Tommy in? I want a word with him.'

Surprised, Emily's jaw dropped. 'Tommy. Why?'

Joe blinked. A hundred reasons for the official visit, from stone throwing, to pinching sweets, raced through his head. What trouble was the little devil in now? Not wishing to be obstructive, but aware that Tommy might be a culprit, Joe answered politely. 'Any questions you have for my family I will answer.'

Affronted that Standish was taking that line, civilly defensive, the constable frowned. 'It's the boy that I want to talk too. Where is he?'

Emily stuttered. 'He's just gone to the privy.'

Constable Williams gave a false laugh. 'Or run away more like.'

Irked by the comment, and the man's attitude, Joe squared up to him. 'And why would he do that?'

Enjoying the moment, the revelation that he was about to deliver would knock this lot back to Manchester; the policeman spoke sharply 'Because he may have had a hand in the rape of Millie Barker.' He watched Emily's face blanch and her husband lose his bluster.

Wordlessly, Joe turned from the man and strode to the back door, wrenching it open he felt the chill air blow into the scullery, he stepped outside. The moon cast a spectral light on the small outhouse, and the branches of the trees swaying in the breeze. Glancing at the stream, the water rushing away to the sea, phosphorescent in the eerie light. Everything was so unbelievably normal, the sound of the water, the trees rustling, Emily indoors, Frank asleep, Tommy up to his old tricks. He could have wept; maybe nothing would ever be the same again.

His eyes grew angry. There was the girl to consider too, the poor wench. That a son of his could be involved in something so base, so disgraceful, and if he were not, why was he hiding in the privy?

With visions of his son, forcing a girl against her will, he banged on the thin wood of the privy door. 'You can come out of there, and answer some questions' His voice rose to a roar 'I'll give you one minute, my lad, then I'm coming in to get you, if you happen to have your trousers round your ankles, bad luck.'

Slowly the latch lifted, and Tommy trembling in the darkness, whispered, 'Is it Millie, or her mother that's looking for me?' As soon as the words were out, he realised his error.

Grabbing him, Joe hauled him out. Now there was little doubt in his mind that the boy had something to do with the calamity.

Tommy shouting his innocence was towed into the cottage. Behind them, the open privy door banged in the breeze.

Pushing the lad through the living room door, Joe, his face red and his breathing harsh, barked, 'Tommy Standish for you.'

Tommy's eyes fell on the great bulk of the constable.

Joe pushed him forward. 'Answer the man's questions, and if you so much as lie once, I'll have your guts and string them around this village for the bloody crows to peck at.' Shaking the boy by the arm, he scowled. 'Do you understand?'

It wasn't the reaction that Twm anticipated. A brushing under the carpet, my son couldn't possibly have anything to do with such a heinous deed, would have been more in keeping with how he perceived these people.

As though washing his hands of his son, Joe said, 'Ask him anything you like.'

Pulling himself up to his full height, Twm Williams looked down on Tommy, eyeing him sternly. The boy looked terrified. It was hard to tell if it was his father, or the law he feared most. Making full use of his baritone voice, he bellowed, 'How well do you know Millie Barker?'

Reddening, Tommy didn't answer immediately, his brain seemed to have ceased functioning. Devious ploys deserting him entirely. Fighting to get control, his voice let him down and he almost squeaked. 'Not very well.' Covering his embarrassment he gave an awkward little cough.

The constable's eyes bored into him, and his next question was barked loudly. 'Where were you this afternoon?'

The air he was holding tightly in his lungs, blew out, Tommy saw that he might not be in as much trouble as he had first thought. Tread carefully, he urged his mind, think, and consider the answers carefully. Ignoring the feeling of sickness lying in his belly, he faked a look of innocent surprise. 'Here.'

Letting go of the mantelpiece, Joe stepped forward, his heart a little lighter. 'We can vouch for that, he's been in the house the entire afternoon.'

Emily, picking at her apron, nodded her agreement. Although it was a mystery to her why the boy had stayed in, generally on a Sunday he was off high jinking somewhere. But if it meant that he couldn't have anything to do with the crime, then she'd be eternally grateful that he had seen fit to stay indoors all day.

Sharing Emily's relief, and the same thoughts running through his head, Joe glanced at the officer. 'Could you tell us exactly what has happened, Constable?'

Twm Williams eyes turned from the boy and onto Joe. 'Millie Barker was viciously beaten and raped this afternoon in the old, derelict mill.

Tommy's fear subsided. He was in the clear. He couldn't be blamed.

Joe's face clouded. 'That's terrible. Poor lass.'

Taking a handkerchief from the pocket of his coat, Twm blew his nose noisily. 'Millie says that it was two of his friends that did it. That she had gone to the mill to meet Master Standish, I believe this arrangement had become something of a habit, and two of his friends jumped her and subsequently raped and beat her.'

Emily sank in to her chair. 'Oh my God.'

Tommy's mind was racing; he had to see Millie, and soon to find out how much she'd told everyone.

The constable barked, 'So who are these boys? Where do they live?

Tommy had the answers but he wasn't telling. When the questions got tough he even managed a few tears.

Unconvinced that the boy was telling the truth, and sure that he would not get any further information from him, Twm Williams left the house.

The night was a long one for Tommy seeking a solution to his problems. The one conclusion he did come to was that he had to reinstate the arrangement with Millie, at least until the heat was off him. With this thought he fell into a restless sleep.

Millie's troubles were far from over. The mistress, calling her into the sitting room on the day of her return to duties, had upbraided the girl for her behaviour. Admonishing her severely, she had said that had Millie been where she ought to have been, namely at work, and not skiving off as soon as her employer's back was turned the embarrassing incident at the mill with two boys would never have taken place. Her wages were withheld against the expense of her recently acquired uniform. A reference was not forthcoming. 'How could she,' her employer had said, 'a wife of a respected businessman possibly give a reference to a girl lacking in deportment, she was a disgrace. Who in their right minds would want their innocent daughters in the company of someone with so poor a reputation?' Depressed and still deeply shaken by her ordeal, Millie returned home.

The following Thursday, Tommy, nervous that the affair may have reached the ears of Mr. Bellamy, walked towards Plas Mawr for his lessons. Expecting a call into the study as he entered the house and asked what his part had been in the debacle, he had decided to play the tearful innocent.

There was no call, and the lessons proceeded as normal. At four o'clock, relieved to have the day drawing to a close, he collected his belongings and made ready to leave.

Counting his blessing he started the long walk down the avenue to the roadway. There had been neither sound nor sight of the special constable since last Sunday, which was a good sign, it must mean that he was off the hook.

Throughout the week, he had kept away from the places the village boys usually congregated, the local woods, the old bench under the chestnut tree near the Methodist chapel, and more recently the bridge crossing the stream.

There was the sound of a blast from the quarry, and he looked up from kicking a pebble towards a thrush rooting amongst the dead leaves for earthworms.

The booming explosion brought his father to his mind. In a moment or so he'd be coming out of the blast shelter; climbing back onto the rock face to begin clearing the precarious rock after the black powder had done its work. It was a dangerous and dirty occupation, at best uncomfortable, a rope hooked around one thigh and suspended perhaps hundreds of feet above the galleries, the rock above likely to come tumbling down, extinguishing life or severing limbs. The rain in the mountains was legendary, if it wasn't tipping it down, it was cold, he smiled, or both, wet and tipping that was the life of a quarryman. Mad buggers.

Kicking a pebble into the undergrowth, he began to run.

He was starving, although he'd eaten a good breakfast and another meal at noon, roast lamb and spuds and a big dollop of blackberry sponge and custard. He was lucky, he ate a great deal better than Frank, no wonder the twerp was so skinny. Runt of the litter, he thought grinning.

Dashing through the pedestrian gate he was startled by Millie as she stepped from behind the hedge. At the sight of her his heart pitter-pattered in his throat, and he felt the rush of blood flushing his cheeks. Embarrassed, he stuttered, 'What you doing here, Millie?

There was a hard line to her mouth that he hadn't noticed previously; she was less pretty for it. He wondered how he had ever thought her desirable, undeniably he had found her so the first few times he'd been with her. Now she looked positively peevish. The bruises on her face and the cut on her brow were livid against her pale skin.

Running her eyes over him, she said spitefully, 'Well look who we have here, Tommy Standish.'

His bottom lip curled in irritation. 'So.'

'So. Is that all you have to say to me?' She almost screeched.

Looking skyward, he gave a long sigh. 'Why did you come if all you want to do is scream at me?'

Through narrow eyes she watched his face. 'I came because I think you owe me an explanation.'

Silently, he stood his ground.

Her voice rose. 'Where were you the other Sunday? Why did you stand me up?' Tears filled her eyes. She shouted harshly. 'And why did you let those horrid boys do that to me?'

Looking incredulous, his mouth dropped open. 'Me! It has nothing to do with me.'

Tears flowed down her face, her mouth stretched and ugly she began to sob. 'If it wasn't you, who told them that I would be there?'

Stepping towards her, his books filling his hands, he spoke quietly, almost whispering, 'Millie, you have to believe me, I had nothing at all to do with it. Honestly. I would never hurt you. You must believe me.'

She sniffed. 'Why must I?'

He paused before answering, using silence to accentuate his claim. 'Because I care for you, that's why.' Placing his books on the ground, he stepped towards her, enfolding her in his arms. He spoke quietly against her ear. 'Because I care, Millie.'

Sobbing, she clung to him. 'Swear to me that you really didn't tell them.'

'Millie how could I tell them anything, when I didn't know myself that you were going to the mill.'

How she wanted to believe him, to banish the demons that haunted her day and night with taunts that he had betrayed her.

Her body trembled against his, tightening his grip around her, he spoke softly 'Millie, Millie, how could you doubt me? You know that I love you, and always will.'

She sniffed. 'If that's true why didn't you show up last Sunday?'

The excuse came automatically and he delivered it smoothly. 'I couldn't, my mother was ill. I had to take care of Frank. Mam was too ill to leave, so I couldn't come to the mill to see you.'

She wasn't feeling strong enough to ask why he hadn't come on the second Sunday. For the moment she needed to believe that he did care, it would soften the terrible pain that was eating at her.

The next free day available to him Tommy walked to Millie's home. He felt that life was hard to him: There was his mother with her endless complaints of his behaviour, and his father, tired after a week at the quarry, expecting him to clean the pig's sty and feed the hens. The furrows striping the two-acre plot, which his father had dug so meticulously now needed the planting finished. On top of all else that was expected of him, he had to suck-up to Millie to keep her from saying anything untoward to Twm Williams. In all it made for a poor entertainment for the weekend. Nearing Millie's home he felt miserable and very hard-done-by. That he hadn't accomplished one of the tasks set by either parent failed to carry any weight with him at all.

Millie opened the door at his first knock. Ecstatic, her eyes shining with delight, she agreed to go for a walk with him. Glad that she had changed into one of her mother's frock's, a grey wool garment with an added fancy collar, cut down to size to replace the lovely blue dress. Throwing a short, brown cape over her shoulders, she was ready in an instant. Ignoring her mother's advice to wear a bonnet against the breeze, she came out at once and fell into step with him.

By some taciturn agreement they stayed away from the mill, walking through the woods beyond the disused old quarry and on to the foothills of the mountains. The day was unseasonably warm, winter giving away to an early spring. Awakening buds were everywhere, adorning the trees, hedgerows and the ground. Ceaseless song from innumerable birds, and a trace of fragrant herbs in the air.

Forgetting her heartache, and lack of employment, Millie clung to his arm, returning his kisses and listened to his assurance and promises.

The following Sunday was dismal in comparison, hoping that he might call Millie stayed at home, the hours slipping by slowly. It was a relief when darkness fell and her mother lit the lamp, for now she knew that he wouldn't come, and she could stop anticipating and leaping up at every sound.

An afternoon of drama and music had been organised by George and Henrietta Bellamy; it was to be held in the large and elaborate orangery at Plas Mawr.

George, a great enthusiast for theatricals had made most of the arrangements, hiring minor actors and actresses, musicians, and a troupe of exotic dancers.

Two days before the entertainment, George was in a flap; sure that he would not have everything accomplished in time. Turning to Tommy at the end of Friday lessons, he begged for his assistance.

Delighted, Tommy stayed at Plas Mawr for the evening, helping to decorate the orange trees with Chinese lanterns. A job that George didn't trust the house or garden staff to do properly. As George predicted, the job was not finished during the evening and Tommy's help was sought for the following day.

Pleased, feeling accepted at last, and sizzling with excitement, Tommy raced home.

The following morning he could hardly wait to get back to Plas

Mawr. George was still in bed when he arrived, Tommy began fixing things without him, eventually he appeared, and working together frantically they finished the bulk of the work during the afternoon.

They were putting the finishing touches to the miniature display, very much on the lines of the new Crystal Palace Great Exhibition, when Henrietta came into the orangery with lemonade. 'Gosh it looks wonderful. Prince Albert himself would be impressed. '

'No thanks to you.' Brushing his grubby hands down his trousers, George sneered.

Smiling brightly, Henrietta put the tray down. 'Now come on, little brother, you know very well that I have been busy, practising on the pianoforte. Papa cleverly got me the music of Tussaud's Great Exhibition Polka.' She giggled. 'So there, that's a surprise for you isn't it?'

Turning to Tommy, she smiled again. 'I suppose that George had you doing all the work? Take it from me he'll steal the credit.'

It looked as though George might stamp his foot with irritation. 'That is positively not true. Tommy has helped me.'

Turning her back to her brother, she looked up into Tommy's face coquettishly. 'Oh I'm sure that he has. So what will you give him in return for all this hard work?'

It hadn't occurred to George's to reward Tommy, but not liking to be outsmarted by Henrietta; he answered hastily. 'You are quite wrong, Hen'. I have invited him to come tomorrow. So there.'

Looking beneath her lashes, she smiled again, and from the glint in her eye Tommy saw that the by-play had been merely for her own satisfaction. Cleverly, she had outmanoeuvred George. Her reasons were not a concern to him. Her capriciousness had gained him an invitation, and that was all that was important. His heart sang with excitement.

Racing home, his feet bounced on clouds, he couldn't wait to tell his news. It was a dream come true, socialising with the gentry. He ran to the cottage door, opening it in a rush, he dashed into the living room.

Wet washing was draped, steaming on the fender in front of the fire; there was a smell of hot ironing, and the peculiar odour of the flat iron heating on the hob.

Looking up from pressing a pair of trousers, his mother gave him a small smile. Her brow was moist from the rising steam. Tiredness, always a problem on laundry day, was etched on her face. She replaced the iron that had now cooled with the one on the hot plate.

It was a world away from Plas Mawr, and the grey eyed, dark haired, fragrant Henrietta. Her fine clothes rustling softly, and gold bangles glinting as she moved her slim, pale wrists.

Muttering a half-hearted greeting, Tommy shrugged off his coat. His glance went to his brother sitting crossed legged and almost naked on the rag rug before the blazing fire. Pasty, thin shouldered, the four-year old looked small for his age.

Glancing over her shoulder, Emily said, 'Your father will be home soon, he's been to see a friend up at the barracks.' Picking out a shirt from the pile of laundry she shook creases from it, then began to iron again. 'The poor man took a bit of a fall this morning, and has taken to his bed. His leg is badly bruised, he'll not get back to his home on Anglesey for the weekend. Poor man.' Folding the shirt, she sighed.

Muttering a reply, Tommy made for the stairs, he had to get out of the depressing room. The evening stretched out before him insufferably, long, slow hours, stretching into the night. He'd go mad if he had to stay home. A minor panic enveloped him, which he felt powerless to check or control. Scrunching his jacket, he flung it at the wall. Tears of frustration were not far from his eyes.

Groaning, he slumped on the bed, head in his hands. There was absolutely nothing to do but read some dull book, or hold a conversation with his family, five minutes of that and there'd be a row; they always accused him of something or another, or thinking the wrong thing. He groaned again.

Putting his thoughts beyond the claustrophobic house, he considered going to the bridge, his mates might gather there. But it could be risky, if the lads that had been involved in Millie's rape was hanging around, and he was seen in their company, there'd be trouble for him and them. Nosy Parker, Twm Williams was sure to be on the lookout.

Beating his pillow viciously, he looked for an alternative.

Arriving home, Joe called up stairs, 'Tommy come down and give a hand.'

With a long drawn out sigh, Tommy beat the pillow again.

Plodding down, he came into the living room. 'What do you want?'

Joe sighed. 'How about hello father, how are you. Instead of, what do you want?' Eyes raised to the ceiling, he muttered 'Boys.'

Tommy's voice rose several notes. 'I only asked.'

Emily, the ironing finished, put the irons aside to cool. 'Now, now, you two. Don't start.'

Amazed to be drawing her criticism, Joe's jaw dropped. 'I'm not starting. I only want the lad to give me a hand putting the fowl away and feeding the pig. It's not too much to ask is it?'

Emily a dab hand at keeping the peace flowing between father and son answered calmly. 'No, Joe, it's not too much.'

Glancing at Tommy, biting his nails, she said mildly, 'Be a good lad and give your father some help, our Tommy.'

Tearing a snag off the jagged nail, Tommy spit it into the fire. Then without a word, took his old coat off the hook and pushed his arms into the sleeves. 'You coming or what?'

Exasperated, Joe slapped his hat on. 'Yes, yes, I'm coming.'

Ignoring their departure, but listening to Joe's sharp comments and Tommy's snappy replies as they walked down the path, Emily picked up the folded ironing, and put it neatly in the cupboard at the side of the fire. She had a few minutes to tidy up, dress little Frank ready for bed, and give him a cuddle, before her two warring warriors returned. Bliss, she thought, planting a kiss on Frank's curls.

The following morning, Joe rose early. After swallowing a mouthful of tea, he went to the two acre field beside the cottage and released the hens from the coop. Three beautiful brown eggs, still warm, awaited him, he put them aside carefully. One would be for little Frank's breakfast.

His thoughts turned to his young son, an adorable little boy who was loving and well behaved. Conjuring up his small face, he smiled. Nothing was too good, or too much trouble, when it came to little Frank.

Whereas Tommy. He frowned, deep furrows ridging his brow. He loved the lad, but my God there were times when the lad himself made it hard to do so. Trouble walked with Tommy. He could be an obnoxious little bugger at times. Then ten minutes later he could be quite different, a kind, loving streak would surface and it was like looking at a rainbow after a storm, brightening the world and adding rare colour.

Beyond the hen run, slate paling surrounded a small plot of land and sty. Entering by the picket gate, bucket in his hand, Joe poured a thick mash into the pig's trough, watching the mixture settle.

Anticipating his meal the incarcerated pig would head butt the sty door, grunting and squealing noisily, a ritual that never ceased to amuse Joe. Wading through the mushy ground, it had rained heavily during the night, and standing aside of the door, the pig was likely to leave the sty at a hasty trot, he lifted the catch.

Racing out, running on short fat legs, the animal made for the trough and buried his snout in the mash.

With the animal immersed in his breakfast, Joe made a swift retreat out of its domain. He had learned the hard way that swine could be dangerous, unpredictable creatures. Hungry, pregnant, or suckling young, they were best treated with the utmost respect.

For a few moments he watched the creature enjoying his breakfast, from the safety of the fence.

Then with a glance back at the hens pecking and scratching the thin grass, he remembered the eggs, collecting them he stowed the fragile treasures carefully in the bottom of the bucket and started for the cottage.

The morning was lovely, a real harbinger of spring. A breeze was feebly lifting the leaves of the evergreen. The hedgerow furze was leeching soft, pale green shoots, and on the blackthorn, tiny, tight buds promised glorious blossom at the first hint of warm sunlight.

It was a perfect day for a long walk; he planned to go up to the high barracks to check on his mate Ifor. He could take Tommy with him. They hadn't had a walk round the quarry for an age. It would be good for them both to spend a bit of time together.

Pleased with this idea, he quickened his pace. When he got into the cottage he'd take a cuppa up to Emily, wake Tommy, and then they could set off.

The cottage was silent when he entered a few minutes later. The fire he'd lit before going out was now blazing, hot enough for the kettle to boil. Putting it to the hot plate he went out of the back door. The bucket he swilled in the stream and left it upside down to drain. The privy door was swinging in the breeze, closing it; he went back into the house.

With the kettle coming to the boil, the new laid eggs washed and in a dish on the table, and a loaf sliced on the wooden board, he climbed the stairs to wake Tommy.

The boy now slept alone, Joe had partitioned the bedroom at the time of Frank's birth. It gave the lad a bit of privacy and raised him in the hierarchy of family life; he was now big brother.

Tommy's rumpled bed was empty. Joe was disappointed. He climbed back down the stairs, the brightness of the day dulled.

A few minutes later he left the cottage on his errand to see the injured man at the barracks. In his canvas bag he had a couple of days supply of tea, a meat and potato pie wrapped in paper, and a round of bread. Food to keep the chap from starving until his neighbours brought supplies from his Anglesey family.

The climb up to the long huts that were the Garddryn high barracks was steep. Perched near the windswept galleries. Erected more than a couple of decades ago, they were home during the week to the men that worked high up in the quarry, and travelled from the villages of Anglesey and the far off villages on the mainland.

Hitching his canvas bag on his shoulder, he didn't use the long sack of white linen, a wallet, like the other workers. This bag he had carried all his working life. Sometimes it reminded him of his old mate Frank, his had been identical.

The going here was steep, the track a switchback. Stopping for a moment he caught his breath and took a moment to look out over the mountains. His thoughts went back to Frank; they had both thought themselves pretty hard done by in the Galloway walking the cobbled streets from home to the pit, six days a week. But that didn't compare with what the workers endured here. Men like Ifor, the chap he was going to visit now, started out from their homes on Anglesey at three o'clock in the morning. They would walk to the ferry, cross the Strait, no picnic when the weather was bad, or in the dark. Coming ashore they still had to get from there to the quarry. It wasn't for the fainthearted, and far from a perfect beginning to the week. The poor buggers still had to climb several hundreds feet up to the barracks, dump the wallets with the weeks food in. A quick brew if they had time, then a climb to the gallery, so the poor sods could work until dark. It made a man out of breath just thinking about it.

In his mind he had spoken all this to Frank, he could see his mate now, laughing, saying, 'So the Galloway were a piece of cake, were it?'

Remembering, seeing Frank buried beneath the rock fall, he answered, 'No Frank it weren't all bloody roses that's for sure.'

He wondered if he had spoken aloud, he often told Frank things, although the man had been dead now eleven years or more.

The thought was depressing. It had been so long since he and Frank had shared a joke, a day's work, and an ale at the end of it. He missed him still, always would.

Sighing, he began to climb, concentrating all his thoughts on the good times they had shared as boys and men. Almost laughing aloud recalling the incident with the feather and the neighbour's privy. What a morning that was, and what a beating he got for tickling the backside of old man Harvey. Old Harvey had leapt off the hole as though a flame had touched his rump. His own father apoplectic with fury, his poor mother ashamed to go out until Sunday fell again. It made Tommy seem less troublesome when he recalled some of the mischief he and Frank got up too.

On the last stretch of the hard climb, his thoughts went to Tommy. 'Where had the little bugger disappeared to this time? He was out of bed sharpish, and gone without a word. Could only mean trouble of one sort or another.'

Stopping to catch his breath, he scanned the scene, it made him slightly dizzy looking up at the pale blue sky, white clouds scurrying across the mountain tops. Looking back the way he had come to the layers and layers of galleried cliffs.

Taking a deep breath, his eyes on the long huts that were not too far away now, he could make out the grey smoke spiralling from a chimney. A good sign, if Ifor was fit enough to keep the fire burning.

Arriving he stamped mud off his boots, and opening the door stepped into the long room, after his exertions the room felt incredibly cold.

Ifor was dozing beneath a couple of extra blankets he'd filched off nearby beds, he'd have to give them back tomorrow when the owners returned, but then the communal room would be a bit warmer with the addition of their body heat. He'd kept the old stove burning as best he could though it pained him dreadfully to hobble to it. Rationing what was left of the wood, eking it out until the men returned carrying logs from outside. A necessary evil the extra burdens, but there were no trees to rob on the mountainside.

Pulling himself up in the bed he grunted with discomfort. 'You shouldn't have come all this way up on your day off, Joe.'

Joe's face was pink with fresh air and the exertion of the climb. Opening his bag he pulled out the pie, the bread and tea, putting it down on the long table by the stove.

'I wasn't going to let you starve up here all on your own. You daft bugger.' Rubbing his chilled hands together. 'It's parky in here, Ifor. Are you short of a bit of wood for the stove?'

'Aye, there's hardly any left, I just shoved the last bit on.'

Joe made for the door. 'I'll see what I can find.'

Parched for a decent brew, Ifor struggled off the bed and limped to the stove, putting the almost full kettle on the hot plate. Through the small dirty window pane he watched Joe, hunkered down dragging a few lumps of wood from a small stack beside the door of the nearest barrack. He had no fear that the wood was too wet to burn, it had been protected from the weather by an old cover. The owner of the fuel obviously a provident man.

Joe came in carry several good-sized logs. 'It's a bit like scrumping apples, or poaching a couple of trout out of Bellamy's stream.'

Cheered by Joe's presence, Ifor laughed. 'Don't tell me you intend to nick a couple of prize fish for our dinner.'

Chuckling, Joe stacked the wood by the stove. 'It might be an idea. It's a long time since I had a nice plump fish. I can see it now, sizzling in the pan, shiny with butter and a smattering of salt.'

'Your making me mouth water just thinking about it.'

'Bugger mouth watering, I reckon I can taste the little beauty on me tongue.'

Both recalled past exploits. There was nothing like a bit of poaching to sassy up a man's nerves. Exhilarating, a prowl through the woods after dark, going careful, minding where you placed your boots, no call to alert a keeper to your presence with cracking twigs or worse, snarling an ankle in a vicious man trap.

Wondering how long it might be before Ifor was fit enough to go trapping again, Joe opened the front of the stove, and threw a log in, pushing it down on the red-hot embers. 'We'll have a good blaze going in a minute.'

'I'm right grateful, Joe, there's not many men would traipse up here on their day off.' Ifor's eyes turned to the pie and bread. 'You must thank your Emily for this.'

'Lancashire through and through is Emily. Her meat and tatty pies are beautiful.'

'Of course, Lancashire, that's where you come from, I'd forgotten that. You've been here a long time now Joe, you've almost lost the accent completely.'

'There are times when it comes back as naturally as Welsh rain falling on the mountains.'

Ifor took the singing kettle off the hot plate and poured the boiling water onto the leaves in the pot. He gave Joe a sidelong glance. 'When's that then?'

'Oh, when our Tommy gets me riled, and sometimes when I'm as happy as a lark about summat.'

'You're a lucky man if you still get bursts of joy. A lot to be thankful for, that.' Ifor smiled. 'Joy, that's a wonderful word for you. In English it has a powerful ring to it.' His eyes glinted. 'Equally beautiful in the Welsh tongue, *gorfoledd,* a great triumphal sound. Rejoice it shouts.'

Joe enjoyed Ifor's company, a literary man with a love of poetry and church music, a Welshman through and through. There were scores of men like him working in the sheds, or up here on the rock face, with their own literary societies and eisteddfodau. They might form a tight clique but it didn't mean that they wouldn't welcome a man if he was like minded.

Joe poured out the tea. 'Are you doing a recitation at the eisteddfodau this year? Same as last?'

'Oh no. This year I'm presenting my own poetry. I have a little gem, it took me a while to get it down on paper, but now it's finished I reckon it stands a good chance of being placed. Would you like to hear it? It's in Welsh mind, there's no translation.'

Listening to Ifor's soft, lilting voice, and understanding some of the words, Joe caught the gist but not the full elegance of the poem.

Shortly afterwards Joe left the barracks. Before he started the descent back to the village he looked back and saw smoke whipping from the chimney, and imagined Ifor propped up in a chair by the stove, a book in his hand.

If his injury was no better tomorrow the doctor would be sent for, it was his decision if Ifor would stay or go back to Anglesey on the first available wagon. Joe was hopeful that he would have improved by then, and with a few more days off the leg, he'd be going back home under his own steam come Saturday afternoon.

The wind had picked up, swinging round to the north; there was a bite to it. It was draughty enough for him to raise his coat collar.

On even ground he would have shoved his hands in his coat pocket for warmth, but it was too steep here, the shale underfoot unstable, hard to stay balanced properly.

Far below, Garddryn village nestled in the valley, cottages and houses straggled the single track roadway, a few clung to the hillside, perched higher were smallholding, the boundaries marked out square and neat. As a whole it appeared as small as a child's model toy, fashioned from mossy material and bits of wood.

Plas Mawr was well lit, he could just make out several carriages parked in front of the mansion, there were another two on the avenue, four horses a piece, making progress towards the house.

It was a relief when he was down, the wind had really whipped up and there was an icy edge to it.

Emily heard him on the path, his heavy boots clinking on the stones, he coughed once then again as he lifted the latch and came in.

Emily in the middle of dusting the mantelpiece stopped what she was doing. 'Are you ill, Joe? That sounds like a nasty cough, sweetheart.'

'It's not much, just a bit of a dry tickle that's all.'

She touched his arm, peering up into his face. 'That might be so, but it's better to be safe than sorry. There's a drop of medicine left from when our Tommy was poorly last. Take a spoon of that before your dinner.'

'Aye, I will.'

Putting her palm to his forehead, she felt for signs of a high temperature.

'Don't fuss, Lass. I'm not ill.'

A frown ridged her brow. 'Perhaps it's the dust from the quarry got into your throat.'

He laughed. 'We are not supposed to suffer from such inconveniences, didn't Bertram Bellamy say that he had it on good authority, medical at that, that the dust on the whole was beneficial to the men.' Slumping in his chair he pulled off his boots. 'Aye and I tell tha something else, they'll be saying that for a long time to come. As long as there is a profit to be made out of mining an' quarrying, no medical man will speak up for the health of the poor sods digging at it.'

It was a measure of his irritation that he had dropped into a Lancashire brogue. Determined to give his children a better chance, he had insisted that when they settled in Wales that they would do their utmost to drop their North Country dialect. The children would be educated and not mocked for their simple language.

Glancing at him, Emily was worried. He looked worn out, he was working too hard, either up at the quarry or on the two acres with the animals, there never seemed enough time for him just to sit still.

'Joe, I want you to take a nap after your dinner. Me an' Tommy will put the fowl and pig away.'

'Oh is the lad home?'

Emily sighed. 'No. I've no idea where he is. No doubt he'll come home when he's hungry.'

Frank was hiding behind the ladder-back chair, clutching a book.

Spotting him, Joe smiled. 'Hello, little fellow, I thought that you were playing with your young friend next door.'

'No, Dada, I'm weading.'

Laughing, Joe opened his arms to him. 'You come and sit on my knee and we can read together. You'd like that wouldn't you?

Scrambling up, Frank climbed onto his father's lap. 'You do this page, Dada, then I'll do this one.' His short stubby fingers held the book tightly.

Pulling him close, Joe settled in the chair. 'Once upon a time there was a little boy named Frank...'

'Does it say that, Dada, really?'

Smiling, Joe lied. 'Course it does. Now are you going to let me read this story or what?'

'Wead it to me, wead it.'

'Right, here we go.' He pulled the little chap closer. 'Once upon a time there was a little boy called Frank...'

The child didn't show the promise that his elder brother had at his age, but he had the sweetest nature imaginable. There was no heartache with little Frank; he'd be a good steady worker one-day. Where as Tommy, Lord only knew where the lad would fetch up.

Putting these thoughts aside Joe concentrated on telling the make-believe tale to the boy.

Busying herself with finishing off the dinner, Emily listened to the wondrous story unfolding.

Much later Tommy dashed in; face red from the cold wind that hadn't abated, and if anything had grown steadily worse as the day progressed.

Dozing in the chair, sewing lying abandoned on her lap, Emily jumped, startled as the door banged closed. It took a moment for her to gather her wits. 'Tommy we were just about to send out a search party to find you. Your poor father has been out several times looking for you. Were have you been? It's after nine o'clock.'

Tommy glanced at the door between the scullery and living room. 'Where is he now?'

'Just gone out to the privy. He's not pleased with you. I really don't know what to make of you. Sunday, you'd think that you would spend some time with your family, instead of running off without a word.'

His voice rose. 'I didn't run off. I had things to do.'

Emily frowned in irritation. 'Things that you didn't wish your family to know about. It'll be that young girl Millie, I suppose?' Reaching forward, she stirred the fire.

'No, Mam. It wasn't.' There was nothing his mother could say that would take the edge off his excitement. What a day it had been. Henrietta had been wonderful; spending time with him and sitting beside him during the high tea that was served after the performance. He wanted to escape to his bed so he could go over the events in his mind, relive every special moment. Mr. Bellamy had been especially nice to him, chatting and asking how he was progressing at his other lessons away from Plas Mawr.

The back door closed and the bolt was drawn. Appearing, Joe gave him a small smile. 'Hello, Tommy, you're back safe.'

Dumbfounded, he had expected a row; Tommy nearly stuttered a reply. 'Yes, Dada.'

Closing the scullery door, Joe came into the room, and retrieving the newspaper he had been reading, said lightly 'Have a good time did you?'

'Yes, Dada.'

Sitting, Joe opened the Chronicle at the centre page. 'Good. Had your tea out did you?'

Tommy viewed his parent with suspicion. Looking slightly baffled. 'I had something to eat earlier.'

The paper hid Joe's head. 'Good. Then you'll be ready for bed, a long day at school again tomorrow. Goodnight, son.'

Emily had heard enough of the nonsense; the lad wanted a good talking to. 'Is that all you are going to say to the lad? "Have you eaten and did you have a good time."'

'Yes.'

Indignant, she stabbed a needle through the hem she was sewing. 'I'm surprised at you, Joe.'

He lowered the newspaper to his lap. 'Well I've been thinking about it and decided that if Tommy doesn't want to tell us when he will be in or out, it's his business. If he no longer wishes to confide in us there's not a lot we can do about it. The boy has well passed his fourteenth birthday. At his age I'd been working above three years, and although I had to tell my father where I was going when I was Tommy's age, I don't recall that I resented it. And I would never have dreamt of not telling my mother, I cared for her too much to leave her to worry all day, specially on the Sabbath, when she should have been relaxing a bit, and enjoying her day.' He drew the newspaper up. 'Goodnight, son. Close the door after you.'

Emily turned her head to hide her smile, would Joe never cease to amaze her.

Baffled, Tommy crossed to the stairway door; he looked back at his parents, already engrossed in sewing and reading. He gave a plaintive 'Goodnight,' then went quietly up the stairs.

Emily couldn't suppress a giggle. 'Joe, you old soldier.'

He grinned. 'It might work. God help us nothing else has.'

Lying in bed Tommy tried to listen to the conversation going on downstairs, but could pick nothing up but muffled words. His father's calmness had taken the edge off his excitement, and as much as he tried to recall the events of the day, it all seemed a bit less important. Turning over, pulling the blanket up over his ears to keep out the freezing draught whistling through the old frame of the small window, he fell into a light sleep.

The first days of the week followed the usual pattern, attending lessons at the home of David Davies, a gentleman, who in former years had been a headmaster of a college in London. Returning to his roots he had taken a smart house on the village square, and to safeguard his nest egg, instructed a few of the brighter boys of the district in Greek, Latin, geography and history.

Tommy tolerated attending, the alternative was to go to a school or college, if he could get a scholarship, in Caernarvon or Bangor, but that would mean living in lodging and coming home for weekends only. Thursdays and Fridays at Plas Mawr were too important to him to even suggest such a move.

It was the subject of his thoughts as he strode towards the mansion on this mild, but grey Thursday morning, the weekend after the entertainment in the orangery. The time was fast approaching when he would have to consider his future; it was hanging over him like a sword of Damocles. Next birthday he would be fifteen, too old for school, he would either have to go to college, or begin work. Whichever, it would mean the end of Plas Mawr for him. It was depressing thought.

The footman opened the door on the first peal of the bell, seeing the tall handsome boy on the step, he sniffed, failing to hide the contempt he felt for the twice weekly visitor, Tommy Standish was a nobody, son of a mere quarryman.

Brushing passed him; Tommy hastened towards the sweep of the beautiful flying staircase.

Entering by the front door, and braving the supercilious glare of the footman, was Tommy's choice. It would have been more sensible to use one of the other doorways into the mansion, but Tommy would have none of that. He might come as a visitor now, but one day, if his ambitions were realised, this great house would be his home. No one would ever say that Tommy Standish had used the back door at one time.

Coming into the schoolroom, he discovered Millie adding coal to the burning fire.

Flabbergasted, he yelled, 'What the hell are you doing here?'

She was in the familiar uniform of a female house servant, a maroon dress with a white frilled collar, a white apron, white and maroon cap, and black boots. Millie, anticipating the meeting, but hoping that it would take place at a more desirable location, the back stairs, or an out of the way hallway, was flummoxed to be caught on her knees attending to the fire.

Getting clumsily to her feet, she answered huffily. 'Don't you swear at me, Tommy Standish. I have every right to be here. Mr. Bellamy hired me as a scullery maid when he heard about me troubles.'

Suspicious, his eyes narrowed. 'What troubles?'

Her voice rose. 'What do you mean, what troubles. That I was raped and fired from me job because I had been. I'd say that was trouble enough. But little you care.' Her bottom lip trembled.

Sensing that if he didn't tread carefully there'd be grief for him, Tommy took her in his arms. 'I'm sorry, Millie, it was just such a surprise seeing you bending to the fire there. That's all.'

Glad that he cared, she nestled against him, picking at one of the buttons on his shirt. 'Tommy, why didn't yer come and see me last Sunday?'

A head taller, she fitted beneath his chin. Looking over the lace on her cap, to the wall beyond, and the picture of the mother and child. He spoke softly. 'I couldn't, I had to mind our Frank, me mam's still not too well.'

Against his chest, she smiled, assured that had it been possible he would surely have called. Snuggling closer, the fragrance of him reminding her of their passionate embraces, and his hardness, her voice was husky with arousal. 'Never mind, perhaps this Sunday then.'

'Yeah, why not.' Alerted to hurried footfalls, he released her sharply.

The door flew open and George entered, grinning. Blind to the presence of a servant, he blustered. 'What a great day we had last Sunday, Standish.' His eyes alive with mischief, he chuckled. 'I hope you weren't getting too close to my sister.'

Looking from one to the other, tears beginning to fill her eyes, Millie grabbed the handle of the coal bucket. Forgetting to bob a curtsey, she dashed from the room. Her boots could be heard by the two youths as she clattered down the uncarpeted back stairs.

Tommy glanced once at the slammed door, then turned to George. 'Don't be daft. Your Henrietta's not interested in me.'

Guffawing, George yelled, 'Not interested, are you blind, Standish? The silly young fool follows you everywhere with her great gawking eyes.'

Tommy hid his smile, but his heart raced with excitement. Lying in his bed, walking the quarry, when he was here in Plas Mawr, traipsing the avenue, working on his father's plot of land, there wasn't a moment that he didn't search his brain for a way to make Garddryn quarry and the beautiful house that went with, it his own. It was a magnificent dream and it had been with him as long as he could remember. Wished for, craved, begged the Almighty for this one great thing. It was his sole ambition, the reason he breathed. And it might come to him on a plate.

His flesh tingled, the tiny hairs on his skin rose, his entire being was ready to grasp that which could be his. It was hard to swallow, to keep his voice even, to hide the thrill that was coursing through his bloodstream.

'You mad or what?' There, he'd spoken, and hidden this great and unbelievable moment from prying ears and eyes. He could do it, contain his excitement, plan, plot, and with careful and magnificent strategy, birth his spectacular dream.

Throughout the morning he was on tenterhooks, listening to the sounds of passing feet in the hallway, trying to distinguish if Henrietta passed the door. At noon, the midday meal was delivered by a girl from the kitchen, and eaten as always on the small table in the bay window. The saddle of lamb and vegetables, apple pie and custard was hardly tasted, so intent was he in watching the lawn below, hoping to catch sight of Henrietta crossing the grass. In his imagination she would turn her face to the window and give him a warm, promising smile, and he would respond with a slight wave of his hand. But there was no sighting; disappointed he went back to his desk, waiting for the return of the tutor and a boring lesson of Latin to commence.

Thankfully George sat silently, engrossed in a borrowed book, explicit illustrations of men and women in flagrant acts, between the plain cover. Any other time he would have shared the joke, chuckled over the less than seemly pictures, but his entire thoughts, breath, heartbeat, were consolidated in picturing his future.

The afternoon drew to a close, and although George rushed to be away from the confines of the loathed schoolroom, Tommy held back making a meal of packing away his books and tidying his desk. Surely she would come to him, if only to flirt for a moment. If she did appear what would he do? Seize her passionately? Kiss her lips? Make grand promises? He had no answers to his questions, just a stomach turned to jelly, and a wild picture in his head of Henrietta naked beneath him.

When he no longer had an excuse to delay in the room longer, he walked away, going slowly to the front door, making more than the usual amount of noise leaving the house, bidding the footman farewell in a over loud voice.

Then he was out in the fresh air, his boots scrunching on the gravel. Suspecting that it was all in George's mad imagination that Henrietta really did fancy him.

In his mind's eye he saw hundreds of impressions of her face and mannerisms. The way she had smiled when she caught his eye on the previous Sunday in the orangery cheered him, for surely she did look interested then.

He heard her voice before he spotted her standing between the trees, her green dress blending with the cultivated vegetation. 'Hello, Tommy.' Her smile brightened her otherwise plain face. 'You're later than usual. I was just about to return to the house.'

His heart sang. She had waited for him. Carefully he calculated his words, it was important to give her an impression that he might be interested, but not go too far and make it look as though he was prepared to make a fool of himself over her.

Pitching his voice low, he looked deeply into her eyes. 'Henrietta, I hoped I might see you before I went back to the village.' He made no reference to his poor home. 'I wanted to thank you for your company last Sunday, I really enjoyed myself. I hope that you did too?'

Although she was the elder by a few years, his maturity and height gave him stature.

Now returning his glance, her hand touched the buttons on her bodice. 'It was a lovely afternoon. Perhaps...' Losing confidence her words trailed off.'

Eager to move things on, to get an understanding between them, he finished the sentence for her. 'Perhaps we might do something together this Sunday afternoon?'

Her eyes glittered. 'I'd like that. But Papa...'

Smiling, to ward off any idea that she might have that he was trying to take advantage. 'Who needs to know. I was only suggesting a walk or something.'

She was eager. 'Where can we meet?'

Taking step closer, he felt her breath on his face. 'Do you know the old mill just outside the village on the Llandfydd lane?'

'Yes I do, George and I explored it last summer, it's lovely there.'

'I'll meet you there, around three.'

Her eyes turned to the house. 'I must get back. Don't mention anything to George will you?'

'What do you take me for. I'm good at secrets.' He grinned. 'See you at three.' Lowering his voice until it had a sexiness about it, he said 'I'll look forward to it. Bye, Henrietta.'

She was gone in a second, melting between the trees.

Tommy watched the flutter of her gown, and the leaves of the rhododendron bush fall back into place as she passed. Grinning, he kicked a stone way down the avenue, and curbing a desire to leap into the air, he went on his way. Millie, forgotten until she sidled up to him on the other side of the pedestrian gate.

Her mouth was narrow with spite. 'Got your eye on Miss Henrietta now? I saw you talking to her.' Tears brimmed in her eyes. 'Tommy Standish you are the meanest boy I know.'

Fighting the urge to slap her, he eyed her silently, his brain racing. No way would he allow Millie bloody Barker to ruin his mood, or his future.

Seeing that he meant to ignore her, she lost control of her tears, her mouth gaping in an ugly way. 'You lied to me,' she spluttered, wailing. 'I'm going to tell Twm Williams that it was you in the mill that day. It was you that raped me.' Her nose began to run and she brushed it with the back of her hand. 'And I'll tell Miss Henrietta and Mrs. Bellamy what you did to me. I'll tell them everything is your fault, and that you're not fit company for the fine people of Plas Mawr. I'll crush you, Tommy Standish as sure as you are standing before me.' Her shoulders heaved, and she crumpled forward, tears streaming.

Panic surfaced, for a split second he was at a loss. Then pulling her behind the shield of the bushes, he enclosed her in his arms. 'Millie, please don't cry. Why do you always forget that I love you? Come with me now and let me hold you properly, let me prove it to you.'

Her voice was pitiful. 'Oh, Tommy if only it was that easy.'

Gathering her to him, he looked over her head to the house beyond. He felt like crying himself. What had he done to deserve this wench and her evil intent? She could crush his dreams. Confine him to a lifetime of living in a bloody little hovel like the one his parents had. Keeping a blasted pig, and a few hens to eke out his meagre wages from the bloody quarry. God help him, he couldn't stand that. His mind leapt ahead searching for a solution.

Clutching her shoulders, he shook her gently. 'Millie, please come with me, I want everything to be right between us. Like it was before.'

He had her attention, but she was still eyeing him with suspicion.

Bending his head so that his face was on a level with hers, he searched her wet eyes. 'Millie sweetheart. Let me run home, give Ma a reason why I'm going out, and then I'll be with you. We can go somewhere private. The old mill, wherever...'

Her eyes brimmed with fresh tears. Almost squealing, 'I don't want to go there ever again.'

Flustering, he hadn't anticipated her instability. He tried to calm her. 'That's all right, we can go somewhere else. Anywhere, you choose, just as long as we are alone for a while.'

Sniffing loudly, she had seen his moment of panic and knew that he was afraid of losing her.

Taking her hand, he lifted it to his lips. 'Is your Ma expecting you back home?'

With her other hand she wiped at her tears, sniffing again. 'No, not really. I often go for a walk at this time .She might even think that I have stayed late at Plas Mawr.' Looking carefully into his eyes. 'Why?'

Trying to look happy, he forced a smile. 'Because, darling Millie, I want to spend as much time as I can with you. If no one is expecting you, we will not need to think about the clock for a while.' Touching her breast gently. 'If you race off towards the mill, I'll catch up with you. If you don't want to go too close to the building, wait behind the wall at the far end of the paddock.' His lips brushed hers.

She smiled wanly. Sorry now, that she had said the terrible things to him, threatening him had been unnecessary, he still loved her. When they were alone she would make it up to him, let him do whatever he wanted too. She gave him another small smile, hoping that he would forgive her, she didn't really want to hurt him. With a little giggle, she said, 'You promise you will not be very long, that place gives me the spooks now, after...'

Sweeping a stray hair off her brow, he kissed her wet eyelashes. 'I'll not keep you waiting, I promise. I just need to go to the house for five minutes, see Ma, then I'll be with you.'

'Why can't I come with you?' As soon as the question was out she regretted it.

A look of exasperation crossed his face. Stifling the emotion, he smiled again. Touching the tip of her nose playfully. 'I'll see you near to the mill.'

She tried to give him a smile, and on tiptoe she planted a kiss on his lips.

He patted her rump. 'You go on, Millie. I'll be there shortly.'

For a moment he watched her begin to trot down the lane, ungainly now she'd put on weight.

Several minutes later he flashed into the house, dumping his books on the table; he was back at the door, shouting up the stairs to his mother, 'I'll go and feed the hens and pig and put them away, it'll save Da the trouble when he comes in.'

Without waiting for her reply, he ducked out of the cottage, racing to the two-acre field.

His eyes were looking in the direction that Millie would be waiting. Lifting the latch on the gate he walked gingerly into the pig's domain.

The animal grunted, snuffling at his knees. Coaxing it with an apple he led it into the sty and closed the door sharply.

Glancing over the hens strutting in the dirt, he moved slowly towards them, herding them towards the coop. He felt a pang of remorse that all would have to go without a meal if he was to accomplish anything this evening.

Shutting the gate, he cast his eyes over the land for stray fowl, not that he could afford the time to put them to safety, they'd be a meal for the fox if they were unlucky enough to have been left out.

With a swift glance up and down the lane, and across the sheep filled fields, he raced towards his destination. His heart leaping in his chest, the thudding heard in his ear.

The rushing water of the millstream came to him as he rounded the last bend. Ahead was the dry stone wall, flanked by massive elms, the branches stirring in the breeze. Picturing Millie waiting for him, growing impatient. The nasty threats bubbling in her mind, ready to strike, to obliterate all his hopes and ambitions, to smash into his future life, and leave nothing but the ashes of his dreams.

Taking a deep breath and focusing his mind on the hatred he felt for her, he came to the wall and slowly climbed over it.

Throughout that night sleep evaded Tommy, and it was with a heavy heart and a banging headache, that he dragged himself off the bed and prepared to go to Plas Mawr for his Friday lessons with George.

Ushered into the house by the parlour maid, it being the footman's day off, he saw the bulky figure of Millie's mother in the hallway.

Agitated, her hands wringing in consternation, she flew across to him. 'Tommy have you seen our Millie?'

'Yes, I saw her yesterday morning, stoking the fire in the schoolroom when I arrived. Why?'

'Cos she never came home last night.' Mrs. Barker held a none to clean piece of linen to her nose. 'I can't think what has happened to her. She hasn't been the same girl since that terrible incident a few weeks ago. I just don't know what will become of her, she nothing but a bag of nerves. Can't stay in the house more than a minute at a time.'

Hearing the commotion, Mrs. Bellamy came out of the dining room, her pearl grey morning gown rustling as she crossed to the distraught woman. 'I believe you are looking for Millie?' She should be in the scullery where she belongs.' She looked down her long patrician nose. 'If she has take time off I'll have severe words with her, she has no sooner started working here and she's creating problems.'

Lazily, George sauntered down the stairs, casting an eye to the gathering in the hallway.

His mother called to him. 'George please show Mrs. Barker to the kitchen and enquire of cook if she has seen Millie this morning. Do try to find the blessed girl, otherwise none of us will have any peace.'

Giving her a languid smile, he said, 'Glad to help, Mama. Mrs. Barker do please follow me.'

Muttering, she tagged behind him, explaining to deaf ears her predicament. 'Mr. Barker has gone off looking around the lanes for her, in case she has been taken poorly, or had an accident. Oh, Master Bellamy I am so worried.' They disappeared behind the green baize, covered door.

Slowly, his legs aching with tiredness, Tommy climbed the stairs to the schoolroom.

It was much later, when the candles were lit in Bryn Tirion that the special constable knocked on the door.

Rising from his chair, Joe sighed. 'Who the devil is that at this time?'

Twm Williams filled the doorway as he entered the living room. He glanced first at Tommy then to Emily, who had begun to rise from her chair.

The rough material of his constable uniform stretched across his barrel chest. 'I'm sorry to disturb you, Mrs. Standish, but we are looking for a missing girl. Millie Barker has not been seen since leaving Plas Mawr yesterday afternoon. I want to ask Tommy if he has any knowledge of where the girl might have gone.'

A look of concern crossed Emily's face. 'Why our Tommy? What has he to do wi' it?'

'Nothing probably, but he might know something. The girl's mother is beside herself.'

Putting aside the book she was trying to read, Emily frowned. 'Oh poor women. She's had more than her fair share of heartache of late. Why would Millie run off and give her more?'

Stepping closer to Tommy, Twm Williams hovered over him. 'Do you know anything about this.'

Looking suitably wronged, Tommy's eyes widened in amazement. 'Nothing whatsoever. I saw her yesterday. I told her mother that I saw Millie in the schoolroom at Plas Mawr, she was stoking the fire there when I arrived.'

Twm Willims coughed. 'Did she say anything to you?'

Tommy caught his father's eye. Then looked back to the special constable. 'Nothing, beside that she had a new man friend, and was looking forward to meeting him last evening.'

Twm's face showed interest, there was an unmistakable glint to his eye. 'Did she say who this man was?'

Shoving his hands in his pocket, Tommy spoke as though he understood little of the coming and goings of men and women folk. 'No she said it was a big secret. I didn't ask beyond that.'

'Did she say how long she'd known him?'

'No, nothing was said about that. All she did say was that there was a man in her life and she was going to meet him last evening. That's all, I can't help you more than that.'

Twm glanced around the room. 'Well that might help. I'll see you again if I have more questions. But I expect she'll turn up soon enough with a reason for her disappearance.

Fixing Tommy with a penetrating stare, Twm asked, 'And where were you last evening?'

Emily answered for him. 'Our Tommy came straight home from Plas Mawr. Then he went out to feed the few livestock we keep, he was back here in no time, and spent the evening here in the house. His father can vouch for what I say.' It didn't seem five minutes since the lad was being blamed for the last incident. It was all very unfair, picking on a young lad like Tommy. He might be a rogue at times, but he was far from bad.

Joe took his pipe from the rack by the mantel. 'Aye. Our Tommy was sitting with little Frank when I came in. I was pleased not to have to attend to the animals, as I was very tired.'

Minutes later, Joe saw him out. Coming back into the room he took a spill from the container and put it to the fire, watching it flame, he said 'Do you know more than you're saying, Tommy?'

'No, Dada, honest. It's like I told Twm Williams.'

It was Saturday afternoon before Millie was found, lying behind the wall of the old mill. The doctor examining her body said that the poor girl had been raped and strangled.

The two mystery boys that had been involved in the former incident were again sought, and two boys from a neighbouring village made a hasty retreat from the scene to escape the hangman. The hunt for them went on for several weeks. It was assumed that they had fled to Ireland, or signed on as seamen, and the hunt was called off.

Chapter Twelve

A year had passed since the murder of young Millie Barker, and for all except her family, life had returned to ordinary routine. Occasionally, speculation would rouse the villagers and questions about the disappearance of the two boys; Billy and Henry Beardsey would be raised, had they fled because they were guilty or just plain afraid that justice would not be served.

Tommy Standish was always reticent when the subject sprang up again, and would take himself off to a corner of the Half Way and drink his ale in silence. The men supping at the bar would remember that he had been a special friend of Millie Barker's and they would not intrude on his privacy but sagely shake their heads in sympathy.

Henrietta Bellamy had been stunned by the young scullery maid's murder. Although a year had passed since the outrage, she still felt a morbid fascination when meeting Tommy at the old mill on Sunday afternoons, the mill being so close to where the body had lain. Crossing the grass to the derelict building, she would look across to the wall surrounding the overgrown paddock and remark to Tommy how spooky the place was. Pulling her close he would tell her not to be so silly; there was nothing there now to see. But often she had caught him glancing towards the slab of slate that bore Millie's name and fate, that the Barker's had erected upon the spot.

Henrietta and Tommy had grown close, a secret that they had succeeded in keeping their own. The clandestine meetings at the mill were the highlight of Henrietta's week, to be anticipated with rare joy and recalled with barely concealed passion. So far they had been careful and though their kisses and intimate caresses had come very close to being consummated, she had so far managed to keep his desire within acceptable bounds. But she was afraid that if she didn't succumb soon he would leave her for a girl that would. There were many young women waiting to catch Tommy, he was handsome, strong, and intelligent.

Now lying together on the mill floor, Henrietta her bodice open and young breast exposed and her lacy drawers unbuttoned, listened to Tommy's whispered words upon the needs of a virile youth. Nibbling her ear, his fingers inched up her thigh to the soft moist flesh of her sex. Instinctively she tried to push his hand away. Shushing her, coaxing gently, he calmed her and his fingers began again to explore.

Shifting slowly, he eased his body onto hers and began to kiss her passionately. Tired of the teasing, his lower belly taut and aching for release, his desire ready to explode, he knew that she desired him as much as he needed her, he unbuttoned his trousers. A second later he pushed into her and the breath left his body in a loud groan of pleasure.

Henrietta cried out in surprise and pain. Her first thought was to her virginity, the second to pregnancy, and overriding both sudden concerns was the image of her angry father striding into the dank water mill.

Above her, Tommy moved slowly, murmuring gentle words of love. Brushing her mouth with his lips.

The honeyed words calmed her, and like steam in a hot room the notion of an enraged parent vanished, and there was just her and Tommy and he was moving inside her, awakening new and exciting sensations in the secret places of her body.

Instinctively she began to move her hips matching the rhythm of his slow strokes.

Pleased at her response he smiled, looking into her open eyes he whispered her name, and then with the tip of his tongue explored the soft flesh of her inner lips.

Above them, the dying light of evening shone through a gash in the broken roof, burnishing his hair with the tints of the setting sun. It would be a picture and a moment she would remember forever, but for now she thrilled in the love she had for Tommy Standish.

Henrietta had been missing for hours; her father paced the library at Plas Mawr, his mood veering between anger and panic as the hours slipped by. He called for George who had spent most of the day in his room recovering from a monumental hangover. The moment that George appeared Bellamy's concern for his daughter turned to outrage, that one child should be so thoughtless and the other, George, profligate, was a reproach on his parenting. Blustering with anger he resolved to save them from the rising tide of their depravity. George would go to college and Henrietta would be married into a suitable family.

George took the news badly, beginning to shout until it hurt his head and disturbed his stomach too much. Putting his case badly he moved around the room like a demented child, then slumped in a chair, legs outstretched, his voice raised and argument flawed. College wasn't for him, what could he learn there that the revered tutor hadn't already taught him, that his father had paid for all these years. A grand tour he tried to convince his irate listener, would be much more beneficial and definitely a sight more educational than some stuffy old college.

Bellamy would not be moved, and although the scene had taken his mind off his wilful daughter for a moment, it was pulled back with a jolt as she appeared in the doorway, dishevelled, and with a rosy glow that told a tale of mischief.

Jumping out of his chair he stormed towards her. 'And where might you have been, young lady?'

Unprepared for the parental onslaught, she had no rehearsed reply. Muttering something under her breath, she turned to leave the room.

Grasping her arm he drew her roughly toward him, his face close enough for his hot breath to fall upon her cheek. 'Not so fast, my girl, we have things to discuss.'

Listlessly she tried to escape his hold. 'Not now, father, I'm tired.'

Shaking his head in fury, his white hair flopping about his forehead. 'Tired. I'm not surprised. By your appearance I would say that you have been up to no good.'

There was fragment of straw in her hair, plucking it out he held it up. Face red with rage, he landed a vicious slap on her cheek.

Crying out, her hand came up to cover the mark already visible.

With no compassion or sorrow for the injury he had inflicted, the first ever on his beloved daughter, he thrust her aside, bellowing, 'Go to your room, you hussy. Don't come out again until I say that you may.' His eyes narrowed maliciously, dark lips specked with spittle. 'Be warned, Henrietta I will have my way. You'll stay there until I have discussed with your mother whom you will marry. And I warn you; I'll have no stupidity of a long engagement.' Glancing at her belly, he smirked cruelly. 'I'll be surprised if there isn't another reason to see you married off. You brazen, madam.'

Roaring loud enough to be heard in the kitchen at the back of the mansion. 'Now go, get out of my sight.'

Sobbing, Henrietta fled to the shelter of her room. Slamming the door she put her back against it. Everything was ruined; the day had been so beautiful. Tommy loved her. They had stayed late at the old mill to make love again. Now, hours later, her father wanted her to marry a despicable stranger. She wanted Tommy and no one else. Her father would never allow her to marry the man she wanted too. Wailing into her hands, she cursed the family that understood nothing of love.

After spending a day alone in her room, Henrietta not the least contrite but very miserable was brought by her mother to join her father in his study.

He was looking grave, his eyes watery from the beginning of a head cold. 'Your mother and I have decided who should be approached as a likely candidate as a husband for you.' Lifting his hand as his daughter began to interrupt him. 'His family will be in possession of my letter in the next day or so. I have invited them to join us for the weekend after next. So you, my girl have time to brighten yourself up, get fitted for a new gown or two.'

Henrietta began to weep again.

Coming to her side her mother held her arm. 'Now, now, Hen' darling, don't take on so. Your father knows what is best for you.' She clicked her tongue seeing the wan look on Henrietta's plain face. 'The young man is very suitable. His family connections are impeccable. Everything will turn out fine.' She brushed a lock of hair from her daughter's hot brow. 'Believe me, Henrietta, it's all for the best.'

Raising her blue taffeta skirt above her ankles, Henrietta fled from the room. Aggrieved, Bertram Bellamy looked across to his wife. 'Well you would think that she might have taken the time to find out who the man is. After all the trouble I have gone too.'

Snuffling into a clean handkerchief, he ignored his wife's reply and went on regardless, 'I'll have George settled at college, and that young Madam married off before the summer holiday, as God is my witness.'

Mrs. Bellamy reached out to him, clutching the arm of his brown jacket. 'Now, now, Bertram dear, don't take on so. You'll make yourself ill with all this fuss and bother.'

Face twisted in a scowl, he shrugged her off. 'I am ill you, silly woman. It's this dratted family that makes me so.' Gripped by a fit of coughing, he slumped into the nearest chair.

Patting his back ineffectually, Louis Bellamy tried to soothe him, coax him into a better humour. Although her efforts were doomed to failure she persisted with her gentle caresses. 'Dear, Bertram, do please try to be calm, if only for me, dear. You know how desperately unhappy I become when you're upset.'

Ignoring her efforts he proceeded to curse the day that he had sired such ungrateful children.

The servants bore the brunt of the family altercation. The butler delivering brandy and water to the wearied man was castigated for slowness and general slovenliness. Upstairs, Henrietta imagining that her maid found the family argument a source of amusement lambasted the girl for her impertinence, threatening to have her removed from Plas Mawr as soon as she could be replaced with a more devoted female. Tearful, the maid hurriedly descended the back stairs to the relative sanctuary of the kitchen, where the other servants had gathered to gossip and exchange information over numerous cups of tea.

The unsatisfactory state of affairs ruined the day; the occupants of the household, servants included, retired at the end of it with a great sense of relief that the long and tumultuous hours had finally come to an end. When all the lamps and candles were extinguished the house settled into an uneasy stillness.

Outdoors, the air was wet with passed rain, a crescent moon rode high behind thin, ink-black clouds. The mansion an indigo silhouette appeared brooding as though protecting itself against the disruptive humanity within.

Eventually, a grey, wet day slowly dawned, the trees and vegetation of the garden detached one from another as the shadows perished, mountains and sky separated, no longer the one dark mass of the night, the sea draped in mist remained a mystery and would do so until midday.

Servants rising early braced themselves for another day of calamity. Soon, spirals of smoke rose from the chimneys, and the aroma of meat frying escaped from the open kitchen door.

Bertram was the first of the family to rise.

Louis made a habit of breakfasting in her bedroom, attended by her personal maid who remained until her mistress's bath had been made ready.

George, nursing another hangover kept his head well buried beneath a goose feather pillow, obliterating the noise of the house stirring.

Henrietta, determined to sulk for a few more hours nursed her grievances alone in her room with only a book for entertainment, which for the moment was discarded in preference to making mental lists of her family's flaws, and past misdemeanours.

It was left to Bertram Bellamy, sitting down to a lone breakfast, to receive the reply from the college and the letter accepting the invitation to visit from the prospective in-laws of his daughter.

Eventually, unable to stand her own company for another moment, Henrietta went in search of her mother or father. Upon learning that the chinless wonder, Archibald Howard was the candidate for her hand, Henrietta flew into a rage. Refusing to be measured for new gowns 'For what use would they be to her in a convent?' she demanded of her distraught and aggravated mother.

Henrietta's resentment was minor when compared to George's very major temper tantrum on discovering that he was to attend Godfrey College in Berkshire as soon as his kit could be purchased and his bags packed.

The following day was much the same with arguments and tears prevailing. Several of the younger staff threatened to leave their employ if thing were to go on like this, but the threats were only heard by other employees in the sanctuary of the warm kitchen.

It wasn't until the approach of the weekend and the imminent arrival of the Howards that the servants became too busy to give much thought to the warring family.

Escaping the house and the miserable atmosphere Henrietta snatched a few moments alone with Tommy, so taken with her own distress she forgot to tell him of the imminent change in George's circumstances.

Blind to the upheaval coming his way, Tommy placated the tearstained and often bad-tempered young woman, promising that whatever happened he would find a way for their love to continue.

George ranted daily, but to no avail. The following week found him in a first class carriage on a train heading south. Leaving his father in Chester to make the difficult return journey to North Wales alone.

Climbing aboard the train George discovered that a young lady and her attractive maid were to share the carriage with him, instantly his mood improved. With a large increase in his allowance to ensure that comforts he may desire in his enforced college life were affordable, he began to look forward to making new friends.

The Howards' visit was an unmitigated disaster. Henrietta had joined the guests on only one occasion for dinner in the dining room, and thereafter sent her maid to inform her mother that she was too unwell to attend further entertainment.

The Howards, thankful when the time came to depart, did so sourly. Striking the Bellamy family off future lists of engagements. Thankful to retreat with their young and impressionable son intact and with no marriage arranged with such a surly girl, they bowled down the avenue, the four horses drawing their carriage at full tilt.

Upon their departure Henrietta had suffered an appalling interview with her mother and father, after which she retreated to the woods to sit in peaceful silence contemplating her blissful future life. For surely they were not foolish enough to try to marry her off again to someone she abhorred? She would consent to one man and one man only. Although she might have to wait until he reached his maturity to do so.

Unaware of the changes Tommy arrived at Plas Mawr for lessons on the following Thursday. Draycott, the footman smirked, looking down his long nose at the young man stepping over the threshold.

Ignoring him, Tommy brushed passed, heading for the wide staircase.

Behind him the elaborately uniformed servant coughed lightly into his gloved hand. 'Standish, the Master wishes for you to join him in the library.'

Tommy's brow lifted in surprise. Without replying he walked

down the long hallway between the dark portraits of Bellamy family members, their painted eyes following him as he went towards the oak door. Stomach fluttering with apprehension.

Knocking he waited for the gruff voice of Bertram Bellamy to bid him enter.

When it came, he took a deep breath and opened the door.

His benefactor was sitting behind the large desk; a high backed chair dwarfing him. Glancing over the top of his spectacles, the elderly man waved Tommy in. 'Don't let a draught in, lad, come if you're coming.'

'Yes, sir.' In the large, impressive room, walking towards the handsomely sized partners' desk, Tommy felt about five years old and no taller than three feet tall. Meeting Mr. Bellamy's eyes he tried to fathom why the man had summoned him. He hoped to God that it was nothing to do with him seeing his daughter, if it was, it would be the end of his lessons, end of the cherished visits to Plas Mawr. Jesus why had he been so stupid? Why couldn't he leave well enough alone? Why did he have to chase every piece of skirt that came his way?

Bertram Bellamy looked tired, harassed; the lines around his eyes were deeper, like strokes from an artist's over burdened brush. Sighing, he cleared his throat before speaking, the recent cold he'd suffered still evident. 'Take a seat, Tommy, I have several things I wish to discuss with you.'

'Yes, sir.' Straightening his shoulders Tommy pulled himself up to his full height and crossed to the desk, back straight he sat opposite the imposing man.

Their eyes met.

Mr. Bellamy cleared his throat again. 'Standish, there has been a change within my home.'

The breath that left Tommy lungs did so noisily. The sense of relief that this was nothing to do with him and Henrietta was exquisite. This was just a routine information meeting…He interrupted his own line of thought – why would Bellamy inform him of anything unless…

In the next second Bellamy delivered a blow to Tommy that the boy thought he might never recover from. Speaking quickly and precisely, he said, 'George has departed Plas Mawr for Godfrey College in Berkshire.' A small self-satisfied smile spread his lips. Linking his podgy fingers he rested them on his corpulent midriff. 'A superb establishment and one that I hope he accomplishes a great deal in. He will not return until end of term. I have informed the tutor that his services are no longer required. So that brings an end to our arrangement. I do hope that you feel that you have benefited by the years spent in the schoolroom at Plas Mawr.'

The news rendered Tommy speechless. It was like being hit with a quarry shovel, the air stopped moving in his body and he was aware that his bowels had turned to water. Stuttering a reply, inaudible even to himself, he moved in the seat and began to rise.

Bellamy waved him down. 'I haven't finished yet.'

The water moved and Tommy was forced to clench his buttocks. He knew about him tupping Henrietta. Feeble words rose in his throat, bumbling excuses forming in his brain. She had plagued him. Followed him with her eyes. Made the running, and arranged to meet him at the mill. Oh Jesus, the mill. Dark-secrets unfolding in his mind released a black fog. The eyes he lifted to Bertram Bellamy's face were full of fear.

Bellamy lowered his voice, 'I have thought about your future, it would be a pity to waste all the education I have bestowed upon you, so what I propose is that you work for me in the quarry.'

A savage dart of pain caught him beneath the ribcage as he pictured himself with a coarse rope looped around his thigh, hanging over the great precipices of the Garddryn, his father dangling beside him grinning with encouragement as they hacked at the immense and nearly indestructible slate cliff together. Drenching rain and a howling gale swinging them away from the rock face. Then the dreadful cabanod high up on the galleries, the men congregating in the crowded and noisy shelter, wet clothes stinking in the heat from the stove. Oh, not for him, that hard, arduous, crippling serfdom.

Without conscious thought he looked down to the palms of his hands, soft, unblemished, slightly pink from the warmth of the room. Unmarked by scars, callous, or dry-flaking skin, like his father's were. Tears of self-pity welled in his eyes.

Believing the boy to be upset by the passing off his boyhood and the beginning of employee, employer status, Bellamy was slightly amused. 'It's not so bad is it, Standish? Earning a living. Think of the help you will be to your parents. No doubt they'll welcome a wage from you. They have been good enough to support you during all these years of extra education. Most boys of your age have been working several years by now.' He grinned. 'So come on, cheer-up, let' s talk of the future.'

'Yes, sir.' Tommy doubted that he would ever feel cheerful again.

Reaching over to the side of the fireplace Bertram pulled the bell-cord to ring for a servant. A moment later the butler opened the door and stepped in.

Sharp with the household staff, as he thought all diligent masters should be, he commanded, 'Bring the Madeira and two glasses.'

'Yes, sir.' Bowing out, the servant cast a suspicious look at the back of Tommy's head. There was no good in the lad. Too big for his boots, thought that he was bigger and better than anyone else. There'd come a time when the young upstart would get his comeuppance. But by all accounts it wasn't to be today, not if the Master was asking for two glasses. What was the world coming too when the sons of working men drank Madeira in the library of their betters? Closing the door quietly, he went for the less than best wine.

With the rich wine warming his stomach, Tommy began to feel a little hopeful. Bellamy wasn't feeding him Madeira so that he could go and work at the rock-face. That job would hardly be cause for such celebration or a shared drink.

His boss, for now it looked like that was who he was to become, twirled the rich liquid round in the glass.

Peering over the rim of his spectacles he watched Tommy's face for any reaction that would mark him down as ungrateful. 'Monday next there'll be a job for you in the office. It hasn't gone unnoticed the diligence you've put into your lessons.'

Leaning forward, his eyes staring into Tommy's as though to read his thoughts and ferret out any possibility of future betrayal. 'I expect your loyalty in return for the investment I have put into your learning.'

'And you will have it, sir.' It was much better than he had expected, at least it was a clerical position, far removed from the rock-face. The earlier fear hadn't dissipated entirely, he felt as though he was recovering from a very serious illness, fragile and tired. He took another mouthful of the wine and felt the warmth crawl to his stomach.

Picking up the decanter and eyeing the contents Bellamy poured more into his near empty glass, then offered the decanter to Tommy. 'Before you begin in the office I want you to accompany me to Penryhn Castle. Edward Pennant is showing the place off. There is also a jaunt to his quarry arranged.' An expression of cunning flitted across his face. 'You might pick up a few pointers as how he makes such a vast profit from the place.'

Expecting Tommy to make a reference to the other sources of the man's income, he went on quickly less he should appear not to have the full facts. 'I know a great bulk of the family fortune comes from sugar.' Dropping his voice conspiratorially. 'Not much is disclosed about the other side of the business though. We'd make a handsome profit at the Garddryn if we didn't have to pay for labour.' He chuckled. 'See us can you Tommy, rounding up a lot of Blacks an' forcing 'em into quarrying?'

Still chuckling he began to sip the Madeira, eyes sparkling with amusement. 'I expect you to remain alert, garner what information you can. We won't be the only ones there with quarry interests, Thomas Assheton Smith, if he can tear himself away from his yacht, is expected. Pennant and he are old friends.'

Tommy's mind was whirling, yachts, castles, fine estates and only moments before he'd imagined himself swinging above the quarry precipice on a stout rope.

Bellamy's voice interrupted his images of grandeur. 'If you haven't suitable attire for the occasion take something from Master George's dressing room, my valet will attend to you there.'

Tommy gave a thought to the great divide between abject despair and joy, it might seem a million miles, but it had taken only a few moments to cross the vast distance.

Within the hour Tommy accompanied Bellamy to the Garddryn offices to meet the people he would be working with. From there the carriage took them to the bank for a meeting and luncheon with the manager. Throughout the afternoon he listened intently as deals were struck, promises made, money accumulated.

Back at Plas Mawr, as the afternoon was drawing to a close, brandy was served in the library; toasts to the future were made in front of a roaring fire for the weather had turned dismal.

Finishing a second brandy Tommy placed the bulbous glass on a side table. Dinner for the family must be imminent, and as he had no wish to run into Henrietta and her mother he began to take his leave. Lifting his coat from the chair where it had lain all day, how long ago it seemed since he had walked into this room. By some strange alchemy he had aged ten years in as many hours, attitude, demeanour and standing in Garddryn society had taken a new direction, his youth had ceased in a flash. His mother might not recognise that he'd reached manhood but he'd have endorsement from all others.

Bellamy pulled the cord near to the mantelpiece to summon a servant. When a man in house livery appeared bowing from the waist as he entered the room, Bellamy ordered brusquely. 'Have the brougham brought to the door. Mr. Standish is to be driven home.'

Draycott's jaw dropped. His eyes flashed from Bertram Bellamy, now standing, to Tommy Standish who had a new air of arrogant authority about him.

It was on the tip of the servant's tongue to say something, it may have been to question his employer's command, but the steely glint in Tommy Standish's eyes silenced him before he had uttered a syllable

Closing the door quietly, Draycott stood for a moment in the hall, catching his master's muffled words.

'Did you think I would allow my new under-manager to walk to the village when he can ride in style? It'll give the lazy blighter in charge of the stables something to do, and when he returns he'll go straight to the kitchen to gossip. Everyone will learn of your new status and treat with you with respect, which is important.'

Minutes later the brougham stood at the main door, an elegant black horse in the traces tossing its head in anticipation of an outing. The footman, aware that Mr. Bellamy was probably watching from the library window, trotted quickly towards the carriage and pulling the door open stood to attention waiting for the passenger.

Appearing, Tommy stood for a moment poised on the threshold of the front door pulling on his gloves, glancing down the avenue as though it were his own personal possession.

The servants, both driver and footmen averted their eyes unable to countenance the meteoric rise in Tommy Standish's fortune.

Slowly he descended the steps to the gravel drive and with a small smile playing on his lips he climbed into the vehicle. The footman clicked the door closed and sniffing walked slowly back up the wide steps to the front door. His thoughts were his own for now, but he proposed to air his grievances at the first opportunity. Still sniffing he made his way to the servant's quarters.

Tommy contained the urge to laugh out loud as the door closed but he couldn't hide his smile as the carriage moved quickly down the avenue, the roll of the wheels and the beat of hooves on the shale were like sweet music to his ears. The familiar trees and groups of shrubs seen through the small window appeared more stately, grander seen from the vantage point of a carriage. He thought of the stones he'd kicked and the mud he'd let fly as he raced beneath them to and from the house. Passing through the high gates he turned his eyes to the elaborate arch above and recalled the first time he had walked beneath it, his young mind filled with awe. Now, today, he was a large step nearer to his goal; it had been almost a lifetime ambition. Careful planning, patience and animal cunning would take him to his final and glorious step. Plas Mawr would be his, and sooner than he had dared to hope for.

Turning onto the lane the carriage slowed then picked up speed, the horse's hooves beating a tattoo on the hard packed road.

Minutes later he ordered the driver to stop and alighting he bade the man goodnight. He had no wish to be dropped outside his home, neither wishing to alert his parents to his stylish arrival or allow the man who had driven him to observe the simple pleasure they might display.

Turning at a nearby farm gate, the carriage began the short journey back to Plas Mawr.

Standing on the wet grass verge Tommy watched it until it disappeared into the grey mist. Then for the last time he turned towards home.

Joe was soaking in the zinc bath, sitting with his knees up to his chin, a cake of coarse household soap held in his hand, inspecting the wound above his knee.

Emily taking the kettle off the hob left it to stand in the hearth. Glancing down at the raw injury, she clicked her tongue. 'That looks really nasty, our Joe. Perhaps you should visit the doctor, let him have a look at it.'

'I'll wait for a day or two, if it's no better by then I'll go. No need to throw good money away visiting the doctor when there's every chance it'll right itself.'

'Yer health's important. You should go.'

Sighing, he trickled bath water over the injury to soothe and cleanse it. 'Aye, an' I will if it's not better by Monday.'

Sitting at the table, Frank was flipping through a book, the room almost too dark to see the pictures clearly. Without looking up, he said, 'Can I light a candle, Mam?'

She glanced up quickly from rubbing soap over Joe's shoulders. 'Don't you dare play with fire, our Frank. I'll light it in a minute when my hands are dry.'

The household soap was virtually sudless what little lather she could raise she spread across his broad back. The paleness of his skin never failed to astonish her it was such stark contrast to his neck, which was dark mahogany, as were his face and lower arms. She would have liked to kiss the small nub of bone at the base of his neck where dark skin met pale, but Frank's presence stopped her. Sighing, she cupped her hand and scooping water rinsed away the suds. Handing him the soap to finish the parts of him that were submerged, she rose, her knees creaking, and wiped her hands on her apron.

Glancing at Frank, his head still in the book, she smiled, he'd be no bookworm her Frank, it was the small pictures that held his attention, the written word escaped him as it did her. Often she would sit with a book and try to fathom the mystery but it was beyond her ken to read more than twenty simple words. Joe would have to try harder in teaching their son if he were to do anything remotely as clever as Tommy.

As though her thoughts of him were strong enough to conjure him out of thin air, her elder son bowled through the door, the draught nearly extinguishing the flaming spill in her hand as she lit the candle.

Tall enough to need to duck beneath the wooden lintel, he stepped into the room. It didn't take the glow from the fire or the light from the candle to see his face shining with excitement.

Blowing out the spill, Emily smiled. 'Tommy lad you look as thrilled as a girl on her wedding day.'

Grinning, he slipped out of his coat. 'Don't be daft, Mam. How could I look like a lass?'

Joe laughed. 'Em' you do say the funniest things. Like a lass on her weddin' day, indeed.'

Frank giggled. 'Our Tommy's not a girl, Mam.'

Flustered, she smiled. 'You all know what I mean. He just looks very cheerful.'

Joe began to rise from the now cool water, the wound on his leg seeping pink watery rivulets.

Holding a thin towel for him Emily covered his private parts. She was uncomfortable when he was exposed to the boys. Though if she should mention it Joe would castigate her for being silly, weren't they all men together, he'd say. And of course she would have to agree with him, but there was a portion of Joe that she considered should not be revealed, it had more to do with her married state and the intensely private time they shared together. As though by being exposed himself he revealed this secret also.

Hurrying to a cupboard she found a piece of clean cotton rag. Folded it would make a firm dressing.

Glancing at the wound, Tommy's nose wrinkled in disgust. 'How did you do that, Da?'

Patting his leg dry, Joe inspected the damage. 'A lump of rock came down, caught me a right wallop.'

'It looks nasty. You should go and see the doctor.'

'Aye, I know.'

Kneeling, Emily gently applied a thick ointment. 'Couldn't you get a job in the sheds, Joe? Splitting or dressing slate would be safer than being on the galleries.'

The pungent mixture stung, wincing he spoke through clenched teeth. 'Craftsmen's work that is. A man has to be born to it. Like father like son.'

She caught his eye. 'But you could try, Joe.'

'No, Emily I couldn't. I wouldn't have a cat in hell's chance of getting work in the sheds. Such jobs aren't for the likes of me, I'm a miner at heart, not a bloody craftsman.'

'I know, sweetheart.' Sighing she rose. 'Get dressed. Then take the weight off that leg. I'll have the supper on the table in no time.'

Reaching for his combinations airing by the fire, he began to dress. 'I'm so hungry, I could eat a scabby cat.'

There was a trace of amusement in her voice. 'Every chance yer might. Who's to know what we're buying at the local shop.'

He laughed. 'Maisy Lloyd might like to make a profit, she's a real chancer but she'd not go that far.'

'Let's hope not.'

Finding the silly humour embarrassing Tommy slumped in a chair beside Frank.

The boy didn't look up, used to being ignored by his elder brother, or worse, pinched or shoved for being around, he kept his head in the book listening to the cheerful banter going on.

The bath disposed off and the wet towel put to air, Emily brought the pan of steaming stew from the hot plate. Her eye was on Joe, in spite of his claiming that his leg was fine she had noticed the grimace of pain that crossed his face as he stood and limped to the table.

'It's worse than you are letting on, isn't it?' She didn't mean to be sharp, it was just her way when she was worrying or nervous.

'It'll be fine, Emily.'

'Tomorrow you get yourself down to the doctor, and whilst you're there get him to look at that cough of yours.'

Joe's eyes turned to the ceiling. 'How's the man going to look at me cough?'

As he settled in a chair, placing his leg gingerly beneath the table, she gave him a nudge with her knuckle. 'Less of your cheek. You know what I mean. Let him look at your chest.'

Frank had been silent for several minutes. Skewering a lump of meat on his fork, he eyed it suspiciously. 'Is it really cat, Mam?'

She answered him brusquely. 'No of course not, it was a joke.'

'I only wondered because Mrs. Griffiths cat, Toby, has been missing for nearly a week.'

Emily drew in her breath noisily. 'It's not Toby or any other cat. It's meat like we always have, from Maisy Lloyd's shop.'

'But you said...'

'Eat your dinner, son.' Amused, Joe tried to sound serious. 'Cat indeed. Just your mother's fancy that's all.'

'You sure?'

Noisily, Tommy dropped his fork onto his plate. 'For pity's sake, stop it, Frank. You'll put us all off eating it.'

'Sorryeee. But I was only asking.'

Tommy's eyes narrowed. 'Well stop it.'

'Boys that's enough. Give your mother a bit of peace at suppertime.'

Picking up his fork, Tommy pointed it at Frank. 'Can he go to bed early?'

Joe sighed. 'No he can't. Stop arguing and eat your meal.'

Frank's face lit. 'Seeeee.'

Joe gave the boy a hard look. 'Don't you start. Or else…'

The meal continued in silence, with Frank giving as many grins as he thought he could get away with before annoying his father, or seriously arousing Tommy's temper.

Joe, curious to discover Tommy's obvious news, and mildly aggravated by Frank's silly behaviour sent the lad off to bed at the first opportunity.

The small protests and loud muttering finally ceased when Joe standing at the stairway door called for quiet, and sounding as though he actually meant to be obeyed. Closing the door he sat in his chair by the fire and began to fill his pipe.

'Well now that little beggar's settled, you can tell us what had you lit like a lamp, earlier.'

Tommy inched the kitchen chair closer to the fire. Failing to hide his elation as he explained Bertram Bellamy's plans and all that had happened that day.

Joe listened with mixed emotions, pride that his son's hard work and determination was to be rewarded, and foreboding. As much as he cared for the boy, he was aware that he was capable of abusing power. There was a ruthless streak in Tommy, and a determination to succeed at any cost. At the back of his mind, he was too good a father to allow the misgiving to be spoken, was how his own working life would be affected. The men he worked with might not take to kindly to the father of a boss working alongside them.

Emily was thrilled, but apprehensive. Afraid that Tommy would make a show of himself at Penrhyn Castle. What clothes was he going to wear? How would he manage for money, should he need pennies in his pocket?' Only a few days were left to her to get his clothes ready, washed, dried and ironed and his shirts white enough to wear in the company of the gentry.

The following morning Joe rose at the usual time, but putting a foot to the floor he realised that his leg would not allow him to walk to the quarry and do a day's work there.

Emily stretched out her hand to touch him and found the place empty. Opening her eyes she saw him sitting on the edge of the bed. 'What's wrong, Joe? Is it your leg?'

Lifting the blanket he got beneath it. 'Aye you could say that. I'm not able to manage work today, Lass.'

'Oh, Joe, how bad is it?'

'It'll be alreeght. Give it a day or two and I'll be as reeght as rain.'

Pulling her shawl off the end of the bed, where it was used as a cover to warm their feet, she rose quickly. 'I'll get our Tommy to mind the pig and fowl. Then he can run up to the quarry and tell Tom that you'll not be there today.'

Joe sounded weary. 'Aye, Lass you do that.'

Tommy wasn't to be found in his small room, the blankets on the bed had been pulled back neatly and the tiny space was tidy. Expecting to find him in the living room, Emily went down the stairs. His coat was missing from the hook and for a moment she thought him in the privy outside, but when several minutes went by and he hadn't appeared she went out to check, but there was no sign of him.

Tommy had left at first light, planning to hitch a ride on David's cart. David often left the village early to get to market with butter and cheese from his mother's small dairy. There was a stash of money in his pocket, won from George. George was a bad poker player; his face to open and full of expression when he had a good hand and equally readable when he had a bad one. Taking his cash had been like taking sweets from a bairn. Now the money would be put to good use, for he intended to purchase new clothes and a leather bag fit to take to Penrhyn. Bellamy's offer of George's clothes had been turned down, how could he carry himself with pride in another man's attire; he'd feel like a sham, a poor relation. George's money won over many months would be ample to kit him out respectably and for him to rent rooms near to the quarry. He'd done with Bryn Tirion and the meagre lifestyle of his family.

He heard David's cart before he saw it rounding a bend in the road. Hailing him he climbed aboard. Listening to the man's chatter and the beat of the horse's hooves, he thought of the style of clothes that might be purchased today and what he would instruct the tailor to make.

Emily dressed quickly, and without a word to Joe that their son was already away from the house, and therefore unable to run the errand to the quarry or tend the livestock, went to release the pig and hens herself.

Crossing the small field, her boots sinking and squelching in the wet soil, the heavy bucket rattling in her hand, she cursed her elder son for his uncaring attitude. Although he knew that his father was unlikely to be fit enough to attend to this chore; he'd taken himself off without a bye or leave. Thoughtless young man, off like a shot and nary a word to anyone. Pity the wife that got caught with him, she'd not know from dawn to dusk what the bugger was up too.

Opening the gate, she glanced at the pigsty, a great lout of an animal he'd grown into, he'd trample anyone to get to his feed. He wasn't to be trusted, very much like someone else that wasn't very far from her thoughts.

Temper rising, she lifted the hatch for the hens. Out they trotted, neatly, politely waiting for the one before them to clear the small opening, so feminine and careful. So unlike, she glanced once more at the sty, the bugger that would trounce her as quickly as look at her.

Lifting the bucket she filled the trough, then making her way across the quagmire, she stood prudently to one side of the door and pulled the thick bolt. As predicted out came the beast at a fast trot, scattering the hens, dashing towards his food. Emily, making a quick escape before his nose lifted from the mush in his trough, ran as fast as the wet ground permitted, to safety. Out of harm's way she saw the silliness of being so nervous. Resting her arms on the top of the gate she watching the pig snaffling his grub. She laughed. If she hadn't got Joe to worry about, it would seem like quite a nice day. Tommy forgotten, she made her way back to the house. The sun was climbing over the mountain, with luck it might be a fine enough day to dry the mire in the pigpen and air yesterday's washing.

Friday morning and the streets of Caernarvon were busy with shoppers. Tommy had already picked out a tailor to visit; often he had admired the lengths of cloths displayed in the small shop window on Castle Street.

Shortly after nine o'clock he entered the establishment. An hour later equipped with clothes to get him through the days and evening at Penrhyn, and measured for a further suit to be made ready before the end of the month, he walked towards the Black Boy public house. He would dine in style, and call for his parcels later.

Mid-afternoon, replete, he walked to the market place where he expecting to cadge a ride back to Garddryn. With luck he would be in plenty of time to look over rooms that had recently become vacant near to the doctor's house. Close enough to Plas Mawr and the quarry to make both places easily accessible in any weather.

The lift went according to plan, and arriving back in the village he went straight to the house where the rooms were advertised.

The accommodation was luxurious in comparison to the damp and small bedroom at Bryn Tirion. Putting his new clothes in the wardrobe and setting his comb and personal things on the dressing table, he looked around this first room of his own. His mind went back to the day that his father had built the partition to make two rooms out of one. Frank had been barely a few days old and squalling night and day. The sound loud enough to invade his head as he tried to sleep in his narrow bed.

Now all that had changed. There was no more of Frank's whining to tolerate. House rules were a thing of the past, as was helping with the blasted pig and hens; all the troublesome chores had ceased. The endless stews his mother concocted, never would he eat another during his lifetime.

Falling onto the bed, feeling the soft mattress sink beneath his weight, he grinned up at the ceiling. He was free to run his own life. Only one last task to accomplish, tell his mother and father that he had left home. They ought to be pleased that at last they had the little stinker Frank out of their bedroom.

Joe wasn't pleased, his face set in a scowl he said that yet again his son had been underhand, going behind their backs, ungrateful, uncaring, and what about the feelings of his mother. Did he not think that she would be hurt? It was all said, and now he was striding back to his own rooms at the end of the village, a fine temper on him and his day for the moment ruined.

He had left Emily crying, weeping quietly by the fireside.

Chapter Thirteen

There had been several invitations to Tommy from Edward Douglas-Pennant to visit Penrhyn Castle. Bertram Bellamy had been excluded from most. Edward had taken a special interest in Tommy Standish, and on several occasions over after-dinner drinks in the exquisite library had urged him to change allegiance from the Garddryn and take a managerial post at the massive Penrhyn quarry.

There were temptations; Tommy appreciated the superb opulence of the castle. From the moment he rode beneath the huge evergreen at the castle gate and along the mile long avenue planted with trees from far-flung and exotic lands he experienced a sense of prosperous security.

The end of the avenue was on a small incline, and opened onto neat and orderly planted parkland, here the castle came into full view and what a view it was, the great limestone Keep towering a hundred feet or more, the principal block stately and grand. He could never look at this aspect without considering the immense wealth it had taken to erect the building and plant the pleasure grounds.

On reaching the Carriage Forecourt he would hope to have a moment before a flunkey dashed to open the carriage door, or if he came alone, to take the reins of his horse. Often he could enjoy a private moment to admire the view at the stone parapet, the Great and Little Orme in the distance, with the isthmus of Llandudno between. Rising out of the sea the rugged headlands of Penmaenmawr and Penmaenbach, ice age mammoths. In the far distance the high plateau of Carneddau and the peaks of Carnedd Dafydd and Carnedd Llywelyn. Although he wasn't born to the district he could name the mountains without hesitation. Away to the left Puffin, a dark and magical isle washed by ocean waves. To the southeast the perilously tidal grey water of the Menai Strait raced between the mainland and the island of Anglesey. He had a fondness for Anglesey, green and vibrant island, the breadbasket of Wales. It was no surprise that George Hay Dawkins had chosen to place the main entrance on this side of his castle, it was fantastic, astounding and beautiful and just for a moment Tommy could actually forget the cost of erecting the monumental building.

It had all been seen a dozen times or more but it still moved him this view of mountain, sea, and islands.

Now, standing on the Carriage Forecourt he watched as his horse was led away. Its hide sweating from the exertion of the ride from Bangor.

The massive oak door to the Entrance Gallery was open and a liveried servant stood to the side waiting for him to enter.

Before obliging the man Tommy gave the mountains a last glance and in his own time stepped across the threshold.

Remembering the first time he had entered the vestibule walking behind the portly body of Bertram Bellamy he'd been struck by the smallness of the low room, a reminder of an old church cloister. Old Bellamy fussing over his old-fashioned red coat, shaking water out of the beaver collar had taken a large portion of the space, attended as he was by two lackeys. He, Tommy, had been obliged to stand in the open doorway the rain lashing behind him.

That first visit had been almost three years ago, he'd come a long way since that evening; he'd matured vastly, no longer the rather gauche young man impressed by every stick of furniture and plate. Not that the Grand Hall he was about to enter didn't have the power to impress him; its majesty still filled him with awe.

Pulling down the hem of his coat, he glanced at the servant.

'This way, sir, Mr. Standish.' Opening the door he gave a graceful bow and stood aside announcing 'Mr. Standish.'

Edward Douglas-Pennant, Member of Parliament for Carnarvonshire was a slender elegant man, a gracious host. Hand outstretched he crossed the York stone floor. 'Good to see you, Tommy. Did you have a good ride over?' Before waiting for an answer he turned to a servant. 'Get Mr. Standish a scotch.' Lowering his voice, 'Now, Tommy let's hear all your news.'

It gave Tommy great pleasure to stand in the great room, which resembled a transept of a cathedral, drinking scotch with a man he admired hugely. It added to the sense of personal worth and well-being that socialising with gentry never failed to arouse. It was a far cry from his early beginnings and he felt pride that he had lifted himself above the quicksand of poverty to the elevated position he now enjoyed. Little thought went to the stable and loving home that Emily and Joe had granted him and the very real start that they had bestowed by encouraging him to attend the lessons at Plas Mawr.

Edward put a hand on Tommy's shoulder. 'John Morgan is joining us for dinner.' He laughed. 'Most people find him too outspoken, but I think you and he will get on fine. As soon as he arrives we'll go to the library have another snifter before dinner.'

A slight commotion in the Entrance Gallery announced the arrival of Mr. Morgan. The Welsh radical's views were well known to Tommy and he looked forward to a heated debate before the evening ended.

In the library, a room a far cry from a typical room of that name as it incorporated the area of the medieval house that had originally stood on the site. The vast room the domain of gentlemen was immense, gorgeously elaborate with great arches that befitted a grand cathedral, large windows looked out over the scenic panorama of Snowdonia. A fire blazed in one of the four ornately carved limestone fireplaces.

Entering, Tommy and John Morgan settled on two Italian high back chairs, Edward preferring a smaller more comfortable chair upholstered in wool velvet, lifted his coat tails before sitting.

Animated, Edward talked of the proposed visit of the Queen and Prince Albert. 'It's arranged that the Messiah will be sung by the Llanllechid choir in the Great Hall.' He grinned. 'I expect that you are too much of a radical to come and join us for that, John?'

John Morgan muttered something about a comment in his newspaper and then sipped his drink thoughtfully.

Tommy knew that if an invitation came his way, however casually it was made, he'd make sure that his answer was clear and precise, the opportunity to dine with royalty was too rare to mumble over an acceptance. The music he could live without, but the chance to be in the presence of the Queen sent little shivers of excitement dashing up his spine.

John had begun a story about an incident in the Houses of Parliament; Edward amused was listening intently. Tommy for the moment was lost in thoughts of the royal visit and when dinner was announced the servant's voice startled him.

John finished his story before the trio began to move, the servants standing patiently behind the chairs to either take the glasses or usher the men through the door.

The dining room was a much more intimate room than the library and although it was large, the elegant table perfectly capable of seating twenty comfortably, the lavish and richly dark tones of the decoration gave the room an ambience of comfort. A fire blazed in the chimneypiece the flames glittered on the polished black stone, and on the mantelpiece a pair of black limestone candlesticks, the candles alight reflected on the heavy gilding of the picture frame above them. The carved buffet nearest to the end of the dining table that had been laid for the three, held exotic fruit in bowls decorated with bronze dolphin stands. Tommy aspired to a room like this one, elegant, expensive, decorated superbly it whispered exquisite taste.

Dinner was simple, soup, a sea bream, saddle of lamb, an iced cream desert, a favourite concoction of the cook who loved nothing more than showing off her skills and making use of the vast ice house.

Hungry, Tommy was relishing the delicate flavour of the fish when his eye was taken by something more desirable, a buxom girl with fire in her eyes, her wonderfully round and soft breasts torturing the material of her uniform.

Glancing at him she gave him a sly smile.

After that he found it hard to concentrate on the rest of the meal and only relaxed when the maid had departed the room.

Edward caught his attention, when he asked, 'How's Bertram Bellamy? I haven't seen him for some time?'

Resting his knife and fork on the porcelain plate Tommy frowned, he was genuinely fond of his old patron. 'He hasn't been well lately, he had a bout of flu sometime ago and he doesn't seem able to shake it off. His surgeon advises that he heads for the Riviera the warmth and dry air supposedly will effect a cure.'

Juliana, Edward's first wife had died at Pisa seeking a cure for a persistent chill but he made no mention of this, but said 'I'm surprised that his surgeon doesn't think him too elderly to be dashing off to foreign climes.'

Tommy smiled. 'Mr. Bellamy is hardly likely to take the man's advice however well intentioned. He's far too busy at the Garddryn to take a month or so off from business. Work is his lifeblood.'

A frown flitted across Edward's brow. 'Commendable but foolhardy when he has a man like yourself to run the place for him. You'll have a hard job, Tommy to climb to the top of the pile and run the Garddryn how you would wish with old Bellamy in charge of the reins.' His eyes sparkling with amusement. 'Time for you to accept my offer and come and work for me at Penrhyn.'

Tommy had heard the offer often but his ambitions lay with the Garddryn and Plas Mawr, the prize that went with it. 'It's generous of you, Edward but you know how I feel about the Garddryn and anyway, I couldn't abandon Bertram he's been very kind to me.'

Stabbing a small piece of fish on his fork, Edward popped it into his mouth and began to chew. 'I know that he educated you alongside his own son, but he wasn't being totally altruistic he saw your potential and knew how to harvest it.'

John Morgan's cutlery clattered to his plate.

'George Bellamy is the only son isn't he?' Picking up his wineglass he sipped the white Bordeaux letting it linger on his tongue.

'I saw an old friend in London the other day, he told me that young George was in a spot of bother. It seems that the young man has accumulated a great deal of debt, gambling I believe, and now he can't afford to pay his notes. Bad do.' He swilled the wine to the rim of the glass then let it settle.

'I expect his father will have to cough up the necessary and not for the first time I'm told. If old Bellamy kicks the bucket and leaves the quarry to George who knows what'll become of it.'

Edward wondered how sick Bertam might be. Could his illness be more than a lingering bout of influenza? There was no knowing what diseases a man came into contact with on a daily basis. Putting down his knife and fork he gave Tommy a serious look. 'It's something to think about, Tommy. What John says is true the Garddryn is sure to go to George.'

Ever the radical thinker John Morgan smiled mischievously. 'Of course it could go to the daughter.'

Edward clicked his tongue. 'Bellamy's too much of the old school not to leave it to his son. He'd just hope that George would straighten out and run the place properly once he was in charge of the reins.' He turned his eyes to Tommy. 'Would working for young George be difficult?'

'It wouldn't be good that's for sure. He has no knowledge of quarrying, he was never interested in the business.'

John Morgan gave Tommy a heavy lidded stare. 'When it's his he might just let you get on with running the business but that doesn't mean that he'll not have his hand in the profits, grabbing what he can to serve his life style.' He paused, his finger tapping the table. 'Opium is a terrible scourge, it blinds a man's prudence. And George I'd say is short on prudence in any guise.'

'Is he addicted to that?' Edward asked Tommy, looking surprised.

Shifting in his seat, Tommy's eyes went from one man to the other. 'He was always taking doses of laudanum to cure his hangovers when he lived at Plas Mawr. I suspected that he was taking something stronger last time he visited home. More often than not he was in a bit of a daze.'

'Drinking heavily too!' John shook his head. 'Sounds like he might pop off before his elderly pater.'

Edward's grey hair fell across his forehead as he shook his head. 'Wouldn't be at all surprising if that is the way he lives, but young men generally have a good constitution.' He looked toward Tommy for confirmation that George was a healthy bull.

'As far as I know he has, but he's not what you might call strong.'

'Eee gods,' John said before finishing his wine in one swallow.

Three servants entered the room to clear the used dishes and silence fell over the three men until the chore was completed and the saddle of lamb was carved on the side table.

With full plates they began to eat and appreciation of the

competently cooked meat held their chatter until Edward asked Tommy 'Have you got the new water pump working yet at the Garddryn?'

Tommy halted from slicing a roast potato. 'We have had one or two problems with it but we expect that it will be up and running before the week is out.'

Nodding sagely Edward gave him his opinion. 'We had problems with one very much like yours, same engineer, in the end we had to ditch it and put another in its place. But that was some time ago back at...'

Interrupting him John asked about the original engineer.

The evening passed quickly and John Morgan was the first to announce that he was for his bed declaring that he'd had a long day and expected another on the morrow.

Standing, Tommy declared that he would also retire and not keep his host from his bed. He had noticed the young maid's glances as she had come to clear the desert dishes away and wondered if her comely smile was a promise of a night of sport. If so he could forget Henrietta for a few hours and her whining about never seeing enough of him. Fornication brought blessed amnesia. Happy with this thought he left the dining room and climbed the wide stone stairs to bed, the castle lamp man walking ahead of him.

Opening the bedroom door Tommy saw at once that a light burned within the room. Dismissing the lamp man he entered quickly and closed the door. She was turning down his bed, how long she had waited for him he could only guess at but a dint in the bedspread where she may have lain was an indication that it might have been sometime.

Her eyes were less wilful, darting nervously from him to the bed. She bobbed a curtsy and leaving the smoothing of the sheet she whipped passed him.

He caught her forearm and pulled her close. 'Why leave now when you've waited for so long?' There was a malicious smile on his lips.

'I wasn't waiting, honest. I just came in now, sir to turn down your bed and make sure the warming pan was still hot.'

Her long hair was in his hand and pulling her head back he kissed her roughly. He began to unbutton the bodice of her dress and for a moment she made little whimpering noises but as he touched her pert nipples she stopped struggling and succumbed to his harsh caress.

The dress lay like a puddle at her feet and he was untying the tapes on her drawers impatiently, threatening to tear the garment. Giggling she assisted him and a moment later the plain white garment lay on top of the dress, carefully she stepped over them.

Sadie was a firebrand in bed, energetic, athletic and willing to try anything to please him. She was like a little plump pigeon, warm, round and comely. Her heavy breasts overflowed his hands.

When the lamp had been extinguished and his body lay above hers, his maleness planted in her wetness, he recalled Millie Barker.

She had gone before he woke, to attend to her early morning chores. On drifting out of sleep he, luxuriating in his solitary state, stretching languidly in the expanse of the bed, considering if he should have her again at some future point. Then he rose and began to wash in the bowl of water that had been left on the stand.

Leaving the castle shortly afterwards mounted on his favourite horse he didn't look back as he trotted down the avenue.

Sadie watched him from the room they had shared for the night. When he was out of sight, lost to the trees, she lay on the crumpled sheet breathing his scent on the pillow.

As he made his way down the avenue and onto the roadway the girl and her emotions were the last thing on Tommy's mind. He was pondering on last night's dinnertime conversation. George certainly was a liability and if he wasn't checked he might wreck everything. With plans and counter plans forming in his head he considered the possibilities of dislodging the young man from his father's affection.

If there was ever going to be a chance of realising his ambitions then he had to make a strong case for laying claim to the Garddryn and Plas Mawr.

Emily had been baking bread; the warm cottage smelled of risen yeast and baked dough. As soon as the first batch was out of the oven and cool enough to handle she pulled off her apron.

Joe came through the door, as she was about to leave the house.

'Emily, sweetheart where are you off to?'

She had a loaf wrapped in a clean cloth in her hands. Flustered, she knew that Joe would not be pleased with her errand, she spoke quickly. 'I've been baking bread.'

'Aye I know that I smelt it as I came through the door.'

'Well I thought as I hadn't seen our Tommy for weeks that I'd take a loaf to his lodgings.'

'I don't know why you bother,' he said crossly. 'That lad hasn't been in sight of this cottage since the day he so unceremoniously departed it. Three bloody years or more.'

Tears filled Emily's eyes. She felt hurt that Tommy neglected to call, the only chance she had of seeing him now was if she bumped into him in the village. On one occasion she had called at his lodgings but

Lillian Little his landlady didn't encourage visitors. Embarrassingly, Emily had been left on the front step to state her errand only to be told in a very patronising manner that young Master Tommy was visiting the gentry at Penrhyn Castle and wasn't expected back that day.

Heavyhearted, Emily had returned to the cottage. That had been almost ten months ago. Now desperate to see her lad she was prepared to take Lillian's scornful looks just to set eyes on her boy.

Holding the loaf firmly, she met Joe's eyes. 'I'm going, Joe and I'll not let you stop me.'

His mouth dropped in surprise. 'I'd not stop you doing whatever you want to do, Emily, but you're unlikely to find him at home, the rascal will be out having a good time celebrating.'

It was her turn to look surprised. 'Celebrating, celebrating what?'

Sighing, Joe slumped in the chair by the fireside and pulled off his heavy boots. 'I didn't know how I was going to tell you this, but our Tommy has been promoted, he's now manager over the entire Garddryn. Bellamy's retiring.'

She knew that she should be pleased for her son, but a pain had come into her heart catching her unawares as it stabbed her beneath the ribcage. That her firstborn didn't think to share his news with his family hurt her deeply. Sitting slowly she pushed the loaf onto the kitchen table. 'No need for me to go down there then.' A fleeting look of hope crossed her face. 'Perhaps he'll come and tell us himself.'

Joe snorted. 'Aye an' pigs might bloody fly.'

She was crying, tears like melting icicles trickling down her cheeks. 'Oh, Joe don't say that.'

He was out of the chair and his arm circling her. 'Oh, sweetheart don't cry for that bugger. Save your tears for them that need um.'

'And who might that be?' She cried.

Breathing into her clean hair, he smelt the sweet scent of lavender. 'You have more than one son, Lass.'

She sniffed into a square of linen pulled from the sleeve of her bodice. 'I know that, Joe and I never forget it. It's just that I see so little of our Tommy.' Fresh tears flowed. 'And I miss him so very much.'

He sniffed himself. 'Aye, I know that you do. I miss the bugger.' His voice rose 'But I get so bloody angry with him.'

Frank came through the door whistling he stopped on seeing his father stooped to his mother, who was crying gently. 'What's up?'

Joe stood. 'Nowt important. We were just sharing a tear or two over Tommy.'

'Why? What's he done this time?'

Joe pushed his hand through his hair. 'Nowt but get promoted.'

Frank's manner was the same as usual, down to earth and matter-of-fact. 'Well that's good news, not a matter to scrike at.'

Joe gave him a weak smile. 'Aye, you're reeght there, lad.'

Sighing, Emily rose from the chair and put the kettle to the fire. Then taking her apron from the back of the chair she wrapped it around her best skirt and tied the tapes before looking at her younger son and giving him a small smile.

Glad to have everything back to normal, Frank was cheerful. 'What's for supper, Mam?'

'There's a bit of meat pie to warm up.'

'Smashing. Hey, Pa do you think our Tommy will give me a job?'

Emily was aghast. 'Frank you've to go to school for another year. You don't want to be thinking of a job yet.'

A frown clouded his young face. 'Mam, I'm no book learner like Tommy, I'm just not made for it. Even if I do go to school for another year I'll still end up in one of the quarries. It might just as well be the Garddryn it's nearest. If I got a job at Penrhyn I'd have to lodge nearby or stay in the barracks. I'd hate not being at home in the evening.'

Planting a kiss on his cheek, she said softly, 'You're a good boy, Frank.'

Rubbing his cheek, he laughed. 'Geroff, Ma, don't go all soft on me.'

Tutting, she said, 'Kids, who'd 'ave them?' A picture of her little daughter Chloe came into her mind and she turned her back to her two menfolk less they saw the tears that came to her eyes.

Things had become uncomfortably embarrassing in London for George Bellamy; several times persons employed to collect the money he owed for his gambling and rich lifestyle had accosted him in the street.

Although his father had bailed him out several times in the past and had sworn that he would not do so again, George decided to take the train and return home for a week. In that time he would hope to convince the old man to help him out just one more time. He would promise to turn over a new leaf and become the hardworking son that his father longed for. If necessary he would swear to model himself on Tommy Standish, the creep.

If he could just extract more cash out of the old man he would steer clear of the clubs where his luck generally deserted him and frequent the ones where his face was less familiar. All he needed was a change of fortune and more money.

A few days later George arrived at Plas Mawr unexpectedly.

Bertram Bellamy was resting in the library when he heard his son greeting one of the staff as the door was opened to him.

The familiar voice raised mixed emotions. He was pleased to have him back in the house, George was a lively chap and he added a touch of sparkle to the old place. But if the young rascal had come begging for more money he was going to be disappointed.

The last thing he needed was a row with his boy; he didn't feel up to a confrontation. He wasn't well, the dratted cough that had plagued him most of last winter was as persistent as ever, disturbing his sleep and drawing every ounce of energy from him. A reminder that he had passed his seventieth birthday and probably shouldn't expect so much from his body as he had in the past.

Putting aside the newspaper he was reading he climbed out of the comfortable chair by the fire, a dry cough hacked in his throat and he wiped his mouth with a soft, linen handkerchief.

Henrietta was coming down the side staircase when she saw George, squealing with delight she dashed down and grabbing hold of him hugged him fiercely. 'Oh you don't know how good it is to see you, things have been so bloody dull.'

Laughing, he hugged her back. 'Hen' don't swear it's not ladylike.'

'Tosh to ladylike. I don't care about such things. Come up to my room and tell me all your news.' She pulled his arm.

'Don't pull so, Henrietta.' He laughed again. 'I have to see Pa first before I do anything else.'

'Fiddlesticks. Come on we can have a really good chinwag before it's time to dress for dinner.'

'No. I must see Pa.'

Her lips pursed sulkily. 'Well if you must be a bore, you'll find him in the library reading the stuffy old newspaper.'

Sighing, Bertram slumped back in the chair. The newspaper lying abandoned on the Turkey rug.

A moment later the library door opened and George entered alone. Bertram caught a glance of Henrietta trotting back up the stairs.

He knew the answer to his question before he asked it. George was smiling too breezily, a trait of his when he was nervous, and he had every reason to be nervous if he had come asking for more money. Bertram braced himself for a row. 'What brings you home George?'

George was over cheerful, smiling ingratiatingly. 'Only a small matter that you, dear Pater can help be with. Just a trifle.'

'Trifle or not boy if you are expecting me to bail you out again the answer is no.'

'But, Pa!'

Bertram raised his hand. Don't you Pa me. I told you last time there would be no more help from me if you were foolish enough to run up debts. Do you remember how much I gave you on that occasion? It was two hundred pounds. That's more than a man working in my quarry can expect to see in a lifetime, more than one lifetime in fact.' Raising his voice he began to cough again. Recovering but his voice still wheezy, he said, 'I told you last time that there'd be no more from me.'

George looked crestfallen. 'If you could help me out just one more time I promise that it will never happen again. Pater I have men looking for me and they are not the sort of people that can be told to just go away. They are threatening and nasty. I am afraid that if I don't pay them soon that they will harm me in some despicable way.'

Bertram was silent, considering this new turn of events.

'Please help me out. I promise...'

Leaving his chair and crossing to the window Bertram looked out over the neat parkland. His voice was cool and level. 'I'll not listen to another one of your promises. It seems that yours are easily forgotten. How much is the debt?'

George was silent then gathering his tattered courage, he spoke quietly 'Five. Five hundred.'

Outraged, Bellamy turned sharply. 'Five hundred! You, bloody fool!'

'It won't happen again I prom....'

'Get out of my sight!'

The library door closed quietly and Bertram left alone in the room sighed and looked out over the land that the fruit of his labour had brought to such perfection. Unchecked, George would run through the profits, then the capital of the Garddryn and eventually Plas Mawr itself. There was Louise and Henrietta's future to think off. George had to be stopped.

George went to his mother to plead with her to intercede with his father. Frightening her when he told her of his fears for his safety. When he departed to seek out Henrietta he left her flustered and with a gnawing headache.

Louise dressed for dinner with the help of her maid and the theme running through her mind as she did so was that Bertram was unlikely to pay out that amount of money. She had very little of her own to offer her son. Nauseous with worry she slipped the pearl and emerald necklace around her neck and as the tiny diamond clasp clicked closed she vowed that she would hand the exquisite piece to her son before he returned to London. Bertram would be furious but that had to be preferable to her darling boy suffering harm.

Dressed, she made her way down to the drawing room and never in her entire life had she felt so like drinking a sherry.

Tommy, Henrietta, and Bertram had arrived in the drawing room a few minutes before and were gathered around the fireplace sipping pre-dinner drinks. Joining them Louise looked pale, the green gown she had chosen to wear giving her complexion a sickly hue.

Ever the gentleman Bertram crossed the room taking her hand he squeezed it fondly and kissed her cheek.

Expecting to find George in attendance, normally an early starter on the pre-dinner drinks, Louise started in surprise seeing that he was absent. 'Where's George?' Her voice was brittle.

Bertram sighed, obviously his wife had heard of the contretemps and the reason behind it. He tried to be patient. 'Louise I don't want you making yourself ill over this matter. George and I will discuss it again tomorrow. There is nothing at all for you to worry about.'

Her hand covered the emerald drop in the centre of the rope of pearls. 'I'm not worried, Bertram. I just asked where George was.'

Sighing loudly and closing his eyes to draw attention to his growing frustration, he said, 'No doubt he's idling in his room or primping himself and will be down the moment he realises that sherry is being served. Please do not fuss, Louise.'

Her face darkened. Turning away she walked to the fireplace, glancing at the butler she spoke briskly. 'Send someone to ask Master George to join us.'

Uncomfortable, the man replied, 'Master George has left the house.'

'Left. When?' Her lips pursed. 'What time was this?'

'About an hour ago, Madam.'

Disappointed and angry Louise snapped at the man, and fixing him with a haughty stare said, 'And did he say if he would be returning for dinner?'

Cross that the brunt of her anger was being directed towards him, his nose wrinkled in indignation. The information he had regarding her erstwhile son would upset her, and enjoying the moment of his little triumph he failed to hide his smirk. 'He made a mention of going to the local tavern to meet friends, Madam.'

Anger that had bubbled away since he heard of his son's debts erupted and Bertram hastily revised the decision he had made regarding the five hundred pounds. Before this piece of flagrant bad manners he had been prepared to give the boy what he needed on this occasion, on the understanding that he would return home and help with the management of the Garddryn. Now all that was changed, the young waster didn't deserve help if he could be so flippant with his mother's emotions. When he did return he would be treated to a piece of his mind. He'd make damn sure that he would stay under the roof of Plas Mawr, or by jove his allowance would be severed.

Frowning deeply, he glanced at the butler. He had noticed him smirking at Louise. If he couldn't remember his manners and station in life then he'd have a boot up the backside and be through the door without a reference. He'd had just about enough of being treated with disrespect by his son and the servants.

Turning his attention to the man in question, Bellamy barked, 'Serve Mrs. Bellamy a sherry at once. I'll have a scotch, and go easy on the water. I'll not have it blasted well drowned.'

After this outburst the drinks were finished in virtual silence with the butler and a maid keeping a respectful and appropriate distance and remaining silent.

When the time came to escort the ladies into the dining room, Tommy took Mrs. Bellamy's arm and led her ceremoniously to her usual place at the long mahogany table. She was still pale and her hand shook slightly as it brushed Tommy's.

The arrangement of dining with the Bellamy's on a Saturday evening when there were no other pressing engagements for either party had become something of a ritual for Tommy. It was usual when dinner was over for he and Bertram to go to the library to smoke and drink brandy and discuss the week's business at the Garddryn.

The ladies would occupy their time as best they could with a little playing on the pianoforte, or a simple game of cards. Then Mrs. Bellamy would go to her room to sleep, and Henrietta to her own to wait impatiently for Tommy to retire to the guestroom allocated to him. When the house fell quiet Henrietta would join him there.

This arrangement suited Tommy, although Henrietta's sighs and muttering that she saw too little of him, and that he was taking advantage of her, took up the first thirty minutes or so of the time that they were together. During this tiresome interlude Tommy would recall the night he had spent with Sadie Pearson in the suite at Penrhyn, and he would crave for a silent, enthusiastic partner, as mentally he undressed Sadie scattering her drawers to the far reaches of the bedroom.

When Henrietta suspected that he was no longer listening to her she would cajole, coax, and promise never to be so unreasonable again, and allow him to make love to her. Although this was often not a satisfactory union for Henrietta, for Tommy it was excellent as he had the lovely Sadie, metaphorically lying beneath him. Finishing he would be determined to visit Penrhyn at the very first opportunity. It had already been several long weeks since he had experienced a night of exquisite and inexhaustible passion.

With his mind on Sadie and her plump thighs he tucked into the venison and rich gravy on his dinner plate.

Bellamy seated beside him, turned his head to check that the servants had left the room before disclosing what was on his mind to Tommy. 'I need you do something for me. The young scamp George has got himself into a bit of bother in London. He needs bailing out. The stupid boy has got himself into debt. I want you to arrange with the bank for a draft of five hundred pounds to see him right. I wasn't going to pay up, I had quite decided that the rascal should learn his lesson and sort himself out. But I am his father after all and I can't see him facing trouble alone.' He gave a benign smile.

Well practised in hiding his true emotions Tommy showed no surprise at the disclosure, although rage began to bubble beneath the surface of his resentment. Speaking calmly, as though he'd been asked to pass the salt and not to surrender a large part of the recent profits of the Garddryn. A profit he had fought hard to achieve. Things were not running smoothly at the quarry, the new pump and all its problems being the main reason for his over expenditure the last few months.

With a steady hand he placed his wineglass back on the surface of the table. 'Of course, Bertram I'll see to it first thing on Monday morning. I'll be at the bank when it opens.' Suddenly he felt vaguely nauseous.

Bellamy, satisfied that he had done the right thing, and by the gracious and thankful look upon his wife's pale and drawn face, she appeared to be pleased too. He gave her a satisfied smile before stabbing a slice of meat and stuffing it into his mouth.

Tommy ate more slowly, his brain whirling.

The whisky downed earlier and wine with dinner had relaxed Bellamy, he was expansive. 'It's the right thing to do, to settle this debt, but I don't propose to let him get away with causing all this trouble scot-free.' He leaned closer to Tommy and spoke quietly as though the conversation was not polite enough for the women at the table. 'George is my only son and I expect him to marry soon and give me grandchildren. He's my heir and it is his duty to do so. In return for the inheritance of Plas Mawr and the Garddryn I expect him to give me boys to carry on the name of Bellamy. With good training from you,' he tapped Tommy's hand affectionately, 'he will learn enough to take over and enrich the quarry and the mansion by his own efforts.'

The words hit Tommy like a bolt piercing his brain. Of course in his heart he had always known that this was the way it was going to be. But somewhere in the back of his mind he had believed that something would occur to make it different. How, had always been a dark mystery, something obscure and tenuous, but he had known that the moment a chance presented itself that he would seize it. Plas Mawr must be his.

Throughout the remainder of the meal Tommy was dead to the conversation. Henrietta's fingernail surreptitious digging at his thigh failed to arouse even a dart of annoyance, and her inane conversation went virtually unheeded. Insentient he downed another glass of wine, longing for the interminable dinner to come to a close.

It wasn't until he was in the library with Bertram, the old man pouring brandy from the decanter that had been left on a side table by one of the staff, that he learned of the extent of George's problem.

Sitting in his usual chair, the heat of the fire warming his leg, Bellamy began to explain. 'George has accumulated a debt that he cannot pay and it seems that wretched debt collectors are after him. They have even gone as far as to threaten his life. I'm worried, terrified that should he return to London something unspeakable will happen to him.'

Tommy looked shocked. 'Oh surely not. They wouldn't go that far would they?'

Bellamy nodded, his grey hair falling across his brow. 'I have no doubt about it. Five hundred pounds is a lot of money by anyone's reckoning. It's possible that the devils have followed him here.'

Tommy's mind lit. The incredible solution, the answer to all his hopes and prayers, his chance had emerged. The word Kismet sprang into his brain and his excitement was so profound that he almost spoke it aloud. Terrified that he may have given himself away, allowed his face to register joy, he glanced at Bellamy, fortunately he was looking towards the window.

If he was to stay in control he must watch his step, the old man might be slow but he was no fool when it came to ferreting out a falsehood.

Turning a helpful but sympathetic face to Bellamy, he made a suggestion. 'If it is that serious perhaps I should go the bank manager's home first thing tomorrow and get him to put the arrangements in place. With a bit of luck I might be in a position to bring the draft to you by lunchtime.' Moving to the edge of his seat, he looked prepared to go immediately. 'I will need a letter of authority to give to the man to let him know it's all above board.'

'Tommy you are a wizard. Of course that's the right thing to do.

Only you would understand the urgency and get things moving quickly. What a gem you are, my boy.'

Glancing at the clock on the mantelpiece, Tommy was brisk. 'If I leave here now, I'll be back at my place in no time. Then I can get a reasonably early night and make a start first thing tomorrow morning. Mrs. Bellamy wouldn't mind if I didn't take her up on her offer of an overnight stay would she?'

'Of course not, old boy. She'll be pleased that you are doing something for George. I'll write the note, then I'll call for the carriage to take you to your home.'

Standing, Tommy buttoned his black frock coat. 'There's no need I have my horse in the stable. I'll alert the boy and be off in no time.'

Tommy watched the clock, listening to the clear tick of the pendulum as he waited for Bellamy to finish writing at the desk.

After two attempts Bellamy sighed with satisfaction, and melting red wax he sealed the letter pushing his fob into the warm blob. Waiting a moment for the seal to harden before handing it to Tommy. 'This should satisfy the man. Hopefully we will see you back here around noon or shortly afterwards tomorrow. Thank you, my boy. Just take care of yourself.'

His hand was the young man's shoulder as they went to the door together. 'I can't thank you enough for your support. It means a lot to me, Tommy. Goodnight, my boy and God bless.'

The commotion of doors opening and closing disturbed Henrietta who was lying on her bed planning what she would say to Tommy Standish the moment he reached his room. He had been definitely less than attentive all evening, she wondered if he might be seeing someone else. The thought brought a stab of pain.

Hearing the beat of hooves she rose quickly and parting the heavy curtains looked out. It was dark, but by the light of the library windows she saw a horse and rider.

With her nose almost touching the cold windowpane, Henrietta saw that the rider was Tommy and her breath caught in her throat with annoyance and a moment later she lay on her bed crying quietly into her pillow.

With the lights of the house behind him his eyes slowly grew accustomed to the darkness. The sky was moonless, heavy cloud threatening rain lay over the tops of the mountains and away to sea. Trees barely moved in the light breeze, and hardly a ripple disturbed the shrubs. The night was silent but for the beat of hooves and a lone nightingale trilling prettily in the distance, but the hoot of an owl silenced it. He took a long, deep breath and felt the wet air do its magic, his taut muscles began to unwind. A quiet command to the horse and it stepped up the pace and as they cantered down the avenue the chill air crept under the collar of his coat, beneath him the heat of the animal warmed his thighs.

Reaching the village he rode down the main street to his lodging and after stabling the horse he let himself into the house.

A lamp with the flame turned down low burned on the table in the hallway, but the stairs and the corridor above were in darkness. He was familiar enough with the layout of the house not to need a light to guide him to the door of his room on the first floor.

On the first tread of the stairs he made more noise than was necessary, dropping the cane he was carrying and deliberately putting his weight on a step that creaked. As he had hoped the landlady came out of her sitting room.

'Oh, Mr. Standish it's you. I didn't expect you home tonight. Weren't you supposed to stay over at the mansion?'

He had stopped halfway up the staircase, his hand resting on the polished wood banister. 'I'm so sorry to have disturbed you, Mrs. Little it wasn't my intention. I dropped this.' He raised the cane and smiled boyishly.

Mrs. Little had a special interest in Tommy, mixing with gentry and high society as he did. Eager to pick up gossip from Plas Mawr she tried to garner a snippet of news. 'So there's been a change of plan has there?'

On this occasion Tommy was happy to oblige her. 'Yes there has, Mrs. Little. Now I have an important meeting early tomorrow morning.' He smiled warmly, eyes alight, purposely flirting with the middle-aged woman. 'I thought I'd get to my bed at a reasonable hour. Lonely and cold as that bed is.'

She made a sound that he had not thought to hear from her, a silly girlish giggle. 'Well I must away to my own, though I fear it is as lonely and cold as yours.'

Eee gods, he thought, she's making a suggestion. He smiled, though his stomach had turned queasy. 'Well goodnight, Mrs. Little.'

She tried to detain him a moment longer. 'You'll not be disturbed. Mr. Goodman and Mr. Leyland have gone away for the weekend, so you'll have the upstairs to yourself. Gone off to Chester they have.'

Impatient to move he stepped on the next tread. 'Oh that's good I wouldn't wish to disturb anyone as I leave in the morning.'

'No fear of that, me and the two daughters sleep like proverbial logs we do.' She gave a short laugh, then with a final goodnight closed the door.

Sighing with relief he climbed the stairs quickly, and reaching his room he flung the cane onto the bed. Changing his clothes quickly, donning an old coat over trousers and a jacket, he stood with the bedroom door open listening for sounds from the Littles' apartment.

When he was sure that the women had retired for the night he left his room, and closing the door quietly he leaned over the banisters checking for sounds from below. Holding his breath, avoiding the creaky treads on the stairs he descended slowly.

The lamp in the hallway had been extinguished. Unsure of the exact distance between the last step and the dresser, he moved cautiously until his hand touched the cumbersome piece of furniture, side stepping it he came to the front door.

A quick glance behind him, ears pricked for a change in timbre of the old house, he drew back the two bolts. A draught of damp night air cooled his face. Placing the palm of his hand flat against the edge of the door, to shield the sound of the lock tumbling into place, he closed it gently.

Hoisting his canvas bag onto his shoulder, he stole down the steps.

Staying within the shadows of the tall hedge he left the garden, and using the alleys behind the cottages he walked cautiously through the village and onto the lane leading to Plas Mawr.

The lay of the land was as familiar to him as the small patch of land of his childhood home. There wasn't a bush, tree, spring or ditch on the road from the mansion to the village he was unaware of, and he headed for a place that would serve his purpose well.

With noiseless steps he covered the two miles and when he was a few dozen yards away from the main gates he moved close to the hedge and scanned the road behind and forward, his eyes piercing the darkness. There were no moving shadows, or half-seen shapes to concern him.

To the left was a thicket of rhododendrons and making for it he hid, the thick foliage closing around him. Hunkering down he settled as best as he could. For a long time he waited, the sickly fragrance of the bushes and the insects on his skin became unpleasant. The ground was damp with a musty smell of fungus, kneeling upon it the moisture seeped through the knees of his trousers.

Time crawled and he began to wonder if George would materialise. There was always a chance that he would be too drunk to walk home, and if he'd didn't fall down at the inn incapable, he might sleep off his stupor at a near-by cottage. George had plenty of so called friends amongst the labourers and low life of the village.

There was a whispered sound in the stillness, and he drew back into the blacker refuge of the leaves, his heart hammering with the torture of suspense. His eyes, fixed and staring in the dark, hungered to glimpse George tottering towards him. Aching for action, to get what must be done over with, he willed the man to show himself. Although the task ahead was distasteful, it was better to get it done than to delay, for never would there be a better set of circumstances that would suit so well.

The night noises shifted, and the few notes that the birds called ceased, a small animal scurried into cover.

Then the tramp of an unsteady walker reached him, and a moment later a man staggering came into view. Tommy watched intently. Every few steps he would stop and lift a bottle to his mouth and drink.

When he was a few yards distant and he was sure that it was George, Tommy left his cover, crouching in the shadows.

George had begun a song but the tune froze on his lips as he turned unsteadily, then a rock clubbed the side of his head. A look of disbelief glazed his eyes, and he crumpled slowly, blood spurting from a raw wound.

A ragged, ugly sound tore from Tommy's mouth. The rock was still in his outstretched hands and he glimpsed the black and glistening stain. With a cry of disgust he hurled it into the bushed.

The initial shock was profound, and his imploding brain rained black mist, a low howling sob wrenched from his belly, and he slipped to his knees.

George's face was death-white, and bending over him Tommy checked his pulse with fingers wet and sticky with blood. Sure that his boyhood adversary was dead, he rose on shaky legs and running to the bushes he retrieved the canvas bag and took to his heels. His breath was hoarse in his lungs, ragged and uneven, and his body shook like an old man's with ague.

Sprinting over a five-barred gate he hid for a moment in the lee of a hedge, struggling to get control over his limbs and heaving lungs. Fear moved him on, and with visions of the hangman's gibbet bedevilling him, he ran across the field to the fast flowing mountain stream. Thrusting his hands into the icy water he washed off the stickiness and then flung water over his face. Panting, his fingers stiff as sticks, he stripped off his outer garments and wrenching fresh ones from the bag, he changed.

Swearing beneath his breath, forcing control back into his mind and body, he worked quickly to make a small fire, when it was hot enough he threw the bundle of bloodied clothes onto it. Making sure that there was nothing left that was recognisable he scattered the hot ash with his boot.

Hunkering down at the stream edge, he cupped his hands and dashed icy water over his head to clear his brain. His lungs no longer laboured and his hands were steady, he took a moment breathing in the damp air.

The night was still and moonless, the birds and small animals silent, watching the intruder, smelling the recent carnage.

Back in control, he stood, and with a quick movement dipped his boots into the fast flow to wash off the evidence of ash.

Glancing over the scene of the fire, he checked that nothing was there to incriminate him. Taking his bag off the bracken where it had lain, he began the journey back to his lodgings.

Across the fields, and then through the back alleys, he made his way carefully. If anyone should see him now he would pay the ultimate penalty. The only souls he met were the cats of the village, slinking into the shadows.

Advancing on his lodging he saw to his relief that the house was still in darkness, but aware that he was still in grave danger he moved stealthily towards safety.

Keeping to the shadows of the trees, he crossed the garden. Glancing back at the roadway he checked that the night was still empty before moving quickly up the long steps to the front door. Holding his breath he put his shoulder against the solid mahogany to deaden any sound, and with his eyes closed turned the knob. There was no resistance; the bolts remained off. Stifling a sigh of relief he pushed open the door. Silently, avoiding the creaks and groans of the treads he ascended the stairs and slunk into his room. He had been holding his breath, and now as he sat carefully on the bed, less the springs should disturb a light sleeper; he let out a stifled sigh of relief. A slow smile spread across his mouth. He had done it, got rid of George and now the world was his. His heart rate began to slow and his breath became even. The shadow of a smile remained.

There was no sleep in him, and until the first ray of dawn flushed the sky he lay on his bed with his face to the ceiling. At a reasonable hour he rose and dressed carefully, he needed to look immaculate and carefree as he passed through the village.

Downstairs he made tea, and drank a cup in the kitchen, leaving the evidence of his being present strewn on the table.

Then with no show of haste, and whistling a popular tune he made his way to the stables. He was mounted and passing through the village before the church clock struck eight.

Completing the business with the bank manager and with a

promise that the money would be ready for collection at start of business on the following day, he made his way towards Plas Mawr.

There was plenty of time on the ride to practice the shocked and sorrowful expression that would be necessary when hearing the news of poor George's demise. Murdered by footpads from London, seeking to reek revenge on a creditor. Notoriously evil were moneylenders, and he thought he might mention this when confronted with the terrible news.

Coming to the place where George had met his Maker, Tommy reined in the horse and looked down for evidence, a pool of blood, a lost shoe, but there was nothing there to show of the night's deed not even a small patch of darkness. The early dawn rain had washed the ground. He rode on.

There was no change in the avenue; no sign that the heir was no more, everything appeared perfectly normal. Damp trees, birdsong, scurrying of small wildlife. A carriage at the door surprised him, he hadn't expected to see a vehicle parked there. Visitors transport always went straight to the coach house. Recognising that it was the surgeon's carriage and the man must have been called to administer treatment to a distraught mother, he stepped up his pace.

Dismounting, he tied his animal. Pulling on the metal rod that would ring a bell within, he listened for footsteps on the mosaic floor. The few moments that passed he reminded himself to control his features, appear normal on entering, he knew nothing about the death, then give a look of horror and disbelief when given the news.

The door opened slowly and he greeted the footman formally.

Bertram Bellamy was descending into the hall as Tommy entered the house.

The man had aged ten years, descending slowly, his hand on the banister shaky and unsteady. He glanced towards the footman. 'I'll deal with this. Please take tea to Madam. At once.' Gone was the voice of authority.

Tommy, appearing concerned moved to the foot of the stairs. 'Are you ill, Bertram?'

Bellamy's eyes closed, and his hand came up to his mouth to stifle a sob. 'It's George.' Tears welled then ran unchecked down the deep folds on his cheeks.

Tommy was at his side, his hand on the old man's arm he supported him down the last few steps. 'What's happened?'

A sob caught in the old man's throat. 'It's George.'

Tommy held his breath, waiting to give his condolences.

'Bertram wiped his wet eyes with a square of linen. 'George was almost killed last night.'

'His voice whispery, Tommy said, 'Almost. But that can't be.'

Sniffing back tears, Bellamy patted Tommy's arm. 'I know, my boy. It does seem preposterous doesn't it? But it is what I feared. The surgeon is still with him.'

A red flood filled Tommy's head. A sledgehammer had struck him in the belly and he felt that he was falling to the floor. His mouth agape he waited for the vomit that was turning in his stomach to erupt from his mouth. Speechless, the breath had stopped in his body. The colourful mosaic floor had begun to spin.

Hanging onto Tommy coat sleeve, Bertram called out, 'Blake.'

Hurrying, the footman saw Tommy Standish as he slipped out of Bellamy's grasp and slid to the floor.

'My God, he's fainted.' Bertram shouted. 'Get someone from the kitchen, anybody. Go, you bloody imbecile, don't stand there gawking, the lad might choke.'

A moment later, with the help of three men servants, Tommy was lying on the couch in the drawing room, a woollen blanket across his torso.

'He's coming out of it. Here put the salts nearer to his nose.'

A pungent acid scent assaulted his nostrils, stinging and unpleasant. He tried to rise but firm hands held him down.

Bertram's kindly voice was in his ear. 'Don't move for a moment, you banged your head as you went down.'

His memory of what had happened was hazy, relaxing back on the cushions he waited for his head to clear. There was a vague pain above his ear, as though he'd been clouted there. The thought brought the nightmare rushing back. George isn't dead.

'No, no. George isn't dead.'

Hearing Bellamy's words Tommy realised he had spoken aloud. Jesus Christ what else had he said. Confessed to trying to kill him?

Bellamy began fussing with the small blanket. 'As soon as the surgeon is finished upstairs I'll get him to look at you.'

With his hand to his head, Tommy rose gingerly. A pain shot through his skull and he groaned.

'Just stay quiet until we have had you checked over.'

'I'm all right, Bertram. Don't worry about me. Just tell me what happened to George. How is he? Is he seriously hurt? Will he recover?'

Slumping beside Tommy, Bertram reached in his pocket and drew out a handkerchief. His voice was flat. 'There's no knowing at the moment what will happen to poor George. He was hit hard, very hard. The doctor seems to think it was a rock or something like that. Caught him just on the side of the head. What a wound.' He began to cry. 'If it hadn't been for the veterinary my George might well be dead.'

'The veterinary, what had he got to do with it?'

'Looking up Bertram saw that one of the men who had helped to carry Tommy into the room had remained, with a wave of his arm he dismissed him. When the door was closed, and what he had to say wouldn't travel to the domestic quarters, he began to explain.

'The veterinary was called to one of the horses. The man stayed late and when he rode up to the gates he found poor George in a bloody heap.' Blowing his nose before he continued 'I half expected trouble yesterday. The bastards that threatened George in London must have followed him here to hound him. When he told them he couldn't pay, they coshed the poor boy. Almost killed my George.' His eyes filled again. 'If only they had waited they could have had the money. I was prepared to pay them this time. But George never knew that, he'd gone off without a word yesterday. If only I had been more reasonable this might never have happened. And now...'

Wiping his eyes, he stood. Pouring two brandies from the decanter he handed one to Tommy, and drank deeply of the other. 'And your trip to the bank manager all gone to waste. Your kindness gone to nothing.' Sighing, he took another mouthful of spirit. Hearing footsteps in the hallway he downed the rest of the brandy and was making for the door when it opened and the surgeon stood on the threshold.

'Come in, man, come in. How is he?'

Bellamy was agitated; his hands shaking as he took another glass and filled it for the medical man, topping up his own he sipped before handing the other to the doctor.

The doctor's long face was serious, a deep frown cutting across his brow. 'It's hard to say at the moment. He's still barely conscious. If he survives the next few days we might be able to predict that the boy will live, but it's impossible to say if he will ever regain his faculties completely. It was a dreadful blow. I'd say that his skull is broken for certain.'

'Oh poor boy.'

Tommy swallowed a mouthful of brandy in an effort to quell the worms of fear twisting in his belly. 'Is there anything at all that can be done for him?'

The doctor looked down his long nose. He knew the Standish family and didn't approve of one of their ilk, a labourer for a father, hobnobbing with their betters. His voice was chill 'Not that needs concern you.'

Bellamy stepped in. 'Tommy Standish is a friend of George's, they played together since they were boys. If anyone can pull George round it will be Tommy.'

The doctor had heard the tale of the education. 'I recommend that the patient be kept motionless in a darkened room. A nurse is in attendance and will be replaced with another to watch over him tonight. Until things improve I suggest that he have around the clock nursing. I will call in again later.'

'So we must wait and see.' Bellamy slumped into a chair. 'It's the waiting that is the hardest.' Sighing 'His poor mother will be hit hard by this.'

'I have seen your good lady and recommended a good dose of laudanum to calm her, she will sleep in a while. I will visit her when I return later.' Placing the glass on the table he made ready to take his leave.

Bertram Bellamy rose to his feet. 'Tommy took a dreadful fall when he heard about George, perhaps you would be kind enough to take a look at him before you go.'

Tommy was adamant. 'There's no need, I feel fine now, it was the shock.'

The doctors narrow nostrils dilated. 'Well if you are sure. I really must be getting along.'

Bellamy had a hand on the doctor's sleeve. 'Let me see you to the door, Doctor.'

Stomach churning, Tommy stood with his hand on the mantelpiece listening to the muffled voices in the hallway. Cursing himself for not checking properly to see if George was dead. By his pallor alone he would have thought so. God he'd been deathly pale. The wound had been dreadful. He shuddered, grimacing, recalling how when he had tried to detect a pulse his hands had been sticky with George's blood, trembling uncontrollably. His hurry to escape had been so great that he hadn't finished the job properly, and now the error might cost him his own life. A shudder ran through him again. At best he could make a run for it, fetch up in Ireland and work his fingers to the bone on some poor farmer's land. If he made the journey undetected it would mean a life in hiding. Glancing at his image in the mirror above the mantel he saw that he was pale, grey with anxiety, his life was hanging in the balance, as he himself might hang yet.

To solve his problem he had to get into the room where George lay, and soon, he couldn't afford to have him regain consciousness.

He went back to the moment when he had crept up behind George, just before he had hit him with the rock George had turned, and Tommy was sure that the man had seen his attacker. God forbid that he should live to tell the tale. A fine sweat slicked his skin beneath his clothes.

Bellamy came back into the room. 'I have ordered the carriage to take you to your lodgings. I don't want to see you in the office for a day or two.'

Tommy began to protest. 'But I have so much work on.'

'Now, Tommy, you just listen to me. Don't make life more difficult that it has to be. I want you to rest for a day or two. Now that is an order.' Looking sternly, brooking no contradiction. 'I don't want you going down with a brain fever. This shock followed by a fall, you never know what it'll bring on. So take yourself off to your bed and stay there until I send for you.'

Powerless, Tommy wanted to rant. How was he to bear the four walls of his solitary room when everything was so uncertain? Confined, he'd go crazy!

The following morning as he walked to the quarry, Joe heard the news of the attack on George. Between the men trudging to work speculation was rife, theories passing from one to another as swift as any plague. Who could have tried to murder the quarry owner's son? The men gathering in the caban at the dinnertime break created a hotbed of conjecture. Ignorant of George's debts or threats to his life they began to question if the culprit of Millie Barker's murder couldn't also be guilty of this new outrage.

Joe remained reticent, and all though the men questioned him, his son being the manager and so must be privy to what occurred in the big house, he had no answers for them or for himself.

On finishing work he strode towards the office, on reaching there he was informed that his son was absent and it was unknown when he might return.

With a seed of worry burning in his belly he walked to Tommy's lodgings. There were several questions racing through his head, the prime one being, what had his lad to do with this calamity. A busybody had been glad to notify him that Tommy had been for dinner at Plas Mawr the night of the attack.

Utterly absorbed he travelled quickly to his son's lodgings. The lad might not like a member of the family calling on him, and the toffee-nosed woman that kept the house might be averse to dusty work clothes messing up her rooms, but he'd not have Emily fretting throughout the night going over the whys and wherefores. He'd have answers and he'd have them today. Reaching the house he pulled the bell rod with more force than necessary.

Indoors Tommy stopped pacing the floor of his room as the bell rang out. Thirty-six hours he'd been in virtual seclusion and the nervous strain was obvious. He was pale, a greyish tinge on his face. For the passed two days his bowels had turned to water, cramping his belly. His head ached with a dull persistent pain, and a purple bruise was blossoming on his brow.

Twm Williams, the special constable had pulled the bell pull just as viciously yesterday when he had called to inquire of his whereabouts at the time of the attack. Staring uncompromisingly, the enormous man had demanded to know what time he had arrived home on Saturday night, and if he'd gone out again before the following morning. Fortunately Mrs. Little had given him a solid alibi, but for that he might have found himself in deep water.

The bell rang out again and a fist beat the door. Tommy withdrew into himself. Then he heard his father's distinctive voice, answered by the soft tones of Mrs. Little. Marking Joe's heavy tread upon the stairs, he stared at the locked door waiting for his sharp knock.

When it came he almost cried out, then remembering that he must not betray emotion he swallowed deeply, preparing himself, and opened the door. A tight, half smile on his mouth.

Shocked by his son's appearance, Joe was alarmed, his eyes flying to the bruise on his face. 'Are you unwell?'

He answered mechanically. 'I'm all right. I took a fall.'

Joe's eyes darkened. 'When?'

'Yesterday, on hearing the terrible news of George.' He gave a weak smile. 'I'm afraid I fainted.' His hand touched the dark bruise. 'I hit my head as I went down. It was the shock.'

Joe's eyes bored into his son's. 'You weren't fighting?'

'No, Father I wasn't fighting.' His voice contemptuous, a supercilious twist to his mouth, he said 'Is that why you're here? To find out for yourself if I was involved in this despicable deed?'

'No of course not,' Joe lied.

'Oh really, Father!'

Joe's face tinged pink. 'I didn't want your mother worrying about you. If she heard that you were not in work, you know your mother, worries herself over every little thing.'

Opening the door, holding onto the doorknob, Tommy said 'Thank you for calling. Now you can report back to mother that I'm perfectly well.'

Tempted to black the other side of his face, Joe stood for a moment his emotion betraying his dislike for the man his son had become.

Ignoring the dismissal, his lip curled angrily. 'I'll not report anything such thing to your mother. At least you might show some respect for the woman that had the misfortune to bear you. You ungrateful pup.'

'Thank you, Father, I'll try to do so.'

Anxious to be out of the room, Joe turned on his heel.

Listening to his father's angry departure, tears welled in Tommy's eyes. Why did he behave so badly when the old man was around? In a prescient flash he answered his own question. Guilt. Shame. His father's high moral standards were hard to live up too. Throwing himself on the bed he stared at the ceiling and in the uneven whitewashed surface Millie Barker and George stared back. Visions of happier days came back to him, Millie running towards the old mill, the long grass pulling at the hem of her blue dress, sunshine glinting on her flying hair. George, a boy in a brown holland suit enjoying the local fair, his young face bright with laughter.

Noiseless, he rose and stood at the window looking down on the garden; the trees were beginning to shed leaves, small flurries of the brown parched debris shifting on the lawn in the increasing wind. Beyond the black railings, on the pavement, several straggling workers were returning home, dusty beards and distinctive hats making them easily identifiable as quarrymen. On the other side of the street a woman struggled to fasten a garden gate, her grey skirt billowing and the ribbons on her bonnet dancing around her face. Two children, hand in hand, dashed across the road a black and white dog at their heels. A carriage rounded the corner, stopping at the house opposite before moving on again.

The scene appeared so ordinary, which was amazing, when only a few yards away from this commonplace he was wondering if he should flee to Ireland to escape the hangman.

Sighing he went back to the bed and sat down on the edge of the mattress and sighed again. What was he to do? Whatever, he had to do something, he couldn't just sit here waiting for the inevitable to catch up with him.

Rising quickly he pulled the leather bag off the top of the wardrobe and opening a drawer he began to pack clothes into it, his movements frantic. Stuffing a shirt over a pair of trousers, he stopped. This was stupid, fleeing before he knew the state of George. He might already be dead. Hurriedly he flung the bag under the bed. Straightening his suit, pulling down his long coat, he took a brush from the dressing table and began to tidy his hair. He would go to Plas Mawr at once. Bertram Bellamy may complain, but he had to find out for himself how the land lay. No longer could he be the victim of circumstances, however much they might be of his own making.

With this thought he hurried from his room and out of the house. At the garden gate he debated whether to ride to the mansion or walk the two miles on foot. Deciding that it would be useful to have the horse if he was forced to make a rapid departure, he made his way to the livery stables.

With the aid of two stable-hands his horse was ready and he was mounted, leaving the yard within minutes. Anastasia, the chestnut bay tossed her brown mane as she and rider approached the roadway. Pleased that he'd decided to ride, the poor beast hated confinement and would become unduly frisky if cooped-up for more than a day. A moment later they were on the road to Plas Mawr.

He felt better almost immediately, the anguish that had plagued him since discovering that George lived began to recede and with it his headache lifted, and for the first time he was able to consider the situation objectively. Surely no man could withstand such a blow and recover his senses completely. If the unthinkable happened, and he made a recovery, it was imperative that he denied leaving the house on Saturday night. The constables had Mrs. Little's word for it.

It was with only half a mind that he became aware that the light was weakening, the hazy sun dropping to the mist on the sea.

He passed the place that George had begun his song, and he spurred the horse on to leave the spot quickly.

As he neared the gates of Plas Mawr he saw Twm Williams searching beneath the rhododendrons. The man's presence there was so unexpected that Tommy reined in suddenly so that his mount danced and turned a half circle beneath him. There was a curse on his lips for the badly behaved beast and the lawman, but he mustered a polite 'Good evening, Constable' as he brought the mare under control.

Straightening, Twm released the branches. 'Tommy Standish.'

It was with alarm that Tommy saw that the constable was dangerously close to discovering the rock used in the assault, he tore his eyes away from the spot. 'Are you searching for anything in particular?'

Twm's glance went back to the dark ground beneath the bushes. 'Anything that can help hang the bastard that did for the young master.'

Tommy felt an immense sense of relief washed over him. With an expression that matched the tragedy, he gave a low sigh. 'He's not dead is he?'

'No. Thank goodness.'

The disappointment was astounding; he had difficulty making his lips move into a smile. 'Thank God for that.' The words nearly choked him. 'So what are you looking for exactly?'

Twm put his palm on the bay mare's neck, patting the whickering animal. 'Anything. What baffles me is why anyone would wait until young Bellamy was at the gates of his home before attacking him.' He turned his eyes to the road that George had walked. 'If he had spent the evening in the village why didn't they attack him there? Why wait until he was this close to home?

Tommy shifted in the saddle. 'I reckon that whoever was sent to whack him probably followed him here to make sure he was the man they were after before striking him down.'

'Hmm. It's possible.'

Hoping that he had set a seed in Twm Williams's slow brain, Tommy pulled on the reins. 'I must be going. Let me know if there is anything I can help you with.' There was sheen of sweat beneath his clothes, growing chill, as he rode up the avenue.

Louise Bellamy received him in the drawing room, her eyes dreadfully swollen and her nose red from weeping. Clutching at his coat sleeve, she turned her wet eyes to his. 'Tommy I'm pleased that you are here.' She began plucking at the material. 'You'll know what to do. You're always so good in a crisis. Bertram is hopeless.'

Steering her to a chair, Tommy lowered her into it. 'I'm sure that Bertram is doing everything than can be done. Please don't upset yourself. The doctor is sure to be doing his very best for George.'

'I know, but poor George looks so gravely ill.' She wept softly. 'His poor head is so sore. Oh my poor boy.'

He shot a quick glance at the door, as hurried footsteps sounded in the hallway, terrified that George had woken and named his assailant. The footsteps receded and he composed himself, and brought his tortured mind under control. Turning to Louise his voice was calm. 'Is he still unconscious?'

Her face crumpled. 'Yes. He lies there as still as a doll.'

Stooping to her Tommy put his arm around her shoulder. Words of comfort remained unspoken; he wouldn't tempt fate my saying he was sure that George would make a recovery when his whole being longed for his death.

Clutching her voluminous skirt, she began to rise. 'You must go up to see him, it might make all the difference having you by his bedside.'

'I don't think that's a good idea. My presence may disturb him.'

'Please, Tommy, do it for me.'

He imagined George opening his eyes as he made his entrance into the room and his stomach lurched sickeningly.

Catching him by the sleeve, she steered him towards the door. 'A friendly voice might be just what he needs to restore him to us.'

'I don't think…'

Deaf to his protests she led him out of the drawing room and up the stairs.

The bedroom had already taken on the odour of sickness; the windows closed to keep the patient from draughts and the drawn curtains obliterating the last of the day's light. On a bedside table a lamp burned, the low flame hardly assisting the physician drawing blood from the patient.

Slumped in an armchair, Bertram Bellamy his face ashen watched the doctor open another vein in George's pale flesh.

Louise went straight to the bedside. With hardly a glance at the doctor performing his surgical operation, she spoke to her son. 'George darling I have brought Tommy to see you.'

George's eyelids flickered.

Beaming through her tears, she turned to Tommy. 'I told you that you being here would help. George is so fond of you Tommy.'

George's hands twitched

Without taking his eyes off his son's face, Bertram rose slowly. 'By Jove she's right. He moved.' Wetness filled his eyes, his voice cracked. 'So all is not lost.'

In his excitement Bertram clutched his wife to his chest. 'Louise you are a miracle.'

'Bertram dear, you have to thank Tommy for the miracle. It was his presence that brought our boy out of his dead faint.'

Beaming, he crossed to Tommy and threw his arm around his shoulder. 'Words can't tell you how much I thank you for this.' His eyes went back to the bed. 'Our George will make a recovery now, I just know that he will.'

The doctor began to wipe his instruments with a cloth before placing them back into the mahogany carrying box. 'He'll still need careful nursing but I predict that he'll come out of his faint before morning.' Smiling. 'The strength of the young, remarkable recuperative powers.'

George's face had been grey when he and Louise had entered the room but observing him now Tommy noticed that the grey tinge had had taken on a trace of blue. He looked across to the doctor but he seemed as hopeful as the Bellamy's did, and nearly as excited as they made arrangements for a roster of nurses to watch the patient day and night.

Bertram beamed at Tommy. 'I want you to move in here with us until George is fully well. You'll be good company for him.' His face sobered. 'It's likely to be a long haul before he's his old self.' Thoughts of what had brought George to this demise surfaced in his mind but he squashed them immediately. George would turn over a new leaf. If nothing else he would have learned an important lesson from this debacle.

It was perfect. If George should begin to make a recovery he was here on hand to deal with the problem. By volunteering to sit with him at every opportunity he could judge the state of George's mind. Of course he might just never remember what had happened that night. Then George would be safe. Aloud, Tommy said 'I'll be glad to be what ever help that I can.'

Bertram patted his shoulder. 'Good, man.' Turning to his wife. 'Louise be an angel and make the necessary arrangements with the housekeeper for Tommy's stay.' He raised his hand. 'Mind now, I want a very good room for the boy. He must be comfortable if he's to be with us for a long period.'

Clearing her long skirt off the floor, Louise looked back to the bed once more before leaving the room.

The doctor snapped his leather bag closed. 'I'll call in again first thing in the morning. The nurse will take care of him now.' He smiled. 'I expect to see a big improvement in the patient when I return.'

Bertram took the man's hand and shook it energetically. 'Thank you, Doctor.'

As the doctor left the young woman hired to attend the sickroom entered and turned the lamp down low until the room was almost in darkness. 'Master Bellamy should rest now.'

Bertram glanced at his son. 'Of course, nurse. We will be in the library should you need us.'

Efficiently she began to straighten the bedclothes. 'I will get someone to fetch you should it be necessary.'

In stark contrast to George's bedroom the library was bright with lamp and firelight. Slumping into an armchair Bertram sighed. 'Well, the day has had a much better outcome than I expected. I don't mind admitting to you, Tommy that I feared the worst last night and again this morning.' He gave another weary sigh.

Tommy at the sideboard poured two large measures of brandy into glasses, and crossing the room he handed one to Bertram.

'Thanks, my boy, I need this.'

Taking the chair on the opposite side of the fireplace, Tommy crossed his long legs. He had an ear cocked for footsteps summoning them back to the sickroom; he didn't share Bellamy's belief in George's recovery. The man looked too much like a corpse to survive for long. He was ashen, cold looking, with that blue-grey tinge to his flesh.

Although he hadn't touched him or come near enough to do so, it was clear that he hardly breathed. There'd be no clawing his way back from the brink of death to denounce his childhood adversary. Hiding his grim smile he sipped his brandy.

A short time later Bertram dozed off in the chair exhausted by the two-day ordeal. Tommy called for his valet and when the man had helped Bellamy to his bedroom Tommy poured himself another brandy, and enjoying the heat of the fire he let his nerves unravel.

Allocated a bedroom close to George's, Tommy heard the coming and going of the staff throughout the night. As no alarm was given he assumed that the patient lived. He woke in the early hours to Henrietta slipping beneath his blankets.

Hours later he awoke to the wind soughing through the tall elms. The other side of the bed was empty, grown chill, and for that he was grateful. The consequences of a servant coming on them together didn't bear thinking about. He would speak to Henrietta about her nocturnal wandering and insist that she curb her reckless behaviour, if she did not he would threaten to return to his lodgings immediately. He felt vaguely irritated that he must see her to deliver the ultimatum.

Rising he flung his legs over the side of the bed, the rug beneath his bare feet was soft as lambs wool. Cherishing hopes that such comfort would soon be commonplace he glanced around the unfamiliar and luxurious room. The fire in the black marble grate had burned itself out. The dark framed mirror above it reflected the green brocade of the curtain and little else save the overhead chandelier and the corner of the wardrobe. Beneath the window, a plain mahogany stand held a bowl and large water jug ornate with maroon and gold decoration. In the far corner a mahogany commode embellished with oak leaves and acorns faded by sunlight. His eyes fell on the green damask couch at the foot of the bed; the clothes he wore yesterday were draped tidily across it. The room was not dissimilar to George's bedroom except that had a desk and an extra wardrobe for his extravagant store of clothes.

George, he wondered how he was, probably worse than yesterday if his colour then was anything to go by. Rising he sighed. It wasn't worth worrying about; George wasn't going to recover. He gave a long yawn then walked over to the washstand and splashed his face with freezing cold water.

Before going down to breakfast he knocked on the sickroom door. The nurse was straightening the bed sheet as he entered; looking up she gave him a warm smile. For the first time he noticed her, slightly built, her long dark hair platted and brought together in a coil at the base of her neck. She was pretty in a soft sort of way, not the sort of prettiness that lasts beyond a twenty-fifth birthday; she'd be motherly and matronly by that time.

Keeping his voice low, he asked 'How is he?'

George's colour had improved, and he wondered how much this should concern him.

She glanced at her patient. 'He's getting better by the moment.'

Tommy scotched the idea of going to the office. If George began to show signs of regaining consciousness, he needed to be on hand to deal with the situation.

It sounded like an order as he said, 'I'll stay with him if you want a break.'

'That's kind of you but my relief should be here at any moment.'

She'd be hard to shift, he could see that, and changed his tactics accordingly. His eyes dropped to George and he played the part of a sad friend. 'If I can't be of any use here I'll go down to breakfast.' For several heartbeats he remained silent, then lifting his eyes to hers, he spoke softly 'I'll ask someone to bring you a tray of tea up.'

His distress touched her and she wished that she had slipped out quietly and left the pair together, it was plain that he cared deeply for his injured friend. She would make amends later and leave him alone with the patient for a while.

'That would be lovely I could do with a cup of tea.' Her eyes went to the pale face in the bed. 'Perhaps later, you could come and sit with him? I could make myself scarce for half an hour or so.'

He couldn't have wished for better circumstances. 'I'd like that. Perhaps if I talked to him it might help. I could remind him of the good times we spent together when we were boys.'

Amused at his naivety she smiled. She wasn't going to be the one to tell him that patients that were unconscious were deaf to sound. 'Who knows, maybe he'll like a reminder of better days.'

'Righto, I'll be back later. If I run out of things to talk about I'll read to him. It must be pretty boring just lying there.' Deliberately he put a note of boyish buffoonery into the statement.

Coming out into the hallway, he glanced back at the closed bedroom door, then walked to the window at the end of the long hallway and looked out over the garden and beyond. The weather had deteriorated, the top branches of the trees were bending in the wind, the sky was greyer than at the beginning of the day, and dark bruised clouds hung over the sea, stretching away to the horizon. Not a good day for straying too far a field. He gave a fleeting thought to the workers on the quarry galleries, there'd be a buffeting and a soaking for man and boy today. It gave him satisfaction that he wouldn't be one of them. With a sly grin on his face he drew towards the stairs, descending quickly he walked to the breakfast room. There was an appetite on him this morning, which was gratifying.

Since the incident he hadn't been interested in food, his worry had played havoc with his stomach.

Bertram Bellamy was sitting at the dining table as Tommy entered. The full plate of breakfast food before him virtually untouched. 'Tommy come and sit down.' He was cheerful but his weariness was easy to detect.

Pulling a chair out, Tommy lifted his coat tails and sat. 'George looks very much better this morning.'

Bellamy's eyes widened. 'Oh you've been into see him already?' Taking a slice of bread from the plate he bit into it and spoke through the mouthful. 'I popped in very early but he was sleeping peacefully.'

Tommy had an urge to squash his optimism. Didn't the old buffer realise that George was on his last legs? There would be no miraculous recovery today or any other day. Eyeing the other man's breakfast plate, the untouched lamb cutlet, kidneys and fried potatoes he pushed his chair back and went to the sideboard where silver domes covered the hot serving dishes. Lifting one he forked a cutlet onto a plate and moved onto a dish of potatoes, spooning a good quantity onto the side of the plate.

What did it matter if he was magnanimous it wouldn't change the outcome. 'I shouldn't be surprised to see him sitting up and taking notice later today.'

The elderly man's beaming smile rewarded him. 'Oh, Tommy, you really think so?'

As he turned back to the table there was a smile on Tommy's face. Placing the full plate onto the tablecloth, he lied 'I certainly do, his colour alone is much better, and he's breathing isn't so shallow. I'd say the signs are good.'

An unhealthy flush rose on Bertram's face. 'You don't know how happy your words make me. You know that I value your opinion and I'm sure that once again you are right.'

A small leafless branch crashed into the window and both men looked up. Pushing back his chair Bellamy crossed the room and looked out of the large bay window. 'The weather's worsening. I hope that it doesn't delay the doctor. I so want to have a word with him.'

'There's not much that'll stop him visiting a patient.' Tommy hooked a slice of cutlet.

'No. I expect you're right.'

Finishing his breakfast Tommy stood. 'I must get to the office.'

Bellamy put a restraining hand on his sleeve. 'Oh not today, Tommy. I really want you here.'

Expecting this reaction, Tommy put up little resistance. 'If you are sure that I will be useful I'll stay.'

The clatter of carriage wheels broke the conversation and Bertram dashed to the door. 'That'll be the doctor now.'

The door of the sick room was closed for more than an hour in which time Tommy remained alone in the breakfast room tortured with the possibility that George had regained consciousness and named his assassin. In this nervous state the hour passed slowly, and by the time that Bertram was heard to go into the library with the doctor, Tommy's stomach was in turmoil once more.

The local doctor had arrived with an eminent man from out of the county, and his opinion of the situation left little hope for George making a recovery. Brain damage he had declared within five minutes of arriving in the sickroom and it was to a stricken father that he gave his news.

Eventually, when Tommy joined Bellamy in the library after the surgeons had returned to the village with a promise to call again on the morrow, the old man was ashen, his eyes red from weeping. Henrietta and Louise had been kept in the dark of the outcome of the examination and the chore fell to Tommy to break the sad news to them. Henrietta took the news stoically but the boy's poor mother broke down and was helped to her room by a maid who administered a dose of laudanum to help her sleep off the terrible shock.

The following day brought the devastating news that fourteen vessels in Caernarvon Bay had been wrecked in a gale. Eventually it would be known that two hundred and twenty three vessels had sunk on the shores of Britain. The largest loss of life was on the Royal Charter when four hundred souls lost their lives when the 719-ton luxury steam clipper sank on Moelfre Head. In all more than eight hundred died on that fateful night.

Hearing the terrible news most of the men left off work at the quarry and went to see ruins and debris that littered the bay. It was a time of funerals and listing of the ships that had come to grief.

It was at breakfast on the morning of the twenty-seven of October 1859 Bertram with tears in his eyes read the roll call of the stricken ships that had been caught unawares in the force 12 gale.

The dark days passed slowly and after a tedious melancholy week, Tommy insisted that he return to his own lodgings.

Henrietta was becoming a pest, wandering around the dark corridors at night and creeping into his bed. Afraid that her behaviour would alert her parents to the state of affairs, Tommy made up his mind to resume his routine at the office and at his home.

Collecting his bay mare from the stables, he rode along the lane thankful to be out of the oppressive atmosphere of the mansion.

Several weeks passed in which George began to shuffle about his bedroom aided by a nurse. His memory was gone and so was the better part of his speech, one side of his face had grown slack and lifeless.

It was in this dreadful atmosphere that a tearful Henrietta gave her news to Tommy. She was pregnant. It was exactly as he anticipated and had planned, Bellamy could hardly disallow a wedding when his daughter began to grow stout in her belly.

Deciding that the news had to be broken, Tommy arrived at Plas Mawr to deliver a further blow to the elderly and now sick man. In the library with a brandy in his hand, his stomach fluttering with nerves Tommy looked into the old man's sad eyes. 'Bertram I'm afraid I have another piece of news that I fear will not please you.'

Resigned the old man sighed. 'Oh tell me anyway.' He waved his hand nonchalantly betraying that this wasn't the first brandy he had enjoyed this afternoon. 'What can hurt me further? My beloved son sits upstairs unable to hold either a conversation or a knife and fork?'

Tommy interrupted him before he began to list the problems within the sick room. 'Henrietta and I have come close during the past few months.'

Bellamy wandering mind focused on his quarry manager, his eyes narrowed.

The steely gaze was disconcerting, averting his eyes Tommy looked down at the Turkey rug. 'We have become very close.'

It dawned on him that Tommy might be about to ask for her hand, it was embarrassing, the young buffoon believed that such a notion would be countenanced, it was absurd. 'You'll not marry her. However much I care for you, Tommy you'll not have my daughter. She's got a good dowry and she'll marry someone of note.'

Angry that he should be considered not good enough, Tommy fought to control his temper. 'It's not quite as simple as that.'

Getting a whiff of how the land lay Bellamy's voice hardened. 'In what way not quite as simple?'

Gathering all of his courage Tommy spoke calmly. 'I'm afraid that your daughter is pregnant.'

'Pregnant!' Bellamy roared. A sound no one had heard from the old man since the demise of his son. 'And by whom? Sir. Who has got her into this sorry state?'

'Me, I'm afraid.'

Rearing out of the chair, face reddening with anger, he blustered 'After all that I have done for you.'

It was with an effort that Tommy remained seated, his voice moderate. 'I am prepared to stand by her.'

Bellamy turned on him, a savage look on his face. 'Over my dead body.'

The door opened and Louise flushed with tears rushed to her husband's side. 'Please, Bertram dear don't be too hasty.'

Turning quickly he nearly knocked her off her feet. 'Oh, so you are aware of this sorry state of affairs?'

'Henrietta has just told me, she's very upset.'

'Upset! I'm upset!'

Turning her tearful gaze to Tommy, she stuttered, 'Go to Hen…rietta, I'll speak to Bertram.'

For a moment Tommy hesitated.

'Please, leave us. Go!'

Like recalcitrant children Tommy and Henrietta sat in the drawing room while Bertram and Louise remained locked in the library. Only the raised voices of both parents reached them and for more than an hour they sat in near silence, Henrietta wringing her hands and Tommy waiting patiently for the inevitable end result.

It was Louise that came to the drawing room and asked that they would both go back to the library. Henrietta was trembling with apprehension. Tommy tight with controlled ill temper.

Standing beside the fireplace his hand on the mantelpiece Bertram looked at them with unfeigned scorn. 'Louise has managed to convince me that this charade will work out.' He turned malevolent eyes to his daughter. 'You have disappointed me beyond my wildest imagining.'

Tears welled in her eyes. 'Papa!'

'Don't you dare Papa me, you brazen hussy.'

Turning his steely glance to Tommy. 'And as for you, I trusted you with my family. I gave you everything in my power to give and you took more. You took and spoiled my prize possession, my unsullied daughter, and by your licentious wickedness you soiled her in my eyes.'

A sob caught in Henrietta's throat, bending her head to her mother's shoulder she began to weep.

Tommy glanced her way then his eyes came back to Bertram. 'I am sorry.' His voice was weaker than he would have liked.

Putting her daughter aside, Louise put a restraining hand on her husband's sleeve. 'Bertram please.'

Shaking her hand off, he spluttered 'Yes, yes, I know, dear.'

Henrietta had her face in her hands, her body trembling to her soft weeping.

Glancing at her Bertram took a noisy breath. 'Your Mother suggests that the two of you marry quickly, and secretly.'

For a moment Henrietta didn't believe what she had heard and her head came up slowly. As his words sank in her face lit, accentuating the dark circles beneath her eyes.

Exasperated, Bertram snatched the idea of a romantic wedding away from her. There'd be no special frock, guests or honeymoon. It'd be the four of them, him and Louise, and the ungrateful pair. It would be an affair as shabby as he could make it. Glaring at her from beneath his untidy eyebrows, he snarled 'Don't think that you'll get away with a special day, Lady. It'll be me that makes all the arrangements.'

There was a tremor in her voice and her eyes shone wetly. 'I don't want an elaborate day.' What did it matter missing out on a beautiful wedding, when she would have handsome Tommy Standish for her husband. Touching her mother's hand she imparted some of the excitement in her trembling fingers.

Feeling bested, Bertram made a scornful noise, then turned his attention to Tommy. 'If you should further injure my daughter by jilting her, or speaking of her sorry state, I will have you removed from my quarry and you'll not work in another quarry or any business in the land. Do you understand me?'

Tommy nodded. Why the old buffer thought that he would ruin this heaven sent opportunity to one day own the quarry was beyond him. Henrietta might not be a prize, but by marrying her, the Garddryn and Plas Mawr would come under his control. George wouldn't mend, and Bellamy was as sick as a man gets without actually taking to his bed. Giving nothing of his thoughts away, there was no need to upset the apple cart at this stage, he spoke softly. 'I understand you perfectly.'

Dismayed by her father's unkindness Henrietta clutched Tommy's arm. 'Tommy loves me. He'll not run away.' She turned doe eyes to her future husband. 'Tell Papa that you love me, Tommy.'

Covering her agitated hand, he smiled. 'Everything will work out.'

Scornful, the old man glared. 'It had better. Before this week is out I'll have the pair of you married. I insist that the child must be born away from this parish so the date of its birth can be concealed. I'll not have our good name besmirched by gossiping servants and curious neighbours.'

The idea of sending Henrietta away for a while to await the birth appealed to Tommy. Imagining his young and tearful bride climbing aboard a train that would bear her to a far off place not to return until the child she carried was sturdy enough to make the homeward journey brought a weak smile to his mouth.

With no intention of accompanying her, he agreed to the old man's demands without question. Affably, man to man, he said 'That's a reasonable request. As soon as we are wed I'll make the arrangements.'

Seeing the shadow that passed across Henrietta's face he patted her hand consolingly. Choose the right location and he would enjoy many months of freedom, enough time to pay several visits to Penrhyn. Glancing down into Henrietta's round face, he gave her a warm smile. 'Cumbria or somewhere in the Scottish highlands.'

The young man's acquiescence galled Bertram. 'Wherever. Cumbria, Scotland or Ireland.'

Mistaking the look of satisfaction that flitted across Tommy's face he endeavoured to expunge the reason for it. 'Standish, you'll not again sleep in my house until my daughter has a ring on her finger. So I suggest you leave now and not call again until the morning of the marriage. You'll be informed of when that will be as soon as I have made arrangements with the priest. Now good day.'

The whole episode was going better than he could have hoped for. There still might be time to ride over to Penrhyn, Sadie's plumptuous thighs beckoned. Thirsting for the servant girl's juicy wetness, he relinquished Henrietta's hot, dry hand.

Reluctant to let him go Henrietta clutched Tommy's sleeve. Turning appealing eyes to her father. 'Oh, Papa you're being very harsh.'

Bertram lashed out. 'Get out of my sight!'

Embarrassed and appalled, Henrietta burst into tears.

Louise was about to intercede on her daughter's behalf but Bertram's anger stopped her mid-stride. Linking her arm through her daughter's she led her from the room.

The wedding took place early on the following Monday morning, the quietest affair the village had seen, so quiet in fact that neither Emily nor Joe got wind of it until the following morning when a worker informed Joe what had taken place.

Throughout the day Joe pounded at the slate cliff with a vengeance, striking at the rock until his arms tingled with the ferocity of the blows.

At mid-day he'd shunned the company of the men and kept away from the cabanod. Hunkered down on a slab of rubbish rock he picked at the slice of bread and dripping Emily had packed for him, eventually throwing it to the scavenging gulls circling overhead.

Blind to the scenery, the savaged mountainside, grey sky and sea stretching out to the horizon, his vista was the past. He was on the *Hardwick Lady* sailing down the Mersey. The sturdy sailing ship meeting the swell at Liverpool bar, spray flying across her decks as she dipped her bows to the sea, tasting the salt of the spindrift on his lip, hearing the crack of the sails ballooning in the stiff breeze.

Emily, nowt but a young girl walking by his side, head thrown back and the ribbons of her bonnet playing around her cheeks as she looked up at the stone walls of Caernarvon Castle. Tommy, a little lad with his tiny hand in hers.

Chloe sprang into his mind and the familiar lump tightened his throat, time hadn't healed the hurt and tears welled as memories seared his heart. Standing beside the small cross that marked her grave, the ground grown flat where her tiny coffin lay. Whispering her name to the wind, he brushed the wetness from his cheeks.

The physical pain brought him back to the present. Years ago he had trained his mind not to remain still for more than a moment when he heard Chloe's voice in his mind. He would divert his thoughts to Frank. Sometimes it worked, and Chloe would go back to the part of his soul that he tried so desperately to hide from.

Frank was a blessing; the boy had never disappointed him, now working in the dressing shed, running around the place on his young legs, at the beck and call of every man there.

Grateful that he was blessed with one good son, he packed away the debris of his meal and made his way back to Jerusalem gallery.

At finish of work he walked to the gates, Frank would be waiting and would fall into step with him much like his namesake had done all those years ago at the Galloway. The past seemed clearer than the present today.

Running from the dressing shed, coat flying behind him, Frank raced towards the gate looking for his father amongst the men standing there. When he saw him he knew from the look of pain on his face that he had heard the news of the marriage, and his heart went out to him.

With barely a greeting father and son fell into step, bringing up the rear of the groups of men making their way to the Half Way public house or their own doorsteps.

As if by some family pact, a closing of ranks, neither Joe nor Frank spoke a word of Tommy. The bitterness and anger might erupt in their own living room, but the Standish family pride didn't allow for grievances to be aired in public.

Frank's eyes were on the brown sparrows flitting from twig to twig in the young elders beside the path. 'I'll feed the pig an' hens while you talk to Mam.'

Joe gave him a sidelong glance. 'That's a good idea, son. I want a quiet word wi' her.' Sighing loudly. 'This lot'll come as a shock to her.'

'Poor Mam.'

'Aye it's poor Mam alreeght. And who is it that makes her sad? Bloody Tommy that's bloody who.' Swearing under his breath. 'I'll swing for that bugger one day.'

Hating conflict or rows of any kind, Frank dropped his eyes to the ground.

Putting his arm around the boy's shoulder Joe pulled him close. 'Don't worry about anything. You get straight to the field when we get home, feed and settle the stock, leave your mother to me, there's a good lad.'

'I'm worried about Mam.'

'Aye I know. She'll be upset tonight but come tomorrow she'll be bloody mad and likely to go up to the big house and take a broomstick to that son of hers.

Frank grinned at the notion. 'That'd be a sight to behold, me Ma battering our Tommy and the butler standing by.'

Joe was glad to see Frank smile; the lad took everything so to heart. He was nowt but a big softie their Frank, not at all like the other bugger.

Arriving at the cottage Frank made for the small back yard to collect the bucket of mash that Emily would have prepared from vegetable peelings. As he picked up the bucket he heard his father close the front door. Sighing he skirted the house and made his way to the two acre field.

Emily was slicing a loaf of bread as Joe came into the living room. Looking up she gave him a smile. 'Is that the time.' She glanced at the clock on the mantelpiece. I don't know where the afternoon gone. All I seem to have done today is iron and mend.'

Joe was thankful that both chores had kept her indoors, no nosy neighbour had had the pleasure of telling her the Standish family business. Sitting in the chair by the fire he unlaced his heavy boots.

Putting aside the knife, she rubbed her hands on her apron. 'You ill or something our, Joe?'

He looked up suddenly.

She was smiling. 'It's the first time in living memory that you have come through that door after work and not asked me what's for supper.'

'Oh is that all.' He pushed the boots to the side of the grate, later he would leave them to air by the fire. Damp it had been up at the quarry, the slate slippery and treacherous underfoot.

Beginning to rise, avoiding Emily's eyes, he didn't know where to begin to tell her. Now he wished that he had come in and blurted out the news quickly. Thinking about the best way to do it had killed his tongue stone dead. On stockinged feet he came to her, resting his hands lightly on her shoulders. A great sadness came over him, much as it had earlier, and he was flung back into the past. Christmas Eve long ago, when it had snowed, Tommy had found small prints in the snow and had run ahead searching for the reindeers. 'Emily I have some news that I'm afraid you are not going to like.'

Her heart fluttered in her breast. 'Oh, Joe what's happened?'

He could have gladly killed his eldest son at that moment seeing the shadow that passed across his beloved wife's face. 'It's our Tommy.'

'Tommy. Is he ill?'

'No nowt like that.'

The tensed muscles in her shoulders relaxed. 'Thank God.'

Joe's face was dark. 'He's wed.'

'Wed! To who?'

His arms fell to his side and he took a step away from her. 'Bellamy's lass.'

'No that can't be. I saw him only a matter of a few days ago and he made no mention of getting wed. He's not even courting. Whoever told you this told you wrong, Joe.'

'He's wed, lass. I'm sorry to be the one to bring such tidings to you, but it's the truth.'

Tears ruined her vision. 'Joe, is he so ashamed of us that he couldn't bear to see us at the church?'

'I don't know. Probably. Tommy has always hankered after a fancy life, the big house and all the trapping that go with it.'

Behind the house Frank stored the clean bucket, ready for tomorrows mash. Entering the house quietly, he took off his filthy boots. Wary of going into the living room, he had no wish to interrupted or become involved with what was going on in there.

'That you, lad?' His father called from the living room. 'Is the livestock alreeght?'

'Aye everything's fine.'

'Well don't stay in the scullery, you'll freeze to death.'

Slipping out of his work-coat Frank hung it on the peg on the back door, then came into the living room. The atmosphere was brittle. Tears still shone in Emily's eyes, and his father was trying to busy himself folding a newspaper.

A loud knock at the front door startled them all.

Joe moved across the room quickly. 'That could be the bugger now.'

Opening the door wide he confronted his son. 'So you've decided to visit at last.'

'Nice to see you too, Father.'

Turning his back Joe walked into the living room, Tommy followed.

There was nothing of the erring son about Tommy's entrance; he looked quite relaxed, almost jaunty. Wearing soft kid lavender gloves and carrying a silver topped cane, a gift from Henrietta, he raised the knob to the brim of his black silk hat, a cheeky gesture, and under other circumstances it might be thought debonair.

Smiling smugly, he said 'You've heard my news then?'

The colour flew to Joe's cheeks. 'Aye we have and I can't say that we are very pleased at being ignored in the matter'

Emily had every intention of giving her eldest son a piece of her mind, but seeing him now she felt nothing but sadness. 'Why did you do it, our Tommy? Are you really so ashamed of us?'

His brows furrowed in irritation. 'No of course not, Mother. Circumstances overtook us.' Looking away from her eyes as he lied. 'Had we had more time I would have been pleased to have you there.'

Joe snorted. 'What 'ave us at the big house don't make me bloody laugh. You couldn't wait to go behind our backs.'

Looking from her husband back to her son, Emily said quietly, 'Why the rush, son?' Then as realisation dawned, her hand flew to her mouth. 'The lass is having a bairn. Oh, Tommy how could you bring such shame on our family?'

Joe laughed rudely. 'Can't control everything then.'

Tommy's eyes narrowed. Thoughts that he had kept to himself for years came in a flood of angry words. 'Shame! Don't talk to me about shame. All my life I've been ashamed by the way that you live.' With a look of scorn he looked slowly around the room. 'In this hovel.'

Beyond anger Joe slipped back into his natural dialect, roaring, 'Hovel is it. I remember a time when thee were pleased to have the roof of it over tha bloody miserable head.

Emily snatched at Joe's shirt. 'Don't, our Joe.' Fist clenched the knuckles ivory; Joe pushed his face into his son's. 'Thou'll apologise to tha mother, the woman that kept this home clean, put good meals on the table, mended and washed tha clothes, bore and suckled thee and for what. Nowt! It were all a bloody waste of her time.'

Furious, Tommy's eyes blazed. 'You just do not understand do you? I hated living here. I hated the slops we ate. The second hand clothes I wore.'

Emily began to cry quietly.

Tommy's eyes flashed to her then back to his father. 'You did nothing to better yourself, nothing.'

Joe slapped his face viciously and instinctively Tommy palm came up covering the red weal.

Joe's hand burnt with the force of the blow but there was no regret in his heart. With a chill in his voice that Tommy was a stranger too, he spoke distinctly. 'I was so busy feeding you, and seeing that you had the best so that you could continue your trips to Plas Mawr, besides paying for your teachers, that I had little time for owt else but to work.' His lips compressed in a thin line. 'Your mother gave up the chance to have our own smallholding so that you could have a good education. If I had ignored her pleading on your behalf she would now have a home to call her own and an income from it. I know that given the time again she would do precisely the same thing.' Snorting scornfully, 'Seeing how things have turned out, I'd have rather dropped you in the gutter as we were leaving Manchester than have you insult the woman that gave birth to you.'

Emily sobbed. 'Don't say that, Joe, he's our son.'

A log in the fire cracked and Joe turned to the grate and said in a resigned and hopeless voice, 'Don't I bloody know it. The Bellamy's are welcome to him. I feel sorry for the woman that has taken him as her husband. She'll have nothing but heartache ahead of her. Treachery and bloody heartache.'

Striding towards the door Tommy snatched it open. And with neither a backward glance nor another word, he walked through it and slammed it closed.

Chapter Fourteen

Emily was melancholy, since the family debacle following Tommy's marriage she'd seen neither hair nor hide of her eldest son. Joe had virtually wiped his hands of the lad and Frank refused to get embroiled in the family argument.

Today, as she washed the slate floor in the scullery, drawing a damp cloth over the uneven flags, she thought of that awful night and Tommy's harshness. Hovel, the word had haunted her, sticking in her gullet like a sharp stone since the moment it had dropped from his unguarded tongue. Sighing, she swished the cloth ones more over the wet floor before wringing it out and leaving it to dry on the tin bath outside the back door, anchoring it with a stone to stop the stiff breeze from whipping it away.

Standing for a moment she let the wind tangle her hair about her face. The sea and mountain heather was on the air, the tang of salt and a haunting fragrance of upland flowers. With her mouth slightly open she breathed slowly, tasting the breeze on her tongue, fresh and energising, lighting her mood instantly.

Before the neighbours spied her acting the mad woman or worse, the mad English woman, she retreated indoors.

Upstairs she stood in front of the specked mirror and pulled a brush through her long hair, grey streaks had begun to appear amongst the once dense locks. Coiling it, she used several pins to hold it tidy. Eyes drawn to the silver-grey strands, she touched the fine hair at her temple. Smiling, she remembered an elderly aunt's words from long ago. "The grey uns are as warm as the dark uns, so why worrit." But could not remember whom the old lady had been speaking to.

Her mind still in the past, she took a clean apron from the pile of ironing on the bed and covered her fawn, woollen skirt.

Downstairs she made a brew, and sat with the tea cooling, pondering on an idea that had been playing on her mind these past few weeks.

Joe arrived home shortly after, and as she poured tea for him she was tempted to talk of her idea, but decided to wait until he'd soaked his aching body in the bath by the fire, and supper was over.

Friday night usually saw Frank at a chapel meeting, or murdering a tune on the fiddle he was learning to play at a retired music teacher home in the village. The evening would be undisturbed. So when the lamp was lit, and the fire burned steadily, without want of fuel for an hour or more, she interrupted Joe's perusal of the Caernarvon newspaper.

'Joe, I've been thinking about what was said the last time our Tommy was here.'

He'd been expecting her to say something all evening; she'd had that look about her, fidgety and distracted.

Lowering the paper, he met her eyes. 'I know that you have thought of little else of late. I could gladly swipe Tommy again for upsetting you so much.'

A frown puckered her brow. 'Let's not go over all that again. I want us to think about something else, something more pleasant.'

'Go on.' The newspaper slipped to his lap.

'Now that Tommy is gone from home and Frank is working why don't we consider building a cottage of our own.'

He felt her eyes resting on him, waiting and expectant. 'Is this because of what Tommy said about us living in a hovel? Is that why you want to up sticks?'

'No of course not.' She wouldn't admit that she hadn't been able to dust or sweep without Tommy's words plaguing her. 'We wanted to do it years ago and we put it off. At that time Tommy's learning was more important. The boys are grown, we could do it now.'

The fire cracked, spitting hot embers onto the rag rug. Leaning forward he doused the tiny red specks. 'It'd be a big undertaking.' 'We'd need a plot of land near to the Garddryn. Big enough to keep more livestock, a few extra pigs, a cow and fowl. Space to grow potatoes and root vegetables. Such a place wouldn't come cheap.'

'Couldn't we do as most other do, borrow money from the Garddryn to build?'

He snorted. 'What! Build our own home. Improve it over the years. Cultivate the land with me own sweat. Then when I die the house is repossessed by the owner of the Garddryn. If I work me guts out I want me own kin to benefit, not the quarry owner's brainless bugger of a son.' Cursing, he grasped the poker and stirred the fire fiercely.

Picking up her crocheting, Emily began to work on the ivory coloured table runner. 'If you rake that fire anymore, Joe you'll have it out.'

'Sorry.' Replacing the poker in the corner of the grate where it normally stood, he sighed. 'It just makes me so mad. It's a man's right to keep what he pays and works for. When he dies the fruits of his labour should go to his family, not be passed on to the bloody gentry. Don't they have enough, and all of it handed down through the generations?'

Without lifting her eyes from her work, she spoke quietly 'There must be another way of doing it.'

'Aye. I suppose if we were to buy Maisie's two-acre field we could put a small cottage up on it. There's plenty of material lying around, haven't we been tormented by the rocks and stones ever since we started renting the field.'

Emily hadn't considered this option. 'Do you think Maisie would let the field go?'

'I don't honestly know, but if not we could look elsewhere. There must be a piece of ground that would suit our purpose that isn't owned by an absent landlord or a quarry proprietor.'

Putting her work in her lap, she smiled. 'It would be exciting wouldn't it, Joe, like starting afresh.' She glanced around the warm, cosy room. 'Mind, I'll miss our little hovel.'

Picking up his paper, he grinned. 'Hovel indeed. Sometimes I think you're as barmy as that son of ours.'

She looked wistful. 'I wonder what Tommy doing now.'

Shaking the paper out, he grunted. 'Summat he shouldn't.'

Tommy was on the return journey after settling an aggrieved Henrietta into a rural house he had rented in Cumbria. Unhappy at being left in conditions that she did not feel were adequate, or comfortable enough, although the house was a large family house with several rooms for servants quarters. Henrietta expected to see her child born into a mansion the size and rank of Plas Mawr. 'Anything less' she had stated in the hearing of her new servants, 'was not only beneath her, but demeaning.'

Promising to return at the end of the month, Tommy had endured another fit of tears before she had relinquished his coat sleeves. Making a hurried departure he covered the miles in an uncomfortable and cold carriage to the railway station, noticing nothing of the discomfort so vast was his relief at being absent from his pregnant wife for the foreseeable future.

He was expected to return to Plas Mawr on Sunday evening, but by taking his leave of Henrietta on a Friday morning, he now had the prospect of spending a delicious weekend with Sadie in a small hotel in Chester. Although the lovers were confined by circumstances to remain in the less familiar hotel dining rooms of the city, their time together was special.

For Tommy to be free of the restraints of an increasingly neurotic wife, who when stressed would take large doses of laudanum, or a hurried sherry in the privacy of her bedroom, this interlude of peace, was as he thought, well deserved.

Sadie, in love with Tommy, measured every precious moment that they were together.

Emily had really got Joe thinking, so much so, that although it was very late he was unable to sleep.

Beside him Emily slept, her breathing faint, and her warm body curled and still.

In the tall tress beyond the stream an owl hooted.

The stiff breeze that had blown throughout the day dropped, and the night grew still as the tide of the sea turned.

Stifling a sigh, he considered the morning. Saturday was a shorter working day, only a few hours to spend at the rock face. All the men would finish at the same time; many would catch the ferry back to Anglesey. What a life, work six days, spend one at home, get your washing done, and the chores that had piled up and then back on the ferry. Back on the mainland in the early hours of Monday morning, rush to the quarry or the barracks, and the bloody cycle would start again.

But on the bright side they were all earning more, there had never been a time like this for quarriers. A boom had begun, output was fantastic, and the men were digging more slate than ever before. The abolition of tax on bricks and the finish of the war in Crimea had improved trade. Pay packets were growing larger.

Was it all too late for him, his fiftieth birthday was little more than a memory. Time knocked on. How long would it be before he wasn't strong enough for quarry work. It was a young, fit man's game.

And God forbid he could be injured or worse, what then for Emily, if she was lucky there might be compensation. There was always a chance that he'd be found negligent and there'd be nowt paid out. Jesus, it wasn't so long ago that a man had fallen and died of his injuries days later. The surgeon said that he'd died of natural causes, and once again the word pneumonia was written on a death certificate, so the quarry wasn't liable. Bastards. Thing never changed. And nothing would improve now Tommy ran the quarry.

Oh yes, output would, and he'd break backs to make it so; there'd be no soft touch for the workers at the Garddryn.

Looking towards Emily, the silver light from the window falling on her face, long lashes dark fans beneath her eyes, she was still beautiful. God how he loved her. Should he try to build her the cottage that she longed for? Did they have the money to see such a project through? Was his health up to working and building?

Stirring, she whispered his name, then called to Chloe.

What could he do but try. First thing in the morning he would make her a brew, bring it to her and tell her of his decision. He had Frank; he was a good boy. He could rely on Frank to help him do this for her. There wasn't a thing Frank wouldn't do for his Mam; he'd keep her safe if the worst happened. With this comforting thought he fell into a deep sleep.

Building started as soon as they had the go ahead from Maisie to purchase the two-acre field. She asked a fair price for it. With what Emily had put by over the time that Tommy no longer lived with them, they were able to purchase it with the addition of a small loan.

Frank worked like a Trojan, rolling great stones to the corner of the field chosen for the site of the small cottage. With the help of the chap in charge of the explosives at the quarry they blew the bigger ones out of the stony ground and added them to the hoard.

The walls went up slowly, four rooms would be the initial extent of the building with plans to add another when Frank wed. The house would eventually be his. Tommy would have no part of it, his father had solemnly declared when enlisting his younger son's help.

Louise Bellamy was having a difficult time. The birth of Henrietta's child was drawing near and she did so want to be with her daughter when the time came to deliver the child. The dilemma was her son, George who grew sad and confused if his mother was not to hand.

Bertram was little help, suffering ill health he had little compassion for his injured son, considering that if he could just pull himself together he might yet grow well again. Fretting at the state of her husband's wellbeing, his breathlessness had increased these passed few months, his heart raced at the slightest exertion and the unhealthy flush on his face would deepen to crimson.

George would become tearful, refusing to allow anyone else to help him with mealtimes if she were not present. How was she to leave both of them with the family in such crisis?

Tommy must go in her place and comfort his wife during her ordeal.

On hearing that he would be required to travel to Cumbria Tommy said little. Louise believing that he meant to go in time for the birth of his child was happy to have the burden of responsibility lifted from her and divided her time between nursing her husband and taking care of her son.

As the days progressed and Henrietta's lying in time grew imminent Louise realised that if Tommy were to be present it would be very much at the last moment. Tearfully she enlisted her husband's help in convincing Tommy that he must leave the running of the quarry to his assistant and go to his wife's side.

Henrietta's waters broke a week before the child was due, and after a short and easy labour she gave birth to a son weighing little more than five pounds. The gardener was sent to telegraph the news to Plas Mawr.

The butler delivered the message to Tommy as he sat down to dinner with Louise; Bertram had taken to his bed earlier.

'What is it? Not bad news I hope?' Louise's face paled.

Reading it, Tommy's face lit with a smile. 'Why does everyone always think that telegrams are portents of bad news and never good?' Waving the paper gently. 'This particular one is good news, Grandmama.'

'Oh Tommy, how wonderful. Is it a girl or a boy?'

'A boy.'

'And is Henrietta all right?'

'It doesn't say. But if she were not it most certainly would have mentioned it. A five pound little boy. Edward.'

'Oh that's a wonderful name. A good English name. A name for kings. Oh I must go at once and tell Bertram, he'll be so delighted.' She stood; excited she began to fluster. 'You must make arrangements immediately to travel to them. Oh darling Henrietta what a clever girl you are. Little Edward what a wonderful boy he will become.' Turning, her face was serious. 'You don't think that five pounds is too small do you?'

'It's certainly tiny but provident.' He grinned, whispering, 'Now we can pass the birth off as premature. There will be no stain on Henrietta's character and we will not have to lie about the birth date.'

Louise clapped her hands lightly. 'Oh clever, clever Henrietta.'

Tommy grinned. 'I thought you were going to tell Bertram the good news.'

I will. I'll go at once.' Picking up her full skirt, she hurried from the room like a galleon in full sail.

Wearing his nightclothes, Bertram came into the dining room, Louise not far behind him. 'Wonderful news, Tommy.' He slumped into the carver at the head of the table. 'You'll be sorry to have missed being there.'

Lying convincingly, Tommy looked regretful. 'Yes, it's a pity. As it was I was prepared to go tomorrow. I'd left Jenkins in charge at the office.' Lifting the glass of claret beside his plate he took a small sip. 'Now of course I'll wait a few days then I can bring them both back with me.'

'Oh, Tommy, Henrietta will be disappointed if you don't go immediately.'

'He was brusque. 'Can't be helped. She'll be home soon enough. And in the meantime she'll have the wailing of a baby to keep her occupied.'

Bertram remained silent, chewing his lower lip thoughtfully.

Several days later, Tommy was driven in the brougham to the railway station. Louise had been sorely tempted to accompany him, but as George had a fever, a chill he'd caught sitting by the open window throughout a cold night, she remained at home.

Baby Edward was almost a month old when he arrived at Plas Mawr with his parents. Louise and Bertram doted on him from the first moment.

Fortunately Joe was busy building the cottage so had little time to fret that his eldest son had not thought fit to inform them of the birth of their grandson. Emily hurt, said little, beside she wondered if the baby looked like any of them.

A month later, on a bright Sunday afternoon, Henrietta visited with the baby. Although she was beautifully dressed in a blue frock and matching bonnet, she looked careworn and thin. With the blanketed child in her arms she knocked at the cottage door.

Surprised to have a visitor Emily flustered and nearly bobbed a curtsy to her daughter-in-law.

Joe took charge, offering the tired looking girl the comfortable chair by the fire; he put the kettle to the flames and began to make a brew.

Within moments Emily had the bairn in her arms, and he was gazing into her eyes as she murmured lovingly to him.

Her eyes shone with tears. 'I'll never be able to thank you enough, Henrietta for bringing him to us. He's so beautiful.' Lifting a pearl-pink tiny hand from the white blanket she kissed the tips of Edward's fingers. 'He looks so very much like Tommy did when he was a tiny bairn.'

Henrietta's eyes darkened. 'Does he. I didn't think that he resembled his father.'

Reading the young woman's thoughts, Joe gave her words of comfort. 'In looks he's certainly like him. Tommy was a lovely little lad. I remember when we first came to Wales he was so excited riding on an old cart, and coming up the cut on a barge.' Laughing. 'Little beggar slept through the sailing from Liverpool to Caernarvon. Quite worn out he was. Much like this one is now.'

The child's eyes had closed slowly, flickered open for a moment, then closed again. Sipping her tea, Henrietta listened to tales of the little wonder that had been Tommy Standish.

When mother and child had departed, collected by the family carriage, Emily made a fresh brew and sat with Joe discussing the event.

'Emily that girl is not happy.'

She agreed with him. There had been great blue circles beneath her eyes and she was pale, her lips hardly noticeable against her skin.

'Perhaps she's just tired, motherhood is tiring.'

Joe raised his eyebrows. 'I don't expect she has to do much for the little one, she'll have a nurse and a nanny, beside the other servants to help her.'

'I expect you're right. She didn't say much about Tommy. Hardly mentioned him at all.'

'Shouldn't wonder that he's something of a disappointment to her.'

She sighed. 'Aye maybe you're right. But she did promise to bring the little one again and soon. I can't wait to see him again. Joe, he's so lovely.'

He grinned. 'Aye, I know. I saw him too.'

'Frank'll be sorry that he missed them.'

'He will, but there's not much that'll stop Frank from laying stone on stone. He'll have that house finished in no time.'

Emily smiled. 'I can't wait for the move. It'll be nicer there for little Edward to come a calling.'

Joe hoped that she wouldn't be disappointed, the picture of a family gathering looked too perfect, considering that Tommy had a say in it too.

Returning from an overnight visit to Penrhyn and finding Henrietta out with the baby, Tommy went to her sitting room to await her return. Furious, guessing what her errand had been, they had talked of a visit to his parents to show them their grandson several times and the discussions had turned into a flaming arguments, and now the moment his back was turned she flagrantly disobeyed him.

The baby's nurse met Henrietta in the hallway and took the baby from her. 'Madam your husband is waiting for you in your sitting room.'

Henrietta's heart sank. 'I'll go to him.' Delaying the meeting, she said, 'I'll just go to my room and change before I see him.'

Hurrying to her bedroom, and making as little noise as possible, Henrietta lifted the lid on the pillbox she kept on her dressing table and took a large pinch of opium. It would help to calm her nerves, give her the courage to meet Tommy's anger, but more importantly it would deaden the pain she felt at her husband's continued infidelity. Moments later feeling calmer, her breath less frantic, she went to meet him.

He was standing as she entered, looming over the delicate furniture, his face angry, mouth a tight firm line. 'How dare you disobey me?'

The drug was working well; she could detach herself from the tirade. Opium was her friend. The sherry or brandy she drank was not, that made her join in the evil game, and she would answer Tommy back, air past grievances, and make threats more foul than his. Now, the magic working she could think of other things, her early girlhood, the chances she'd had to marry someone else. Her father would have married her to Count Vladafitch. What would her life have been like had she done so? He was handsome in a dark way, and very rich, richer than Papa. With Tommy she had Edward; he was reward enough for anything she might suffer at the hands of his father. She had once loved Tommy Standish with all her heart, now looking into his uncaring eyes she wondered why she had. He was handsome, but he wasn't kind or good.

Unable to face her empty eyes Tommy stormed across the room, knocking over a delicate side table, smashing the glass horse that had stood at the centre. Ignoring the debris he slammed the door. In the hallway he stood holding onto the balustrade at the top of the stairs, breathing hard, anger a tight knot in his belly. Who could feel anything for a woman who just stood and said nothing?

Bertram Bellamy came out of his room, stood for a moment in the doorway, then stepped back, closing the door quietly.

'Damn! Damn! Damn!' Tommy slapped his hand down on the polished wood. This was all he needed; alienating her father just wasn't clever.

Chapter Fifteen

Louise, Henrietta and Tommy were sitting in the library at Plas Mawr, Louise tearful, Henrietta in shock and Tommy hopeful at the outcome of the reading of Bertram Bellamy's Last Will and Testament.

The solicitor sat in the chair behind Bertram's desk. A tall, white-haired man, clean-shaven around the mouth, ruddy cheeks and tidy side-whiskers. He faced them calmly; little suspecting that one amongst them would be dangerously angry at the outcome of the reading.

For the third time he glanced at his watch, as though he awaited another person.

Tommy made an impatient gesture. 'I believe all the relevant parties are here.'

Giving the upstart, as he thought of Tommy, a sour glance, he began in a low, quiet voice. 'Mrs. Bellamy you have my deepest sympathy for your very sudden loss.'

Louise peered through the heavy veil she had worn at the graveside. 'Thank you. Mr. Withinshaw. My husband will be much missed. I am only glad that he had a chance to know his grandson, he was extremely fond of Edward. Sadly he had less than a year to spend with him.'

'Indeed.'

He gave a sympathetic nod to Henrietta. 'Mrs. Standish allow me to convey my deepest sympathy to you also. Your father was very fond of you; he spoke of you often when he called to my office on business.'

Henrietta sniffed into her embroidered handkerchief. 'I loved him dearly and I miss him so much.' She began to cry quietly.

Turning his eyes to the package before him, he broke the wax seal, his thumb quivering slightly. Coughing lightly, Mr. Withinshaw began the preliminaries.

A ghost of a smile appeared on Tommy face. It would only be a matter of minutes now before he owned the Garddryn and the property that went with it. Bellamy had only Henrietta to leave it too. George was out of the question; he was nothing but a blubbering idiot. Bellamy would no more have thought of leaving it to Louise than abandoning it to the workers. The woman couldn't manage her household let alone a business. When it came to idiocy she wasn't far from her son, and Bellamy had known that. The whole shooting match would certainly go to Henrietta.

The solicitor lifted his eyes to Louise. 'The house in Liverpool and an income of two hundred a year...'

Tommy shifted in his chair. He'd been right, the old man knew that his wife was incapable. She'd got what she deserved, the mediocre city house and a small income for life. Fortunately for her she actually loved the house and the social life of the city.

'And to my son, George, an income of two hundred... To remain in his mother's care until such a time that his illness...'

Tommy could have laughed out loud. So the sod that had lay in wait for him and beaten him on the avenue of Plas Mawr on the first day that he had gone for lessons there had lost Plas Mawr and the Garddryn. It was sad that he would never realise who he had lost it too. Ha, ha, ha.

'To my dear daughter Henrietta I leave an income of two hundred plus the Chester house.'

Tommy almost leapt out of his chair. So the old man had come up trumps. He's been fonder of his old friend Tommy than he'd given him credit for.

Raising his eyes to Tommy, Mr. Withinshaw paused for a moment.

Tommy felt his heart beating.

'To my grandson Edward, I leave Plas Mawr the Garddryn Quarry, the seventeen cottages in the village of Garddryn, the six houses in Llandfydd and all the monies in the...'

The bastard had got the lot. And if it hadn't been for him marrying his mother that is what he would have been, a bastard.

'The Garddryn Quarry to be managed by my son-in-law Thomas Standish and overseen by my solicitors who shall have control of the finances and the...'

Tommy didn't wish to listen to more. Pushing his chair back he retreated from the library, dashing upstairs to the sanctuary of his private suite, where he collapsed on his bed. He ached physically, his throat was as tight as a drum, and to breathe, he sobbed.

Chapter Sixteen

For several days Tommy remained alone in his bedroom drinking brandy, his rage out of control. On the fourth morning he woke with a massive headache and denying himself another drink he fell into a troubled sleep.

Waking during the early evening he lay watching the sky darkening, the ceiling above his head deepening from ivory to dark grey. The turmoil in his mind lessening as the day drew to a close.

Falling into a more peaceful slumber, he woke again during the early hours and by a subconscious miracle he had passed through the fire of his anger. As the fury subsided and the torture of losing the Garddryn to his son became less agonising, he was capable of rational thought.

Rising, calm now, he lit the lamp, then threw wood from a basket by the fireside into the grate and built a fire. Sitting in the comfortable armchair, watching the leaping flames and feeling the warmth he considered his position.

The boy was only just twelve months old; it would be another twenty years before he would take control of the quarry and all its assets. Twenty years was a long time, but he would still be a comparatively young man. In the meantime he could channel the boy's education. Music and an appreciation of fine art could be the theme of his learning. The theatre, philosophy, literature his interests. Priests and bishops could instill a religious aspect to his life. Taught to appreciate serenity and beauty it wasn't likely that he'd desire to mix with roughneck workers and the business end of quarry life.

It could all be managed. Lord, hadn't he managed bigger and more hazardous problems? Millie Barker, George, his parents, Louise and Henrietta, one small boy wasn't going to beat him.

Twenty years to build his fortune, he'd take what he could from the Garddryn, squeeze every ounce of profit there was to be had out of the place. The trustees and the parasitical solicitors he could manage, there wouldn't be many honest men amongst them. Most men could be bought or blackmailed. Smiling for the first time in days he thought of the ultimate price honest men often paid, George was one, and Bertram another in his way.

A watery gold dawn was breaking, the sky pale as a robin's egg. Extinguishing the lamp he rose from the chair. At the washstand he poured cold water into the bowl, after dousing his head he dried his hair on a soft towel. Dressing carefully, choosing the elegant clothes that he would wear, he left the house.

Rousing the stable-hands he had his new black stallion harnessed and ready in minutes.

Mounted and without a backward glance he left the yard at a trot.

The early morning was glorious, sparkling. The trees and shrubs in the avenue fresh after last night's rain, droplets glittering in the grass like priceless gems.

Riding steadily he made it to the Garddryn entrance before any of the men had begun to file up the track. Remaining mounted he waited, then he heard them coming, their voices carrying on the still air like the slight buzz of summer insects.

The horse barely moved, but for a restless shift of a leg and an iron shoe clinking on the shale. So he waited. Motionless.

The first line of men stopped, falling silent at seeing him there. Then behind them other men drew up. No one spoke. All eyes were on him. He recognised the looks of apprehension, hesitancy, subservience and hatred written in their faces.

Tightening the reins, he steered the horse to the side of the track, then waited for the men to move on. Every face turned to him as they passed, all but that of his father, and Joe looked purposely away.